Fortunes
of the
Dead

Fortunes of the Dead

A NOVEL

LYNN HIGHTOWER

ATRIA BOOKS

New York   London   Toronto   Sydney   Singapore

ATRIA BOOKS

1230 Avenue of the Americas
New York, NY 10020

ISBN: 0-7434-6389-7

First Atria Books hardcover edition September 2003

10   9   8   7   6   5   4   3   2   1

ATRIA BOOKS is a trademark of Simon & Schuster, Inc.

Manufactured in the United States of America

For information regarding special discounts for bulk purchases,
please contact Simon & Schuster Special Sales at 1-800-456-6798
or business@simonandschuster.com

For Laurel

My beautiful, intelligent, talented daughter,
who makes the world a better place.

ACKNOWLEDGMENTS

To Tracy Hite, Program Manager, Washington, D.C., Alcohol Tobacco and Firearms . . . for opening the doors and paving the way, for answering questions and making me welcome.

To Jim Cavanaugh, Special Agent In Charge, Nashville Region, Alcohol, Tobacco and Firearms . . . who was gracious and generous enough to take time out of a busy schedule to answer all of my questions, to advise me on criminal investigation, and to educate me on the workings of the fascinating and hugely under-appreciated agency of Alcohol, Tobacco and Firearms.

To all of the ATF agents who give the job their best, then step back to let others bask in the limelight.

To Gary Cordner, Ph.D., Dean of the College of Justice and Safety at Eastern Kentucky University, who spoke with me at length and answered all of my questions about his impressive law enforcement program. It was a pleasure to talk to someone from home.

To Gene Lewter, of Fayette County Legal Aide, an attorney with heart, as well as a talented writer, who was always available to advise me on the workings of the legal system—in the courtroom and behind closed doors.

To Aaron Priest and Lucy Childs, Lisa Erbach Vance and every single person at the Aaron Priest Literary Agency, who take care of the business end and take the weight off my shoulders so I am free to write and enjoy it. Thank you for keeping me out of trouble (a big job, no?) May I never disappoint you.

To Joy Ritchey, for invaluable help on artwork.

To Adam Ritchey, the enormously talented graphic artist who created my beautiful cover art. You are every author's dream.

To Gina, Maggie, and Shelley, for girl talk, good food, and introducing me to George, a truly amazing dog.

To Randy, for friendship and backup.

To Judith Curr, publisher of Atria Books, for being so great and amazing to work with.

To Amanda Ayers, who is perceptive, creative, and hardworking, and knows the book as well as I do. And to Christina Boys, for all her detail work and input.

To Kay, my partner in research adventures, and to Jerry, for cooking.

To Victor, for listening, reading, cooking, and dancing.

To my sister, Rebecca, who knows what to say at every stage of the book, who listens till she falls asleep, and who never lets me down. May we squabble forever.

To Julien and Arnaud, who have taken me under their wing and taught me soccer, bowling, and football. I can still beat you at Ping-Pong—but for how long, I don't know.

To Alan, Laurel, and Rachel, who make me proud . . . and who know the process better than anyone and are always there for backup.

And, above all, to Robert, who has captured my heart, and shown me that the last love is the best one of all.

In the pursuit of illegal gun sales, the federal enforcement agency of Alcohol, Tobacco and Firearms analyzes the time period that occurs from a weapon's date of sale to the date the weapon is recovered from a crime scene. This interval is referred to as . . . *time to crime.*

CHAPTER ONE

I have had nightmares all my life. I do not know if this is unusual. But sometime late last September, when the leaves were on the verge of turning, and the sun was still strong in the afternoons, I started sleeping the night through. Gone were the two A.M. sweats; the late nights surfing the Net; flipping channels to catch a movie at four A.M.

It felt like happiness.

I stood on the front porch of a gray stone cottage on a gentrified and tree-lined street. I held a newly made key in my right hand, a bucket of paint in my left. The wind blew rain at my back and a sudden gust toppled the Sold sign in the middle of the yard.

Joel and I started looking for a place to buy together six months ago, in September. I knew as soon as we pulled into the driveway of 1802 Washington Avenue that this cottage was *it,* and before Joel had even stopped the car, I told him this was our place.

Joel never gets excited. He glanced up at the porch where the realtor was waving and said, "You want to make an offer now, or should we take a quick look around?" Joel's humor is so low-key and dry that he has friends who don't know he makes jokes.

Our little cottage is in an eclectic neighborhood called Chevy Chase. Due to the ever-rising real-estate values in Lexington, Kentucky, this means we pay top dollar for our square footage. We are close to the university, not too far from downtown, and a ridiculously short drive from Billy's Barbecue. Chevy Chase Inn, a watering hole popular with divorcées in their forties, is right across from

Billy's, as is an ice-cream store, a doughnut place, and a bar that used to be called The Library. The bar has burned down twice that I know of. After that the name was changed to Charlie Brown's, and it hasn't burned down near as much since.

If you want to go dancing you can hit the Blue Moon Saloon, which is on the opposite side of the road from Charlie Brown's. Some nights they have a line of people waiting to get in. This strikes me as funny. Lexington is not big enough to have clubs with long lines, but at least they don't have velvet ropes.

It took a moment for me to work the key in the lock—old doors always have little tricks. The door was a solid oak arch with black hinges. Inside, to the left of the foyer, a staircase went straight to the second floor, or you could go right, through an arched doorway that opened into the living room.

I went right.

The smell of fresh paint made the cottage seem like a brand-new gift. The house was built when ten-foot ceilings were run-of-the-mill, all floors were wood, and heating registers blew warm air through scrolled metal grilles in the floor. My boot heels sounded loud. They echoed.

It was chilly in the house and I looked at the fireplace, wishing. It was the last day of February, the rain was cold, and I was damp and shivery. February is the worst month of the year in Kentucky.

Rain pounded the windows—broad, heavy panes of glass that stretched from midwall to a foot below the ceiling. The glass was so old it looked wavy. The fireplace was flanked by built-in bookshelves enclosed with diamond-paned wooden doors, in the style of barristers' bookcases. It was the shelves that sold Joel the house.

And I was missing Joel, who was supposed to help pick out the paint. He was in charge of drop cloths and brushes, and today was his scheduled day off. But Joel was a cop, a homicide cop, and days off were a maybe at best. He'd left in a hurry this morning without saying why, and I'd been edgy all day, because it was the Cheryl Dunkirk case that he worked. Joel had spent eight sleepless weeks on the trail of this girl, and had yet to come up with anything other than her car—neatly parked in the lot of her apartment house, stained with traces of blood and bodily fluids, and ravaged by a web of newly made cracks in the windshield. Her trail ended abruptly at a Pilot gas station on Richmond Road.

Joel did not know that I was considering taking Cheryl Dunkirk's family on as clients. And I saw no reason to tell him until I made up my mind. I will have no argument before its time.

Cheryl's stepfather, Paul Ellis Brady, a Pittsburgh developer who dealt in multimillion-dollar commercial and government projects, was dead set on hiring me to "do anything" I could. He and his daughter, Miranda, who lived in Lexington, were due in less than an hour to work out the details—as in look me over, and bring me a check. Brady was very clear on the phone. He wanted me to keep the investigation going until I could find out every detail of what happened to his daughter. He wanted me to take up the slack in the official investigation.

The first thing I told him was that there wasn't any slack in the police investigation. This I knew firsthand, though I didn't tell Brady that. I tried to talk him out of hiring me. Uncertainty is the hardest thing to live with, but in the case of Cheryl Dunkirk, I didn't think she would ever be found.

I was uneasy about Joel's reaction to me working this case. I'd almost told him the night before, when he came to bed after working late, and had been deciding exactly what to say when he pulled me close, my back to his front, and put his arms around me to keep me warm. The truth is that I chickened out, but what I told myself was that it was better to make a decision on my own, uninhibited by the thought of his disapproval. Because that's how women get lost in relationships—pleasing everyone but themselves.

Joel and I had been together for two years and counting, and I found that the longer we were together the happier I was. We bought this house jointly and were scheduled for official cohabitation in two days. Our loan folder was so new it was still piled in some In-box, waiting its turn to be filed. The mortgage papers had been signed, the closing, always tense, had been endured, and everyone who was anyone had taken a percentage from our fees.

It took me two years to completely commit—to Joel, or to happiness, or both. Joel, ever patient, was delighted, if you can use such an energetic word for his understated ways. I was good for him. In the months we'd been together, his face had filled out and he looked younger. The lines of fatigue in his brow had smoothed; the stress creases that ran from his nose to his lips had faded.

We began our evenings in the kitchen. Joel cooked and I watched. We talked long into the night about the things that interested us—why people kill, why men beat women, how a mother could be so drug addicted she would aid and abet a nightmare childhood for her kids. We talked forensics and DNA, and our most heated arguments involved either the death penalty, or how much garlic should go into the pasta. Joel is a "less is more" kind of cook, and I am a "more the merrier." So we talked and argued about food and work: the merits of wheat beer over ale; Joel's job in homicide; and mine as a private detective—a woman's equalizer, specializing in cases involving women and children who fall between the cracks of the legal system.

I set the paint bucket down gently so as not to mar the floor. The heating control was a simple round dial, likely installed before I was born. Turning it on reminded me of the combination locks you use in school. There was that moment of hesitation, when you think, *Hey, does this work?,* then a rumble and a sigh as the compressor kicked in; the noise of air rushing through cramped, old-fashioned vents; and the toasty smell of burning dust.

And I was home. More at home than in Joel's austere warehouse loft; more at home than in my sister Whitney's haunted suburban ranch—recently sold to make a substantial down payment on this cottage. Joel and I had agreed that I would make the down payment and he would handle the bulk of the mortgage—a reasonable arrangement. Joel had a regular salary, generating cash flow and good credit. I was paid by economically challenged women in the midst of domestic chaos. I survived by a form of medieval barter.

It's a complex system that generates satisfaction, a million-odd privileges, but very little ready cash. There is no financial security, and none of the sort of documentation that impresses mortgage companies or any reputable bank.

On the other hand, my freezer was stocked with homemade

meatballs, chicken casseroles, and Chicago steak fillets. My car insurance would be provided for the next eighteen months. I could walk into the Asian Pearl and have free martinis, which was a shame, since I didn't drink martinis. My yard maintenance would be taken care of for the next year, a bouquet of flowers arrived from Ashland Florist every two weeks, and I had gift certificates on hand to spend whenever I wanted: one from Lazarus for $175; another for Victoria's Secret for $50; and one I had just cashed in at Joseph Beth Booksellers for a Miles Davis CD. One very grateful client had signed over a 1994 Mazda Miata with 85,000 miles and a tear in the tan canvas roof. Another had a brother who kept the Miata in good repair. Clients cleaned my oven, brought over casseroles on a scheduled dinner plan, offered me the professional services of family members who moved furniture, worked in restaurants, and repaired antiques.

The arrangement has advantages for the lazy at heart. That would be me.

I thought about making coffee while I unwrapped the new CD and put it in the portable stereo. Coffee would require me to go back outside. On the other hand, it was coffee.

I went back out to the car, avoiding the lawn and the mud loosened between the drowning blades of grass. Rain had been steady for six days straight and the ground was saturated. It had been a miserable soggy month, nothing but gray skies. The scent of wood smoke was so strong that it seemed every household must be using a fireplace or wood-burning stove.

I hauled my essentials out of the car—a corkscrew, a bottle of Chilean Merlot that met my exacting qualifications (under ten dollars, eye-catching label), a bag of salt and vinegar potato chips, coffeemaker, cream, my favorite New Orleans coffee mug that said American Belle on one side and Absolutely Pure Coffee on the other. I picked it up at Kroger's just last week. I was drinking Yuban coffee because it had been on sale, but it was nothing like the rich black Italian roast that is full-bodied rather than bitter— and currently out of my price range.

I shut the door on the rain and slipped out of my wet shoes— red alligator high-heeled boots I had no business wearing in this weather. I left my stuff in the foyer and headed for the kitchen. Joel had left his toolbox on the Italian marble countertop (another strong selling point), anticipating, as was his habit, exactly what we would need to have on hand for the move. In the refrigerator was bottled Dasani water, Becks, Miller Lite, and chocolate biscotti. Joel had come alone to bring these few things roughly a week ago and had not set foot in the house since. I'd wandered in almost every day.

Like his pantry, his closet, even his underwear drawer, Joel's toolbox was neat, organized, and spotless. The tools were worn, but clean, as if Joel wiped them down with a soft cloth every time he used them, which he probably did. I found a screwdriver in a plastic tray that held several screwdrivers arranged according to size. I mixed them up on purpose, grabbed one, and snapped the lid shut.

I rustled through my pile of stuff until I found the bag of potato chips, then sat cross-legged to consider the bucket of paint. Joel and I had sorted through a hundred and one color strips and set-tled on leaving the trim in the living room Manhattan Chalk White, and repainting the walls Lido Beige. I had been perfectly content with the Lido Beige. But standing in the paint aisle at Home Depot, the Sienna Sun Red called my name.

I had always wanted a red room, but red was something of a tricky color. Candy-apple red would be disgusting, and I would loathe any shade that looked the slightest bit orange, which let out everything with a Southwest motif. Maroon was unacceptable—a good color for a high school marching band, but not my living room.

And then I saw it—the red I had always imagined, the red that would be dramatic and elegant, the red I could live with day in and day out. The big question was did I have the right to paint the living room whatever color I liked. Living with someone meant compromise, and I had agreed without agony to the Lido Beige.

I turned up the music and opened the bag of chips. Fingers sticky with salt and vinegar, I used the screwdriver to pry open the paint.

So beautiful. I ripped the plastic off a brand-new paintbrush, and dipped the bristles into the placid and virginal surface. I made an arclike smear on the wall, followed by another swath of red, this one bigger. Drips of paint slid like oil down the side of the can and dropped to the newly buffed wood floors.

Joel says that disorder follows wherever I go. It's not intentional. But it is true that I have never decorated on my own before, and never picked out paint, or furniture, or dishes, without someone weighing in with a heated opinion. My ex-husband, Rick, had a place of his own when we moved in together, and we didn't change much after we got married. And when my sister was murdered, and Rick and I split, I moved into Whitney's little suburban ranch and changed not a thing that didn't involve cleaning or replacing the carpet and baby bed that had been soaked with blood and tears. It took me by surprise, this strong vision I had of how my house should look.

I set the paintbrush on the metal rim of the bucket, and stood back from the wall. Two coats would do it, and I'd leave the woodwork as it was.

The doorbell rang twice. This was the first time I'd heard the doorbell in the house, and I liked the way it sounded—it's the little things that make you proud.

I was not looking forward to having to explain that it was entirely possible we would never know what happened to Cheryl Dunkirk. The family never gives up. Paul and Miranda Brady still had hope. But Cheryl had likely been dead for the last eight weeks, and her passing, much like Whitney's, was not an easy one; this much I knew, and very little else. I also knew Cheryl's death would haunt her sister, Miranda, the same way Whitney's violent murder haunted me.

The bell rang again—that made three. I wiped my hands on the back of my Victoria's Secret Five Button Fly Boyfriend Jeans and went to open my arched front door.

My client was not what I expected, and it was clear from the way her mouth hung open that the reaction was mutual. She was young. If I were a bartender I would card her as a formality only before I escorted her out the door. I looked over her shoulder but did not see her father. Miranda had come alone.

She stepped forward to look at me more closely, and I could see that she was still struggling with those tricky issues of complexion. The small spray of whiteheads on her forehead were barely visible, buried beneath a generous application of cream-based foundation. She had likely selected the color during the summer when her skin was brown from the sun. The shade was too dark now, and gave her face an orange cast, though with her coloring—medium dark hair and green eyes—the orange wasn't all that bad. She was about my height, which, in terms of Internet shopping, is a sort of medium—a five-foot-three or -four, average to short.

"Excuse me, I'm looking for Lena Padget." Her voice landed in the upper registers, which meant she didn't smoke.

"I'm Lena Padget."

She stared and made no comment. If she hadn't been quite so young I might have found her on the wrong side of annoying.

"Maybe you could tell me who you are?" I only asked this question to get her on track. I knew very well who she was. I looked over her shoulder one more time. Still no sign of the father.

"I'm Miranda." Her tone of voice let me know that I should have been expecting her.

"Paul Brady's daughter?"

"That's right."

"Your father isn't with you?"

Her voice went flat, eyes downcast. "He's still home in Pittsburgh. He can't get away right now."

I shook her hand. "Nice to meet you, Miranda. Please come in."

The invitation was unnecessary, as she was already two steps through the door. I wondered if she realized that hiring a detective was not quite the same thing as interviewing a servant.

She walked through the foyer, glanced at the staircase as if deciding whether or not to take the time to go up for a look, then moved into the living room, where she spun in a slow circle to take it all in.

"I love your house."

"Thank you. Let me get a couple of chairs." I fetched two folding chairs in from the kitchen and set them facing each other in the middle of the room. "I spoke with your father yesterday."

"I know." Miranda tore herself from the view outside my

living-room window. "He told me you didn't want to take this on. He told me to convince you to do it anyway." Miranda's chin came up. "You don't have to worry about dealing just with me. I know I'm only twenty, but my father trusts me to handle things. He relies on me, he always has. And I talk to him every day. He really wants you to do this."

"Sit down," I told her. The first thing we were going to have to establish was what Paul and Miranda Brady defined as "this." And dealing solely with Miranda was going to complicate matters. She was young to be taking things on alone.

"Can I get you a cup of coffee, or a bottle of water?"

Miranda shook her head and sat on the edge of the chair. Her confidence was fading. She adjusted her skirt, which was filmy and cut on the bias. She wore clogs and her legs were bare in spite of the cold. The sleeves of her blouse flared over her pudgy hands. Her hair was either naturally curly or permed, and had been generously gelled or was in need of a wash. Her fingernails were bitten to the quick, and she wore shiny metallic lip gloss over a full bottom lip. She had a backpack instead of a purse.

College student, college student, college student.

"I'm very sorry about what happened with your sister. I know how hard this can be."

"Do you think she's dead?" Miranda looked me directly in the eyes. "I like to get things out in the open."

I did think Cheryl was dead, and I wondered about this Paul Brady, and why he hadn't made the time to come. I wondered why he would put this responsibility on the shoulders of Cheryl's younger sister, and not take care of things himself.

"Do you think she's dead, Miranda?"

Miranda bit her bottom lip, and did not answer. But silence made her uncomfortable, and she ran a finger along the material of her skirt, avoiding eye contact.

"Just so you know, Daddy got your name from Chick Ryder. He works in Legal Aid."

"I know."

"He recommended you very highly. He said you guys were friends."

"Ah ha. We are, but Chick knows lots of detectives. He give any reason why he settled on me?"

Miranda twirled a curl of hair between her short, thick fingers. She was a heavy girl, by current standards, but not unattractively so.

"Mr. Ryder says you've got a good reputation."

I hid my cynicism behind a smile. No doubt Chick also made Paul Brady aware that I was sleeping with the cop who headed up the Cheryl Dunkirk investigation. If I were in Brady's shoes, I'd hire me, too.

Brady's instincts were sound, because I did have a wealth of inside information and I wouldn't be going into the situation cold. The disappearance of Cheryl Dunkirk had shaped into one of Joel's most frustrating cases, one that had riveted the entire state of Kentucky and even splashed periodically through the national news when they were having a slow day. We'd been on *Nightline* and CNN.

Cheryl Dunkirk, a college student at Eastern Kentucky University, was enrolled in the Criminal Justice Department with a major in Police Studies. She disappeared eight weeks ago and was last seen leaving her job as an intern at the Alcohol, Tobacco and Firearms outpost here in Lexington, Kentucky. Cheryl Dunkirk never made it home.

She was a top-notch scholar with a 3.7 GPA, consistently high test scores, and the respect of almost all of her teachers. If she had a fault, it was that criminal justice major or not, she followed a personal code that sometimes coincided with by-the-book rules, and sometimes did not. The one black mark on her academic record was an incident the first semester of her sophomore year when she admitted to cheating on a take-home test. Cheryl had given exam answers to a borderline student who did not have the patience or the IQ to pull the cheat off, and who took Cheryl's answers verbatim, using and misspelling vocabulary that was out of her normal realm of word usage, when compared to her previous tests.

Cheryl had been unrepentant. The dean had been careful; Cheryl had too much potential to waste, and he was the kind of dean who took an interest in every one of the students. He had delved into the details, finally deciding the situation to be one of Cheryl helping a fellow student who was having a hard time balancing work and studies in a class where the professor did not play fair. This teacher was a member in a club of one who did not like Cheryl Dunkirk; there had been complaints about him before.

Securing the ATF internship for Cheryl had been a coup—the cheating incident had almost squelched it; ATF had high standards. But the dean backed Cheryl's application, and that, combined with her grade point average and the glowing recommendations of her other instructors, landed her an internship that was highly prized among the students at EKU.

Miranda pushed hair out of her eyes. "Daddy told me to give you this check. I just need you to tell me what to fill in for the amount."

"I think before we start getting into fees we'd better establish exactly what it is that you and your father want me to do."

Miranda wrinkled her nose. "That's kind of a no-brainer, isn't it? We want you to find my sister."

"The police are all over this, you know that."

"Yeah, and still no Cheryl. That's why Daddy wants to hire you."

I leaned back in my chair. This was exactly what I was afraid of, and I saw my fee slipping away. "I have a high opinion of the cops on your sister's case, Miranda. They're doing a good job."

"Yeah, okay, but they have intern tunnel vision. They think Cheryl is some kind of Monica Lewinsky or Chandra Levy. And look what happened there. They got so sidetracked on the intern sex drama they didn't find out what happened to Chandra Levy until too late."

"It was always too late for Chandra Levy."

"Look, I see what you're saying." Miranda leaned forward, arms wrapped around her waist, as if her stomach hurt. "Daddy already talked to me about all of this. He feels guilty, okay? Like he owes her. Let me explain something. You've noticed that Cheryl and I have different last names, right? She's a Dunkirk and I'm a Brady, like my dad.

"Cheryl and I are stepsisters. I mean, we were always close and all that, just like real sisters. It's just that she wasn't as close to Daddy as I am, and I think he feels guilty about that. He shouldn't; I mean it's perfectly natural. My mother died when I was just a baby, and all Daddy had was me. So we've got this bond, you know?"

I nodded, but I still wasn't liking Daddy.

"And he meets Cheryl's mom, who's a nurse, and she's in Pittsburgh for some kind of workshop conference training thing and . . . it's funny the way they met. My dad had just bought the hotel where she was staying. It wasn't the greatest building in the world, but it was worth what he paid for the location. Of course, to Violetta—that's Cheryl's mom—this hotel looks pretty good, considering where she comes from and all of that. Only the service was bad and there was no hot water, and she's down talking to the desk clerk about it, and getting nowhere. So she asks who owns this place, and the guy points at my dad, who is walking through the lobby.

"Violetta goes right up to my father, telling him, in a nice way, all the stuff that's gone wrong on her stay. Daddy always laughs about the things she told him. He always says how she was even charming about her insults. Then she tells him how she had to save for the workshop, and it's a big deal as far as she's concerned, and one thing leads to another, and Daddy winds up taking Violetta to lunch. His excuse is that she can give him suggestions on what he needs to do to renovate the hotel." Miranda laughed, and crossed her feet. "As if Daddy needs help in business. But she's from this small town in Kentucky, and really thinks he wants her opinion. It's romantic, isn't it? Like one of those old movies with Audrey Hepburn or Cary Grant."

I admitted to being a Cary Grant fan.

Miranda tilted her head to one side, staring down at the floor. "Just think how everything would have been so different, if my dad hadn't been walking through that hotel lobby at that exact moment. They probably never would have met. I would have finished growing up in Pittsburgh, instead of Danville."

"I didn't realize your dad ever lived around here."

"Violetta was a Kentucky girl, and she wouldn't live in Pittsburgh. So dad bought a place in Danville, and just commuted back and forth. He can do a lot of his business from an office at the house. He moved back to Pittsburgh after Violetta died."

"How long has Cheryl's mother been dead?"

"Four years. I was sixteen, and Cheryl was eighteen. I lost two mothers before I was twenty, which is pretty sad when you think about it. And both of them died of breast cancer, isn't that weird?"

"And your father moved the two of you back to Pittsburgh?"

"Daddy waited about six months, so Cheryl could finish her senior year at Danville High School. And he didn't want me to have to move in the middle of the year. He was worried about how I'd adjust. He just kept the status quo for a while for both of us, because of Violetta and all. Then when Cheryl graduated, and wanted to go to EKU, Daddy decided to go back to Pittsburgh. Cheryl could have come with us, but she wanted EKU because of the law enforcement thing."

"But you came back to Kentucky?"

"Yeah, it's weird, isn't it? Because I had been dying to get back to Pittsburgh. But a place is never the same after you go away and come back. And Daddy was busy working and getting engaged again, and I was missing my sister, so I came back here to go to college."

"You go to UK?"

"No. I started at Centre in Danville."

"Good school."

"Yeah, but it wasn't a good match for me. My grades were a little . . . disappointing. Probably a freshman adjustment thing, Daddy says. My passion—my absolute passion—is art history. I already know how I'm going to make my mark. I want to open a gallery in Pittsburgh, not in L.A. or New York, and I'm going to find artists that nobody has any interest in, but that are really good, and I'm only going to sell their stuff. Every piece of art in the gallery will be from one of my personal discoveries. Once that gets started, then new artists will come to me, and the buyers will come to me because I'll be cutting-edge, because they'll know that I have the sensibility to appreciate what is true, you know? Art from the heart, I call it. I think that's what I'm going to name my gallery." The far-off look in Miranda's eyes faded. "But anyway, to answer your question, I'm taking the semester off and then next fall I'm going to enroll at Transy."

"Another good school," I said. Centre College and Transylvania University were private liberal arts schools, both with hefty price tags.

"And Daddy's paying all of Cheryl's tuition, too. He didn't adopt her or anything, but he treats her just like a real daughter. And he was glad, too, that I had someone who could kind of look out for me, going away to school for the first time and all."

"It looks like somebody should have been looking out for Cheryl."

Miranda slumped in the chair. "My dad isn't going to stop until he finds out every detail of what happened to my sister. Daddy was proud of her, he bragged on her all the time. And he isn't going to put up with her disappearance being written off as some dumb coed shacking up with a married loser and getting killed."

"You do realize that it looks like that's exactly what did happen?"

"That's only because no one gets Cheryl. And anyway, I'm her sister. She wasn't having an affair with Cory Edgers. She would have told me for sure."

"You were close?"

"Oh, extremely. I used to introduce her to my friends, and include her in things, because sometimes Cheryl could get a little housebound. She was like, one day confident, and the next day a mess. We were good for each other; we were real sisters."

"Did she ever talk about Edgers?"

"Sure she did. All the time. They were both kind of outsiders, there, in the ATF office. She's a college student, doing an internship. He's a sheriff from London, Kentucky, on loan to some kind of task force. My sister was smart and opinionated and always had a million questions, and Cory Edgers was encouraging her; he showed her the ropes. Believe me, if there was more to it than that I would have known. I told the police all this, but I don't think they believed me."

I could confirm that observation. It was frustrating being relegated to the sidelines, listening to Joel's theories about the case. I had a few ideas of my own, hunches I would have followed up, and it was tedious just to hang on the fringe, while Joel nodded and ignored everything I said. As a matter of fact, I was kind of ticked at the way he had dismissed my opinions, as if I didn't deal with this sort of thing every working day. I took a moment to indulge the thought of getting to the bottom of Cheryl Dunkirk's disappearance, and passing the killer on to Joel.

But that was no excuse for misleading a client.

"My point is, Miranda, I need to make sure you and your father understand that I'm unlikely to come up with anything the police haven't already. They're giving this everything they've got."

"That may be so, but they're not sharing any of it with my dad."

And this, of course, was the clincher; this convinced me I could contribute without misleading Miranda and Paul Ellis Brady. By necessity the police had to shut the family out, but I'd been the family, and it's a frustration I remembered very well. I caught the shrewd look in Miranda's eyes, and I knew that she realized I was hooked.

"Okay then, Miranda. You know what I can't do for you; here's what I *can* do. If nothing else, I bring a fresh viewpoint, and I'll look at some things differently than the police will. I won't withhold any information. Whatever I find out, I'll tell you, provided that's what you want."

"Why wouldn't I want it?"

"It means I won't censor anything to protect your feelings; it means I'll give it to you straight. But you better think about the possibility that there may be details you don't want to hear."

"I want to hear everything. I want to know. The things I imagine . . . look, you know how I feel. Chick Ryder told me what happened to your sister. So you know what it's like, right?"

"Yeah, I know."

"You're the closest thing to a peer I've got, did you ever think of that?"

I had thought of that. It was one reason I wanted the job.

"So no holding back no matter what. Agreed?"

"Agreed," I said.

Miranda leaned across the floor to shake my hand. I might waste her father's money, but I'd give him some sort of control and satisfy his conscience, if I accomplished nothing else.

"Now what?" Miranda said.

"The first thing I'm going to tell you is that I'm almost positive Cheryl is dead."

Miranda chewed the nail of her little finger. "But you can't really know that."

"You know the police found her car, right?"

"It was still in the parking lot at her apartment. That's what they told me."

"The police think Cheryl was killed in the car."

Miranda's face lost color, and I stood up.

"I'm okay," she said, but she wasn't.

I went into the kitchen and took a bottle of the Dasani Joel had stashed in the fridge. There were no glasses, so I unscrewed the cap and took her the bottle.

"Water?"

"Thanks."

"Can I get you a cup of coffee?"

"I don't like coffee. This is fine, really, I'm okay."

"Why don't we call it quits for today, and I'll give your father a call tonight."

Miranda covered her eyes with her hands. "Don't do that to me, don't call my dad. This is as important to me as it is to him, sometimes I think more important. I'm the one who's here, you know? He's up in Pittsburgh, working and getting fitted for a tux."

"All right, then. I won't shut you out. I expect you to tell me if it gets to be too much."

"Is there any way I can take a look at the car? I want to know what the police see when they look at it. I want to know what it is that makes you so sure Cheryl's dead. I need to know, one way or the other."

I considered. It was pretty far on the rogue side, but I knew how being shut out feels. Sometimes you can't believe things until you can see them, or touch them, to make them real. And the car was the last point of contact, the place where Cheryl Dunkirk died. I could take Miranda right now, if I wanted to. And if she was sure she wanted to go.

She said yes, of course. That's what sisters do.

CHAPTER TWO

Miranda was childishly pleased with my beat-up Miata, though she said that, like Cheryl, she was a Mustang girl herself. She didn't think twice when I suggested we ride together, and there was no reason to point out that after seeing her sister's car, she might be in no shape to drive herself home. Miranda didn't even ask where the car was. She had yet to grow out of the childish expectation that she would be taken care of by the grown-ups in charge.

I had to think about where I was going, the twists and turns of the neighborhood were new, but once I was on Tates Creek Pike, I was back in familiar territory. I headed east toward downtown and that magical place where the road changed its name to Euclid. Lexington, like many cities, often succumbs to the schizophrenic habit of changing street names from one side of an intersection to another.

Miranda peeled the cuticles on the fingers of her left hand and stared quietly out the window. Having her in the car felt like taking a nervous dog for a drive.

I'd left Paul Brady's check covering a twenty-five hundred dollar retainer by the kitchen sink. Real money strikes a note of reverence when you see as little of it as I do. Clients like Paul Brady don't come along often enough. I wondered if I would have agreed to take Miranda to see her sister's car without that check. I decided I would have no matter what. I also decided Joel would be furious if he knew. I'd have to make sure he never did. The thought gave me a pang, as if I had put some distance between us.

The rain started up again, and I veered around deep puddles, cursing the SUVs that sprayed mud on my windshield. I muttered quietly so Miranda wouldn't hear. Joel says I am an aggressive driver, but I think he's just not used to the passenger's seat.

Traffic moved like slow agony on Main Street. The stoplights were flashing yellow. In a perfect world this would mean that each intersection would be treated as a four-way stop, but actually meant every man for himself. A drop of water splashed Miranda's left shoulder, and I noticed that the duct tape I had used to repair the tear in the roof was sagging with condensation.

I reached around the back of my seat for the semiclean navy blue towel I had stashed, and passed it to Miranda. I pointed to the roof and the drips. She shrugged and wadded the towel in a ball, holding it like a pressure bandage against her stomach. She'd run out of conversation.

The corner of Broadway had turned into a lake, and water fanned both sides of the Miata, coating the plastic slit that serves as the back window with mud. Traffic was thinning, and the stoplights ahead were functional as downtown Lexington petered out into storage units, discount gas stations, strip malls, and vacant buildings. Traffic picked up again once we headed east on Leestown Road. We were almost there.

Miranda's sister Cheryl drove a vintage '64 Mustang, navy blue with rust spots. It was out of sight and out of reach behind a chain-link fence topped with three separate strands of barbed wire. I pulled the Miata across a gravel drive, getting as far to the right as possible.

"Is it too muddy over there for you to get out, Miranda? I can pull up some more if you want."

"This is fine," she said, without looking.

I let it go. She had boots, and the mud was near impossible to miss. "Stay put for a minute."

She didn't answer or look my way, and I gave her a second look, wondering if this was such a good idea.

But we were parked, and I could see the uniform out of the

corner of my eye, and I was going to have to get out and talk to him no matter what. The rain fell steadily, and I grabbed a ball cap from behind my seat, and left Miranda alone in the car. I'm not sure she noticed me leave.

"Hey, Chris McFee, how you been?" I was in luck. I knew this guy.

McFee wore a plastic cover over his hat, and a poncho over his uniform. He stood in front of the chain-link gate, oblivious to the rain. This meant I had to be oblivious, too, since Chris had left the dry comfort of his little wood hut to see to my business.

"Hell, Lena. I didn't recognize you with your hair stuffed up in that hat. You a Steelers fan now?"

"This?" I flicked a finger at the bill of my cap. "Got it from a grateful client."

"Spoils of war?"

"Don't knock it. I got a jersey, a jacket, and season tickets that brought me a nice sum on eBay."

"No shit?" McFee rocked back on his heels. His hair was normally sandy and light, but today it was dark with rain. Chris had a build like a bulldog and a face that looked like it had been hit with a shovel; this exterior covered a tender heart.

I was counting on it.

"Mendez send you out here?"

"Mr. By-the-Book? I think not."

McFee gave me a look that could only be described as wary. "So what brings you out here, Lena, on such a nice afternoon?"

"Chris, you see that girl over there in the car?" Rain dripped off my ball cap. My jacket was already soaked, and the thighs of my jeans were wet.

"What about her?"

"Her name is Miranda. She's Cheryl Dunkirk's little sister."

"Man. *Jeez.*" McFee caught Miranda's eye and gave her a sympathetic but masculine nod that managed to somehow be courtly. McFee had presence.

Miranda raised a hand. At least she was responding.

"She wants to see the car, Chris."

"Oh, hey now, Lena, come on."

"Yeah, I know. It's a lot to ask. I'll take no for an answer and no hard feelings. But if you'll do it, I promise we'll follow you at a distance, we'll stand where you tell us, and we won't touch a thing. We'll keep our hands in our pockets the whole time."

"What's the point, Lena? Seeing the car isn't going to change anything."

"Sure it will. It'll change Miranda. Right now she's just trying to deal with it, you know?"

Chris did know. He'd lost a boyhood friend to a mugger when he was a seventeen-year-old living in Chicago.

"You really think it's going to help?"

"Does anything help, Chris?"

"I have to believe it does."

I liked this guy more every time I saw him.

"Hands in pockets, Lena. Okay?"

"At all times. We won't jam you up, Chris."

"Listen, Lena, be straight with me. Does Mendez even know you're out here?"

"Hell, no."

"Did she hire you? Are you working this now, too?"

"The daddy hired me. I signed on this afternoon."

"Does Mendez know?"

"I didn't ask permission, if that's what you mean."

McFee gave me his penetrating look. "Aren't the two of you engaged or something?"

"We just bought a house."

"One step at a time, eh? Congratulations. Invite me over for the housewarming, okay?"

"Will do." I hadn't thought of a housewarming, but now that Chris brought it up, I liked the idea. Joel would have to cook.

McFee led the way in a golf cart. Rain funneled off the canvas roof and brown water splashed up from the gravel road. If he hadn't already been drenched, he was now. Miranda and I followed in the Miata.

"This is where the police store their evidence. Cheryl's car will be in one of these warehouses." I glanced sideways at Miranda and wondered if she even heard me. She sat forward, seat belt stretched, clutching the navy blue towel. I had no doubt that Miranda was sure that seeing Cheryl's car would give her some kind of insight—maybe even a gut feeling on whether or not her sister was alive.

The golf cart veered left, and stopped beside one of three corrugated metal Quonset-style warehouses. I stopped the Miata behind the cart. McFee raised a hand and headed toward the inset door, fumbling with a fistful of keys. The rain came down harder, pattering the roof of my car.

"You ready?" I asked.

Miranda nodded. She did not seem able to talk.

"Okay, then. Ground rules. Once you get in there, the only thing you're going to care about is Cheryl's car. You're going to want me and Chris to go away and let you sit in the front seat and think a little, and be private. I wish I could arrange it that way. The car is evidence, and if your sister was murdered—and you know that's what I think—the physical evidence in the car is what's going to nail her killer. We can't compromise that."

Miranda made no sign that she was taking anything in. She was leaning so far forward in her seat she could stick out her tongue and lick the windshield.

But I did take everything in, and I was thinking I made the decision to drive out here a little too fast. I was thinking I might be in over my head. It was too easy for me to identify with Miranda; but she was young, and I didn't know her all that well. And what might have been right for me in this situation was not necessarily right for her. If Joel ever found out I brought her out here, I was toast.

I took the ball cap off and brushed hair out of my face. "Okay, Miranda, here are the rules. You can't touch the car. You can't even stand close to the car—keep back at least six feet. Keep your hands jammed down in your pockets. I'll be doing the same.

"Understand, Chris is sticking his neck out letting us in here. When he looks at us I want him to feel comfortable. I want him to see two women well away from the car, and with their hands in their pockets. Just so you know, Chris could lose his job for doing this."

"Then why is he doing it?"

Her voice was faint, but at least she was listening.

"Think of Chris as another one of your peers. You can't tell anybody you were here or let on to the police that you've seen Cheryl's car. Just remember you're among friends. Agreed?"

Miranda turned so she could meet my eyes. "I won't tell a soul."

The Mustang sat on the concrete floor like a showroom exhibit, the rusty blue metal cold but clean. Joel continually referred to the car as a "nice ride," and most of the guys, even Joel, spoke wistfully about the '64 "Stang." And always with an annoying reverence in their tone.

Miranda halted midstride when she saw the Mustang, and she stood rigidly, like a woman in a trance. After a moment of watching her, I had to look away.

The one person I hadn't worried about in my long lecture to Miranda and my plea to Chris was me. I wondered how Joel stood this sort of thing, day in and day out. I realized how happy I'd been the last few months, how light. I didn't want to watch Miranda Brady storing up memories of her big sister's death car. People say it's time to get out of the business when things stop affecting you, when you no longer care; but to my mind that's leaving it too long. Maybe I didn't want to know every bad thing that happened in the world.

The warehouse was noisy with the echoes of rain clattering on the tin roof. It was crowded inside, but organized, like the attic of a pack-rat control freak. Miranda turned and looked at me, ready to hear what she did not want to hear.

"The police think Cheryl's killer disposed of her body, and then drove her car back and left it in the apartment parking lot." I started to point, then remembered that I had to keep my hands in my pockets. My jeans were heavy with rainwater and felt tight and miserable on my legs. I thought of the upstairs bathroom in my new little cottage, of the claw-foot bathtub that I had been fantasizing about since Joel and I made our offer on the house. I imagined a tub of bubbles and scented oil, the water hot enough to steam up the mirror, a stack of thick white towels.

"Do you think you could explain the evidence to me, like you said?"

Miranda was leaning toward the car, a speculative glitter in her eyes. I thought through what I needed to say, trying to remember how Joel and I worked out the whole scenario. I considered how best to word things.

"If you look hard, you can see fresh scratches in the paint on the passenger's door." I walked to the side of the car, watching Miranda out of the corner of my eye, making sure she kept her distance, making sure her hands stayed in her pockets. "It's a crisscross of tiny scars, like you'd get if you drove your car into the brush.

"The last person who drove the car back was pretty tall. The seat position pegs the driver at a height range of five-ten to six-three. As you know, Cheryl was only five-six. There are smears of lipstick on the bucket seat, passenger's side, along the edge and on the back cushion, leading to the conclusion that Cheryl was on her back, lying in the front seat, twisting her head from side to side. The lipstick matches exactly a tube of Berry Red MAC lipstick found on the bathroom countertop in your sister's apartment. There were hair and scalp fragments on the door handle that match up with strands of hair taken out of Cheryl's brush. There was enough scalp material and blood for a positive ID. It's pretty clear that Cheryl's attacker slammed her head into the car door at least once. The signs are she put up quite a fight. No trace of semen anywhere. That doesn't rule out the possibility of the attack being sexual, but it's not definitive that it was. We ... the police, I mean, think she knew this man. From the way the physical evidence charts the struggle, the police think Cheryl let the man in the car willingly, and that she moved to the passenger's seat, and he drove. That's all speculation, frankly. Body fluids found on the seat cushions indicate the strong likelihood that your sister died in the car."

"Body fluids? Was there a lot of blood? Did he cut her up?"

I scratched my cheek, wishing Miranda could figure some of this stuff out on her own. "The presence of feces and urine often occurs at the time of death, due to the total relaxation of the bladder and bowel muscles."

Miranda looked away.

"There's a well-defined heel print on the inside of the windshield. The location is consistent with the placement of a five-foot-six female on her back in the front seat, head toward the passenger's door. The size of the print indicates a size eight shoe. A swatch of pearl white silk was found snagged on the seat-belt buckle, and fibers of pink cashmere were present on the upholstery of the front seat. The police have asked you already, haven't they, if you can identify the clothing owned by your sister well enough to tell what's missing from her things?"

"They did," Miranda said. "But I couldn't figure it out. I don't even know my own stuff that well."

I nodded. Too bad, but understandable. "A size eight shoe—a black, two-and-a-half-inch stiletto heel—was found in the trunk of the car. Just the one shoe, and—"

"Which shoe was it? Right or left?" Miranda had inched closer and was staring down into the front seat of the car. Her hands were still stuffed in her pockets.

I took a quick look at Chris McFee, who was so still and quiet he seemed not to draw breath. Then he sighed and shifted his weight, hipbones cracking.

"Right shoe," I said, pointing. "The heel print on the windshield matches up. I don't know if you can see it, but there's a hairline crack in the glass that emanates from the shoe print. It looks like Cheryl kicked the windshield, hard, while she struggled with her attacker. The theory is that she was strangled, but that conclusion comes from a lack of other kinds of physical evidence, and it may well be wrong. Three hairs in the trunk of the car are a positive match to Cheryl." I took a quick breath. "The police think that Cheryl was meeting a man. She was pretty dressed-up just for work, but not overly so, so that's another thing that's not definite. But the silk, the heels, the fresh lipstick . . . all indicate a lover.

"Cheryl meets with the man, he's someone she knows, and she lets him into the car. Short strands of dark hair were found on the floor mats up front, as well as the seat of the car, and the police think it's likely they belong to Cheryl's attacker. The gas tank was on empty, so unless the guy filled the gas tank after killing Cheryl, which is certainly possible, wherever they went was in a range, there and back, of roughly two hundred fifty miles. We do know that Cheryl filled the tank late that afternoon at five-forty-five at the Pilot station just before the I-75 interchange off Richmond Road. Again, nothing definitive, and there are too many variables, but the mileage is something to look at.

"The police are holding to the theory that your sister met a lover, the man drove the two of them to an undisclosed location, and something went wrong between them. The man strangles Cheryl, puts her body in the trunk of the car, drives somewhere and disposes of her remains, then returns the car to the apartment parking lot."

"But why take the car back? Why not keep it?"

"He doesn't want to be found with the car. He doesn't want to leave the car where he's disposed of the body. A car is hard to hide and if he leaves it, then it's a connection that leads right to Cheryl's remains. Making a case is a whole lot easier with a . . . with the victim on hand. And there would be a wealth of forensic evidence from Cheryl herself."

McFee leaned toward Miranda. "Anywhere the car is found, other than your sister's apartment, is a trail that leads right back to her attacker."

Miranda looked from me to McFee and back again. I wasn't sure she got it.

"Unless somebody saw the killer in the car, having it back in Cheryl's parking lot leads us nowhere. And there's a bus line that stops right down the road from Cheryl's apartment, so the guy could drop the car and get home pretty easily."

"Okay," Miranda said, "but *did* anybody see him? Did they check with the bus driver? What if something came up there?"

"The problem is, they're not sure what night the car came back. It might have been the night Cheryl was killed, it might have been later. It took two days for her to be missed and another to get the investigation rolling."

"That's my fault," Miranda said. "I should have known something was wrong."

I gave her a minute to mull it over. I did not try to talk her out of her guilt. In her heart, she knew better, and arguing tended to make victims emotional. I didn't want Miranda any more emotional than she already was, not in the evidence warehouse, and not with McFee pushing his luck.

"So how come the police haven't told me any of this stuff? Why hasn't it been on the news?"

"Most of what I've told you isn't common knowledge. You and your father would have been informed eventually, particularly if your dad has been keeping in touch and pushing."

It occurred to me that Joel hadn't said much about Paul Brady. I wondered if it was reticence, disinterest, or if Brady hadn't been as aggressive as I'd have thought. That could be why he hired me, because he felt he wasn't doing enough. I wanted to meet this man face-to-face.

"At this point, Miranda, the police are working closely with the Commonwealth Attorney's office. They'll be the ones making the case, if there is one, and taking it to trial. They'll go for the indictment before a grand jury. You might want to tell your father to start making contact with their office, if he hasn't already."

McFee glanced at his watch and I took the hint.

"Miranda, it's time to go."

But Miranda did not move. She stared at the Mustang as if it was her last connection with Cheryl, and she seemed not to know how to leave. I was at a loss.

But Chris McFee wasn't. He put his arms around Miranda and she relaxed into his giant hug. He held her for a long moment, and she sighed deeply. Arm around her shoulders, and shielding her with his jacket, he led her out into the rain to my car.

Chapter Three

I was alone in the house, sitting in front of the empty fireplace, listening to the rain. I didn't feel like painting any walls. Miranda had stumbled home hours ago; dinnertime had come and gone. A single lamp sitting in the center of the living-room floor cast a bronze glow that did not quite reach the corners of the room; otherwise the house was dark. I was cleaning out a favorite purse—red, made of soft Italian leather, with a shoulder strap and a brass latch, and two interior zip compartments sized perfectly for makeup, Advil, a cell phone. I turned the purse inside out, scattering the dusty contents. When I get tired of a purse, I toss it to the top shelf of my closet, vowing to go back the next day and clean it out. At least this time I didn't leave an apple inside. Six months of dead apple does terrible things to silk lining and leather.

Rick bought me the purse on our honeymoon. Neither one of us were big on beaches and piña coladas, so we took a week in London in a small hotel in Soho that had a separate name for each musty suite.

I shut my eyes and tilted my head up toward the ceiling. I could remember everything about the place but the name—that it was built in the 1700s, that the ceilings were impossibly low, the floors uneven, and the furniture of an age that puts the American concept of antique to shame. Each suite had a private bathroom (pricey in London), and competent plumbing (also pricey in London). The price of a room included a tea tray at the door each morning and afternoon. The hotel would have been ideal if there had not been scaffolding attached to the front façade and jack-hammers to greet us early each day.

We stayed in a tiny suite on the second floor, solely accessible by a twisting and narrow back staircase. A four-poster bed took up most of the floor space and sat opposite a fireplace that had been sealed since 1910. Actually touching the foot of the bed were two worn but well-padded chairs divided by a small marble table that sat on the hearth. A mahogany bureau occupied the whole of the opposite wall.

The bathroom was oddly spacious. A claw-foot tub squatted dead center on the yellowing tile floor. Rick and I, thinking our-selves wise, brought an electrical conversion kit so he could use his electric razor and I could use my hair dryer. The dryer lasted three minutes, then blew a fuse and shot flames. I can still see Rick's stunned look as he turned from the mirror where he was shaving; I can hear him shout, *"Bathtub, Lena. Throw it!"* Which is what I did, chipping a piece of glaze off the cast-iron tub. With typical grace and panache, Rick spun like a dancer, ripping the dryer's cord from the outlet before he bent over the bathtub faucet and turned the water on full blast, laughing so hard he stumbled against the tub.

Rick and I are comfortable now, the after-marriage friendship no longer so edgy. I have Joel and Rick has Judith, and Rick is so far distanced from the feelings of our past that he recently asked me if I thought we would have stayed together if Whitney's mur-der had not changed us—me, really—so that we became strangers to our life.

An image of Miranda Brady came to mind; how she stared at her sister's death car while I sketched out the final minutes of Cheryl's life.

I wished Joel would come home.

I turned to the crumpled detritus on the floor, starting the trash pile with a business card for Bright Side Storage, where I bought boxes to move from my apartment with Rick to Whitney's house. I unfolded a crumpled receipt from the American Express gold card I had when my credit was steady and I worked a regular job. Along with the fine etch of numbers and my signature on the sliver-thin scrap of wrinkled paper, I could see that it was from the Atomic Café for thirty-two dollars and sixty-eight cents. How strange to remember the occasion—me, Whitney, my nephew Kevin, all sitting on the back patio under a string of colored lights, listening to reggae, eating jerk chicken, my sister and I drinking Red Stripe beer. Kevin had been too young for the revelry on that patio, but even then, Whitney had been uneasy about leaving him alone with Jeff.

The receipt joined the trash pile, along with a petrified stick of red cinnamon gum. I tossed an old hosiery club card from Lazarus department store; a folded loan application for the financing I took out on the crappy Cutlass Supreme I used to drive; a flyer for Armstrong Flooring I got for Whitney when she was redoing her kitchen.

I unfolded a dingy business card, with Joel's name and rank, the address of the Lexington-Fayette County Police Department, and Joel's home phone number written in my sister's handwriting. Joel had been kind to Whitney on that first visit she and I made to discuss Jeff with the police. He had listened patiently, taken copious notes; he'd understood immediately what we were up against. He'd made two things clear—the limitations on what he could do for us, and the recognition that our fears and worries were well founded. It is one thing to know your sister's husband is dangerous; it is another to protect your sister. Talking to Joel was too little too late, but all of us tried.

It was Joel I called when I found the bodies of my sister and her child; it was Joel who worked the case.

I tucked the card back into the purse.

A FedEx air bill went straight to the trash pile (divorce papers sent to Rick) followed by a folded piece of yellow legal paper with directions to Joel's north-side loft—a list of twists and turns notated in purple ink, and in my handwriting. Next in the heap went a parking receipt from the downtown garage I used when I went, time after time, to talk to someone in the Commonwealth Attorney's office about Jeff's trial and subsequent conviction for manslaughter—a desolating step down from the multiple murder convictions I had counted on. Two paper clips went next, along with one tarnished silver hoop earring. The last item, a to-do list:

2:00—Commonwealth Atty. Office
dinner, 7, meet Rick at Portabella's
cat to vet for shots
Xanex prescription refilled
Need paper towels
Figure out WHY check bounced at Kroger's

How strange to feel nostalgia for those months of hell. Strange
to look back and see good things; Joel for one, the crazy things
Rick did to pull me out of lethargic depression. Outrageous he
might be, full of a thwarted actor's ego and pissy envies, but for
sheer set-your-hair-on-fire fun, Rick is hard to beat.

Back in what I think of as the Age of Innocence, my sister, Rick
and I went out together every Friday night—Saturdays were couples only. Jeff had been run off early in the game, unable to with-
stand the onslaught of Rick's wit and energy, and uncomfortable,
as always, with the unity between my sister and me, the female
kinship forged by quarrels, shared childhood, and goddess power.
When Whitney got pregnant with her second child, we moved
out of the bars and into restaurants—Shoney's midnight breakfast,
Applebee's half-price appetizers.

In the last months of my sister's life, our Fridays were devoted
to strategy sessions for getting Whitney a divorce, full custody of
Kevin and UB (unborn baby), and keeping everyone safe. We had
no idea what we were up against. We made a lot of jokes. Whitney
was seven months pregnant when she died.

Afterward, when reality shifted and nothing was ever the same,
I spent every waking moment in the grip of Joel's investigation. I
enjoyed the hunt; the smallest thing I could do to fuel the chase
constituted the sole pleasure of my life. And when, at last, Joel's
swift but meticulous investigation ended in Jeff's arrest, I lived for
the moment when I could sit in a courtroom answering question
after question, tireless, and careful to make sure the jury understood Jeff Hayes.

Whitney, Kevin, the unborn child—they have been peaceful
now for over eight years.

★ ★ ★

A car door slammed. I looked out the window, but it was too bright inside and too dark outside for me to see. Staring from the darkness into the light brought an image—that last night Rick and I spent in London, walking out of a bookstore onto the narrow sidewalk, stepping off the lip of the curb. The pubs were lit and filling up with Londoners stopping off on their way home from work in search of lager and daily specials; in the working-man's pubs one could find karaoke and a meat raffle for a pound a throw. It is a wistful feeling, standing in the dark and looking in at people drinking, talking, eating.

I did not need to see out the window to know whose footsteps those were on the walk. I heard Joel's key turn the lock, feeling that mix of thrill, relief, and safety I get whenever he walks in the door. I looked forward to taking Joel for granted someday, and though I was nowhere close, I had progressed to being comfortable around him in my most horrible shredded sweatshirt and no makeup.

Joel peered around the archway, smiling gently, tired but relaxed, tie loose, not a hair out of place. It was only because I knew him that I could detect the relief that clung to him like a scent. Home is Joel's sanctuary, the one place he is allowed to relax. At home he actually takes off the tie.

"Good God, Lena, what did you do to the wall?"

Joel, knowing me as he does, had stopped on the way home for a double order of Pad Thai, a bottle of Casa Diablo Merlot, and, even better, Maynard the cat. Predictably, Maynard was deeply offended by being put in a carrier, no matter how comfortable, and he ignored me and did his stiff-legged walk across the room to sniff and explore. He wandered in and out of the living room for a while before he tucked himself up on the cold hearth to work out the rest of his sulk. It was what he didn't do that made me realize he was slowing down—no racing up and down the stairs, no howls from the kitchen, or experimental climbs up the doorjamb.

He was losing weight, suffering from arthritis in his back legs; but he was still up for a master sulk. I wondered how he would adjust to the house. His patience had already worn thin from being transported back and forth from Whitney's house to Joel's loft, where he endured the indignity of not being allowed to eat Joel's lizard. Maynard tolerates Joel, as he does most people, but he loves only me. And Rick.

Joel and I prefer style over substance, so we used chopsticks instead of forks. Also, we didn't have forks. Joel opened the wine, then built a teepee of splintered twigs and balled up paper towels in the blackened fireplace grate. A tiny flame ignited. Joel blew on it until it spread and flickered higher, then he added the smallest piece of wood in the bundle he bought from the Pilot station down the road.

"Man make fire for woman," he said, softly, without beating his chest.

He'd had the foresight to bring a blanket, because he is Joel, and Joel thinks of everything, and he sat cross-legged beside me to eat. Maynard, who had fulfilled his obligatory pout, checked out the fire before curling up beside me, purring whenever I stroked his head. It struck me that there was a time that the minute Joel and I got together there would have been sex before food. I wasn't bothered. I was hungry.

"So tell me," I said. "What was the big deal that you had to go in today?"

Joel was chewing, and I knew he wouldn't answer till the end of his bite. A methodical man, my Joel.

"You remember that scene in *The Wizard of Oz* when swarms of Monkey Men came down out of the skies and snatched Dorothy and the Tin Man, etcetera?"

"Yeah, and the little dog, too." I picked up my wine, leaving sticky fingerprints on the rim of the glass.

"The Feds have found us. They're interested in the case."

"When you say Feds, you mean ATF?"

"Alcohol, Tobacco and Firearms."

"I thought you were already keeping tabs with them, because of Cory Edgers's connection."

"We were, but that was with the local office. And they've been cooperative—not happy, since Cheryl Dunkirk was their intern, and running their own investigation—but I never had the sense they were working a seriously adverse agenda. But now we've got a new guy on his way in from California, and I think the agenda is . . . evolving. As it stands I'm out of the loop. That makes me nervous."

"Why an agent from California? Why not one of the locals?"

"Don't know. Maybe to keep clear of any personal loyalties or relationships."

"But Edgers hasn't worked with them that long, has he?"

"Nine months."

"On loan from the sheriff's department in . . . where was it?"

"London, Kentucky."

"Is that usual?"

Joel poked through his noodles. He looked depressed. "Happens all the time. They need extra staffing, they beef up with natives. They like to work *with* rather than against local law enforcement. And it gives the local guys some extra pay. But on the other hand, it can generate resentment. You got the Feds making fifty, sixty-five thousand. And a guy like Edgers lucky to pull down twenty."

"I know you talked to the sheriff in London. What did he say about Edgers? He seem surprised about the whole Cheryl Dunkirk thing?"

Joel grimaced. "Not really. I got the impression Edgers was a screwup and they were glad to get him off their hands for a while. Their gain being ATF's loss."

"What about the intern angle?"

Joel shrugged. "Guy's got a wife, one kid. I've talked to the wife. Intelligent, attractive . . . down to earth. I liked her. She obviously didn't think Cory could have had anything to do with Cheryl Dunkirk's disappearance. She says he's a workaholic who never comes home and she doesn't think he'd have time to fool around."

I rolled my eyes. "That's exactly the type that would get snarled up."

"I know. I refrained from rubbing her nose in it. When she's ready to face it, she will. But I did establish that on the night Cheryl disappeared, Edgers wasn't home. And he didn't mention Dunkirk to her, or say a word about it until she brought it up. Evidently her mother called her to clue her in as soon as the story broke."

"What an idiot. How could Edgers think she wouldn't find out?"

"'Think' seems to be the operative word. The complication is that it looks like the ATF has another case that this one crosses, I'm just not sure where. I don't know if it has something to do with Edgers or Cheryl, or if there's something more complex here than a love affair gone bad."

"The family's viewpoint would support that."

"We got our court order, so Edgers is going to have to donate some DNA. And the Commonwealth Attorney's office is kicking around the possibility of going before the grand jury, but right now that's just talk. They don't have enough to make a case. And now the ATF is doing an about-face, and asking me to lay off Edgers for a while."

"Huh." I noticed floating particles in my wineglass. No wonder Joel never liked to drink after me. True love only took you so far.

Joel refilled my glass. "Could be this guy's coming in from out of town just to make it abundantly clear that nobody is protecting anybody, and that the investigation is completely aboveboard. Which wouldn't be a bad idea."

"But that's not what you think is up?"

"No."

"Are you okay with it?"

"Assuming I have a choice?" Joel sorted through his noodles, found a piece of chicken and put it in his mouth. "I'm not going to bring my investigation to a standstill, but I'll cooperate when I can."

"Spoken like a guy who grew up in the Watergate years."

Joel's lips tugged to one side. I had amused him.

He caught my eye, and raised one brow. There is something very sexy about the way he does this, and I know exactly what he is thinking. He took my chopsticks and the Pad Thai cartons, moved the wineglasses out of range, and deposited Maynard in front of the fireplace. Then he smiled and settled close beside me on the blanket.

"And how are you?" he asked. He put his arms around me, and kissed me. His tongue tasted like wine.

"I missed you today."

Joel moved a hand up under my black sweatshirt. "I missed you, too."

With a quick flick of his wrist, Joel executed the singularly male maneuver that disengages a bra in the space of a second.

He kissed my ear. "That's better, isn't it?"

"Um-hmm."

"And this?"

"Yes."

"How about that?" He was smiling, watching my face. "Better without the clothes, don't you think?"

I did, but I was too breathless to say so.

"Let me help you with that."

Joel has a way of getting a woman out of a pair of tight jeans that is impressive unless I dwell on how this method was developed. I was cold without my sweatshirt and blue jeans, and he pulled the blanket up around my shoulders. I noticed the firelight reflected in the wood floors, the living room dark save the flicker of flame. It was as simple as that, a certain man pulling a blanket up over my shoulders because he worried that I was cold. Happiness, I mean.

Joel held me close to his chest, running his fingers up and down the inside of my thighs, kissing the side of my neck, sucking my lower lip into his mouth. I closed my eyes and relaxed against him and was acutely aware when his muscles tensed, and he went very still. I opened my eyes. Joel's face was a fingertip away from mine and he was looking at me in a way that was more speculative than loverlike.

"What?" I asked him.

"What you just said, a little while ago. When we were talking about the possibility that Cheryl's murder has something more to it than an intern being seduced and discarded. You said the family viewpoint would support that angle."

He settled away from me, lying on his side. I pulled back from him, propped myself against the wall and wadded my sweatshirt onto my lap.

"Yeah, that's what I said. I've spoken to Paul Brady and saw his daughter, Miranda, today. They want to finance their own investigation. I think the main point is to ease their mind, so that they know they did everything they could. Get an independent opinion about what happened to Cheryl."

"And you turned them down." Joel was so still as he watched, as if my decision answered a question he didn't want to ask.

"I took the case."

He looked away from me and exhaled sharply. Then he stood up and reached for his pants and shirt, dressing methodically, wordlessly.

"I'll sleep at home tonight," he said.

"Does that mean here or the loft?"

"The loft."

He was just as aware as I was that a new bed had been delivered and assembled yesterday afternoon, and that we had planned to sleep in it for the first time tonight.

"You don't want to discuss this?" I asked him.

He glanced down at me, hands working deftly to knot his tie. "If you'd wanted to talk about it, I assume you'd have brought it up before you took the case."

"Joel—"

"Have you accepted a fee?"

"A retainer. Yes."

"How much?"

"Twenty-five hundred."

"I hope it's worth it."

Joel never got angry with me—even when I got angry with him. His calmness diffused things between us; kept us running on an even keel. I'd never understood how he could be so even tempered and gentle with me. I'd even wondered if it meant he was emotionally lazy or something ridiculous like that. Leave it to me to make a good thing questionable.

But he was angry now.

"So what, Joel, you're just going to leave?"

He started picking up the boxes of Pad Thai, gathering up the two wineglasses.

"Stop cleaning up, dammit, and talk to me."

Joel paused, but did not look at me. He set the glasses and garbage down very gently on the floor and headed toward the door.

"If you're going to go to the trouble of putting your tie back on for the drive home, why don't you tighten it up a little and choke yourself with it?"

Joel closed the front door and made a point to turn the key in the lock.

I could not believe he was going to walk out like this, and my hands were shaking, my stomach full of butterflies. I didn't mind arguing things out, but I can't stand it when a man walks off and won't deal with things. I hate uncertainty. I want confrontation and closure.

I grabbed the front door and twisted the doorknob. "I don't need you to lock me in, Joel. If you're leaving, just go."

I knew he was standing right outside the door. *Come in here,* I thought. *Come back and talk to me.*

"I'm tired, Lena. I need to go home and get some sleep."

"Fine then, go."

I heard footsteps on the sidewalk, a car engine catch, the grind of tires on the drive.

Would he really be able to sleep? Could he just set this aside and go on with his routine, because I knew that I'd spend the next ten hours agonizing and punching my pillow.

At least now I knew what made him mad.

Chapter Four

I woke up early the next morning with a tight feeling in my eyes and throat. Maynard was asleep at the foot of the bed, and he opened his eyes to slits, stretched and yawned widely and rolled over on his back. It was still dark outside, but going grayish. The phone hadn't woken me, so Joel hadn't called. Time to get up and go to work.

But first I was going to have a long soak in the tub.

There wasn't any bubble bath, and there was only one towel and it was one of Joel's old ones—a dingy sky blue. I turned on the faucet, wound my hair up in a clip, and padded downstairs after Maynard, trying to remember if Joel had brought cat food.

He hadn't. I looked down at the cat who looked up at me. "Ummm," I said. And then I remembered the potato chips—my cat, like me, had bad eating habits.

I gave them to him whole so he could bat them around and kill them before he ate them alive. I peeled a Styrofoam cup down to about an inch high, filled it with water, and set it down on the floor. A large, curled chip skated past my toe and stopped just under the overhang of the cabinet next to the stove. I turned and headed back upstairs.

It is amazing how deep a claw-foot tub is. The water level rose slowly. If I'd turned the faucets on just before I went to bed last night, I'd have a bath ready right about now. I climbed in, winced and added a little more cold water to the mix. I leaned into the back of the tub and sighed. My legs floated free and I slid and would have gone under if the water level had been higher. The tub was too long.

I wondered what Joel would have said if I'd told him about taking Miranda out to look at Cheryl's car. I wondered about Miranda, thinking that I had made McFee and myself vulnerable to the discretion of a twenty-year-old girl I had known for less than twenty-four hours. Of course, if she was less than discreet, we could deny everything.

The water finally reached the halfway mark, and I added more hot to the mix. There is nothing that matches the embrace of a hot bath as it leaches the tension out of your body. But it was hard to relax when I had to hang on to the edges of the tub to keep my head above water. I turned sideways—cramped, but I could rest my head with no fear of drowning.

I rested my forehead on my knees and tears leaked down the sides of my cheeks. I could spend my life in the bathtub, alone, because Joel would never speak to me again. I missed my cup of coffee. Every morning Joel made coffee and brought me a cup. I wondered if he would ever bring me a cup of coffee again. Maybe he would be taking a cup of coffee to some other woman, one of those women who say, *I don't know, I have to ask my husband first.*

On the other hand, if Joel wanted to spend his life with a woman like that, best to know early. He didn't know about the warehouse, and he'd still gotten furious and refused to talk and made me feel like my paycheck was the equivalent of thirteen gold coins. Unreasonable and unfair. It didn't show respect for my work or my judgment; it didn't show respect for me. Was this Joel's way of getting out of the deal? Had he changed his mind about buying a house with me? Maybe he'd gotten cold feet.

Maybe I should turn the water off before I caused a flood.

The door to the bathroom opened abruptly and I looked up, startled, to see Joel hesitating in the doorway. He knelt down by the side of the tub, and put his arms tightly around me, getting his suit, tie, and shirt wet.

"Are you crying?" he said.

"No."

"You lie."

★ ★ ★

Joel had gotten his tie off, as well as his shoes, and I was wrapped in a towel that he was peeling away while kissing the back of my neck when the doorbell rang.

"Ignore it," I said.

The bell rang again.

"I'll get it," he said. I tossed the wadded towel to the end of the bed and got back under the covers. Unlike Joel, I didn't have to worry about being late for work.

I heard his footsteps in the hall, heavy and precise. "Lena?" Joel stood in the doorway, hanging back. His face looked closed and he seemed miles away again. "Miranda Brady is here to see you."

"What?"

"Mir—"

"I heard you, I just don't believe you. It's . . . what time is it, Joel?"

"Seven-forty."

"What in the hell is she doing here at seven-forty?"

"Why don't you ask her?"

"I will, dammit."

I pulled on jeans and a sweater over my damp skin, and ran barefoot down the stairs. Miranda wasn't in the doorway. No doubt Joel had invited her into the living room, though it seemed pointless, as there were no chairs. But Miranda wasn't in the living room, she was in the kitchen staring out the back window in the little dining nook.

"Miranda?"

She paused for a long moment before turning around, as if too absorbed in my soggy backyard to register my voice.

"Has something happened?"

She smiled and extended her hand. "I stopped by to give you the key to Cheryl's apartment. I talked to Daddy last night and he asked me if I'd remembered to give it to you." She paused, registering my lack of makeup, no bra beneath my sweater, bare feet, and the curling damp edges of my hair. "Did I come by too early?"

I didn't answer, just took the key. Miranda was clearly one of those unfortunate and annoying people whose timing and social skills could use some fine-tuning. I saw no sign of the stunned girl who had left my house late yesterday. Miranda looked well rested, and wore low-rise khakis and the same clogs. No backpack today.

"Daddy wanted me to give you this, too." She handed me a folded slip of paper. "It's just a note that says we authorize you to be in the apartment. Daddy didn't really sign it, he had me do that."

"Thanks. Ask your father to give me a call, will you?"

She smiled brightly. "Sure."

I studied her. "And nothing's happened? You haven't thought of anything else you want to tell me? You're okay after . . . yesterday?"

"Yeah, I am really. I'm sorry, I—" She looked over my shoulder and I turned my head and saw Joel in the doorway.

"Lena, I'm headed out." Joel's voice was leaden.

"Don't you want some coffee?"

"I'll get it at the office."

"Detective?" Miranda said.

She didn't look surprised to see Joel. My theory had been correct; I'd been hired because of my relationship with Joel. I didn't even want to think what he'd say if he figured that out. He wouldn't hear it from me.

Miranda was twisting the end of her shirt and looking up at Joel. "Since you're here, I mean, is there anything new on Cheryl?"

"No, Ms. Brady. If there was, I'd have called you."

Miranda watched him like a crow tracks a shiny object. "Well, I guess two heads are better than one."

I didn't have the nerve to look at Joel after that comment, and I decided to keep Miranda and Joel apart for the duration of the investigation. I also decided that I needed an office out of the house, and wondered if I could possibly afford it. On the other hand, I didn't think I could afford not to have one.

Joel nodded at her. "Good-bye, Ms. Brady. Lena."

"Stay in touch," Miranda said.

She was not at her most charming this morning, but I recognized the tendency for someone in her position—a position of helplessness and frustration—to try to exercise some kind of control. Joel didn't kiss me good-bye, and I didn't blame him.

"I'm having coffee, Miranda, would you like some?"

"I'd like to stay, but I've got to go to work. Sorry, that's why I'm here so early. I'm already late."

"Where do you work?"

"Michael's Sporting Goods, off Man-of-War. We're taking inventory, and I'm supposed to be there at seven-thirty."

"Thanks for coming by, Miranda."

"Sure. I like your backyard."

"I do, too."

"You don't have to walk me to the door."

"I don't mind," I said. I figured it was that or let her roam the house.

CHAPTER FIVE

Cheryl Dunkirk's apartment was on Euclid, a red brick fourplex set between bungalow houses built in the twenties and thirties. Some of the houses were residential, but most of the ones facing Euclid were offices or small shops. I knew the police had gone through everything in great detail, but I always like to see for myself.

Certainly there was more to Cheryl Dunkirk than her love life. She was an ATF intern, she had ambition, she had goals, she had opinions that were loud and clear. On the other hand, when a woman disappears or turns up dead, more often than not there's a sexual connotation to the crime, which is usually committed by someone in her life: a lover, a husband, an ex. Reality 101.

I parked the Miata and made my way up the stained concrete steps, wondering why Cheryl lived in Lexington and not Richmond, where she went to school. I'd ask Miranda next time we talked. Better still, I'd ask Paul Brady.

Cheryl lived on the second floor, and I followed the concrete walkway around to the back of the building. Two guys in sweats and heavy trainers were playing an intense game under the hoops, the basketball mud-streaked from pounding the wet, grimy pavement. As soon as I opened Cheryl Dunkirk's door, they stopped and looked up. I waved and went inside.

No doubt the rent was cheap. The apartment had the basic layout: living room, with the regulation worn mushroom-colored carpet; an opening into a small kitchen—stove, refrigerator, no dishwasher; two bi-fold doors separated the washer and dryer from the hallway between the bedroom and the kitchen. On the other side of the living room, a small hall, with the bedroom on the left and the bathroom on the right.

I smiled just a little. Cheryl and I were kindred spirits.

To the untrained eye, the eye of one who is not a connoisseur of disorder, the living room would be shrugged off under the classification *mess.* Those who are compulsively neat are too distracted by panic to see a mess for what it is, or what it can be. Being disorderly myself meant that I was not blinded by conventional opinions.

It was clear that Cheryl enjoyed her mess. The result was not so much a sloppy lifestyle as a personal expression of comfort. It was likely Cheryl's pretense that the disorder was unconscious. But for those of us who are appreciative of the art, Cheryl's mess was as studied and intricate as calculus, and inhabited space as boldly as red lipstick on a white ceramic mug. Her disorder had logic that would be difficult for anyone other than Cheryl to replicate.

My number one observation: Cheryl's state of disorder pushed others away, keeping them at the edges of intimacy, where they would fall or stick according to their nature, level of stubbornness, and sheer ability to endure. She had obvious standards. Garbage and old food were a violation of this unnatural order, and I would not expect to see either unless Cheryl was feeling particularly outrageous, generally hostile, or purposely trying to annoy someone, or possibly just very short of time. Cheryl's priority in life was her work, made clear by the stacks of manuals on the floor, the neat piles of notes, the computer that was only lightly layered with dust and completely absent of clutter. The web of wires that come with technology were not disguised or hidden; judging from the proliferation of this intricately entwined population, the cords and plugs seemed "in your face" enough to be downright celebrated. There were ATF manuals, and several books on forensics and crime scene investigation, all with an EKU bookstore sticker on the spine. Textbooks.

An open phone book, one of my personal cluttering favorites, was facedown on the floor no more than eighteen inches from the front door. I picked it up, gratified to find it open to a list of pizza places. I was liking Cheryl now; she was no longer in the category of good-looking and vulnerable young victim. She was real.

An EKU sweatshirt hung over a lampshade, an arrangement that was perfectly safe as there was no bulb in the socket. My guess was that the shirt was a reminder for Cheryl to pick up lightbulbs the next time she was out.

A second stack of books, including the *Revised Legal Statutes of Kentucky,* were piled just left of center of the computer where they were visible, ready to hand, and in no danger of being toppled. Location, location, location.

An absolutely mad disarray of opened, half-folded, and occasionally wadded and smudgy newspapers seemed to be a useful and inexpensive way to fill a corner. Magazines added a welcome touch of color—*Vogue, The Economist,* and two law enforcement journals. Clearly, Cheryl was a well-dressed conservative.

Coffee mugs (inevitable) were placed around the room with a harmonious randomness that smacked of feng shui. All of them were stained but drained. Bills, paid and unpaid, were filed beneath the top book in the tallest pile. The danger, and I know this from personal experience, is that this bill paying system frequently goes awry if additional books are added to the top of the pile. But the book stack method is at least as effective as the drawer toss of a more orderly soul.

Faceup next to the computer was a hot-pink class and assignment schedule. I flipped it open, wondering that the police had left it behind. No personal entries—everything school related. It was sobering to see the hoops Cheryl went through to get the ATF internship in the first place, all noted in a detailed list that included her adviser's approval before she could register, an interview with a being dubbed "the coordinator," a formidable list of forms to fill out, and a note about a waiver. Requirements, once the internship was acquired, included a minimum forty-hour workweek and a professional work journal to be handed in to Cheryl's professor at the end of her internship. The journal would be used to determine her grade.

I wondered where the journal was. Joel hadn't mentioned it;

neither had Miranda. But Joel either had it, or was looking for it. An interesting tidbit he'd held back.

The kitchen was disappointing. Cheryl survived on bee pollen, CQ 10, black cohosh, soy capsules, iron pills, and Chocks Chewable Vitamins. I would bet her mother gave her Chocks when she was a little girl. I had grown up on Flintstones vitamins, and my favorite were the purple ones shaped like Dino the Dinosaur.

A cloud of energetic gnats circled three deflated and blackened bananas that were beginning to make a puddle on the countertop; the trash can had the vintage odor of garbage that has gone beyond ripe. The sink was clean save a coffee cup and juice glass. I counted enough knives in the drawers to assume none were missing. The fridge had catsup, mayonnaise, one open can of Dr Pepper, and a pizza box from Papa Johns. The crisper held a packet of soy, several spongy-looking apples, and an unopened container of limp, dispirited bean sprouts. The small freezer held Lean Cuisines, banana Popsicles, and two empty ice-cube trays. Wheat germ, Cheerios, and a small pillow of blue mold that looked to have once been multigrain brown bread were all that occupied a sparse pantry. I wanted to throw the bananas away, but it seemed pointless, as the trash can wasn't going to be emptied anytime soon.

The bed was neatly made, which surprised me. The bedspread was inexpensive white chenille with pink rosebuds. In the corner was a small pressboard desk that had been turned into a vanity table by nailing tacks along the edges to hold a ruffled pink skirt. I pictured Cheryl and her mother sewing the skirt and nailing it to the desk, years and years ago. My sister had something very like it that she and my mother put together when Whitney was eight. Whitney was the *froufrou* member of the family. I still feel strange buying clothes without her approval.

I sat down on the bed. A bamboo bedside table held two pictures, one framed and holding pride of place: a candid shot of Cheryl and a woman who was surely her mother. Cheryl got her good looks from Mom, both of them auburn-haired and slender, their faces attractive and catlike. A loose photograph of a blond male, college-age, in a green polo shirt and beige Dockers, had been torn in half and then taped back together. I turned it over and saw that Cheryl had drawn two hearts on the back, framing the name Rob. I vaguely remembered Joel mentioning an ex-boyfriend, also at EKU. The ex had been out of town attending a forensics workshop at the University of Tennessee in Knoxville when Cheryl first disappeared. He had been seen constantly by numerous people while there and Joel had crossed him off the suspect list early on.

I got up off the bed and opened the vinyl bi-fold door that hid the bedroom closet. The interior was interestingly neat, except the floor, which was a deep snarl of mismatched shoes, purses, a black shawl, several paperback novels involving government conspiracies, and an overturned hamper of dirty clothes. I sorted through the pile of clothes. Dirty socks, jog bra, yellow towels.

Hanging on pink and ivory padded hangers were just enough dresses, blouses, skirts, and slacks to make up, at most, four different outfits. The labels were illuminating. At the prices Cheryl must have paid, I was amazed she had that many.

I moved to the matching bamboo dresser that sat across from the bed. It was stuffed with sweats and jeans, and T-shirts rounded out the mix. It seemed strange that Miranda did not know what Cheryl wore the night she disappeared. There weren't so many possibilities in this closet. I saw no snapshots of Miranda, or Miranda's father, but I learned long ago that closeness did not necessarily measure depth of feeling.

I took a quick look under the bed. Dust and a basketball, scuffed and stained. I remembered the guys shooting hoops in the parking lot and wondered if they were still there.

I was on my way out when I decided to go back to the bedroom and take the photographs. I put them in my purse and locked the door behind me. The sound of a ball slamming against asphalt meant the players were still out on the court. Neither looked up as I clattered down the stairs, but I could tell they were very aware.

They looked like college students from middle-class or well-to-do families—their teeth were straight and their haircuts expensive. Both were wearing logo ridden sweatpants and layers of undershirts, T-shirts, and jackets. One was tall and one had a knit cap on his head. Their faces were flushed, noses bright red.

"You guys know Cheryl Dunkirk?"

They turned and faced me. The tall one ran a hand through his hair. "Are you with the police?"

"No, I'm private, hired by Cheryl's father." I showed them the paper Paul Brady had signed.

"Cheryl doesn't have a father," the guy in the knit cap muttered. The tall one gave him a look that said *shut up*.

"Anybody found her yet?" the tall one asked.

"Not yet, no. I thought maybe Cheryl might have played basketball with you guys. If you have a minute, there's a coffee place down the road—"

"Common Grounds," Knit Cap said, to make it clear exactly whose turf we were on.

"Right. We could have a cappuccino or something, and a cinnamon roll, my treat."

"We've already talked to the police."

Knit Cap rolled his eyes at his buddy. "And she already told you she's not a cop. Come on, Ray, let's go. We could both use a cup of coffee. Aren't you cold?"

Ray rolled the basketball into the grass and zipped his jacket.

Ray and Knit Cap, whose name turned out to be Van, wanted to see my license, which I dutifully provided. The tax ID and fifteen-dollar fee for the license had been a good investment. Both had been playing hard on a cold morning, and they ate accordingly. It would have been hard for me to imagine how anyone could eat two cinnamon rolls of monstrous size, but if you have to see it to believe it, I got to believe it twice.

The food and the coffee made them mellow. I made small talk while they ate, giving them in-the-know and harmless details about the current state of the police investigation. It never hurts to give a little before you ask for help. Both of them listened with the sober air of two worried friends. Ray wiped icing off his chin with a napkin, and asked me what I wanted to know.

I ran a finger around the edge of my coffee cup. "How well you knew Cheryl. How often you saw her. Who she was dating, were there problem boyfriends, did she act like something was on her mind."

Ray looked at Van, who looked at me and settled his elbows on the table.

"Cheryl used to date a guy named Rob, pretty serious, but he didn't have anything to do with this."

I nodded without agreeing or disagreeing.

"Rob and Cheryl dated a long time. Rob was an ATF intern two years before Cheryl." Ray stacked his coffee mug on his plate. "He's a good guy. Sometimes he'd play pickup games when he was over, you know, at the apartment. Most of the time, though, when we played it was me, Van, and Cheryl, and a bunch of other people who'd hang out once in a while at Woodland Park. You know where—"

"Yeah, right down the road. Cheryl pretty athletic? She good at sports?"

Van scratched the back of his head and laughed. *"Hell* no, Cheryl sucked at basketball. It's funny, because see, the first time she came out and wanted to shoot baskets I was blown away. I figured, a girl walks up to a couple of guys at the same apartment complex, she's going to be pretty good before she puts herself on the line."

Ray was smiling. "Cheryl was from a small town—"

"Danville," Van said.

"Yeah, Danville. And she was used to having a neighborhood gang. She watched us off and on for a while after she moved in, and she decided we were going to be her new gang."

"She's even worse at softball. Oh man, does she stink. But she doesn't care, you know, she falls on her ass, she just laughs it off. She's kind of a guy's girl. Not a jock or anything like that, but a chick you can hang out with and be easy. And it was cool because then other girls start coming out to play, 'cause Cheryl is there, so it's like girls are welcome, and next thing you know we're all showing up regularly and we got a group."

I took a sip of my mocha espresso. It was cold, but because it was full of chocolate, still worth drinking. "What do you guys think happened? You got any idea?"

Van went still and tense. Then he shrugged, stretched, and yawned. "Person you ought to ask about that is Robbie."

"Why don't you shut up and butt out?" Ray said.

"Look, Ray, I'm not saying Robbie did anything. He's a pretty straight-up guy and Cheryl was crazy about him." Van looked at me. "She really was. They'd been living together for two years, and he broke up with her because he didn't want any attachments. That's why she moved into the apartment. They'd make up—break up. Cheryl was always getting upset, you know, because he didn't spend enough time with her, and stuff. And Robbie, he wants to work for the Feds, and he figures he'll be moving a lot, and I think for a while there he was just figuring himself as the loner with no ties."

"He was stupid," Ray said. "And when he figured it out and wanted to get back with Cheryl that last time, she didn't want him back."

"Nah, she was having too much fun. Lots of guys asking her out. She was pretty attractive."

"Either of you guys ask her out?"

"Naw, I'm taken," Van said. "And Raymond here is gay."

"I am not. You're an ass, you know that?"

"I ought to, you tell me often enough. He's not gay. Not that there's anything wrong with that."

Ray leaned forward. "Cheryl and I were just friends. Any time one would be out of a relationship, the other one of us would be in one. It got to where we were sort of break-up buddies. We'd hang out and listen to all the whining and trash the ex, go to movies and all of that."

"Why do you think I need to talk to Rob?" I asked.

"You remember you said something about Cheryl having something on her mind? There's something to that," Van said. "She was acting kind of upset, but kind of excited. She stopped dating, and started working just all the time, and she asked us if we thought she could talk to Rob again, and get his advice. And we told her, sure, go for it. And Robbie starts coming to see her again."

"Just twice," Ray says.

"Okay, just twice. But I got no idea what was up with them."

I wondered that Miranda hadn't mentioned any of this. "What about Cheryl's sister?"

"What, you mean Miranda?" Van said.

"Miranda," Ray echoed.

"The nutcase."

"She's just eccentric."

"Did she hang out with Cheryl a lot?" I asked.

"Even a little bit would be too much," Van said.

Raymond leaned close. "Miranda had a crush on Van a while back, and she caused him some trouble with his girlfriend. So he's a little down on her. But the thing is, Miranda was jealous of Cheryl. She hated that her dad married Cheryl's mother, she hated moving away from Pittsburgh, and she was basically a pain in the ass."

I tried not to frown. I wondered if these guys would lie about Miranda. I couldn't think of a good reason. Which didn't mean there wasn't one. Unless Miranda was lying.

Van shrugged. "I can see her viewpoint—Miranda gets up-rooted to go live with people she hardly even knows. But after a while, you get over it. And Cheryl was good to Miranda. Tried to introduce her to the kids in Danville, bought her makeup when they were little. Cheryl taught Miranda to drive, and took her to her college orientation. After Cheryl's mom died, nobody was really looking after Miranda. The dad's a self-centered dick—sorry—and a workaholic, and Cheryl never liked the guy."

"I thought he was paying her school tuition."

"Cheryl wouldn't take it. In her way, she was just as upset about them getting married as Miranda was. Neither one really gave the mom and dad a chance. It might have worked out sooner or later, except Cheryl's mom got really sick. Some kind of cancer."

"You know, I've talked to Miranda," I said.

Van looked at Ray.

"She tells me she looked after Cheryl. Said Cheryl had a habit of studying and being kind of a loner. That the two of them were very close."

"Total crap," Van said.

"Why would she lie?" I asked.

Ray shrugged. Neither of them said a word.

"Look, guys. I'm not judging, but the more I know the better chance I'll have of finding Cheryl."

"How much chance is that?" Ray asked.

Van made a fist. "Slim to none."

"Dammit, Van—"

"No, he's right," I said.

"You think she's dead?" Van asked.

"Yeah, I do. Sorry, but that's how I read it."

"So how come you're looking for her?"

"Because I want to know for sure. And I want to nail the guy who did it."

Van leaned forward. "Miranda is the social misfit, not Cheryl. Miranda's been moved, and uprooted, and all that sad stuff, and I don't think it makes a bit of difference, I think she'd be Miranda no matter what. She was jealous of Cheryl. Cheryl was smart and pretty and made friends easy. Miranda gets under your skin. She pisses people off. She doesn't mean to, but still. She's no Cheryl."

"But they did hang out sometimes," Ray said. "Maybe twice a month sometimes, until about a week or two before Cheryl died."

I put a picture of Cory Edgers on the tabletop. "How about this guy? You know him?"

Van smirked. "He's the old guy. Playing mentor, but trying to get in Cheryl's pants."

"Did Cheryl tell you that?"

"No, we told her."

"How did she react?"

Van looked at Ray, then at me. "It pissed her off. The guy had what you might call an impact. He's a deputy sheriff from somewhere in Kentucky, and Cheryl thinks he's some kind of hero."

"London, Kentucky," Ray said. "Cheryl had an internship with the ATF. You know about that?"

"I know about that."

Van shook his head. "Guy's shady, you know? I mean, you could just tell from stuff Cheryl was saying, and she totally wasn't onto it. She's talking about him all the time, about how he shows her stuff, and introduces her to people, and really thinks she'd be good in law enforcement. She's thinking about using him as a reference."

Ray rolled his eyes. "Van warned her."

"But she didn't agree?"

"When I told her he was just trying to get some, her face went all red, and I took it to mean he already had. I made the mistake of asking Cheryl and she bounces a basketball off my head." Van rubbed his face. "Damn near broke my nose."

Ray leaned toward me. "Yeah, but later, Cheryl backtracked. She told me her boss at ATF—what do they call him?"

"Special Agent in Charge or something like that," Van said.

Ray shrugged. "Anyway, the supervisor or whatever took Cheryl aside and warned her to be careful, things could get out of line, and it wouldn't look good. I remember Cheryl was really upset, because she thought she'd screwed up the whole internship and her career was over."

"She had a crush on the guy," Van said.

"She did not."

"Aw, come on, Ray. It was like she thought she had this secret thing about him, but in reality, the whole world was onto it. She was pretty humiliated, if you ask me. I know I would have been."

"You ought to be used to it by now," Ray said.

"What about Miranda? What did she think of Edgers and Cheryl?"

"Miranda?" Van blew air between his teeth. "Man, she hated the guy. Told Cheryl he was bad news and to stay away from him. And for once, Miranda called it right."

I was trying to remember exactly what Miranda had said about Edgers. That he was showing Cheryl the ropes. That Cheryl and Edgers hadn't been having an affair, that she would have known if they were.

"You guys tell all this to the cops?" I asked.

"Uh, some of it. They were more interested in whether or not they could pin it on us. When they decided we weren't good enough perp material, they kind of lost interest." Van grinned and leaned across the table, brushing the back of my hand with his fingertips. "And nobody was putting together the questions like you are. You're pretty good, you know, a good detective."

"Uh-uh. Don't hold my hand."

"No?"

"And don't be hitting on me."

Raymond laughed and punched his buddy in the shoulder. "Stop messing with her, you're being an ass." He looked at me with a hint of apology. "He's just playing. He's already got a girl-friend."

"Okay, now, you just broke my heart. Tell him not to toy with my affections. And give me Rob's address."

Ray looked at Van with something like panic. "I'm not sure we should do that."

"I promise not to hurt him," I said.

I left Common Grounds with the warm and charitable feeling one gets when one helps to feed the hungry children of the world. Ray and Van and I parted on good terms, and we ex-changed promises; they would get in touch if they thought of any-thing that might be helpful, or saw anything out of the norm at Cheryl's apartment, and I would keep Van in mind if I found my-self with an overpowering urge to spend one lost night with a much younger man.

I also left with the address of Cheryl's ex-boyfriend and confi-dant, Robert Little. He lived on Rosemont Garden, a block down from the Rosemont Baptist Church. Van had written the street ad-dress on my hand when I said I needed to write it down to re-member it.

I decided to drive out, hoping Little would be home. I was wondering about my client—Miranda had not expressed any ani-mosity toward Cory Edgers, which, under the circumstances, seemed a little off. She'd described Cheryl as bookish and intro-verted, something of a loner—the exact opposite of what Van and Ray told me.

So who was lying? On the surface, Miranda, as the sister, was likely to know Cheryl better. But Cheryl and Miranda were stepsisters, thrust upon each other in disharmony. And Cheryl did have a battered basketball under her bed, giving credence to Van and Ray's version. It would be interesting to see what the ex-boyfriend had to say.

Robert Little lived in a smallish, snug little house that was made of Whitestone, from Kentucky quarries. A tiny yard was enclosed by a white picket fence that stood no more than two feet tall. There were no cars in the narrow driveway. I parked in the street, opened and closed the short wood gate, and rang the bell. My only answer was the staccato bark of a smallish dog, and the scrabble of doggie toenails on the door.

CHAPTER SIX

The Los Angeles branch of Alcohol, Tobacco and Firearms is on South Figueroa, and as usual, Wilson McCoy had to park in the underground garage. The morning sunshine was neon yellow, and as oppressive as the lighting in a pool hall. There was no humidity to speak of, unless you count ocean breezes, which couldn't be felt on South Figueroa anyway.

Wilson was early; most business in L.A. did not start until after ten. He had a nine A.M. appointment with Vaughn Chesterfield, the assistant to the Special Agent in Charge.

For an ATF agent, Wilson was amazingly laid back. But then, Wilson was that rare creature, the California native; third generation at that. His parents had long since abandoned Los Angeles for San Francisco, where his mother made huge sums of money as a broker. His father taught spatial geographical analysis at Berkeley, and his grandmother lived in the valley. His grandfather had passed on several years ago and resided in an urn at the Forest Lawn-Hollywood Hills location, no more than ten yards from Lucille Ball's burial slot. Wilson had no doubt his grandfather was happy there—he was always crazy about Lucille Ball.

The California blond jock aura dropped away from Wilson when he walked. His limp was impressive. It had been years since the Waco holocaust put him in the hospital and rehab for over seven months; years since his leg lost nerve, bone, flexibility, and strength. He knew one of the four ATF agents who was killed while trying to serve a warrant on David Koresh and the Branch

Davidians, and has no regrets about being involved. That he considers himself one of the lucky ones is what he tells people when they bring it up. He doesn't feel lucky, but hell, it sounds good, and keeps people off his back.

Wilson passed through the glass doors into the high rise office building, took an elevator, and headed left for the ATF offices. He passed his ID card in front of the mechanical censor outside the door, glanced up at the cameras trained on the hallway and smiled. The receptionist buzzed him in and gave him a laconic wave. Like many L.A. residents, she didn't really spark until noon.

It was an effort, but Wilson managed to smile rather than grimace when he said hello. Today was a bad day for pain, a repercussion from yesterday's excursion wandering the hills between Valencia and Lake Elizabeth, thirty-five miles northeast of the city, but still in Los Angeles County. He'd walked for miles uphill, at dusk, in order to confirm a cache of ten MAK-90 firearms buried under an old galvanized water trough. As hoped, the trough was right where it was supposed to be—rusting away on a small horse ranch that had been abandoned so long the stalls were marked by nothing more than a collapsed tin roof, the house reduced to cinder block foundation.

Wilson's informant had been on the mark. A minimum of digging uncovered the cache—stolen in the broad daylight heist of a UPS delivery truck parked on Ventura Boulevard. The guns were now waiting for the sales transaction to a dealer in Gardenside who would then turn them over to Colombian guerrillas.

Informant Code Number 379S—a hooker who made extra cash as a straw purchaser of Lorcin and Bryco handguns—had been in way over her head. Wilson had caught her with the goods, as she was en route to make a delivery to one of the ubiquitous hives of office suites in Brentwood. Her mistake was giving her real address to the gun dealers when she made her buys. In Wilson's line of work, stupidity kept everyone in business.

Wilson had the paperwork to document the woman's purchase of seventeen handguns in the last thirteen months, one of which had already been used in a homicide in South Central, time to crime less than a year. The serial number had been sanded off, but the lab was able to raise it again with acid etching, and that was the beginning of the trail Wilson had been following. He could nail Code 379S on §922(a)(6) for willfulness to deliver a firearm to a person where possession would violate state law or ordinance (five years); §922(d) for disposing of a firearm to a prohibited person (ten years); and §922(a)(1)(A) for engaging in the business of dealing in firearms without a license (five years). Ninety percent of the cases Wilson put together were prosecuted. There was no parole for a federal crime.

The informant had two kids, both under six. Wilson had pushed the paperwork through in record time, gotten department approval to use her as an authorized informant rather than to prosecute, and personally moved her into public housing forty miles from where she'd been living. Forty miles was a universe away from her usual contacts and haunts. She was in Riverside now.

She had baked him cupcakes the day after the move. Wilson thanked her kindly, then ate all of them on the way home, a violation of rules that were explicit about what kind of personal give-and-take was allowed between an agent and an informant (none). But he sure as hell wasn't going to say no to her cupcakes.

He would have liked to round up some clothes and nursery books for Code 379S's kids, but that wasn't allowed either—too easy to slide into a personal rather than professional relationship. But there was no reason he couldn't leave a box of things on her doorstep, anonymously, at Christmas—providing she hadn't returned to the old neighborhood, and the old habits. People often did.

It had been full dark by the time Wilson made it back to his car. The quiet of a desert mountain after nightfall was eerie to a man who grew up rollerblading at Venice Beach. He hadn't had to use the flashlight—once he got his bearings he had no trouble finding his way.

The ATF agency begins the process of weeding-out candidates with a written test; one of the major features of that test is spatial analysis. Wilson's advantage came from the four years he'd spent attending college and delivering pizza. By the end of his sophomore year, Wilson could stand outside a six-story building and determine where an individual apartment was located, hit the right stairwell on the first try and go unerringly to the front door. His university years hadn't been a waste after all, no matter what his mother said. When anyone asked Wilson how to get hired on in federal law enforcement, he always recommended a minimum of three months delivering pizza.

Wilson threaded his way through clusters of cubicles until he found his own tiny kingdom. The light on his phone flickered—five messages. He settled himself into his chair in such a way as to take the weight off the bad leg and ease it into the most comfortable position. He watched the orange light at the base of his phone flick on and off.

He was worried about tonight's stakeout. Wondering how he was going to hold up. He'd been pretty much off active field work since he'd come back from Waco, and was grateful no one had taken him off the case. Yet. They hadn't been expecting the paper trail to lead to stakeouts, field work, and Colombian guerrillas.

Assistant Special Agent Vaughn Chesterfield was standing outside his office door, looking like he'd been waiting awhile. Wilson wasn't rattled. He knew he was on time. Vaughn was just up to his games because Vaughn didn't like him. As Wilson heard it, secondhand of course, Vaughn thought Wilson was some kind of beach boy, a California dude, and was of the opinion that Wilson was unfit for the job. Wilson did not think it helped that his mother had named him after her favorite singer in the Beach Boys. He wondered if she had any idea how much trouble this name had caused him. Knowing his mother, she would have done it anyway.

Wilson made the effort to get along with Chesterfield, careful not to say "totally" or "like" or "dude" in front of the assistant S.A., careful to wear very good shoes. His efforts made no impression, but Vaughn was from Connecticut and rumor was he would not be in L.A. much longer. ATF moves people around.

Vaughn motioned Wilson into a chair facing the desk. Wilson, invariably fair, would be the first to point out that Vaughn was smart and savvy, and the thing he admired most about the man was his refusal to give Wilson special treatment for being wounded in the Waco mess. Wilson thought that showed integrity.

Chesterfield was immaculate in a white shirt and charcoal slacks, and an oddly patterned tie. Wilson would bet money that Vaughn had not bought the tie in California. He wondered how far a man would have to go to find a tie that ugly. Well, Hollywood.

Vaughn sat straight in his chair, as behooves a man from Connecticut. He tapped a finger on the desk. "I'm pulling you off tonight's stakeout."

Wilson gritted his teeth. He had spent a long time laying the groundwork for what had become a net for a major player. Now they were pulling him off?

"I've put a lot of hours in this, Vaughn."

"Remember Alex Rugger out in Nashville?"

Wilson blinked. "What?"

Vaughn's face deepened into a webwork of stress wrinkles. "Alex Rugger. From Nashville."

Wilson wondered what Alex Rugger had to do with anything. Was there some kind of Tennessee connection he didn't know about?

Last night, out in the hills behind Valencia, he had stopped to rest his leg, taking a moment, out in the desert and mountains, just to be still, just to think. There had been a three-quarter moon, and lights from the city created a belt of illumination that had an effect even out there. Wilson heard a coyote, close enough that he'd looked over his shoulder. This far out in the San Fernando Valley, the sky was an open book, with the stars as distinct as streetlights.

It had been like that in Texas, his first night there, before the FBI guys strung the lights, blasted the music, and drove everyone out of their mind. *Waco.* He didn't remember much about the last night, when the fires were burning. He was dead to the world when they cleared the compound of bodies, undergoing his first surgery, then intensive care, then another surgery, the next to the last. The final surgery, what the surgeon humorously called "tweaking," was yet another two weeks after that.

The recovery time shocked him. He thought for a while there was something else wrong with him, something no one was telling him. He thought that until a veteran agent from Tennessee, Alex Rugger, flew in from Nashville for the sole purpose of sitting by Wilson's hospital bed for a chat. Rugger had appeared in the doorway of Wilson's hospital room, cheerful and curious. Wilson had been edgy and in pain. He had noticed the man favored his right leg when he walked into the room. Wilson thought that if he could just walk and be up on his feet again, he could put up with a limp.

Rugger said *Don't get up, ha,* rolled a well-padded recliner in from the hallway, and pulled a bottle of Jack Daniel's out of a brown paper bag. He settled in, leaving his right leg unflexed. They drank from Dixie cups—the blue-and-white paper ones used in Sunday school classes to serve juice at snack time. Rugger—a thin man in his early fifties, vibrant blue eyes and a face just now showing wrinkles—moved the leg again, crossing it over the good one, and finally seemed comfortable. He had an easy presence, and you knew without being told the details that he liked his job, his family, his whole damn life.

Rugger stayed at Wilson's bedside the whole afternoon telling stories, as if he'd been hired to provide the entertainment. Wilson told Rugger he could have a second career in stand-up. Rugger said only if Jack Daniel's was his official assistant.

Some of the stories weren't so funny, talk of the trade in that shorthand experienced agents develop. Clearly Rugger had done his time in the dark places, but it hadn't marked him, not that Wilson could tell, and seeing this reassured him.

Halfway into the bottle Wilson was as free of pain as he had been since he'd been wounded. He floated in a drug and alcohol induced haze and Rugger just kept filling up the little cups. Wilson had been puzzled for a while, then realized that there had not been a single interruption since Rugger had appeared in the doorway. Not a nurse, not a CNA, no techs, no tests, no blood work, no meds—just Rugger and that bottle of Jack Daniel's. Wilson had been feeling friendship and gratitude toward the man, and now he was enveloped in awed respect. Orchestrating an interval of peace and rest in the midst of hospital chaos, bringing in contraband and serving it in little cups without a backward look—Rugger's presence was deceptively low-key. He was clearly a powerful man.

About the time these thoughts permeated Wilson's weary and buzzed brain, Rugger had leaned back in the chair and mentioned that he'd been hit by the same kind of bullet in his *right* thigh a decade ago, that it had taken him over a year to get back on his feet, and that he'd recovered pretty well but it was three years before he was really back to normal. He opened his wallet to show Wilson pictures of his kids, his dog, his brilliant university professor wife, a woman he clearly adored. He had a wealth of stories about his wife's absentmindedness, her skewed way of looking at the world, her left-wing politics that clashed with his conservative standpoint. Rugger then began listing one hundred and one reasons not to own a sheepdog—none of them convincing when matched with the man's obvious affection for the beast. Wilson knew the Agency had flown Rugger to Texas in order to give him peer support, and the amazing thing was that it had worked.

"Agent Wilson?" Vaughn was leaning across the desk, staring at him.

Wilson rubbed the bridge of his nose. "Sure, I remember him. He came to see me when I was in the hospital out in Texas. We compared scars."

"He liked you okay."

"I liked him."

Vaughn radiated annoyance. It did not matter to him who Wilson liked. "What I mean is, you made a good impression on him. He's the assistant S.A. out there in Nashville. You knew that, didn't you?"

"Right." He hadn't.

"He wants to use you."

"In Tennessee?"

"You got something against Tennessee?"

Wilson knew as little about Tennessee as anyone else in southern California, but he was pretty sure he would have a lot against it once he got out there. Clearly, he was being transferred. His first thought was of Sel. He didn't think she'd really grasped the concept that a federal job in law enforcement equals relocation. Wilson had only lately been working up the courage to ask her to move in. It might be a better idea to marry her. Although marriage was an option Wilson had given very little thought to, this was Sel, and he might like to marry her either way.

"Agent McCoy, are you with me here?"

Wilson shrugged. "I don't know that much about the South. Just that it's the Bible Belt—guns and Moses. I take it I'm being transferred?"

Vaughn shook his head. "Temporary assignment."

Gun shows and flea markets, Wilson thought, immediately followed by *Why me?*

"It's not gun shows and flea markets, if that's what you're thinking." Vaughn leaned back in his chair. "Son, I guess you know I've had my doubts about you. You don't act like the kind of agent I'm used to, but I've developed a lot of confidence in you."

This was news to Wilson. He was pretty sure it was news to Vaughn, too, but Chesterfield was a company man and if the job required a temporary respect for Wilson McCoy, he'd have it.

"I think you handled that Waco business pretty well—"

Wilson looked away. "Handled well" and "Waco" were two phrases he'd never thought to hear in the same sentence.

"You've been slogging along in the trenches, doing a lot of sideline work since you got hurt out there, and I haven't heard word one of complaint."

Wilson looked the man in the eye. They both knew that Chesterfield had been giving him low-end assignments, and that the only reason Wilson did anything halfway interesting was because he drummed up the business on his own. But then, that was how ATF operated anyway. No initiative, no career.

"I think Alex has a point. A guy like you, kind of different from the average federal bear, can have an advantage in certain situations. And we've got a situation."

A situation. Two magic words. Wilson was newly alert to Vaughn's tone of voice and he felt a tiny jab of excitement at the base of his spine. *Hallelujah mama, let's hope this is good.* As soon as Vaughn started talking, Wilson realized how good.

★ ★ ★

"You ever hear any whispers about a guy called Rodeo?"

Wilson maintained a blank look, something he was good at. Yes, he had heard, just a hint, but he had no intention of admitting what he'd heard or from whom. In the aftermath of the Waco disaster and the finger-pointing, there was a brother- and sisterhood between the ATF agents who'd been there, the bond impenetrable, unspoken, permanent. And strictly out of any official influence. They watched each other's backs from every direction, including the "friendlies."

"No? I thought maybe you had. We're fairly certain we've got an assassin at work. As a matter of fact, at this point we're sure."

"An assassin? Who are his targets, sir?"

"His targets are agents—ATF and FBI."

"FBI?"

"Yeah, FBI. And the targets all have one thing in common."

"Waco?" Wilson had heard the rumors, dropped in his lap as a faint but possible warning, but had put it down to paranoia. Two agents murdered in the last eight years—bad, but not a trend. Unless you added dead agents from the FBI. That might be a trend.

"So you do know. Yes, Waco. Every single one of them was there."

"How many?" Wilson asked. He drifted away, mentally, connecting bits and pieces. He had an advantage over other men in that he was not a linear thinker. What Vaughn had always considered Wilson's *California moron look* was really the face of a creative thinker. Wilson could shift from subject to subject, moving in and out to consider an inexhaustible range of possibilities—an ability that gave him the same cerebral advantages as a woman.

"Three from the FBI, two from our side; five total. We know he's got an agent in his sights and we know the agent is located in the Southeast—either Tennessee or Kentucky. We're going to get him first."

"And the name of the perp is . . . Rodeo?"

Vaughn rubbed his chin. "Nickname, obviously. Had some guys in D.C. working with a marine intel group out at Pendleton in geographical forensics. They came up with an unmistakable correlation between the location of the hits and several select annual rodeos. Right now we've got it narrowed down to the U.S. Pro Am Markus Bourbon Rodeo, but he seems to move around."

Wilson waited. He scratched his nose. "This is all we've got after both agencies have been on this five years?"

"Three years. That's when we decided we had something going and connected it up with Waco."

"Killer doesn't leave any little notes or anything?"

"No notes. No variation in the method of execution." Vaughn removed a legal-sized file from an accordion folder. He laid crime scene photos in a square on his desk. Very precisely, no overlap.

Wilson scooted his chair closer. He didn't recognize any of the faces, but he wouldn't, even if one had been his brother. Looking at the row of victims he was reminded of those little puzzles in elementary school where you looked at a series of pictures and tried to pick out the differences.

The faces were alike—eyes half-lidded, face puffy, tongue lolling, neck swelling almost comically over the wire that was used to strangle them. They'd been shocked with a high voltage Taser or prod, which had been powerful enough to knock them out, leaving a significant burn mark. Merciful in the long run. Their hands and feet had been bound with baling wire, and they'd been strangled from behind, wire wrapped tightly around their neck. The killer had only to cross the loose ends and pull tightly, and the wire would bite through the flesh and deliver a quick, brutal execution. There were no defense wounds, no signs of struggle, no histamine levels that showed high and extended pain levels before death. All five were male, and had been incapacitated and killed quickly, the whole procedure over in five to eight minutes tops.

Wilson settled back in his chair. He realized his leg was aching. He'd been too absorbed to feel it.

"Taser—cattle prod. Baling wire—large animals. Rodeo. That can't be all."

Vaughn leaned back in his chair. "It's not. We've spent the last two years chasing a network of loosely connected conspiracy groups. Up until about six weeks ago, we were sure they were the major players."

"What kind of conspiracy groups are we talking about?"

"Most of them are survivalist wanna-bes. They're not holed up in Oregon, like the serious hard cores, but they have a nasty edge and they talk the talk. They've got a gun rack in the basement, a fishing boat in the backyard, wouldn't be caught dead drinking bottled water. They get on the Internet and play with conspiracies and the teachings of Rush Limbaugh like computer nerds play Dungeons and Dragons. They're convinced the government is collecting all their receipts from the local Kroger's and Wal-Mart and keeping a file on what they buy. They're still talking about Ruby Ridge."

They had a point over that one, Wilson thought.

"Plenty of these guys have enough weapons to make them dangerous no matter how stupid they are."

The stupider they are, the scarier they are, Wilson thought.

"Most of the time they can't get organized enough even to meet regularly, and if they do, they stay up all night and drink beer and whiskey, tell dirty jokes, beat their chest. Pajama parties with the NRA. But with every victim but the first, one of these so-called organizations has put out notice on who will get hit, usually before we even find a body. It's been a different group every time, local to the dead zone—and their stream of information comes simultaneously with the execution. They broadcast like sports commentators at a ball game. It's weird and it's creepy and now, for the first time, they're giving hints about who's next."

"When you say broadcast—"

"Audio streams on the Internet. Easy to trace. We have time and location and I'll get you a download of the files so you can listen."

"Shit," Wilson said.

"In a word."

"They identify the target by name?" Wilson wondered when his would come up. If it hadn't already. There'd been a lot of ATF agents in the mix of law enforcement, military advisers, and civilians.

Vaughn shook his head. "No names. Yet. They give the state, and now the city where the agent lives. Their information is a hundred percent accurate every time. And it's coming out earlier and a little more specific in the detail, with less time between."

"Escalating."

Vaughn nodded.

"So if they're not doing the killing themselves . . . the assassin is using them to draw our interest?"

"That's the general consensus. Rodeo uses the groups as a shield, so he can do his thing without us on his ass. The groups take the credit and feel like they have a hand in the affairs of the big bad world, knowing that if it comes to court they'll be safe—unless, of course, there's a conspiracy to have them framed. So the goofs get to splash around in the big boy pool and make a lot of waves while the assassin does his work. We don't know who the killer is or why he's doing it, other than the obvious Waco connection."

"And they've made another broadcast? That the next hit will be on a Tennessee or Kentucky agent?"

"No."

Wilson waited for Chesterfield to do the song and dance that would indicate an informant so vulnerable no one was admitting his existence. Which was invaluable but would also complicate things, when it came down to warrants.

Vaughn pulled another set of pictures out of the open file and handed them to Wilson.

She reminded him of Sel. Slender with luxurious, dark hair that hung over her shoulders.

"One of ours?"

Vaughn nodded.

"It usually is," Wilson said.

"We've had agents infiltrating groups we targeted as likely. Hoping to get lucky. And we did."

Wilson turned the pictures facedown on the desk.

"She was good. I'll give you a copy of her report, but it boils down to this. The assassin arranges a meet with a group. He doesn't go himself; he always sends an intermediate who meets with a select member of the organization in an out-of-the-way place, gives them the information, and they never see or hear from him again. The last thing our agent came up with was the U.S. Pro-Am Markus Bourbon Rodeo. Since she was killed less than twenty-four hours later, we figure she was on the right track."

"Where's the rodeo now? Are they on the road?"

"They're in South Carolina."

"Is that typical? The distance?"

Vaughn peeled a piece of skin back on the edge of his thumb. "Sometimes more. That's why it took us so long to tag the rodeo connection." Vaughn cleared his throat. "Alex Rugger will be running the op from Tennessee and he wants you on the Kentucky end of the thing."

"ATF outpost there is Louisville?"

"And Lexington. That's where we want you. There's been a complication. An ATF intern, female, college student at Eastern Kentucky University; she's been missing for two months. Her car was found in her apartment parking lot, looks like she was killed in the vehicle. No body, one suspect. A deputy sheriff from London, Kentucky, named Edgers, who was doing some temp work for the Lexington office."

Wilson groaned. He did not envy the Lexington S.A.

"Local police investigation is being run by a Detective Joel Mendez. Lexington outpost says he's good. No arrests imminent, but the theory is the sheriff and the intern had a thing, and the sheriff killed her, crime of passion, blah blah blah."

"But not one of our guys?"

"*Hell* no. As it turns out, the London cops were kind of unloading this guy. He's a hotdog, not good at following orders, sure there's only one way to do things, which is his way. Kind of guy works lots of hours and gets nothing done. Kind of guy you avoid when you're heading out to lunch."

"Where is London, Kentucky?"

"Roughly an hour and a half drive south of Lexington."

"What was he doing with our office in Kentucky? Other than . . ."

"He's a local boy. He was pointing his finger at the illegal gun buyers, most of whom he went to high school with. They had him going to flea markets making gun buys from guys he's known all his life."

"So how does being local help him? People will know right away he's a cop."

For the first time ever Wilson heard Vaughn Chesterfield laugh. "It's a peculiarity of this part of the country, Wilson. These are the gun states—"

"Texas, Alabama, Georgia, Kentucky, Tennessee."

"Obviously they've got the hard cores, but Rugger says half the time they arrest these ol' boys they're indignant as hell and swear they weren't doing anything wrong. They don't see what the government has to do with their God-given right to sell arms. They've been known to send their kids to college with the proceeds. Son comes home over a long weekend, hugs his mama, has some home cooking. He hangs out with his buddies and has a high old time, and on his way out his daddy packs fifty handguns in the trunk of his Camaro to sell when he gets back to school in the Northeast. Buy a gun in Kentucky, pay fifty dollars. Sell it in Chicago for five hundred."

"Adds up to a lot of tuition." Wilson stretched and flexed the muscles in his right leg. "Fifty guns in one weekend, comes to twenty-two, twenty-three thousand. Beats working at El Polo Loco." He closed one eye, wondering if Southern criminals were as strange as they sounded. "So then we've got this sheriff guy, fingering his buddies, all the people he grew up with and went to high school with, right? He's going to be pretty unpopular when they start picking people up."

"Yeah, it bothered me, too. Hardigree, the Lexington office S.A., thinks Edgers has been counting on moving from a temporary assignment to a permanent position with ATF. Guy is ambitious and told Hardigree from day one that he wanted to get off the local sidelines and into the federal end. Hardigree encouraged him. On first evaluation, Edgers looked pretty good. Put the hours in, was cooperative, happy to do anything they asked him to do. Hardigree says he did really good work, except for wanting to do things his way. Says the guy was starting to wear on him a little when the intern thing came up."

"What have we got on her?" Wilson asked. "Other than she

went to EKU, which sounds good." Even in California, they knew the law enforcement program at EKU.

"The university is about a half-hour drive from Lexington. The girl, Cheryl Dunkirk, was a top student, had recommendations from all her teachers and the dean."

She'd have to be good, Wilson thought. The ATF female population holds steady at nine percent. "What's the story on this girl?"

Vaughn rubbed the bridge of his nose. "She's young and eager, highly motivated, jazzed about actually getting into some work. They had her doing the usual—tagging evidence and entering it in the log. Hardigree says that Edgers started up on the mentor tack, helping the girl, introducing her to local cops at the watering holes, showing her the ropes. Next thing you know, Edgers is taking her to lunch two or three times a week, and trying to get Hardigree to let her go with him on flea market buys."

"An intern?"

"Hardigree vetoes. But he's got the situation in his sights now and he's getting concerned. She's a nice girl, and he takes her aside and gives her a little advice. She thanks him, avoids Edgers from then on out. As far as Hardigree knows, that's the end. He keeps her busy, and out of Edgers's orbit."

"So then?"

"So then she disappears. Her car turns up, physical evidence says foul play. Lexington homicide is as sure as they can be without a body that she's dead. Cops start taking a look at Edgers, which does not thrill Hardigree, but in all fairness he knows Edgers had been working her."

"How sure are they? Grand jury going to indict?"

"They don't have a body, remember, so it's getting long and drawn out. They don't indict for homicide in Lexington unless it's a slam dunk."

Wilson pulled at his bottom lip. "What's this got to do with the assassin?"

Vaughn shifted sideways in his chair. "A few days after Cheryl Dunkirk disappears, one of her friends, an EKU grad student who used to be an ATF intern himself, goes to Hardigree. He says that Cheryl had come to him for advice because she thought Edgers had some kind of information about an assassin who was targeting federal agents."

Wilson sat up in his chair. "What?"

"Yeah. Imagine. She told this guy that Edgers had been bragging to her. Said he had a contact, another old high school buddy, who was involved somehow, and that he, Edgers, was going to track down the assassin and hand him over to Hardigree, who would hopefully use his influence to offer Edgers a permanent job with ATF. Cheryl tells all this to the friend, tells him she's not comfortable sitting on the information, doesn't know what to do. She liked Edgers, but he'd said enough to convince her he was really on to something, and she felt like keeping quiet compromised her ethics. On the other hand, what if the whole thing was just a load of crap? Ergo, the friend—a little older, an ex-intern himself, the closest thing she's got to a peer—says *Holy shit,* and makes her promise she'll go straight to Hardigree. He never saw or heard from her again. Two days later she'd disappeared."

"So what's the theory? Edgers was bragging, trying to impress her, finds out she's going to go to Hardigree, and kills her?"

"Or Rodeo finds out and kills her."

"What does Hardigree think? He's talked to Edgers, obviously."

"Said Edgers acts like a wide-eyed innocent. Hardigree doesn't know about Rodeo, and neither does Edgers."

"Lexington homicide in on any of this?"

"They've pegged it as a sex thing—affair that got out of hand. Thinking maybe she was pressuring him to get a divorce. Or maybe she was trying to dump him and he wasn't going to sit still for it."

"Which is possible," Wilson said.

"Hardigree handed it to Rugger, who wants to watch Edgers, see if he's really involved or just blowing smoke. The problem is that the detective, Mendez, wants to go to the grand jury and ask for an indictment. And Ruggers wants to know what Edgers really has before he gets shut down."

"So is this detective, this Mendez—he going to play ball?"

"Hell, Wilson, that's your job. Tell him what you think he

needs to know, get him to cooperate, and figure out what the hell Edgers is up to. Unless you want to stay put, and chase Colombian guerrillas. Otherwise, you take a flight out of LAX at six forty-five A.M. tomorrow."

"I'll take the flight."

Chesterfield handed Wilson a flimsy piece of paper. "Electronic ticket. Here's your itinerary."

Chapter Seven

The cowboy looks like someone she knew years and a lifetime ago. Janis can't remember exactly what happened to him. This one is young, like Hal was when she knew him. He has black hair and brown eyes, and thinks he's God's gift to women. But you can't help liking him—he is wide open and ready for anything and something about him just sparkles. Rumor has it he was a college boy four years ago, then dropped out, at the strenuous objections of his father. People tell all kinds of stories, so there's no telling if this is true or just a legend. But things are interesting when this kid is around. And Bones Jones, the traveling veterinarian, reminds Janis that life will knock the stuffing out of the kid more than soon enough.

Janis thinks the vet can turn any subject depressing, even if she agrees.

The kid's name is Dennis Kelly, and he grew up in South Dakota. He's been smoking the competition in team roping for the last two years, and tonight he rides his first bull. The prize money is good, and the rush even better. Janis figures he won't make four of the required eight seconds, and that somebody will have to rescue his cute little cowboy ass.

That's her job.

She scratches the end of her nose, trying not to smear the bright red greasepaint. Red and yellow are her signature colors. The silky material of her polka-dot shirt is coming out of the sides of her overalls, like it does in every rodeo she works. She likes the job, likes having a character to hide in. She likes the horses and the cows and the cowboys; the smells and the crowds and the life on the road. And she likes being the center of attention when she goes in that ring to play tag with a bull, to put herself between a cowboy in trouble and an extremely pissed-off animal who weighs in excess of a ton and has horns. Janis knows she is impressive. She knows people talk about her and wonder if she has a death wish. She doesn't, of course. She's forgotten how to be afraid. That's not a concept you can really explain to people; it's not one she even understands herself. Besides, that's rodeo life. It's part of her legend.

She hadn't been afraid of that other guy, either, the enemy, and he had hated her for that. No fear, no control. She knows now that those kinds of people, ones like the Branch Davidians, are all over Texas and everywhere else. The innocents, captives is how she thinks of them, stay holed up somewhere doing all the work, while the bad ones are everywhere, just waiting for someone on the wrong side of vulnerable and then they're right there to pounce.

She was in Dallas when she first got tangled. Following up a lead on a quarter-horse paint that had been sold cheap and quick and might be her Dandy. Dandy was a prize-winning barrel-racing horse, and he'd been stolen right out of his stall in the dead of night. People who didn't understand about horses might think it strange that she would quit her old life and spend all her energy tracking Dandy, but anybody who felt the way she did about horses would probably shake her hand. They would understand that some horses depend on you, like Dandy depended on her. She knew how to clean his stall a certain way, with the bulk of shavings in the upper right-hand corner because that's where he liked to stand and look out the window in the back of the stall. She knew to give him corn oil in the spring when he was prone to colic. She knew he was afraid of pitchforks, that he liked red delicious apples cut into chunks, that his favorite song was "Smile." He would wonder where she was. He would wonder if she'd abandoned him. He might be back to the old nightmare life he had before she'd found him.

And Dandy wasn't just any horse. Dandy had champion quarter-horse bloodlines; he was a massive and flashy paint, and she'd trained him since she was thirteen. He was probably the third best barrel-racing horse alive, if he still was alive. He'd be past it now, all the action. But that was okay. She just wanted to take her baby home.

These days Janis was out of ideas, and had been for years, and she'd finally let him go. Sometimes she would imagine finding him, working the rodeo circuit like she did. She could see him nickering to her, imagining how surprised and thrilled she would be, and how everyone in the rodeo would be amazed. That's him, that's Dandy, that's the horse she's been looking for and worrying about all these years. Isn't it funny how life works out?

Janis rarely indulges this fantasy, but it stays in the back of her mind—she can't let go of all her hope. She lets the pain take hold because running from it is worse, and it washes through her and away, a wave of regret that is almost a memory. Then it goes, and she can focus. She needs to focus.

Bull riding is the last event of the night, because it is the most dangerous, and the most exciting. It is also the most profitable. The cowboys who ride bulls will take any risk to win. There will be three clowns working the ring tonight: David Hopper, who provides the entertainment and looks after the barrel clown; "Clipper" Arnold, who rides the barrel; and Janis herself. Janis is the bullfighter, and one of the five most requested bullfighting clowns on the circuit. If it weren't for her uneven temperament, she'd be number one.

It's cold out tonight; people are hanging together and drinking coffee. The lights in the arena flicker, and come back on. Janis is plenty warm enough in her padding and "bull"-proof vest. She sees the kid look her way and wave, cheeky thing, but she knows his heart has got to be pounding. No doubt he expects to stick the eight seconds through, but Janis knows better. Half of the experienced guys don't even make it. If she was generous, she'd give him four seconds. She waves back and gives him the thumbs-up.

"Hey, there, little Janis."

It's a familiar voice, and Janis turns and lifts a hand to a cowboy named Jaco Walker. He rides a paint just like Dandy, and the horse nickers as he passes by Janis. Walker shrugs and shakes his head. He's never understood the bond between Janis and his own prized horse, but he accepts it.

He didn't at first, not when he found Janis feeding the horse an apple. Janis knew better, of course she did, but this paint gelding reminded her so much of Dandy, with that same devil look in his eyes.

Walker's bellow could be heard all the way to the other side of the fairgrounds, and he had run at her like a Brahma bull.

"Honey, I don't let nobody even pet my horse, I'll be damned if you're going to *feed* him."

Knowing she was in the wrong just made Janis more angry, that ice-cold rage she saw no reason to swallow. She balled up a fist and she punched him. It hurt her as much as it hurt him. Next time she took a swing she would leave her thumb outside the fist, because the way it felt, it was probably broken.

Jaco Walker was so taken by surprise, he lost his balance and fell over, then stayed put for a minute staring up at her and rubbing his chin.

"Dammit. I can't believe you did that."

"So hit me back, I'll stand still." Janis is too angry to be aware of the spectators, but this is the best show in town and the cowboys are gathering.

"I don't hit women, and I'm not going to start today because some pipsqueak like you has no manners. But you ought to know better than to feed somebody else's horse, and this one here has a mean streak. You're lucky he didn't take your hand off."

"Don't talk to me like I'm some tourist. I had a horse just like this once, except maybe a little meaner and faster."

One of Jaco's buddies sticks out a hand, and helps pull Jaco up off the ground.

"I severely doubt that, ma'am."

"And why is that, Cowboy?"

"Because you couldn't last on the back of my horse for two minutes without me holding the bridle and telling him to behave for Daddy's little girl."

Janis is so angry, she is looking for a weapon, but Jaco takes her silence for retreat. "What's the matter, little girl? Afraid to ride the big horse?"

The horse is dancing sideways, reacting to the tension. No one here has ever seen Janis ride. She made a vow not to ride again until she found Dandy.

"That's what I thought," Jaco says. Some of the men are folding their arms and laughing.

"How about you put your money on it, Cowboy."

He is untying the horse from the fence, and frowns at her. "A hundred bucks says you can't ride the horse over to the bullring and back. That'll be just about worth the trouble of raising these stirrups."

"Hey, Jaco, don't do it, she'll pull his mouth."

Janis does not even look to see who said it.

"Not for long she won't," Jaco says.

She thinks about telling him to take the saddle off and riding the horse bareback, but there is something left of common sense. She hasn't ridden in years and years, and she has no idea what kind of tricks this animal might have.

She hears a voice pitched low behind her. "Go on, Janis, you can ride him. Jaco's always bragging on the horse, but the only thing he really does is wheel and bolt after the first few lengths. So long as you let him know you won't put up with that, you'll be fine. He's just a young horse, that's all."

Wheel and bolt, Janis thinks. *Wheel and bolt.* She turns slightly to see who is giving advice. It is Clipper the barrel man, who has ridden more horses in his lifetime than Janis and Jaco put together. Working the barrel in the bullring is a sort of retirement. Dangerous enough, but no running and jumping on old bones that have already been broken at least once.

Jaco leads the horse where there aren't so many people and there's plenty of room to fall. "Here you go, little girl, can I give you a leg up?"

Janis takes the reins gently, and swings right up. She is fluid and graceful after all these years, and it almost brings tears to her eyes, being up on that horse.

"Out of the way there, Mr. Walker."

Jaco looks up at her and is puzzled, like he is beginning to suspect he's been had.

A guy in the back howls with laughter. "Jaco, you dumb ass, don't you know who she is? She's that bullfighting girl."

"Yeah, Jaco, don't you recognize her without all the makeup?"

Janis chucks to the horse, who springs into a fast trot, and she eases him back just a little to see that he pays attention. She feels it right away, the way the muscles in his hindquarters tense, just exactly like Dandy used to do before he'd wheel and bolt. Janis slams her heels into the horse's ribs as hard as she can, and the horse chuffs air and moves sideways. Janis kicks him again, only not so hard, just to get him busy with moving forward, which he does now, as if that had been his intention all along.

"Thatta girl, Janis."

"You keep that feller in line."

"Hell, she knew what that horse was going to do before he decided to do it."

"Best start unbuckling that money belt, Jaco."

Janis pays no attention. It is pure happiness riding this horse. She squeezes him just a little bit, like she would a tube of toothpaste, and he bypasses the lope for a full-fledged gallop. This horse has two speeds, all or nothing, and Janis thinks, *Hell, ride it out.*

She runs him around the outside of the ring three times just to get the exuberance out, then pulls him back to an easy lope, then a trot, and has him prancing smoothly around the ring.

Jaco climbs up on the fence and waves his hat. "I give up, little girl, you got that hundred dollars."

Janis takes the horse in a figure eight around the barrel, then rides him sedately back to the fence. She is breathless and bright-eyed, and there is pink in her cheeks.

"You can keep your money, Mr. Walker, it was a pleasure just to ride your horse. And I was out of line, giving him that apple."

Jaco grins and slaps her back. "Anytime, little girl, anytime."

Janis is sweating through the padding. The riders have been falling like acorns out of trees, and a couple of these bulls have been serious handfuls. Clipper is perched on the barrel, ready to help a rider onto the only safe oasis in the ring, and David is one of the best at protecting the barrel guy. Janis has seen an inexperienced clown let the bull run right over the barrel, and worse still, seen the barrel guy abandoned and hung out to dry. Clipper is no fool, and he has only a handful of people he'll work with.

The kid is up next, and she is wondering what bull he'll get when she hears the announcer say *Godzilla*.

"Jesus Christ," Janis mutters. The kid will be lucky to make it out of the chute.

She puts a wad of purple gum in her mouth, and blows a furious bubble—another one of her personal trademarks in the ring. She exchanges looks with David and Clipper, and they're all pretty much on the same page, which reads very simply: *The kid is toast.*

Godzilla is a twenty-four-hundred-pound Brahma bull. Like most bulls, he's fairly smart, and though they will look wild and out of control when they're bucking, the bulls know just what they're up to. If a rider anticipates the move of the bull, maybe shifting his weight, the bull will lunge in the opposite direction, leaving the rider in the dust, then switching back to go get him. Massive as they are, the bulls are amazingly agile, and they seem to get bigger and stronger every year. The worst is getting them off the cowboy when they are close in and tight, because she'll have no room to maneuver for attention. The bulls are color-blind, no matter what anyone says, and the only thing that gets their attention is motion. It's her job to get between the cowboy and the bull, not flap her arms around and call the animal bad names like some clowns without guts.

Janis can see the kid positioning himself on the edge of the chute, and the crowd goes tense and quiet. They know some history of the bull, Godzilla, and they know that the cowboy is a first-time bull rider.

Janis figures that the kid has so much adrenaline in his system his stomach will be roiling and nauseous. His first problem will be even getting on the bull in the chute. And when the chute flies open, and the bull leaps out, he will have to stay on his back for eight seconds.

Eight seconds, with one hand free, and the other one wrapped in a braided rope that circles the animal's belly. Eight seconds, with both legs clamped tight to the bull, and spurs dulled and not locked into place. Eight seconds of hands down the most dangerous sport there is.

The judges will award one hundred total points, split between the rider and the bull, according to how they perform. No points at all for less than eight seconds. Not for the cowboy, anyway.

The gate goes up. Godzilla makes a sound like a roar, and comes flying out of the chute already spinning.

Lean forward, Janis thinks, *stay over the hand, stay over the hand.* But the kid has snapped backward and the next buck sends him whipping forward, then pinwheeling off. Janis is already running.

"It's a train wreck for the new guy," the announcer shouts, and the crowd stands up and moans. "Looks like this boy is in trouble, his left spur is caught in the rope and . . . good Lord, that bull is dragging him around like a rag doll."

How quiet it seems, to Janis. Just the thud of her heart and the world on mute, because she is supremely focused, and her mind is moving quicker than sound waves, as the brain plans what the muscles need to do. There is only one damn way to pull this off, and it's been done many times before, by herself included, but not with a monster like Godzilla. She'll be lucky to get away with just a hooking.

Godzilla has spotted her across the ring, and Janis runs straight at him. He finds the motion infuriating, and just as he lowers his head to charge her, Janis has a foot on his nose, and is running up and over his head. The crowd in the stands is screaming and cheering, and the bull is ready to kill.

It is like being in the middle of a hurricane in an ocean of high waves and surf, and her brain cannot sort the sensory overload. Janis knows she is straddling the bull backward, with both hands on the rope. She sees the boot and the spur, and all it takes is to pull the rope loose on the side. Damn, okay there, she's got it. The kid kicks and pulls his leg free. Janis sees this just as the bull whips her sideways, and she falls head over heels in the dirt. She is aware of her head slamming the ground, and the vibration as the bull charges her way. She should roll, and it's a crapshoot on which way to go. Left, she decides, giving it all she's got, and the bull churns the dirt where she was. And he's way too fast, Lord have mercy, how can a bull that big whip sideways and get back at her so quickly. The ground is thundering again, and she is scrambling to her feet. She will try and vault over the fence, but she knows there is not time to make it.

She catches motion from the corner of one eye, and sees that David has moved the barrel back and forth on the side of the ring, and is screaming *"Come get me, Godzilla, you son of a bitch!"* Clipper is up and waving his arms like a windmill. The insult is too severe for the bull, and Godzilla turns and charges after them. Janis looks behind her to see that, yep, the kid is out of the ring, then hears the impact as Godzilla connects and sends the barrel with Clipper on it spinning. David will need some breathing room to get Clipper out. She runs back toward the center waving her arms, and Godzilla, gratified by the blow to the barrel, is wheeling and ready to take her.

The funny thing about this bull is that you know he's going to move like a freight train, but you still can't believe it when you see it. She waits him out for a second or two more, then whips sideways and heads for the fence. But this monster bull is way too smart—he has already turned and is heading not where she is but where she is going to be. Janis knows she cut this one a little too close, and as soon as she is in range of the fence, she vaults herself over and out of the ring.

She is aware of the crowd in the background, the beat of her heart, the rasp of her breath. The ground shakes as the bull circles and tosses his head. He has dumped the cowboy and chased the clowns from his ring, and he is Godzilla, the King.

He seems almost cheerful as he is herded on his way to generous feed, and a vet check.

Janis closes her eyes for a moment and there's not much in her head except the observation that the ground can sometimes be fine just to lie on. God, but she is covered in dirt and sweat and when she spits, there's bull hair in her mouth.

"She lost her bubble gum," a familiar voice says, and she opens her eyes to see Clipper and David.

"You going to lay there all night, you slacker?" David gives her a hand and pulls her up.

Janis brushes dirt from the seat of her overalls. "How the hell many more bull rides we got left for tonight?"

CHAPTER EIGHT

The kid drifts toward Janis's trailer one night when most of the bandages are off. He knocks softly. Janis closes the book she is reading on the Buck Branaman method of horse communication, and marks her place with a receipt from the Southern States Feed store. She looks out between the curtains of the window to see who waits so patiently.

Her first thought, when she opens the door, is *I was wondering when you'd get here.* But what she says is, "Hey, how've you been?"

"Alive, thanks to you."

It is the young cowboy, who reminds her of Hal. He's brought a six-pack and a bouquet of flowers.

"You mind if I come in?"

Janis opens the door, and he steps up and ducks and stands in her tiny living room and kitchenette.

"You want a glass for your beverage?" she asks.

"Bottle is fine."

"Sit down then, won't you?"

"I brought these for you, Janis. You drink beer, don't you?"

"Yeah, Hal, I drink beer."

The cowboy opens two bottles, hands her one, and raises his.

"To Godzilla, the biggest, meanest bull in the circuit. And to Janis, who literally walked all over him." He takes the bouquet of roses and puts them in her lap. The flowers are fresh-cut and fragrant, their sweet scent already flavoring the room. "I got red, because that's the color for passion."

"How old are you, Hal?"

"Old enough, Janis."

She puts one of the roses in her beer bottle, and opens another to drink. "Old enough for what, Hal?"

"Old enough to be your love slave."

Janis gives him points for making her laugh.

She takes her time making a decision while the night wears down, and the fairgrounds around them grow still. The kid seems happy to talk or to listen and once his intentions are clear, he waits for her signal, and doesn't push. He looks at her chest when he thinks she's not watching; looks at her hair in the light, like he just wants to touch it, and that is good enough for him. He is easy to be with. He stops at two beers and won't be tempted with a third.

Janis scoots her chair just a little bit closer, and rests her bare feet in his lap. A little half smile tugs his lips, and she bets he's a good kisser. Kissing is important to Janis, and a man who won't kiss her and do it properly gets thrown out with no second chances.

Dennis traces a finger along the creases of her toes. "I never knew a bullfighter who painted their toenails red."

"That's because you never knew me." Some of the toes are black and blue—night before last a bull was camping on a cowboy and she had to get closer than she liked.

Dennis lifts the ankle bracelet up from her skin, and runs a finger in a circle under the chain. Janis leans back to see what he will do next. To see if she will have to kick him out for being in a hurry.

But this one's got nowhere else he wants to go, and nothing else he wants to do, and she is the focus of his entire attention. Which is how Janis likes things to be.

He presses the soles of her feet with his thumbs, his skin rough from heavy labor. He is careful of the hurt parts, and she relaxes finally and closes her eyes. He takes one foot between both hands, stroking the toes lightly with one, and grasping and massaging with the other. She smiles because it is a very good feeling.

"I'd do anything to make you smile like that."

Janis opens her eyes. Dennis has such dark brown eyes, and he is halfway to falling in love. Janis can't be accused of breaking hearts. She always stays put; it's the cowboys who drift away.

His hands go up under the hem of her jeans, and he is warm, and she is drawn to that. She asks him if he'd like to see the bedroom.

The "bedroom" is behind a curtain on rings, but it might as well be a suite at the Waldorf-Astoria for the way Janis pushes away the curtain and motions him in. She curls up on the bed, then stretches, lying sideways, and smiles up at him. "Take your clothes off, real slow, will you do that?"

He hides it if he's feeling embarrassed. He doesn't go really slow, but he doesn't go fast, and he is matter-of-fact about everything he takes off. He folds everything neatly and puts it on a chair at the foot of the bed.

Janis chuckles at his neatness, no doubt his mother would be proud. Dennis covers himself with his hands, and pretends to be insulted.

"Hell, don't laugh at it, will you?"

He is so very lovely in the light that shines through the bedroom window. So muscular and taut, young and ready. And she isn't as old as she feels like she is, which is something that Janis forgets. She is drifting, and thinking how it would be if Hal could be here, and she looks up and sees Dennis has stretched out beside her on the bed and is watching the way her eyes go dreamy.

She sees him now, she is aware, and he takes her face between his hands, and starts a kiss slowly, drawing it out, not letting her go. And she doesn't want to be let go. She strains toward him and he pulls the shirt over her head, and undresses her slowly, admiring each item of clothing she wears. The jeans—they show off the swell of her hips. The sweater—that clings so tight to the most beautifully shaped breasts he has ever seen. The bra, so sweet, so sexy; the panties, so delicate and feminine that he would like to take them home in his pocket. He folds each piece of clothing, and lays it on top of his things in the chair, and ever after they begin this way.

Dennis takes a minute to study her, really study her, and seems sincerely pleased with every inch of her body. Janis thinks that the world would be a happier place if every woman had a man like this one.

He pushes her down to the pillow; he is not through looking. He traces the scars up and down her body, some of them still red and inflamed, others white and silvery, faded. He is intrigued, as if they are beauty marks. She has one leg bent, and he takes a hand and strokes the skin of her inner thigh.

"You talk like you're a hundred and two, but I don't think you're all that much older than I am."

"It isn't just age that makes you old."

He kisses her knee. "Are you too old for this?"

She shakes her head.

He runs his fingers down between her legs. "And this?"

The kid holds her afterward, and she buries her face in his neck, and tries to think of nothing but how pleasant it feels, the way he is stroking her hair. They lay together, legs entwined. "Can I ask you a question, Janis? I can call you Janis, can't I?"

"What else would you call me?"

"Oh, Mary or Cleopatra or Veronica Lake. You call me Hal. I didn't know if I was supposed to make up a name for you."

She says nothing.

"I don't mind if you call me Hal."

Janis traces his left ear with her fingertips.

"I was wondering about all that stuff you got on the wall—the newspaper articles, the building burning . . . and the guy with the devil horns and the target on his shirt?"

"That's the enemy."

"What enemy? Is he bothering you? I can take care of him if you want me to."

Janis does not laugh because Hal is in earnest, and she respects it when a man seriously offers her his protection. "That's David Koresh, Hal, and he's already dead and in hell. Don't you recognize any of those pictures? That's Waco. Waco, Texas."

Dennis lies back, head on the pillow next to hers. "Waco. Yeah, I remember something about that, but hell, Janis, that was a long time ago."

"Not for me it wasn't."

"Are you writing about it or something?"

She gives him a half smile. "Why do you think that?"

"All those stacks of legal pads. I mean, you almost got a whole book there, looks like to me."

"It's just my thoughts, Hal. And some of my memories so I don't forget. Sometimes I forget."

"We all do, Janis."

"Yeah."

"There's a secret here somewhere."

"Want a bedtime story, do you? It's not going to help you sleep."

"I want to know. It looks important."

Janis rolls over on her stomach and props herself up on her elbows, and Dennis strokes her back while she talks.

She starts with the horse, with Dandy, and how she was still looking for him then. And Hal, bless him, finds her quest completely natural. Someone steals your favorite horse, of course you go after him. It's what he'd do in her shoes.

It was early days then, and she was tracking a paint that had been sold and moved quickly, and the farmer thought there might be something funny about it. Janis doesn't have a lot of money, and she is wondering what best to do. So of course, she calls Emma.

"Emma?" Dennis asks. He is paying close attention to all the names, wondering if a Hal is going to come up.

Janis nods. "Emma was my sister. We were as close as two sisters can be. And she had a little boy named Joe, only she called him Crumpet."

"Why do you say 'was'?"

"They're dead now. Went up in flames."

"At Waco?"

"Yeah," Janis says. "At Waco. It's hard to explain about my sister. She was soft."

Dennis gives her shoulder a kiss. "You're soft."

"I mean in personality. How tough a person she is."

"As in you're not going to find her bullfighting in clown makeup?"

Janis squeezes his hand and nods. "Emma's husband died in a car wreck the year after Crumpet was born, and she just never got over it. I didn't realize how bad off she was till I started living with her. Mark left her a house and a lot of insurance. She should have been set for life. But by the time I got there, she had 'donated' all her investments and money to Koresh's people, and she was ready to sign over the house."

"To Koresh?"

"David Koresh. The cult leader at Waco."

"The Branch Davidians, right?"

"Right."

"And he knew your sister? It sure is a small world."

"Don't talk like he was some kind of celebrity. He was evil, a predator. He made it a point to know vulnerable people with money. He would take people like my sister—smart people, Hal, everybody in this world is vulnerable at some time in their life—and he would make them think he could give them whatever it was they needed. Love, family, Jesus. He'd use it to get some kind of hold over them. Then they'd give him all their money and everything they had, and go live in that hell compound he called Mount Carmel. Mount Hell is what it was. Emma was determined to go there. I never could figure out why, except that maybe because she thought if she gave them everything she had, they would take care of her. She wouldn't have to think or make decisions or be alone all the time. And they surely did take care of her."

"I don't get how people are sucked up in all of this."

"Oh, Hal." Janis runs her hand through his hair. "It's shocking how well this stuff works. They start out slow, telling you that what you believe is all wrong, or how come you're not happy? Then they just get to where you come and listen. And first they tell you where to sit, and when you can go pee, and when and what you can eat, and it happens so fast, suddenly you're stuck. It's mind control, and the scariest thing is how well it works. That's how it happened to Emma. She took Crumpet one day, and I could not get her back home. I would go to the compound, and at first they let me come all I wanted, because they wanted to recruit me, too.

"A lot of those people in there were just scared—scared to face what was going on, scared to rock the boat. The Enemy made them scared of the world, of going to hell; they didn't know which end was up. The men lived with the other men, and the women with the women, and Koresh . . . he had sex with anybody he felt like. Even the little girls."

Dennis says nothing, but Janis sees revulsion in his eyes.

"Emma was thin when she got there, but she kept on losing more weight. I know they weren't getting anything to eat, anyone except the Enemy, and he was a pig. That's what he was like, an evil pig who just wanted to eat, sleep and fornicate, and they just treated him like a prize pet that can't be crossed and did whatever he said to keep him happy. It was the universe of Koresh.

"I went everywhere for help. The police, the FBI, everybody. And no one could or would help me. Those people had guns in underground rooms. They stockpiled ammunition and water and food, they lived like the end of the world was around the corner, and nobody cared.

"I got told to just abandon Emma and let her live her life. But she was my sister. So I went to live in the compound with her. And I just started working on her a little bit every day, pointing stuff out. Like how come the Enemy does this and does that and he's supposed to be divine. And she started to come out of it a little. Started to see things with a better judgment. Particularly when they took Crumpet and made him live with the men. And she knew he wasn't getting fed. She knew about their 'discipline'— how they would beat him with a spoon if he cried, or did the things all little babies do. And Emma . . . at least what she couldn't see for her, she could see for her child.

"We made plans to leave, but we didn't want to just walk out, because I knew, and Emma did, too—we knew she wouldn't be strong enough to leave if the Enemy came out and talked to her. She was scared of him. I think she would rather have died, literally died, than make him mad.

"But finally we got a chance for all three of us to go. We were leaving at dusk, but we got delayed, and it was dark, and Emma . . . she just couldn't quite do it. She couldn't go.

"So I said, Emma, if I go get Chris and Dale—those are our brothers. If I go get Chris and Dale, will you leave with them? And she said she would. And she said get Mama to come, too. And I knew that would work. She promised me. So I left her behind, because it was the only way we could both get out of there, and I was going back for her.

"The last time I saw my sister, she was just standing there on that flat plain, waving at me; and she looked so hopeless and worn out, just holding on to little Crumpet."

"And then what? Waco?"

Janis closes her eyes and snuggles down beside Dennis.

"Well, hell, Janis. I think that's the saddest thing I've ever heard."

CHAPTER NINE

Having ready cash in my wallet and more in my bank account had gone to my head. A wiser woman would hoard that money, keeping finances on an equal footing from week to week. But I had gotten used to the periods of boom and bust, and while I was content enough either way, there is no question that I know exactly how to enjoy the good times.

I was having lunch at Ed and Fred's Desert Moon, and after eating half of the Thai pizza and drinking most of a glass of red wine, I had ordered the chocolate fudge cake and coffee with cream.

I flipped through the pages I had printed up from Internet downloads—Cheryl Dunkirk's name had brought up a lot of entries on the google search engine, but most of them were post-disappearance.

Earlier hits brought me the following information: Cheryl was a member of the Pep Club, the Spanish Club, and president and founder of the Pizza Appreciation Club at Danville High School. She sang in the senior chorus.

She had been an avid member of online chat boards, and I read through dozens of her latest chat board posts.

"Listen up, Porcelain Dog Mike. It is not the right of any human being, in any circumstance, to take the life of another human being except in self-defense. Anything else is playing God. I don't know about you, but I have enough to do running my own life. I can't be responsible for deciding to extinguish another.

★ ★ ★

"...*Why? Because I'm in law enforcement? I won't change my mind. I don't let people tell me what to think and peer pressure doesn't bother me—I don't care if I please people. And by the way, you sure are jaded and bitter for a shoe salesman.*

"*You can't get around it, Kiss and Run. It takes time to get over that kind of a relationship, and if you think you can save it you should. Forget who calls first—that kind of connection doesn't come along every day. Don't let it go without a fight.*"

Cheryl seemed to have been an outgoing, opinionated, and idealistic young woman who was passionate about law enforcement, Mayan ruins, and pizza. Added to the expensive clothes in her closet, the sum did not equal the awkward loner Miranda described. Maybe Miranda was describing herself.

I wondered why she would lie in a life-or-death situation.

The fudge cake arrived, with a scoop of vanilla ice cream melting beneath a pool of thick hot fudge. I took a bite—the cake alone was so rich and heavy I could be sated with that one taste, not that I'd let it go at that. I stirred cream into my coffee, thinking back on my conversations with Miranda.

The first thing she'd told me was that Cheryl had *not* been having an affair with Cory Edgers and that her sister's disappearance had nothing to do with a love triangle. She said she'd know if Cheryl had been having an affair with Edgers. She'd even defended Edgers, saying he was a departmental outsider, and that a friendship between Edgers and Cheryl had been perfectly natural.

Miranda might lie to convince me to look elsewhere for Cheryl's murderer. If she really believed that Edgers had nothing to do with Cheryl's disappearance, she wouldn't want me going over the same ground the police were covering. I could see Miranda telling me what she wanted me to know, in an effort to control the investigation. Particularly if she thought doing so was in Cheryl's best interests.

I took a sip of coffee and wiped a dot of cream off the table with my napkin. Was I kidding myself? Making excuses for Miranda? People rarely tell the truth. They tell you what they want you to know.

The waitress eased my bill onto the table. I took another bite of cake, paid in cash, and left a generous tip. The only difference between me and other people with money was that mine wasn't going to last. Which also meant that I enjoyed it more.

Today there were two cars in the narrow driveway beside Robbie Little's house on Rosemont Garden—a mildly crumpled Toyota Celica that was blocked in by a beige Ford Ranger, almost new, a rental. I parked the Miata at the curb one house down, and walked up the sidewalk.

A white trellis covered the right side of the little house, and in the spring the brown growth snarling through the slats would no doubt erupt in dozens of roses.

Very quaint for a single male grad student.

My knock on the door was answered in due time by a small woman, comfortably padded, who could not be an inch over five feet. She was slightly bent, as if her back hurt. Her hair was sparse, soft looking and white. Her glasses were silver, and she wore a nubby white sweater and an apron over red sweatpants. Her tiny elfin feet were tucked into a pair of hideous Dearfoam house shoes that clueless relations give for gifts at Christmas.

"Hello, my dear, are you one of Robbie's friends?"

"My name is Lena Padget, I'm a detective, working on the disappearance of Cheryl Dunkirk. If Robert's home, I'd like to talk to him. Robert and Cheryl were close friends, weren't they?"

"Oh, yes, honey, they used to be 'together.' In fact, for a long time, Cheryl lived right here with me and Robbie. I'm June Holden, by the way, Robbie's grandmother, on his mama's side. Come in now, honey, it's too cold to stand outside."

The living room was overheated to the point that it was more comfortable outside. I shed my jacket in self-defense. The unseasonably warm February had segued into a warmer than usual early March. Winter was over.

"Sit down, sit down, I'll be right back, just let me go tell Robbie you're here."

I settled on an ugly but comfortable couch that was covered in a gold-and-blue floral-print fabric. It had a gathered ruffle across the bottom and there seemed to be at least nine pillows lined up across the seats, two that matched the fabric on the couch, the rest a mix of satin, crocheted knit, velvet, and cotton. The living room was tiny, and crowded with an amazing conglomeration of furniture. A highly polished piano took up an entire corner, and a television perched on a metal rack covered up a window, which could not let much light in anyway, sealed as it was in heavy drapes of gold brocade. A walnut veneered bookcase sat next to the TV, shelves heavy with *Reader's Digest Condensed Book*s and stacks of heavy yellow issues of *National Geographic*. There were two chairs, a recliner and a rocking chair, and a rectangular coffee table whose surface was covered with porcelain dogs of all sizes and shapes.

The murmur of male voices drifted in from the kitchen, which was no more than three feet away. I listened shamelessly, but couldn't really catch the conversation. I heard the faint noise of a bell, which seemed odd, until I noticed a miniature white poodle in the doorway. The dog wore a pink rhinestone collar with a small silver bell.

"Hello," I said.

The dog quivered nervously, then bounced across the floor and stopped at my feet.

I admit a preference for cats or large dogs, but the poodle let me pet her head, then jumped onto my lap. She was light and trembly, but when she curled up in the crook of my arm I could see her attraction.

The slide of Dearfoam slippers across carpet signaled the return of Robbie's grandmother, who gave me a smile and a puzzled look. "Who are you talking to, my dear?"

"The dog."

Mrs. Holden caught sight of the dog in my lap and laughed, settling into the rocking chair. "Oh, Beatrix Potter, you've made a friend." She leaned forward and whispered to me. "I thought she was still taking a nap on her pillow."

Beatrix Potter abandoned me, and ran across the room to her mistress.

"Robbie will be right in. He's just finishing up some business with somebody from where he used to work. Robbie was an ATF agent, you know, like Cheryl. I mean student agent, or what do they call it?"

"Intern."

"Yes, intern. Robbie would get so fussed when I'd tell people he was an *agent,* but the gentleman who's in there with him now, he *is* an agent."

"Really?" I said. This was curious.

"It's been quite a morning for visitors."

"Sounds like it. Mrs. Holden, I was interested when you said Cheryl used to live here."

"Oh, yes." June Holden scratched Beatrix Potter behind the right ear. "She and Robbie were dating, you know, had been dating for a couple of years. They were all set to get an apartment together, here in Lexington, so Robbie could be close if I needed him. He spent half his summers here with me while he was growing up, so he and I are comfortable. And I thought, well, I don't care who lives with who, so I told them both that the offer to move in here with me was open if they wanted to try it out, but that there would be no hurt feelings if they wanted to sign that lease, because couples need their privacy, and I understand that.

"They were both working, and going to school, and trying to get grants, like the kids do these days. And they seemed to like the idea. Now I won't say we didn't have our little adjustments. Robbie uses just an awful lot of hot water, and isn't much for hanging up towels; and Cheryl, she is the sweetest girl, but it takes a little getting used to the way she likes to leave her things around.

"But that's just family, you know, and having them here was lively, and we sure had us some fun. The kids didn't have to work so many hours, because they didn't have to worry about rent, and they insisted on paying for the phone and the utilities. They wanted to pay for groceries, but I put my foot down there. I'm the resident grandmother, for heaven's sake; I don't charge my babies for food. They helped around the house, and did all the outdoor chores, except my roses, I do those myself. And they were always full of fun, those two. We'd spend many a night watching those rental movies and eating microwave popcorn. Beatrix Potter loves popcorn, don't you, girl? She can jump up and catch it in her mouth.

"Like to break my heart, when the two of them broke up. I was sure they were going to get married. Cheryl cried and cried when she moved out and told me she was going to miss me as much as Robbie. Well, poor thing, her mother dying like she did when Cheryl was a senior at high school. That's a hard age, for a girl. And when she and Robbie would come home and see I had cooked them a dinner that was on the stove, her eyes would just light up. Those two years were good for Cheryl, no matter what. She was too shy to come over to visit me because of Robbie and all, but she used to call me up on the phone. And lately, the two of them seemed to make up into friends, and she was just starting to come over again when she . . . when she went away."

June Holden pulled a folded tissue from the sleeve of her sweater.

"Mrs. Holden, I was hired by Cheryl's stepfather, Paul Brady, and Cheryl's stepsister, Miranda."

I stopped talking, because the noise of chairs scraping linoleum was loud even in the living room. The voices got louder, and two men came in from the kitchen.

Robbie leaned across the coffee table and shook my hand. He looked just like his picture, clean-cut and buttoned-down. "Sorry to keep you waiting, Ms. Padget."

"Not a problem." I gave him points for remembering my name.

I glanced at the other man who stood behind Robbie. He was handsome, in a surfer boy sort of way, mid-thirties, and wore a well-cut suit and the kind of tie you could not buy in Lexington.

"I'm Wilson McCoy."

"He's from California," Mrs. Holden said.

McCoy shook my hand. He hair was bleached nearly white, with a lot of dark root showing. He was tan, and built, and stood at an angle that took the weight off his left leg.

"Wilson is an old friend of the family," Robbie said.

June Holden looked at her grandson over her shoulder. "Now, Robbie, I've already told her that Wilson works for the ATF, and if that was a secret you ought to have warned me."

Robbie turned red to the tips of his ears.

Wilson McCoy grinned and shook my hand again. "Wilson McCoy, ATF, and old friend of the family."

"California cousin?" I asked.

McCoy smiled down at Mrs. Holden, then turned back to me. "You're working for Cheryl Dunkirk's family, that right?"

"That's right."

"Cheryl was one of ours, you know. And Robbie was very close to Cheryl. Anything we can do to help you out, let me know. We're all on the same team here." His smile was devastating.

McCoy sat down in one of the armchairs and Robbie settled on the edge of the piano bench. It seemed Robbie had a baby-sitter for the interview.

"Just a couple of questions, Robbie."

His eyebrows went up, like a facial question mark.

"I've talked to some of Cheryl's friends, and they seem to think she had something major on her mind before she disappeared. They seemed to think she might have confided in you."

"Oh, that." Robbie set his lips together, and grimaced. "She was just freaked because the Lexington S.A., her boss, I mean, took her aside and warned her about that deputy sheriff who was firing on her all the time."

"*Firing* on her?" June Holden said.

"I mean making a pass, Gram. Cheryl was afraid it made her look bad, and she asked me what I thought she should do. I told her that the S.A. was just looking out for her, not giving her a hard time, and that it was pretty clear she was young and green and the deputy guy was a sleazebag." Robbie glanced over at McCoy—for approval, I thought.

"That it?" I asked him.

"That's it."

"I had the impression there was something more than that."

"Not that I know of," Robbie said, but his ears were turning red again. He'd never work undercover.

"What happened to her journal?"

"Her what?" Wilson said.

"Her professional journal," I said slowly. "The grade for the internship is based, in part, on a professional journal." I looked at Robbie. "You had to keep one, too, didn't you, when you did your internship?"

"Oh. Oh, that. Yeah. No, I haven't seen it. The police probably have it, don't you think?"

"I guess I'll ask." I stood up; my foot was asleep, but only mildly. I nodded at each one of them in turn, to give the circulation time to get moving. "One more question, Robbie. What do you think happened to Cheryl? Do you think it was just her getting mixed up in an affair with the wrong kind of guy?"

He wouldn't meet my eyes. "No, I don't think that's it."

And though Robbie was looking at his feet when he gave his opinion, he did say it in front of myself and Wilson McCoy, and I admired him at least for his integrity and loyalty to Cheryl.

CHAPTER TEN

It was clear that whatever Robbie Little knew, he was an ATF loyalist and wouldn't be sharing information. It was also clear he agreed with Miranda—that Cheryl's disappearance was more than a sex scandal. The most obvious possibility was that Cheryl had stumbled onto something touchy in her work with ATF. I knew the Feds sheltered their interns—I knew they weren't allowed out in any field situation that might prove the tiniest bit dicey.

And yet. Wilson McCoy, ATF agent from California, was suddenly in Lexington, talking to the one person most likely to know what was on Cheryl's mind.

Joel had not said a word about McCoy, or any details on the ATF angle. Which didn't mean he didn't know about it. But I knew Joel well enough to know he thought Cory Edgers was guilty of something. It wouldn't be a bad idea to meet the man, and make up my own mind. I scrolled through the directory on my cell phone, pausing over Joel's work number. I didn't want to ask him for Edgers's location, and I wasn't sure he'd tell me.

I scrolled through again, and stopped at Rick's name. Rick could find Edgers, if anyone could. And I wouldn't have to go to Joel. I imagined finding out what happened to Cheryl before Joel or Wilson McCoy. It would be nice to score points for the good ol' girls.

★ ★ ★

Surviving as an actor is difficult anywhere, and as far as acting is concerned, Lexington, Kentucky isn't even anywhere. Rick counts himself lucky to do the occasional role for Actors Theatre of Louisville, or Showboat Theatre in Cincinnati. So far his most successful role has been as the man-eating plant in *Little Shop of Horrors*. He does Shakespeare in the Park, and works summer stock. These jobs bring him great satisfaction and no income.

Up until four years ago, Rick worked as a skip tracer for debt collectors; his "moonlighting" job, as he called it. He was good at it—actors are. If Rick couldn't find what he wanted on the computer—easier and easier every day—he could charm someone in a home office into parting with information no matter how confidential. His genius was in knowing exactly what persona to take on to get what he wanted.

The problems started when his sympathies began to sway toward the prey. Rick was a bundle of continual money problems—he simply wasn't born with the budgeting gene. Like any really good actor, Rick paid close attention to the people he met, and no matter how much he tried to gloss things over and pretend otherwise, he learned day by eye-opening day that the majority of people he collected information on, unlike himself, worked hard, tried to make ends meet, and got ground down smaller every day.

His defection started simply—a matter of withholding a bit of information here and there when he felt sorry for the prey. It escalated into direct phone calls made to the hunted giving them tips—often nothing more than pointing out their rights under consumer protection laws. Naturally these calls were made on company time at company expense, and this sort of double game amused Rick so much that he might never have quit if it hadn't been for a brutal home invasion in Cincinnati.

Cincinnati is a mere ninety-minute drive from Lexington; a quick trip across the bridge over the Ohio River. The blood-soaked slaying of an entire family who happened to cross the path of a psychotic check-cashing operator (or as Rick calls them, the Gambino chain-store loan sharks) changed Rick's life. He decided to play on the other side of the fence.

Rick now runs a debt rescue business called You're in the Right

Place. Unlike debt counselors, he has no chummy relations with the credit card companies. He negotiates debt settlements for a percentage of the settlement, arranges payment schedules, and has two bankruptcy attorneys on part-time retainer.

Because Rick has spent most of his life in debt over his head, and has dealt with every possible variety of debt collector as he used to be one himself, and because, frankly, he is Rick, his clients have a high level of customer satisfaction. Rick is nonjudgmental, inventive, and occasionally kind. Most of his clients consider him family.

Although it was entirely unintentional, Rick makes a lot more money now than he used to. His office is next door to the Atomic Café—a Caribbean restaurant where he treats me to jerk chicken at least twice a month—and except for the constant parking problem is a dream workplace in a small house built in 1793. Rick and his beloved Judith live upstairs.

As always on Mill Street, parked cars lined both sides of the road. During the day, the cars belong to students who attend Transylvania University, which is in walking distance of Rick's office. At night, the cars come from restaurant patrons, late-night students, and fraternity overflow.

I drove the Miata up over the curb onto the small lawn. It was colder today than yesterday, but at least it wasn't raining.

The front door of Rick's building was unlocked. A sign beside the brass bell button said You're in the Right Place. The hallway was bare, the wood floors dusty; the walls and woodwork were freshly painted. A sign read Elephant Rides 5¢—I was with Rick when he bought it at a garage sale for a dollar. Rick's private office was the first room off the hallway on the left. Even with the door only partially open, Rick's voice flooded the hallway.

"No, my sweet thing, no, do not pay them a cent. The time is not yet right. I know, they call and call and call, that's what they do. Fish gotta swim, birds gotta fly, collectors gotta call." Rick paused, head nodding. He made a clucking noise. "It's just the phone, my dear Vidalia, it can't hurt you. Do you have the little speech I gave you? No, it's in the folder you got on your initial interview. Right, the first time you were here. Yes, that's it."

I gave the door a little shove, and it opened far enough for me to see Rick pacing majestically, in the way of royalty, if royalty were to pace. He wore a headset and held a tape recorder.

Other voices floated in from across the hall, the gentle gurgle of a brook compared to Rick's crashing ocean. There were three U-shaped desks in what used to be the living room. One man and two women tended the phones. They were dressed in business casual—no jeans and T-shirts. Now that Rick runs his own business these details matter. He keeps a fine balance—employees dressed professionally enough so that a client feels respected, but not so formally a client feels intimidated.

The intimidation is saved for the creditors. Rick, who worked the other end of the game, knows exactly what he can get and how. He usually reduces credit card debt to a settlement of thirteen cents on the dollar, as he is well aware that such debts sell for eleven cents on the dollar on the open market. He goes after any and all violations of federal consumer law. He advises bankruptcies when necessary, negotiates like a pit bull, and rallies his clients, some who arrive at You're in the Right Place so beaten down they can hardly meet his eyes across the desk. His business involves talk talk talk. He basks in the glow created by the sound of his own voice all day long. The smell of overbaked coffee hangs heavily and the heat is turned up too high for comfort. One of the women shoots a rubber band at me and waves.

Rick's voice carries, which I suppose is good unless you are a neighbor sharing apartment walls.

"Keep it by the phone, my love, and read it whenever they call. Who? Well, any of them. Make a note of it, and if they don't stop we can sue them. But yes. No, no, it's your right under the law, the federal law. Uncle Sam does not like people harassing nice ladies who are doing their best.

"No, don't cry, now, how could anyone possibly hate you, gentle and genuine as you are. I don't, my sweet, and I'm very important. I think you are very brave and you've done your best. No one can ask more of a fellow human being. Of course you did, all your life, these things get out of hand quickly when one is on the fixed income. I know you will, but until then—" Rick waved me in.

"Until then you just read them the little speech. Think of it as a game. If they keep after you we can take them to court and they'll pay a fine of twenty-five hundred dollars plus legal fees, won't that be fun? If you have time, you can come and watch. Yes, it is a lot of money. No, my dear Vidalia, this is my job. Call me anytime. Be kind to yourself. Kiss, kiss.

"Lena Bina! My favorite ex-wife!" Rick took the headset off and raced across the red Oriental rug to give me a hug.

"Rick, did you say Vidalia?"

"Like the onion."

"This rug is very thin. It was expensive, wasn't it? Is Vidalia really her name?"

"Lena, lovely as it is to follow your refreshingly scattered thought patterns, pity my poor skills of concentration and limit yourself to three subjects at one time."

"Is this real?"

"You're standing on it. Or do you think you imagine it? Could your fantasy life be that dull? Could anyone's?"

"Yours."

"It always excites me when you're bitchy." Rick put his arms around me and kissed me on the mouth. He leaned back a few inches. "Tongue?"

I caught the scent of the bay rum cologne he gets from the J. Peterman catalog. He wore Levis and a white cotton shirt, with the sleeves rolled carefully back. His thick pelt of light brown hair had been carefully cut, blown dry, and sprayed.

"Not today, thank you."

"I live in hope."

I stood on tiptoe and looked at his hair. "Highlights, Rick? You put in highlights?"

"My dear, yes, and might one suggest that you could use just a hint of red?"

"No, one might not."

"Sit, sit." Rick perched on the edge of his desk, glanced out the window and stood back up. "Lena, you *didn't*. Right on the front lawn?"

"There weren't any parking places."

Rick closed his eyes. "Is it enough to just imagine strangling her? Or should I—"

"Rick, stop playing." I glanced down at the rug. Thin on the verge of threadbare.

"You did pay a lot of money for the rug, didn't you?"

"And if I did?" Rick sat back down on the desk.

"That shirt set you back eighty-five bucks. The rent here . . . Rick, you're doing very well."

He frowned, sighed. "I can't help it, Lena. I thought I'd take a cut in income. Make maybe nothing at all, I wasn't sure. And even when I give people discounts and waive a fee here and there . . . I still keep making all this money."

"It's okay to make money, Rick."

"I always wanted to make money. Not to worry about bills . . ."

"Rick, you never worried about bills."

"But I *should* have, so it's still the same. Then I told myself that there were more important things than money."

"Rick, honey. Were you ill?"

"I know, I know, but I had conviction, Lena, plus what fun to kick fat-cat butt. You have no idea how much I enjoy what I do. But I was wrong."

"About what?"

"The money. It does make me happy."

"I'm glad. Spread the good will around, Rick. I need a favor. I want to know where I can find Cory Edgers."

Rick leaned across his desk and picked up a phone book, which he handed to me. I tossed it on the floor and sat on his couch.

"He won't be listed. He's a deputy sheriff on loan to the ATF. Currently a suspect in the disappearance of Cheryl Dunkirk."

Rick swiveled so he could face me. "Yes, Lena, I do read the papers. I saw him ignoring the cameras on CNN. Why does Joel send you when he could ask me himself? Or ask CNN?"

"It's isn't for Joel, it's for me."

Rick raised an eyebrow.

"Cheryl's family just hired me."

"Is Joel okay with that?"

"No."

"Ah. Sounds like fun. I'll give you a call late tonight or tomorrow—"

"I need it now, if that's possible."

Rick waved a hand. "Are you asking me to drop everything?"

"Yes."

"She's been missing two months, Lena."

"I want to solve this thing before Joel does."

"Ambitious of you, darling, considering the police have an eight-week head start."

I closed my eyes, dozing, while Rick muttered to himself and pounded away at the keyboard.

"By the way, how do you like my laptop? It's a MAC Power Book, and it's got . . . Lena, did you fall back asleep?"

"What do you care?"

"Because I'm talking to you."

"No, you're muttering to yourself, and you find yourself so amusing you can't believe I don't want to listen in."

"Well, don't you? Lena, do you think I'm a narcissist?"

"The term is a little watered down, as far as you're concerned, Rick. Is there a higher level?"

"Not officially. No doubt I'm one of a kind." Rick leaned close to the computer display. He slid a pair of glasses over his nose.

"Those are new."

"Had them for months."

"No, I mean that you need them, Rick."

"One grows ever less able to read the fine print." Rick raised his head over the top of the laptop to facilitate my view. "Rather dashing, don't you think? I was afraid they'd make me look old, but really, the effect is one of intelligence with just a faint hum of serious intent. Cary Grant with a Ph.D."

"Mickey Rooney with bad vision."

"Remind me later to hurt you, Lena Bina. Ah. Thought so. Got you, little sucker."

"You found him?"

"I did."

"How, maestro, how?"

"Like many cheating son-of-a-bitch husbands—I can't tell you how predictable these men are, it's like someone gives them a manual. I figured he'd have a private little account with Victoria's Secret, and he does, and luckily he's been late on a payment from time to time. That's common, too. Got to hide the outgo of monies from the wife. The address of the account is a post office box."

"Great. I have to stake out a—"

"Hush, my love. The zip code on the P.O. box leads me to the closest Kroger, and a Kroger card with an address and phone number. Naturally, our hero is not worried about the little form he fills out for a grocery card. Caution is discarded and frugality prevails. Shall I write the particulars down for you or tattoo them on my—"

"I don't want to see it and you can't make me. Write it down on paper, and thanks, Rick."

"It's going to cost you, Lena."

"Cost me what?"

"Ah, that wary tone, how well I know it. I'm out of Pez."

"Pez?"

"Yes, Lena, Pez. Don't tell me you didn't have those little Pez dispensers when you were a child? You were a child once, weren't you? My favorite flavor is grape, followed by cherry, lemon, and then orange, but only if there's no other choice."

"Pez?"

Candies for Pez dispensers are one of those odd items that might be sold almost anywhere, but on the other hand might not. I had to go to three stores before I found them at Target. I bought Rick every flavor they had, as well as a new Spider Man dispenser in appreciation of a job well done.

Cory Edgers listed an address on Cooper Drive—a small rental house literally next to the railroad tracks. His name wasn't on the lease. Most likely a semiofficial sublet, in Rick's estimation. Most of the houses clustered here were rented, some to college students. The yard was tiny—the only one without the charm of big old trees. While every other house nearby was well kept, this one had the air of a property that spent a lot of time unoccupied and unloved. The paint was peeling, one of the windows had lost a shutter, and I could see window screens stacked by the side of the house. Newspaper darkened the bedroom windows, a depressing but economical alternative to curtains or blinds. The yard was muddy from the days of rain that had overtaken the weak sprigs of grass, and the small narrow driveway had very little gravel over packed-in dirt.

There was a car in the driveway, a two-year-old Saturn that had clearly just been washed. It was the only vehicle in sight that wasn't splashed with mud. The license plate was from Laurel County—London, Kentucky was in Laurel County.

I parked the Miata on the curb, and went to the door.

The bell wasn't working so I knocked, waited, and knocked again. The front porch looked like it had been recently swept, and the glass in the storm door was clean.

Edgers was out, or he was ignoring me. If he was ignoring me, I could have him out of the house in minutes. No man in the world can tolerate a stranger messing with his car.

I stepped off the concrete porch and approached the car. Even the tires were clean. Just inside, on the dash, was a portable blue light and siren. Sunglasses were splayed on the front seat, along with a small vinyl notebook full of papers. I crouched down and looked under the car for no particular reason, then walked slowly, staring, circling the Saturn, which was beige, and so well cared for it looked new. I heard the creak of a door, and footsteps.

Edgers had that state trooper physique—tall, with broad shoulders and physical presence. He had a law enforcement haircut, short and close to his head. His smile surprised me. He had blue eyes, very clear, very alive. He walked with a wiry grace unusual in a man of his size, and was cop enough to do the visual sweep that made him aware of who might or might not be on the street, in my car, along the side of the house.

"I'm sure you have a reason to be here." He even grinned. He talked pure Kentucky and gave me a sideways look and if I didn't know better I'd have thought he was flirting. The boys at Cheryl's apartment could call him an old man all they wanted. He didn't look a day over thirty, even though he probably was, and I could see why Cheryl had been attracted.

"I'm not trying to steal your car."

"That's good. Never steal a car from a cop."

He said it with a quiet pride, as if it defined him. He folded his arms and leaned back against the Saturn like he had all day and talking to me was the most interesting thing on the agenda. I got the feeling that he had been bored until I walked up to the doorstep, and that strangers were welcome here.

"Cory Edgers?"

He nodded.

"Lena Padget."

We shook hands. His grip was firm, his palm warm and dry; he wore a thick gold wedding band on the left hand.

"You with the Commonwealth Attorney's office?"

"No. You're welcome to see the ID." I opened my purse, well aware that he was watching just in case I had a weapon—ridiculous, because there was barely enough room for what I already had in there—the leather wallet, the lipstick and hairbrush and the extra pair of hose. I showed him my driver's license and investigator's license. He looked at them long enough that I knew he was paying attention, then handed them back.

"What brings you here, Ms. Padget?"

"Cheryl Dunkirk. I understand you were a friend."

His smile went away, and his eyes looked sad. "Come on in and sit down. I just made coffee, if you'd like a cup."

The last thing I expected was to be invited in. He led the way up the cracked gray sidewalk, and I glanced out onto the street. Cars went by; there was a lot of traffic. My Miata sat in full view in front of the house.

He was a big man, Cory Edgers. He stopped and motioned me forward and opened the storm door by reaching over my head. I felt very small. I stepped up into the living room, which was clean, though the walls were an ugly mint green and full of nail holes and finger smudges. The wood floors were dull and scratched, but swept clean. The place had a sort of barracks feel about it, as if these were the current quarters of Deputy Sheriff Cory Edgers and were ready for inspection at any time. Edgers was like a retired soldier, newly released from military service but still caught up in the regulations that haunt veterans their first months of civilian life. Edgers was in the law enforcement army.

"I'm here on temporary assignment. The house belongs to a friend. He's been having trouble with vandals, and he's happy to let me stay here free just so there's somebody around. Come on in the kitchen."

The kitchen was the heart of the house. The linoleum floor was as clean as old linoleum can be, which means the current layers of dirt were mopped away, leaving the ground-in dirt that defied string mops and reasonable effort. I wasn't sure if a scrub brush and hard labor would get that kind of dirt up, because I had never tried.

The kitchen walls were also mint green, like toothpaste, dingy and depressing. But the appliances, all matching harvest yellow, were squeaky clean and the stainless steel sink was bone dry and spotless. A Mr. Coffee burbled, the only thing on the scrubbed Formica countertops, and the house smelled like coffee, Pine Sol, and Irish Spring soap.

Edgers took two new brown mugs out of an otherwise empty cabinet and looked at me over his shoulder. "Coffee? Go ahead and sit, if you'd like."

There were three matching maple chairs around the table. Edgers put a mug of coffee at my place, and set a box of Dixie sugar cubes on the table, alongside a tiny carton of heavy cream. He handed me a plastic spoon.

Edgers hooked a chair with his foot and pulled it out in a practiced motion. "So you're looking for Cheryl. Who hired you, if I may ask?" He scrupulously maintained eye contact, voice steady and sure and maybe just a touch wary.

"Her family."

"They have my sympathy."

"You still with the ATF, Mr. Edgers?"

"Technically. I'm on enforced leave until the paperwork goes through so they can get rid of me. It's the federal way. Back home they could have fired me a lot faster."

"Did they?"

"Fire me? No reason to. I guess they know me better down there."

"Why are you still in Lexington?"

"Like I said. Doing a favor for a friend."

"Occupying the house?"

"Occupying the house. Cops do it all the time. It's good for the neighborhood."

I glanced out the kitchen window, noticed a sagging wood garage at the end of the driveway. The door was boarded up with planks.

"That's the first place they looked," Edgers told me. "She's not in there."

I put cream in my coffee, mainly to have something to do with my hands. The constant eye contact was getting creepy. I took a sip from my cup. The coffee was hot and very good. Edgers's foot was a few inches from mine, his chair an arm's length from my chair. His smile was artistically genuine, sincerity vibrating like a jackhammer.

"How can I help you, Lena?"

I did not like it when he said my name. I did not like the sensation I had that he *noticed* me. I saw how intentional it was, the close physical dominance, the unrelenting focus and attention. I looked down the shadowed hallway to the front door. A heavy door; no window at the top. The deadbolt was latched and the chain lock was in the metal slot. When had he done that?

"You know, I appreciate the coffee." I pushed my chair back as if I was trying to get comfortable. Edgers slid his chair forward in pursuit. "But I'm wondering why you'd take the time to talk to me. You don't know me."

Edgers tilted his head to one side. "I don't know about the way you grew up, but down in London we help out when we can, and there's always time for a coffee or a Coke in the kitchen. If you're working for Cheryl's family, why wouldn't I help? I thought the world of Cheryl and it breaks my heart what happened to her."

"What did happen to her?" I asked him.

He reached into his back pocket for a wallet and a leather case.

"This is my badge. These . . ." He flicked pictures out with a practiced air. "These are pictures of my family. That's my little boy. His name is Leo; he's four. Looks like his mama, I think, don't you? That's my wife on her old horse she's had since she was a little girl."

I glanced at the pictures. The little boy was dark-haired, not looking at the camera, as if he hadn't noticed the photographer. The woman was interesting. An honest face, a capable physical presence.

"I'm just a small-town boy who wanted to be a cop all his life. I've got a family, a wife I love and a little boy. I don't need a lot of money; I don't want to work in New York City. I just want to look after the community, to protect and serve the people I grew up with, and if that's corny, then too bad. I want to watch my son grow up, maybe with a brother or a sister. I want to make my wife happy she married *me*. I'm not all that interesting, I'm sorry to say. I don't hunt and kill animals; I don't smoke cigarettes; I drink Jack Daniel's from time to time and that's about it. I'm saving up for a boat to put on Laurel Lake to take my wife and son out on the weekends. Is there anything else you want to know?"

I leaned across the table. He didn't give ground. His face was so close to mine I could feel his breath, and my heart slammed, that sick feeling of nerves rising in my stomach.

"I want to know what you think happened to Cheryl."

"I don't think we'll ever find out."

"When was the last time you saw her?"

"In the office, the last day she was there."

"What was the nature of your relationship?"

"I was her mentor."

"Did that include sex?"

He smiled. "No."

"Was she in love with you?"

"No."

"Anything in her work situation that might have led to her disappearance?"

"She was an intern. No. Cheryl was probably just in the wrong place at the wrong time." He tapped a finger on the table. "You and I both know there are a lot of predators out there who target women. Bad men, bad world."

"Yeah. I'm wondering if you're one of them."

"Take a number and get in line."

I stood up. "Thanks for your time."

Edgers smiled at me, walked to the front door, removed the chain lock, released the deadbolt. Edgers touched my shoulder as I walked through the door.

"Maybe next time, Lena."

CHAPTER ELEVEN

I spent the rest of the afternoon at the movies, trying to shake the feeling Edgers had given me when he'd touched my shoulder. I got home between seven-thirty and eight. There were two missed calls from Joel on my cell. His car was in the driveway and the porch light was on. The front door was unlocked.

The fragrance of olive oil, garlic, and wine permeated the house. I left my purse beside the staircase.

"Hey." Joel stood in the arched doorway between the kitchen and living room, drying his hands on a dishcloth. He had changed into a sweatshirt and drawstring pajama bottoms.

"Smells good," I said.

"It's ready whenever you want to eat." Something kept him there in the doorway. I supposed what kept him there was me. We were awkward tonight. "I've got a bottle of wine open. You want a glass?"

"Maybe in a minute." I headed upstairs to the bedroom. I sensed that he was watching me, but I didn't look back.

Joel had made the bed. It's a black iron bed, graceful and curved in an old southern design called Savannah. We have a stark white duvet and lots of pillows. Joel always throws the pillows off the bed. I always pile them back on.

I wanted to change, but I still hadn't moved most of my stuff over. I wondered how many years it would take us to move in at the rate we were going.

One of Joel's old dress shirts was hanging in the back of the closet. A week ago I would have pulled it off the hanger and worn that. I kicked my shoes off and headed back downstairs.

Joel was in the kitchen, back to me, stirring something in an iron skillet. A panful of boiling water spilled over, hissing and steaming as it hit the hot elements.

"Ready to eat?"

"Sure. Thanks for cooking."

Joel looked at me over his shoulder, puzzled. I took the glass of red wine that sat in front of my place at the card table, and stood in front of the window that faces the backyard. I couldn't see anything except my reflection in the glass. It was dark outside, light inside. Behind me I heard the scrape of a wooden spoon, the splash of water in the sink; mundane little cooking noises I found to be a comfort.

"I tried to call you," Joel said.

"My cell was turned off. I went to a movie."

Dishes clattered, the refrigerator door opened and closed. I would like to cook with Joel once in a while, but he won't let me help. It is as if he has the meal preparation planned like a military campaign and dinner is a mission in which there is no room for amateurs like me.

The week before we moved I served him a casserole that has kept me fed many a night—creamed corn covered in a layer of potato chips. It bakes in a quick half hour and you can vary the flavor depending upon the kind of potato chips you use, so it is both easy to make and adaptable. I think the casserole, combined with a new kitchen that Joel likes, may mean that I'll do very little cooking from here on out.

"Lena?"

Joel stood behind his chair and waited for me to sit down. There were cloth napkins on the table, more pots and pans. Clearly he'd brought over some of the kitchen things. There were new dishes—a blue, yellow, and red pattern, very Mediterranean looking, very swirled.

"New plates?"

"Pier One." Joel used a clawlike server to spoon fresh linguine on my plate. "What do you think?"

"They're very pretty."

"I should have checked with you first. Let you help pick them out."

"No, no. They're great. Really."

Joel had made a dish we call Linguine Mendez. He puts olive oil in an iron skillet, and browns garlic and shallots. Then he puts organic baby spinach (or so it says on the package) in with sliced red peppers, portobello mushrooms, sun-dried tomatoes, Kalamata olives, capers, and a copious amount of white wine. While the vegetables simmer, he grates fresh Parmesan cheese, and puts that in the skillet followed by plain yogurt. He squeezes a fresh lemon over all of this and adds some more wine. Everything simmers, then goes over pasta.

I was there the night he made it up and it is one of my three favorite dinners, the other two being chicken and dumplings and hamburgers from White Castle.

I sat down in front of my plate of pasta, and Joel put warm bread on the table, a French baguette he'd bought at Sloane's. He buttered one piece and handed it to me.

"*Bon appétit,* Lena."

"*Bon appétit.*" I studied the bread, took a small bite.

"What movie did you see?" Joel asked.

He knew there was something on my mind. I knew he'd be patient until I was ready to talk. I cannot even imagine the self-control it takes to sit back and talk of other things. When I think Joel has something major on his mind, I want to pounce on him and jump up and down until I get the details out of him. That hasn't ever worked.

I didn't expect to be able to eat much, but halfway through a glass of the red Rhone wine that Joel had picked out, I began to feel an appetite. Joel ate steadily, telling me about a movie he'd seen when he was a little boy, some kind of mummy movie that gave him nightmares. He carried the conversation and let me sip my wine and eat when I felt like it. His quiet acceptance of my mood, my lack of appetite, my lack of conversation were a relief. I felt the tension in my shoulders start to ease. I realized I had been sitting with my shoulders high, arms clamped to my sides. Tonight

I did not want to be questioned or pressed and I was grateful to be left alone.

Joel refilled my wineglass, and I closed my eyes, enjoying the buzz.

"I miss our table," I said.

When Joel and I decided to buy the house, we also decided to buy a new bed and kitchen table. He didn't like my table and I didn't like his, so we compromised and got rid of them both. We ate on TV trays until we found a mission-style oak table that had been mistreated enough to be affordable, even in an antiques store. We don't bother to lie and tell people we are going to refinish it one day, and it will be perfect for this kitchen if we ever get it moved out of Joel's apartment.

He folded his napkin and put it under his plate. "I called some movers today, and found a local company that seems reasonable. They could pick up and deliver in three days."

"Wind chimes, too. I miss wind chimes."

Joel frowned at me. "We didn't have wind chimes, Lena."

"Wouldn't you like some?"

"I hate wind chimes."

"You hate wind chimes? How is it you never brought this up before?"

"I was hiding it from you. I was afraid you would leave me if you found out."

"I guess you think you're funny."

"I guess you think I'm not."

I drank more wine. So did Joel.

"Wind chimes are important to me," I said. "They make me feel at home. There were wind chimes at Christy's house. Right outside the kitchen window."

"Lena, wind chimes drive me insane. I can't sleep, I can't concentrate. . . . I always end up yanking the damn things down."

"So, what you're saying is, if I hang them up you'll take them down?"

"I won't be able to stop myself the first night we get some real wind. Look, you'll feel more at home when we get the furniture here. Do you think we could be ready for the movers in three days?"

"You mean, get everything packed?"

He nodded.

"Were you planning to help with the packing?"

"As much as I can. I have another meeting scheduled with Wilson McCoy tomorrow afternoon, so I'm not sure what my schedule will be."

"Wilson McCoy is an ATF agent from California."

"You've been busy."

"And you're working with him?"

"I didn't say I wasn't."

I let silence fall, wondering if Joel would tell me anything. He didn't seem to mind the silence.

"That's fine, Joel, but I have a paying client, so I don't know what my schedule will be like either."

Joel refilled his wineglass. Added some more to mine.

"Why do you do that?" I asked him.

"Fill your glass with wine?"

"No, no, the thing with the napkin. You do it every single meal."

"What?"

"You know, fold it in half and put it under your dinner plate after you're done."

Joel nodded his head at me. "Your way is better, of course—balling it up after you get it all sticky, then tossing it over your shoulder to decorate the floor. . . ."

"I pick it up later."

"*I* pick it up later."

"I would if you didn't."

"You forget I saw your kitchen when you lived alone."

That pretty much shut me up.

"So you don't want me to schedule in three days?" Joel asked.

"Go right ahead if you think you can get everything packed by then." I touched my lips with my napkin and tossed it over my shoulder. "Dinner was great, Joel. If you'll leave the dishes, I'll get them later. I'm going to take a hot bath."

"I'll get the dishes."

"Joel, I'll be happy to do them. You cook, it's only fair. I'm just not going to do them right this second."

I took my glass of wine and headed upstairs, trying to ignore the sound of running water and the clink of silverware in the sink.

Despite the wine and the long hot bath, I didn't fall asleep. I was in bed when Joel came upstairs, and pretended to be asleep. I had my back to him when he stretched out on the other side of the bed and I crept as far over to my side as I could get.

It had come between us, the business of Cheryl Dunkirk, in ways I did not anticipate. I did not expect Joel to be so angry when he found out I was on the case, though in retrospect I see his point. I compromised his investigation that first day. We'd made up and forgiven the words that passed between us; it was the intangibles between us, much more difficult to pinpoint, that I did not expect. I felt like his distance and refusal to talk were his way of punishing me. The ease between us, so natural, so effortless, was slipping away.

The bed creaked and the mattress shifted and I knew Joel was propped up on an elbow, facing me. He watches me sometimes when I sleep. He doesn't know that I know. I don't tease him about it, even playfully. Joel has a certain reserve that, once breached, makes him uncomfortable.

Sometimes I think he watches in order to gauge my feelings. In my opinion, he thinks he can puzzle out my internal dialogues from the expressions I have when I dream. He thinks he is being unobtrusive. He still does not understand that all he has to do is ask. Sometimes I think he *does* know this, but that watching me sleep is less time-consuming.

I sighed and rolled onto my back. I scrunched up my eyes, and did a sort of thing with my lips that I know from looking in the mirror is pretty alarming.

"Why are you making those faces, Lena?" Joel was looking down at me, I could feel his breath on my forehead.

"What faces?"

"Ah. Thought you were awake."

"Insomnia is a crime now?"

He put his head on the pillow next to mine. "What's on your mind, sweet? Something's got you upset."

I looked up at the ceiling. "I saw Cory Edgers today. I was alone with him in his house. He was kind of scary."

"Don't push the envelope with this guy, Lena. He's a stone sociopath."

"You could have told me that earlier."

Joel gave me his favorite response, which was nothing.

I pulled the sheet up to my chin. "You know, I don't feel like I can talk to you anymore."

"You can talk to me about anything, Lena. You just can't expect me to push the ethics on this one."

"Cops talk to private investigators all the time, Joel."

"You're working for the victim's family, and like it or not, I can't tell you anything."

"Fine. Whatever you say is right."

"That's got to be sarcasm."

I turned sideways, away from him. "Right or wrong, I have a lot of feelings about this. If you really want to sort it out, we can talk it through, but it's going to take a while."

"I think we've already talked too much."

Joel put a hand on my hip, very lightly resting on the white shirt I ended up stealing from his closet after all. His hand span was large, and he was able to pull at the buttons without moving his wrist, which still rested on my hip, but not so lightly now.

He grabbed me suddenly, pulling me up to meet his mouth, kissing me hard and pulling me close and grinding his hips into mine. I wrapped my legs around his and pulled him down beside me on the bed. There was no gentle back and forth between us tonight.

Joel turned my head sideways to move his mouth over mine, thrusting his tongue, sucking my bottom lip. He held one of my hands tightly, fingers entwined with my own, and we moved against each other more like wrestlers than lovers. He was inside me quickly, pushing hard as if he couldn't get close enough.

After all our time together, we still surprised each other.

CHAPTER TWELVE

She told herself she was happy. She wasn't. The realization of just how unhappy lurked in the corners of her mind, her subconscious trying to break through. She had hidden from this knowledge for years. She was good at it.

Her name was Kate and she was tall, big-boned, and leggy. Her metabolism burned calories like a match to a fuse. Her face was angular, with high cheekbones, and she had green eyes. Her hair was that color of blond mixed with brown that most women highlight. Kate's hair has not been highlighted, and it hadn't been recently cut.

Kate held tight to her son's hand as he stepped off the front stoop, then let go as he pulled away. Leo ran out into the grass, making circles around Kate as she walked down the driveway toward the barn.

"Horsey," Leo said.

Horsey was one of the few living, breathing subjects that claimed Leo's attention. He preferred Lego's, Brio train sets, or watching the video *Milo and Otis* in endless repetition. Kate was lonely at the top of the mountain; Leo was content.

The afternoon sun was strong, and Kate turned her face to the light, luxuriating in the warmth. It had been a surprisingly warm February on the mountain, and she was looking forward to spring. She'd been thinking that she and Leo might go up to Kentucky for a while, visit her parents. She realized that she'd been curtailing her visits home. It always seemed that things went badly with Cory when she spent time away. She could never decide if it was because he was purposely difficult, to punish her, or if a few days of being happy made her relationship with him harder to bear.

There was no friendly little grocery store anywhere near the mountain, no vet to look after the horse. The closest feed store was forty-five minutes away; they didn't deliver, and they only sold co-op feeds. They didn't sell hay and their stall shavings were over-priced. Kate had to drive all the way to Oliver Springs to get the right feed for Sophie, who was twenty-seven years old. The mare, in many ways an easy keeper, thrived on Purina Equine Senior, but lost weight and colicked when fed anything else.

To add insult to injury, Anderson County was a dry county, which meant a forty-five minute drive for a simple bottle of red wine.

Kate had lost weight up on the mountain. Her jeans were so loose she could take them off without undoing the button-up fly. Her weight loss was obvious, even beneath the layers—a T-shirt under a flannel, both covered by a thin, oversized sweat-shirt. The sweatshirt was gray, a loose boxy cut, and the seams of both shoulders had split. It was Kate's favorite piece of clothing, even though it was stained and dingy from endless afternoons cleaning Sophie's stall, rinsing out water buckets, and polishing the expensive, well-used tack. Over the layers of clothes, Kate wore a loose, dark green barn coat she bought three years ago at Southern States Feed.

Kate thinks wistfully of the feed stores in Kentucky. She thinks about the early mornings she spent stomping around in her barn boots with the farmers and other horsemen, discussions about what feed puts the shine in an animal's coat, and what supplements put weight on an older horse. Nothing like spring and Kentucky bluegrass, was the usual consensus. She wandered through every aisle, looking at the water buckets, the feed bins, the fly masks; basic medical supplies, for the farmer on a budget, which is every farmer she's ever known. Even the hardware in-terested her, the metal rings and hooks, screws and racks. The store was cold in the winter, the doors opened and closed too often to keep the heat in. Stale cigarette smoke mingled with fresh-lit cigars, and the camaraderie of people with common bonds.

The patter of Leo's footsteps made Kate look up. He was running straight down the hill.

"Don't fall," Kate said, just as Leo toppled over.

He was back on his feet before she could get to him. His palms were bleeding from skidding in the gravel, but he did not cry. Leo was intent on the horse and would not be distracted.

The mare stuck her neck over the metal-pipe gate hung in the doorway. Sophie's deep-throated nicker sounded like a purr. She liked her afternoon rides, and she knew that Kate would be pocketing carrots.

The barn was really a storage shed/workshop built by the original owners to house power tools and endless piles of junk. The house has been for sale for eight years. In lieu of buyers, the owners occasionally hooked the unwary renter, and had agreed, when pressed, that Kate could house her horse in the shed. The owners would agree to anything to secure a tenant. The last ones left in the middle of the night.

Cory had spent their first weekend on the mountain ripping out the shed's built-in shelves, tossing the pieces of lumber behind the shed, making a scrap heap and covering it over with an old rug. Kate had been stunned at the remoteness of the house, the dirty bathrooms, the sticky kitchen, the old food in the refrigerator; the faltering well that made the bathwater run brown. Cory had stayed home three days, calming her fears, emphasizing how wonderful the place would be with Sophie right behind the house, surrounded by woods, populated by deer that grazed by the driveway, a raccoon that had nested on the porch. He had stood with her on the deck outside their bedroom, marveling over the view, which was stunning, and promising to cut back his work hours and be home with the family more often.

He'd cleared the tree limbs and debris in front of the shed, pronounced it a barn, and promised to help her clear out the inside on the following weekend.

Cory never got back to it, of course. Like many men in law enforcement, he worked long hours, and Cory worked longer than most. He believed that he would accomplish great things.

He was competitive with the younger men, who were ambitious, full of enthusiasm, and single with few ties. Cory told Kate that he was the best there was, because he combined the energy and commitment of the younger guys with the wisdom of maturity and experience. He was contemptuous of the older officers who were slowing down; many of them had flared and burned, the memory of their younger enthusiasms a lifetime away.

It took Kate four days to clear the shed out; four days in heavy gloves, driving endlessly up and down the mountain, hauling the shredded car-seat cushions (red faded to orange and grimy to the touch); the oily pieces of metal engine parts; the tricycle with the broken wheel; and countless open bags and canisters of toxins—chemicals to kill wasps, roaches, ants, weeds, fungus. Everything had to be loaded up and taken to the dump across from the Anderson County High School; there was no trash pickup in the country. If your car did not have Anderson County plates you were questioned. Not just any trash was welcome. It had to be Anderson County trash.

Kate was happy with her barn, particularly the tin roof that was painted a brilliant metallic blue. The curve of the roof made the barn look like a tiny horse chalet tucked beside the driveway, protected from the wind, on one of the few level spots cleared out on the mountain.

The shed worked better than one might have suspected, though Kate knew her father would not approve. He was particular in his views on fencing, stall shavings, the right feed and hay. When he'd shown up out of the blue four weeks ago bringing fifty bales of top-notch alfalfa hay for old Sophie, Kate was torn by her pleasure and relief in seeing that tall, familiar figure in the driveway of this hell house, and the uncomfortable anticipation of his disapproval.

But he'd nodded his head at her little barn, and she read approval, not censure. She saw him note the tools neatly hung from hooks on the side of the barn, the red wheelbarrow on tiptoes, handles up. The heavy pitchfork, the rake, Kate's gloves looped over a nail, the lead rope neatly coiled and hanging beside the stall door, well out of Sophie's reach.

He winked and said mildly that it certainly would not do for one of his thoroughbreds, but contained Sophie very well.

Kate had smiled. Nothing was good enough for Daddy's Kentucky thoroughbreds. Kate wondered if it was the horses and ensuing lifestyle that had first attracted Cory. From the outside looking in, Kate's family seemed wealthy, though they were not. But they did have a place in the world of horse farms, the Kentucky Derby, smooth bourbon, and good ol' boys. Kate had grown up taking for granted the Whitestone house, easily four thousand square feet, with three fireplaces and a long kitchen that ran along the back; the circle drive and the separate garage built to resemble the barns, including a cupola. Easy to make assumptions about the people who lived inside.

Her growing-up years were a vibrant cacophony of endless chores, hard times and good times, though in the last decade or so her family has seen more good years than bad. Her father kept sound business practices, and was conservative about spending money. It was only recently that Kate realized her childhood had been extraordinary.

Kate and Leo stood side by side, brushing Sophie's heavy winter coat, which was so thick and rust-colored the mare resembled a donkey. Flakes of dried mud mingled with the musky smell of horse. Kate noted that Leo kept his free hand along Sophie's flank so he could sense tension and impending movement—just as she'd taught him. She was pleased but perplexed. It made no sense that a four-year-old could be so unswerving in the application of rules. It was clear that Leo was unusually intelligent; it was also clear that he was different in disturbing ways.

As always, Kate's mind eased away from the things that bothered her while she groomed the horse. Leo shared her contentment, and carefully put away the brushes while Kate lifted Sophie's hooves to dig the dirt and gravel out of the crevices. The mare had arthritis in her left hock, and Kate ran a slow easy hand over the contours of the leg, checking for swelling and heat. Sophie twisted her head to one side, and nudged Kate softly in the ribs. The mare had kind brown eyes, with ridges of wrinkles in the skin above—the sign of a good soul, according to the wisdom of Kate's father.

The leg seemed sound enough for an easy ride, and Kate lifted the saddle up and over the mare's back, easing it down gently over the spine. Leo did not want any help mounting the horse. He stood on the mounting block, very small and fearless. Kate lowered the leathers so that he could tuck his foot into the stirrup and swing himself over. He held the reins while Kate raised the stirrup leathers, tightened the saddle girth, and made sure the helmet was fastened properly to his head. Kate walked beside the horse as they followed the ridge that led away from the barn and into the woods. Kate did not allow Leo to take Sophie at more than a walking trot—the path was steep and hard on the mare's arthritis. Kate wished there was a more level place to ride; both she and Sophie were used to the gentle slopes and rich pastures of Kentucky bluegrass country.

Before they were out of sight of the barn Sophie checked and turned her head. Leo started to kick, but Kate put a hand on his leg. Ahead on the ridge stood a black dog, head down, watching. Sophie was an excellent trail horse, and in her younger years had been a seasoned cross-country competitor. She brooked no nonsense from strange dogs and would duck her head and charge if she felt the need to make a point. She had intimidated and scattered dog packs more than once.

But after a careful scrutiny, Sophie continued along the ridge, not bothering to give the dog another look, even when he fell in behind them, even when he followed them home.

After the ride, Kate finished up the barn chores and climbed into the hayloft over Sophie's stall. The wood ladder was new, no rungs to avoid or rotting edges to skip over. It was warmer in the space under the blue tin roof. Hay naturally generates heat, and sunlight poured in the small square window. Kate inhaled the sweet grassy smell of alfalfa and orchard grass—a full hayloft made her feel rich.

Leo's voice came to her, faintly. As long as she could hear him, she knew he hadn't ventured down the hill to the pond—deep enough to fish in, beautiful skimmed with ice, treacherous to small children. On move-in weekend, Cory had promised her long lazy afternoons sitting on the dock, fishing, having a picnic lunch. The sort of thing they never actually did.

Leo was either talking to Sophie or wrapped in interior dialogue, deep in thought processes and internal logics that were unique to Leo alone. Her son's words and inflections had echoes of familiar phrases, but added up to something only Leo could fathom. He only talked to Kate to relay a particular request or satisfy his curiosity. There was a jumble of words he'd string together every night when she tucked him in that Kate took as a declaration of love.

Like everything else in Kate's barn, the hayloft was neat. There were sixty bales of orchard grass from the second cutting of the season stacked on the right-hand side of the loft, and forty-seven bales of finely pressed alfalfa on the left. Her father had the alfalfa shipped in from out west at twenty-five dollars a bale. They'd worked side by side stacking it into the loft, and he'd grumbled, unconvincingly, about the expense and trouble of alfalfa for an old girl like Sophie-horse. In truth, bringing the hay was a pleasure and an excuse to see his Katie, and to take a disapproving look at this remote house out in the mountains where the road lay in Union or Anderson County, depending upon the severity of the curve. He was worried by the stoic look of endurance that had replaced the easy and gentle contentment he was used to seeing on his daughter's face.

He invited her to come home with him; held his breath while he waited for her answer. He was prepared to take her home that day—he'd brought a trailer for Sophie and little Leo could sit between them in the truck.

Kate had turned him down, and though he'd expected her to say exactly what she'd said, he was surprised by the intensity of his disappointment. He left before Cory came home, looking in the rearview mirror of the truck at Katie as she stood at the top of the steep driveway and watched him go. His eyes were not as sharp as they used to be, and rearview mirrors were not known for clarity, so he didn't see the tears that ran down his daughter's cheeks. But he had a sudden fear that somehow Katie was lost and needed his help to find her way, and it was all he could do to keep inching the truck down the gravel drive when his instincts told him to make her come home, now, and no nonsense.

He did not know how badly she wanted to go. Even she didn't know. Kate was still trapped in the worst kind of confinement, the mental box of convention and expectations that constitutes a prison as hopeless as it is common. Kate was committed to her marriage, to her family, to the years she had spent with Cory. She was loyal, bound by a sense of responsibility that was as strong as it was misplaced.

Kate lifted the hair off her neck and tied it back with a length of scratchy baling string. A vague uneasiness sat like an unfamiliar hand upon her shoulder. There was something off, here in her loft. She took the utility knife from its place on the windowsill, exposed the blade, and sliced through the tough fibrous string that bound the flakes of hay in the heavy, rectangular bale. She paid no attention to what she was doing; she could cut a bale open in her sleep. The hay collapsed and Kate gathered up the two end flakes and tucked them under her arm.

She paused in front of the ladder, glancing once more over her shoulder. And realized that the hay bales had been mixed. Someone had stacked three bales of alfalfa hay in with the bales of orchard grass, leaving a trail of loose alfalfa stems and pieces across the middle area Kate kept swept and clean.

She walked the length of the loft, knelt down in front of the stack of odds and ends tucked under the eaves—a water bucket, a feed bin, a scraper and some brushes, an old hoof pick. Someone had been through them. She opened the old tack box, where she kept bandages, Bute, vet wrap . . . didn't she have a new roll of duct tape in the box? She latched the tack box, trying to remember, saw a slip of plastic beneath one of the bales—the packaging from the new roll of duct tape. Someone had been in her hayloft.

Kate counted the hay bales, mentally subtracting the ones already used. None missing.

Why would anyone come up into the loft and take duct tape? Maybe the neighbors, Don and Kathy Madison, at the end of the drive? They were friendly, helpful; they'd had Kate and Leo to dinner a couple of times, taking Leo's eccentricities in stride. Between the two of them and their ex-spouses, they'd raised seven children of their own. Kate always got the feeling the Madisons felt sorry for her, up on the mountain all alone, and were always ready to lend a hand, insisting she call if she ever had any problem at all.

Maybe Don had stopped by and she hadn't been home. He would know she wouldn't mind him taking the tape, though he'd never helped himself to anything before. And why move the hay bales around?

Kate glanced out the loft window and checked on Leo—she knew where he was and what he was doing every minute of the day.

Leo had not been talking to Sophie after all; he'd been talking to the stray black dog.

Kate dropped the hay flakes, and climbed down the ladder, feet touching every other rung. Sophie was nose-deep in her feed bin, and Kate opened the gate and scooted out, clicking the latch behind her. She moved slowly, eyes on Leo and the dog. She was aware of the lead rope, almost to hand, and the pitchfork still propped by the wheelbarrow where she'd been cleaning Sophie's stall.

The dog was coal-dust black, part Lab, part chow, a little of something else. He had a dark purple tongue, a large triangular head, a bushy tail curled up over the back of his narrow hips, and he was so close to her son that Leo, squatting beside him, could likely feel the dog's breath on his smooth baby-tender cheek. The animal looked lean in the way of strays and wolves in a bad winter. Healthy and fed he would likely weigh upward of eighty pounds.

The dog ducked his head and retreated when Kate took a step away from the gate. Leo reached for him.

"Leo, no. Don't pet the dog."

Leo stayed on his haunches but pulled his hand back, glancing at her over one shoulder.

"Here, boy," Kate said. "Let's make sure we're all friends here." The dog cringed and watched her. But his tail was still up, if not wagging. Kate kept talking softly, good-naturedly, trying to reassure everyone including herself, moving slowly to put herself between her son and the stray.

There were dog packs in the area; Kate heard them at night. A foal in a pasture down the road had been savaged not five weeks ago—tendons severed and belly ripped out—and Kate could not get the thought of the foal's last moments out of her mind. From then on she had kept Leo's old baby monitor in Sophie's stall, and listened all night to make sure the mare was safe. Sophie would be vulnerable, trapped in the small space of her stall.

"Okay, pretty boy, you're all right. Nobody's going to hurt you."

The dog retreated, and as soon as Kate was in front of Leo she stopped moving. She could see the animal was quite old, muzzle streaked with white and gray, back legs trembling with advanced dysplasia. He was panting heavily, flecks of foam around the corners of his mouth. But his eyes were black, clear, and healthy. A worn leather collar hung loosely around his neck, testament to a significant loss of weight. He lowered his head when she put a hand out toward him, palm up, and touched the mud-splashed tags, one of them the familiar rabies certification, the other a heart-shaped ID. Somebody somewhere loved him.

"Looks like the doggie is thirsty, Leo. Get me that bucket by the side of the barn, and let's fill it up with the hose."

Leo instantly obeyed; proving, once again, that he understood when he wanted. Again, Kate had doubts. Perhaps her son was not autistic. His skills of interaction and understanding skyrocketed whenever an animal was involved.

The dog was mindful of the hose. Once the bucket was half full, Kate stopped the stream of water, and set the bucket just a little closer. The dog waited a long minute, but neither Kate nor Leo made a move, and he inched closer, lapping the ice-cold water with a frantic grace.

"Hungry," Leo said, and ran back to the house.

The dog stopped lapping, finally, and shook his head, slinging drool and water across the bottom of Kate's jeans. She dropped to her knees and opened her arms. The dog hesitated, then went straight to her. She was flattered by his trust, and stroked his neck and back, feeling the ribcage beneath the coarse black fur. She took hold of his collar, and saw that his last vaccination was eighteen months ago, that his name was George, that he lived at 307 Cedar Lane.

Kate heard the crunch of gravel in the drive, and looked up to see Leo carrying one of the casserole pans.

"What have you got there, Leo?" Her son didn't answer. Kate realized that he had the meatloaf she'd put together early that morning. "Honey, no."

But Leo had already set the dish before the dog, and George pushed his snout into the carefully molded loaf of raw meat. Kate sighed.

She took a certain satisfaction from George's appreciation. The dog did not hesitate over the bits of onion, red pepper, and Worcestershire sauce, and was clearly delighted by the raw eggs and bread crumbs. Kate hoped George would keep the sudden influx of raw meat and spices on his stomach, but figured on the high probability that he would be sick at any minute and throw it all up.

George, however, did not seem to be distressed by the size and richness of his meal, and wrapped it up by shoving his nose back into the bucket of water and sloshing liquid on his coat, Leo's foot, and Kate's knee. He checked one more time to ensure that the Corning Ware was licked clean, then veered suddenly away, heading for the edge of the woods.

"Doggie . . ."

Kate looked down at her son, who wrapped both arms around her leg and watched George disappear into the woods. Her jeans absorbed Leo's tears.

"It's okay, sweetie. He just needed some food and water, and you and I were there to help him out."

Leo tilted his head back, looking up at Kate.

"What is it, Leo? Ask me in words."

Leo would not say, but Kate knew what he wanted to know.

Her son's direct gaze and full attention were more than she usually got.

"He'll be back, Leo. Feed a dog and he's yours—it's written down in some rulebook somewhere. He may even come back tonight. We can make him a warm bed on the porch. Let's get that rug in back of the shed, and fold it up. That would make a nice doggie bed."

But when Kate and Leo circled to the back of the barn, the rug was no longer there.

CHAPTER THIRTEEN

For Kate and Leo, one of the highlights of the Norris/Clinton area was a log cabin restaurant called Golden Girls. For less than five dollars you could choose from the list of dinner specials and get a home-cooked meal, and a basket of homemade yeast rolls, cornbread, and biscuits.

Kate and Leo liked to sit in the back section because it was nonsmoking, and because Leo could look out the windows to the parking lot behind the restaurant. Golden Girls was one of the few restaurants where Kate felt comfortable. By their third visit the staff knew Kate and Leo well enough to seat them at their favorite table.

Tonight Kate had run out of groceries, which gave them a perfect excuse to eat out. It took twenty minutes to guide the battered Jeep Wrangler seven-tenths of a mile down the steep gravel driveway, then along the two-lane road past houses, mobile homes, and the occasional small farm. This effort got Kate to the tiny town of Norris. From there it was another twenty to thirty minutes to Knoxville, or an easier fifteen to Clinton, which was also a small town, but bigger than Norris. Kate found it an effort to go anywhere, particularly with a four-year-old in tow.

Even when her husband was not in the Jeep beside her, Kate could hear him tell her not to ride the brakes as she inched down the steep driveway. She didn't know how else to get down the mountain safely.

Cory's objections echo in an endless loop in the back of her mind. Kate can't get his opinions out of her head, so she argues with him mentally even when she is alone, to prepare for the real fights that come swiftly, with little warning.

Kate hated their arguments—long tedious harangues where Cory kept at her with a relentless adamancy. She dreaded the way he crowded her, how he clutched her arms or pressed both hands on her shoulders. He cared as much for the small issues as the large and there were no limits to what he would do to prove a point. He once spent eighty-five minutes trying to convince her to slice lemons in quarter sections rather than eighths. Kate saved her resistance for the large issues—her son, his suspected "autism," whether or not they should try and break the lease on this rental. She, who had lived happily in the countryside all of her life, hated the house, the remoteness; she was homesick for Kentucky. She would pay anything to leave.

The majority of the clientele at Golden Girls fell into an age range between forty and ninety, a significant number of them used walkers, and Kate once saw a set of teeth left behind on a table. Golden Girls had no pretense whatsoever, and came as close to eating with the family as you could get without actually seeing your relatives. Wearing jeans was just fine. Being dressed-up after church was fine, too. It was one of the few places Kate could take Leo and relax.

Leo was not at his best in restaurants. He was unfocused, restless, prone to rocking in his seat and emitting sudden loud noises; sometimes he just stared, refused to eat, and kicked his feet very hard. Never once had anyone in Golden Girls asked Kate what was wrong with her child, or stared at him or seemed uncomfortable having him in the room.

Two men, the older one in overalls, the other in a brown sweater and khakis, were seated in a booth in front of the television—currently tuned to a ball game somewhere that was not Tennessee. Kate always seated Leo with his back to the screen. She never liked the way TV hypnotized her son, and she never let him watch unless she was really pressed, or he needed calming down. And even those times made her feel guilty.

Leo was in constant motion tonight, and unusually connected. Probably the result of time spent with George.

The dog had reappeared at sundown the day after they'd fed him meatloaf, trotting straight up to Kate, the obvious pack leader, and dropping a mud-stained sweater at her feet.

"Ah," she had said. "A scavenger." She picked up the sweater, as George seemed to expect, holding it by the edge with thumb and forefinger, wrinkling her nose. It was at one time a rather delicate pink cardigan with tiny pearl buttons, cashmere, expensive, and petite. No doubt the owner had been desolate to lose it; but the stains were copious, crusty and dark, and Kate left it draped it on a peg, out of George's reach, outside Sophie's stall near the refuse bin. The sweater would go to the dump on the next trip out.

Kate began by making it clear to both boy and dog that George, no matter how welcome, would be an outside dog. She had gathered up two old towels for a makeshift dog bed, and George slept contentedly on the front porch the next two nights.

Kate, meanwhile, called the Anderson County Animal Clinic who had issued the rabies tag hanging from the dog's worn-out collar, and learned that indeed, George was one of their patients, though they were under the impression he had emigrated. His owner, Clarise Hardinet, had lived just a few miles from Kate's mountaintop. Upon her peaceful death in her sleep some ten months ago, her son had cleared out the household, sold the antique cookstove, and taken charge of the dog.

"You think maybe George escaped and was trying to go home?" Kate asked. If George had an owner, they would have to give him up.

The woman on the other end of the line was honest and opinionated. "Most likely the son just turned him out. Dirk Hardinet's just like that—he's not much on dogs, or any other kind of animal that's not dinner."

Kate's intention to part with George died a swift and unrequited death, and just like that she and Leo had a dog for real. According to the entire staff of the animal clinic, George was a candidate for canine sainthood, and, even better, up-to-date on his shots. It was suggested that Kate bring George in for a checkup, where he was found to be seriously underweight, happily negative on heartworm and lime disease, and sadly suffering from the various infestations that plague a homeless dog who is down on his luck. He also had a painful and itchy ear. Kate and Leo left the clinic with ear wash, healing antiseptic ear gel, heartworm pills, and flea protection, as well as a thirty-pound bag of Hill's Science Diet for Seniors. So far George had run up a tab of one hundred eighty-nine dollars and a meatloaf. Kate put the vet bill on her Bank of America Platinum Visa.

An impending thunderstorm the third night set George to pacing up and down the front porch. He did not ask to come in. His expression was one of stoic uneasiness; he was clearly expecting the worst. Kate brought him inside to the basement, where he stayed quietly for one hour and twenty-three minutes, pacing up and down the hideous gray-and-brown-flecked indoor-outdoor carpet the owners had put down on the concrete floor. Kate, not immune to George's air of discomfort, let the dog out of the basement. He ignored her invitation to sit near her on the living-room floor, and proceeded straight upstairs like a dog who knows exactly where he is going, and settled in the hallway outside Leo's open door.

Kate stayed upstairs for the next two hours, cleaning the master bathroom and keeping an eye on the dog. Hours later, exhausted from sentry duty, both George and Kate fell asleep. The next morning Kate discovered George on the throw rug beside Leo's bed, which was where he had slept ever since.

Kate looked at the list of specials on the menu and laughed. "Here, Leo, they've got meatloaf." She turned the menu where Leo could see the handwritten list of choices in the back plastic sleeve. "See, Leo? That spells meatloaf."

"Doggie," Leo said, without looking up.

"Okay, there's meatloaf, broasted chicken, pot roast, and chicken livers."

"Chee-kin," Leo said.

"Broasted chicken? Like fried chicken, Leo?"

But she'd lost him. "Okay, Leo, I'm going to order you the chicken unless you say different. And mashed potatoes and green beans. And milk." Kate immediately heard an echo of Cory's voice, telling her that Leo didn't talk because she talked for him.

"It's Kate, isn't it? Kate Edgers?" A familiar woman stood shyly at the edge of the table.

Kate smiled automatically. "Let's see, you're—"

"Your insurance agent. Rebecca Turner? The Turner Agency?"

"Oh, yeah. Sorry, you're out of context. But I knew you looked familiar. Sit down, come on."

Rebecca Turner looked wistfully over her shoulder at a side booth where a cup of coffee steamed next to a crumb-crusted puddle of water. A half-filled glass of ice water sprouted two straws, and a lemon slice had been tossed to the other side of the table. An enormous purse of astounding ugliness was open on one seat. Kate wondered where purses like that were sold, imagining a special section in a musty department store. A yellow legal pad, pages covered in large loopy script, sat at an angle from the sugar packets and salt and pepper shakers.

"Just for a minute," Rebecca said. She looked cautiously at Leo, as if he might fly out of his chair and bite her neck. Kate recognized the look of a woman who was childless by choice.

"Hello," Rebecca said.

Leo ignored her, and Rebecca turned away, social obligation to child fulfilled. She leaned forward, shoulders rounded. "I was wondering if you got the letter I sent."

Rebecca was a pretty woman, green-eyed, with long brunette hair pulled back in a sloppy chignon. She wore red lipstick over full, bee-stung lips; no eye makeup. Her brow was creased, as if she'd been worrying or had a headache; maybe both. She had a gentle, nonthreatening demeanor and seemed to be totally absorbed in her work.

I hope she's not going to try to sell me life insurance or annuities, Kate thought.

"I was concerned," Rebecca said. "I didn't get an answer and I wanted to make sure everything was okay, and that you got your coverage taken care of somewhere else."

Kate frowned. "Did the policy lapse or something? I think I'm paid up, but I can make sure and look at my checkbook when I get home."

"No, no no, do you think I would bother you about that in a

restaurant? No, girl, but your husband . . . you know he took you off the auto policy when he added the life insurance?"

"What life insurance?"

Rebecca frowned. "The policy he took out on you last month. Your signature was on the app. He said when he brought the check in for the life insurance that you were going off the joint auto policy, because even with the discounts it was going to be cheaper for you to have your own policy with another company."

"I'm sorry, I don't know what you're talking about. Are you saying that Cory took me off the car insurance policy?" Kate did not voice her other thought—that Cory could take a life policy out on her without telling her.

Rebecca leaned across the table and there was a knowing look in her eyes. "Kate, he took you off the auto policy three weeks ago, and if you didn't get another one somewhere else, you're not covered." It was clear from Rebecca's tone of voice that she considered no auto coverage on a level with jumping out of an airplane sans parachute.

"Can he do that? Just take me off without my permission?"

"Yes. That's why I always send a letter, just to make sure the other party knows. Sometimes, usually when there is a divorce or a separation involved, the spouse doesn't realize they were taken off the policy."

"I didn't get a letter."

"He had me send it to a P.O. box, instead of the home address."

He has a post office box? Kate thought.

"I can get you a quote first thing in the morning, or you're welcome to stop in. You should get a pretty good rate. As I remember, it's Cory who has the accidents on his driving record."

Kate wondered how to explain a situation she did not understand herself, but evidently Rebecca did not require an explanation. It was clear she had seen this sort of thing before.

"If you haven't ordered yet, the meatloaf is good tonight," Rebecca told her.

Kate put a hand out. "Thanks, by the way."

"I'm just relieved we got it sorted." Rebecca stood up. "Let's talk tomorrow, Kate. I can spin you off on your own policy, if that's what you want. I'll call you with a quote."

She went back to her booth, picked up the small blue-and-white ticket left on her table, rummaged through a wallet and left a generous tip." 'Night, Lennie."

" 'Night," Leo said, pouring salt into his hand.

A small part of Kate's mind registered a shocked pleasure that Leo had responded, especially when called by the wrong name, but for the most part she was thinking about what Rebecca had just said. That one, Cory had taken her off the auto policy; two, he'd taken a life insurance policy out on her; and three, he had mentioned neither. No doubt, if she brought it up, she would find that he had put her on another auto policy with another company, and that the life insurance was some kind of joint policy, that left her well-provided for, and covered funeral expenses for them both. Cory was high-handed with the finances, though Kate did most of the day-to-day bill-paying and budgeting.

Money embarrassed Kate. She had that ingrained Southerner's reticence about finances, and had always understood from childhood that one does not ask for things.

But she knew she'd paid the auto insurance premium, six months in full, and wondered if a refund had been issued. Maybe it had. Issued and mailed to Cory's post office box. What other things had he directed to his private address? When was the last time she'd received a statement on their joint mutual fund?

Kate was no longer hungry. She wanted to go straight home and look through the bankbooks and check statements and see what else Cory had been up to. It would be easier and more immediate to keep track of the finances online, but Cory had always been adamant to the point of paranoia that they not access or put out any financial information over the Internet. It occurred to Kate that by preventing her instant access to their accounts, it would be easy for Cory to initiate transactions that would take her weeks to discover.

The dinner crowd was beginning to stream in for an early supper, and the empty tables were filling up. Kate's waitress, Renée, came by with Kate's tea and Leo's milk and took their orders for the daily specials. The woman was slender, with short hair, salt-and-pepper gray, and she brought Leo a package of saltine crackers.

"You having chicken again tonight, Leo?" Renée wore easy-fit jeans and a Tennessee Vols T-shirt.

Leo wrapped his fingers around the package of crackers, crumbling them in his fist.

"Leo," Kate said.

Renée laughed. "So long as they keep him busy, it doesn't really matter if he eats them." She patted Kate's shoulder. "I'll put your order in."

It was the sudden drop in noise level that made Kate look up. Two men in suits stood in the doorway of the dining room. One was young, with a blond crew cut and dark roots. Not local. The other was nearing sixty and had a relaxed self-assurance. Both of them looked at her. Kate turned away, but was aware that they were crossing the room toward her. Her hands began to tremble and she looked up and watched them. Everyone in the dining room stared.

"Mrs. Edgers?" The blond opened a leather ID. Kate took the time to look it over. Agent Wilson McCoy of the ATF. The other, Alexander Rugger, Assistant Special Agent of the Nashville office.

Kate stood so abruptly her water glass toppled sideways. Water flowed across the table and dripped to the floor.

Cory had told her to expect this, and she'd already talked to that police captain, Mendez. Maybe it was the surprise that was rattling her. Being approached in a public place with no warning.

Kate took a deep breath. Her knees felt rubbery and she sat back down. She picked up the water glass, looked at Leo, who was still smashing crackers. The cellophane had split and beige crumbs accumulated on the plastic tablecloth.

Kate was aware that the men asked permission to sit, that Renée came by with a thick cloth to clean up the water, that the men refused any offer of food. She felt disconnected, like she'd taken a double dose of antihistamines.

The men took up space, their knees under the table too close to hers, their polished black shoes taking more than their share of room. Kate tucked her feet under her chair, and watched Leo closely. If he started swinging his feet, he'd hit both of the men in the knees.

Kate shut her eyes just for a moment. For some stupid reason she was thinking about the chalkboard on the wall next to the TV listing the dessert menu. There was butterscotch pie tonight, which she'd been looking forward to, but she couldn't order dessert with those men staring at her, she couldn't eat with the men staring at her, and when they left, she wouldn't be able to eat knowing everybody in the dining room was staring at her.

She had a terrible hostesslike compulsion to offer to buy the men dinner. Did she have enough money? She was pretty sure Golden Girls took debit cards, but what if Cory had taken money out of the account and she didn't have enough?

The two agents exchanged looks, and Kate wondered if they'd asked her a question. The blond, McCoy, shrugged. "Mrs. Edgers, we're investigating the disappearance of Cheryl Dunkirk, who as you know—"

"I'm aware of the situation." Kate looked over her shoulder. No one was out-and-out staring, but people were aware.

She felt a hand on her shoulder, realized Renée was beside her, balancing a round tray of food in her free hand.

"I'm sorry, Renée. Can we . . . can we wait on the food just for a few minutes?"

"Everything okay here?" Renée asked, keeping a hand on Kate's shoulder.

Kate felt steadier. She realized that everyone in the restaurant who was a regular had taken her side, whatever side that was. Two men in suits against a woman and a four-year-old child. She had mysteriously become part of the community.

Rugger looked at Renée. "I don't think we need anything just now."

"You want me to go get the owner?" Renée asked Kate.

"No, Renée, thanks. Everything is okay."

"You sure, honey?"

"I'm sure."

"Just wave if you need me. I'll be watching."

"Thanks," Kate said. She waited until the woman was out of

earshot. "I would have appreciated a phone call from you setting up an interview, and I'd also have preferred to talk to you somewhere other than a public restaurant."

"We were on the way to your house, and stopped across the highway to ask directions. Guy at the Git and Go said you'd just filled up your Wrangler, and had stopped in here. He suggested we could catch up with you a lot easier here. He said we didn't have a chance in hell of finding your house."

Kate wasn't surprised how aware people were of her every move. The good and bad of small towns.

"I've talked to Detective Mendez from Lexington. I've talked to Agent Benden of the Knoxville ATF. I don't have anything new to tell you. And you are, after all, talking about my husband. I don't have to make a statement or testify against him."

McCoy ran a hand over his close-clipped hair. "If you think your husband is innocent, Mrs. Edgers, why are you worried about testifying in court?"

"Don't patronize me." Kate had endured the humiliation of hearing about Cheryl Dunkirk from her mother, though Cory swore he'd been on his way home to tell her in person. He'd dismissed the hints of suspicion about his part in the disappearance as ludicrous, something the Lexington police department was using to hide their own inability to come up with Cheryl's whereabouts. He'd reassured Kate that he was still working with the Lexington ATF office, and hinted that there was a deeper investigation going on, involving something Cheryl had been tangled up in—and that he himself was a major player in the ATF investigation, as he'd mentored the girl quite a bit. It wasn't anything he could talk about; Kate would have to trust him. And he'd told her, with unmistakable smugness, that it would not be long before he was in the clear . . . even a hero, though he hoped the publicity wouldn't come to that. Some things needed to be kept out of the public eye, just for the sake of professionalism.

Cory had been livid when he found out she'd talked to Detective Mendez. She had told Cory she'd left the detective standing on the porch, but in truth she had invited the detective in and given him a cup of coffee and a homemade chocolate chip cookie.

Detective Mendez had called first, arrived on time, and been oddly reassuring—quiet, comfortable to be around. He seemed to understand a lot without being told and had gone out of his way to make it clear that he would not mention their conversation to her husband unless it was necessary. She hadn't had any information for the detective. He'd had a long drive for nothing. She had wondered, afterward, why he had assumed she wouldn't tell Cory about it. Later, she wished she hadn't. Maybe he'd been giving her advice.

Kate looked at the two men sitting at her table and did not think that her husband was on his way to becoming an ATF hero.

"Mrs. Edgers?" Ruggers said. "Would you like us to come back some other time? When we're not disturbing your dinner?"

Smart, Kate thought. *Good police work. Make the witness feel like she has control.*

"Ask your questions," she said. "I'll cooperate as much as I can. I didn't know Cheryl Dunkirk, but I hope you find her, I hope she's okay. Anything I can do to help."

"How is your marriage, Mrs. Edgers?" McCoy said.

"Just ducky," Kate said. She knew they had to ask, but she didn't have to like it.

McCoy flipped open a notebook and wrote. "Just ducky. Thank you for your candor."

Kate covered her mouth with her hand. The urge to laugh was nerves, she knew.

McCoy cleared his throat. "When was the last time you and your husband had—"

Rugger put a hand on McCoy's arm, shook his head, glanced at Leo.

"Sorry," McCoy said.

Rugger leaned across the table toward Kate. "Mrs. Edgers, obviously, if your husband is innocent of any involvement in Cheryl's disappearance, whatever you say can clear him and get the investigation focused elsewhere. But if he was involved . . . and you know something about it? Do you really think you're safe?"

"What's that supposed to mean?" Kate thought about the insurance policy.

"We have no doubt that Cheryl Dunkirk is dead, and that she was attacked, brutally."

"How do you know that if you don't know where she is?"

Rugger's eyes were kind. "You know I can't answer that. But hypothetically speaking, Mrs. Edgers, a man who would attack a woman that way doesn't have limits. And it isn't usually his first . . . moment of brutality. I'm serious about what I said concerning your safety. I have a wife, and kids of my own."

"Would your wife talk about you to the police?" *On the other hand,* Kate thought, *would Rugger take out a secret life insurance policy on his wife?* She thought about bringing it up, to see what they said. But they would likely just stare at her. She would feel stupid.

McCoy tapped a finger on his notebook. His tone was clipped and bored. "Let's just get through this, okay? Your husband ever hit you?"

Kate glanced over her shoulder, wondering if anyone in the restaurant could hear. "No."

"You ever been afraid he might?"

"No. I don't let men hit me."

"Good for you. Was he home the night Cheryl Dunkirk disappeared?"

Kate tilted her head. "That week, Cory was in Lexington. He wasn't home with me."

"So you can't give him an alibi?"

"No."

"He always away from home that much?" Wilson cocked his head sideways, voice suddenly conversational.

"Yes. How often are you home? Or aren't you married?"

"I'm not married, ma'am."

"No love life at all?"

Wilson smiled at her. He wasn't the least bit offended. "My girl-friend has been known to complain. About the hours."

Rugger laid a picture on the table, avoiding the beads of water Renée had missed. "Have you ever seen this woman?"

Kate picked up the photo. Her first thought was how pretty the girl was. Intelligent-looking, fresh. The only pictures she'd seen before were grainy newspaper reproductions of Cheryl's driver's license photo. Her second was that Cheryl was just the kind of leggy brunette that Cory looked at when he thought Kate didn't notice.

"I don't know her," Kate said.

Chapter Fourteen

No woman could ask for a more amusing ex-husband than mine. Being unconventional is like oxygen to Rick, which is why I am sitting behind the desk in his office downtown. Paul Ellis Brady finally returned my phone calls, and landed at Bluegrass Field late last night. He wanted to meet me at my office. I don't have one. And I do not want Brady and Joel to cross paths, which is likely, since Brady could not be available until seven P.M. tonight. Meeting at the house was out. And besides, neither Joel nor I had backed down, which meant there had been no packing, no movers, and no delivery of furniture. I knew I could hold out longer than Joel. He didn't have a chance at waiting me out—the man who craves order against the woman of chaos?

It was Rick's suggestion that I use his office. I had asked if I could meet with Brady in one of the empty rooms downstairs, but Rick had run away with the idea—no surprise—and not only was I sitting at Rick's enormous leather-top desk (the shorter the man, the bigger the desk? Rick was no more than five-five) but Rick was primed and ready to be my secretary. He had dressed up. No jeans, but rather elegant, wool-blend black trousers and a black cashmere sweater. Rick looks very striking in black, which is why he'd chosen the slacks and sweater from "costume," otherwise known as his walk-in closet.

I was spinning in Rick's chair, managing to circle three times on the power of one good push, when the office door opened.

Rick had wandered out to make coffee, and he threw up his hands when he saw me and gave me an exasperated look. His other looks include *wounded feelings; brave martyrdom; twisted amusement; hopeless love; murderous rage; sleazy thoughts;* and *sudden perception.* There are more, but these are his best ones. I know because I was the one he practiced on when the looks were in development.

"Would this be pointless?" he asked.

I propped my feet up on the desk. "Would what be pointless?"

"The trouble I am going to so you will look the part—successful, cutting-edge private investigator. Jaded but savvy woman of the world."

"Jaded, Rick? You think?"

"What if Brady had been with me? What if he'd seen you spinning like that? Do you *want* him to stop payment on the check he gave you for the retainer?"

"Don't be silly, Rick. It's already cleared the bank."

He shook his head, picked up my feet gently and put them on another part of the desk.

"What are you looking for?"

"My glasses," Rick said. "The Intellectual Prissy's."

Rick had several pair of glasses, all with clear lenses; he had the vision of a hawk until the fine print got him. Each set of frames has a "character."

"I thought you would wear the Rising Young Broker."

"Oh, God no, not since Enron. I might as well throw *that* pair away." Rick moved a folder, opened a side drawer, and sighed. The next drawer he yanked open, and the contents slid backward. "What time is it, Lena?"

I looked at my bare wrist, and made a guess. "Seven oh three."

"My God, he's overdue, and I'm not *ready.*"

I looked up warily. The tone of Rick's voice worried me. I knew better than to argue with him about whether or not he needed the glasses. He was already halfway into character. And since he'd chosen Intellectual Prissy, a detail-oriented personality if there ever was one, the glasses would have to be found. I opened the center drawer and shoved stuff around.

"Ah," Rick said. I could hear sincere relief in his voice.

"Where were they?"

"Under your foot." He cleaned the lenses absently on his sweater. "Ready?"

"Ready."

"No *spinning,* Lena."

"Break a leg."

Brady was late, as befitted a man of importance, and I grinned when I heard Rick greet him at the door.

"Oh, Mr. Brady, really? We'd assumed you weren't going to make it after all."

"I'm sorry, I didn't mean to keep you late." Brady had a deep voice.

"Not at all. If I could ask you to sit? Yes, there is fine. May I take your coat? I'll just hang it here. Would you like a cup of coffee, Mr. Brady? I just made a fresh pot for Lena. Between you and me, she has way too much caffeine in her diet."

"Actually, coffee would be very nice."

"Black?"

"Sugar, if you have it."

Brady sounded subdued. Was Rick overdoing? I should never have let him talk me into this. I was feeling like a pretentious idiot. My ex, God love him, was a snob at heart.

I heard Rick talking again, but could not make out the words, so he was likely in the kitchen getting Brady's coffee. Would Rick balk if I asked him to get me a cup?

A discreet knock and the door opened a crack. "Lena? Mr. Brady is here."

I stared at Rick, who somehow looked nothing like his usual self. He raised an eyebrow at me, but waited patiently.

"Ask him to come in."

Rick opened the door wide and Paul Ellis Brady walked in slowly, taking in the details of the office. He had light brown hair, well cut, gelled back. He wore khakis and a dress shirt—a vibrant French blue—and a well-cut suit jacket. No tie, and he seemed comfortable, as if he'd just had a nap and a shower. I stood up and shook his hand across the desk.

"Please, Mr. Brady. Sit down."

Rick set a mug of coffee on my right, making sure it sat on a coaster.

"Thank you, Rick." I took a sip. Lots of cream, the color barely tan, exactly as I like it. Rick's talents were wasted here in Lexington. I felt like he'd been my assistant for years.

Brady sat on a red fainting couch that Rick had shipped in from Nouveau Classics in Knoxville. He settled not quite on the edge, but not leaning back, comfortable but alert. He had presence, no doubt about it, and though he was not pretty, his face had a certain strength of feature and I could see how women would find him attractive.

"I didn't ask Miranda to join us on purpose. I've been worried about her. This is not the kind of thing she should be doing on her own."

This took me by surprise. "Actually I agree with you, Mr. Brady. Your daughter told me you were . . . bogged down in business and wedding arrangements and didn't have time for the details."

Brady gave me a half smile. "Did she? I postponed my wedding, Ms. Padget. Miranda wanted to do this on her own. I thought it was a bad idea, but—when Miranda asks, I usually say yes."

"Ah. Has Miranda brought you up-to-date?"

Brady tapped a finger on his knee. "She said she'd given you a key to Cheryl's apartment. Filled you in on the family background. She said you thought Cheryl was dead, and had been killed in her car."

I nodded. "You do know the police found Cheryl's car parked in the apartment lot?"

"Detective Mendez called me when it turned up. And told me the same—he thought she'd been killed in the car. I wanted to fly in and take a look, but he said he couldn't let me, not yet."

I took a sip of my coffee. Miranda had been discreet, anyway.

"What else did Miranda tell you?"

He finished his coffee in one gulp, set the cup on the floor. "Miranda said that initially you agreed with the police. That Cheryl had had an affair with a coworker, that it had been some sort of mentor thing, and that she'd been murdered by the guy, Edgers."

I ran a finger around the rim of my cup. "That is what I thought at first, Mr. Brady."

"Paul, please."

"Call me Lena. As it stands now, I'm not convinced that Cheryl was the victim of some kind of love triangle."

"How so?"

I wondered how much I should tell him—the paying client. "Paul, were you and Cheryl close?"

"No," Brady said. "Cheryl was never happy about the marriage between her mother and me. For that matter, neither was Miranda. It was sudden, I admit that, but Cheryl's mother . . . we were deeply in love. Both in need of someone in our lives. We probably should have taken things slower. As it was we got married on the spur of the moment, didn't invite the girls, or tell them what our plans were, and then we combined households. Can't really blame the kids. Miranda suddenly pulled out of school, Cheryl with a new sister invading her social group. It was a mess for a long time. We were finally pulling together when my wife got sick. She suffered for two years. We all suffered with her.

"Cheryl couldn't help but associate me with her life turning upside down, her mother dying. She lets me into her life, but only so far. I wanted to pay for her tuition; she wouldn't let me."

That caught my attention. Miranda had made a point of telling me that her father paid for Cheryl's tuition—a direct lie.

Brady put a hand on each knee. "Cheryl wouldn't take any kind of allowance for living expenses from me while she was in school. She'd accept birthday and Christmas presents, and sometimes we'd get together on minor holidays. I tried to stay in touch, but I was busy, she was busy. We weren't talking on the phone more than once every couple of months. I always told her I was there for her if she ever had any trouble. She never called. She knew I was going to get married again. It was planned for mid-March. We've postponed indefinitely. Janet, my fiancée, she understands. And I'd like Miranda feeling a little more . . . settled. The wedding plans have upset her. She's told me she won't attend. I'd like her to change her mind."

"Why did Miranda want to handle this by herself?"

Brady shrugged. "She was close to Cheryl, in her own way. She's a take-charge kind of girl . . . well, you've met her." He chuckled. "Headstrong since birth, but very insecure. She's vulnerable, my little girl. I imagine she's pestered you three times a day with phone calls."

"Not really."

"Well, that doesn't surprise me either. Miranda gets enthusiasms, but she doesn't always follow through."

"What did you mean when you said Miranda was close to Cheryl 'in her own way'? She told me she and Cheryl had a very close relationship."

"Frankly, Lena, Miranda admired her big sister, but she was jealous, too. Cheryl was always sure of herself, and what she wanted to do in her life. She was unusual that way. A planner. Smart and pretty, plenty of boyfriends if she was interested. I don't see her falling into the married-man trap. On the other hand, she was young, and I've seen a lot of bright women get snagged like that."

I wondered if he'd snagged some of them himself. "At least we're all three in agreement, then. I don't think this is a matter of an intern romance gone bad. I think Cheryl was involved in something that was over her head, something connected with her job at ATF, and I think Edgers was involved, but frankly, I'm not much further along than that."

"What do the police think?"

"I don't know. They police aren't speaking to me anymore, about Cheryl Dunkirk anyway."

He nodded as if he understood.

"Do you want me to continue the investigation?"

He frowned. "Did you think I flew down here to fire you?"

"I've had the impression that you wanted to cover all bases, but there's no point in false hopes. I'll be honest. I still think Cheryl is dead. But I don't know if I'll be able to find out anything more than the police will. I'd like to stay on it if you're still game, but I could understand you wanting to leave it with the police."

"Are they going to let the investigation stand where it is?"

"I can't speak for them. You'd have to talk to Detective Mendez."

Brady nodded. I was sure he knew that Joel and I were involved, but he clearly wasn't going to bring it up.

"I'll drop by his office tomorrow. How are funds holding out?"

"Oh. The retainer?" This was a question I rarely got asked. "Fine. Funds are fine.

"Paul, forgive me for being direct, but a lot of the background Miranda has given me has been less than truthful. Which doesn't make sense to me. Do you have any idea why she'd lie?"

The word "lie" didn't go over well, though Brady didn't actively flinch.

Brady crossed his legs, gathering his thoughts. "When I decided to hire someone, to hire you, Miranda was upset about it. Then she changed her mind, and wanted to take care of things herself. She said she thought it would help her to have something constructive to do, something proactive. But I think it's been too much for her. The point is, she goes off like a Ping-Pong ball on these emotional things.

"I think maybe my daughter was telling you things the way she wanted them to be. It's not such a terrible thing, really, to say you're closer to a sister than you really were."

I tapped a finger on the edge of the desk. Brady's answer dodged the issue—Miranda had lied about some odd things. "Paul, does Miranda have any history of emotional problems?"

"Of course not. But your question bothers me."

"Miranda gave me a completely different account of Cheryl from the one everyone else has. You included."

Brady sat forward. "I think it's clear that Miranda is having trouble coping with this—perfectly understandable. I think from here on out I'd like you to talk exclusively to me. If Miranda gets in touch, you can bring her up-to-date, but this way if she doesn't want to face things, then she doesn't have to. We'll leave it to her to find her comfort level."

He wasn't asking permission. "I'd also like to know . . . Miranda told me you think Cheryl was strangled." He studied Rick's carpet. "How much do you think she suffered?"

I sat back in my chair. I do not mind this sort of question the way other people do, because I know how important it is for the family to have information, good or bad.

"She suffered. If things happened like I think they did, she knew her killer. She trusted him. She was taken by surprise and she fought him, really fought him. She wasn't afraid and terrorized beforehand, which is to the good. And the fight from the time she was attacked until the time she died . . . I'd say the whole thing took between eight and fifteen minutes. Being strangled is painful, but the shock and lack of oxygen kick in pretty quickly. A medical examiner could give you better information."

"Fifteen minutes." His tone of voice said *fifteen years.*

"That's from start to finish."

"Was she raped?"

"My guess is no."

He let a breath of air escape through clenched teeth.

"And she wasn't tortured. As far as I know. But at least she died fighting. That's something."

But he and I both knew it wasn't much.

Rick stood in the doorway of his office. "You look pissed, Lena."

"Just thinking. You see him out?"

"You doubt me?"

"No. If I could afford an assistant, you'd be hired."

He grinned. "Afford *me?* You live on that ridiculous barter system, my love." He took the glasses off, and sat on the edge of the desk. "Want to go next door for some dinner? I asked Judith but she's painting and won't be disturbed. Any further, ha ha."

I thought of cold beer and jerk chicken. "Okay."

"You know, Lena, you and I could work together. You could have an office here, I could do your background work, you could pay me with sex."

"Why am I not tempted?"

"I don't know. It's not like I didn't use to get it for free. . . . Ouch. *Jesus.* That *hurt.*"

CHAPTER FIFTEEN

London, Kentucky, is a friendly town. Not very big. There's a tire store, several restaurants, and Laurel Lake, which has several marinas, places for canoe camping, and a wild-bird sanctuary that allows no motorized boat traffic to disturb the osprey and mule deer.

The marinas in London are well run and beautiful and attract boaters from Ohio to Tennessee. It is well known in bordering states that Kentucky boating laws are lax; people come to Laurel Lake to party hearty and contribute to the local fatality rate.

What isn't well known is the London, Kentucky underground railroad, a stop-off for women who forgo the legal system for a myriad of reasons, and start a new life somewhere else. It works like the federal witness protection system, with fewer glitches. Joel knows nothing about this group. He won't hear about it from me.

I met Adrianne eight months ago when we worked opposite sides. My client was a graduate student, working toward a Ph.D. in archaeology. Two years prior, his sister, a single mother, died in a car accident, and he became the instant father of a three-year-old daughter. He'd had a messy breakup with a girlfriend after a year of cohabitation, and she'd taken off with his daughter. When I caught up with her, she was trying to convince Adrianne to take her on, and help her to a new identity and life in Seattle.

My client was lucky. There was no question of custody to complicate the rescue. And Adrianne swears that the girl would not have cleared their background check, and never would have made it through the program. I always hope she's right.

I know of specific circumstances where Adrianne's clients, as they are called, would be dead now, without the help of the group. Many of them had children who would also be dead. In spite of this, I always worry when a woman runs. Prey runs.

Every situation involves a judgment call and some of the women who work with this group are too comfortable with their judgment. Some of them have gone from dedication to fanaticism. I sometimes wonder if once in a while a woman goes through who shouldn't. A woman taking revenge on a man.

On the other hand, nobody's perfect. And the group's track record is significantly better than the Kentucky domestic court system.

When I arrived at the Cracker Barrel in Corbin—twenty miles south of London—Adrianne Lindstrom was sitting outside in one of the rocking chairs on the front porch of the restaurant. The chairs sold for about a hundred dollars apiece, and were looped together with a discreet steel cable.

"Enjoying the sunshine?"

Adrianne smiled up at me. "I was hoping you'd be on time."

"Always the incurable optimist."

I let Adrianne go ahead of me through the restaurant doors. She was in her sixties, had degenerative arthritis in her hips and knees, and she walked according to how badly she ached. She was a short woman, hair still red with the help of L'Oréal, and overdressed for the weather in a navy blue pea coat over a sweatshirt that had large reindeer on it and said I Love Grandma. She wore black polyester pants, low-heeled shoes that tied, and a maroon knit hat with a bobble on the top. Her small hands were covered in matching gloves.

Adrianne is firm but motherly and I find her presence comforting; she has a gentle sense of humor, and more common sense than anyone I've ever met. I've asked her to adopt me, but she only laughs. I wouldn't adopt me either.

We sat in the nonsmoking section close to the seven-foot hearth, and the crackle of a real wood fire. Business was slow; we'd hit the dead time around three in the afternoon. No one was sitting at the checkerboard, no one was waiting to be seated. A waitress took our drink orders, and Adrianne shifted her weight carefully, trying to get comfortable.

"You look good," I told her.

She smiled. "You look happy. Things going well between you and Joel?"

I rubbed the hollow beneath my right ear. "We just bought a house together."

"Ah. I was wondering why you glowed. Except something's bothering you."

"Adrianne, are you sure you're not the reincarnation of my mother?"

I picked up the little wood-and-peg puzzle that sits on every table at a Cracker Barrel.

"Lena, don't start with that thing. Do you still hold the record?"

"Of worst score in the memory of my last Cracker Barrel waitress? Yes. She said she'd never seen anybody leave seven pegs and that she didn't think she could do it if she tried."

"I remember, I was with you."

The waitress arrived. Neither Adrianne nor I had looked at a menu. I ordered unsweetened tea, chicken and dumplings, hashbrown casserole, and carrots. Sourdough toast.

Adrianne went for the catfish. "Same order as always, Lena?"

"I haven't been here since you and I had dinner together back during you know what."

"Don't mention any names, my dear."

"Sorry, Mom." Adrianne doesn't like what she calls "post mortems," which she considers bad manners as well as a security risk.

"Lena, are you going to keep worrying that puzzle, or tell me what's bothering you?"

"Joel and I are both working this Dunkirk investigation. He's the pro, and I'm private, hired by the family. He was furious when I took the case, and he won't share his inside information, which makes me mad, even though I know it shouldn't. It's making things weird between us. We haven't even moved all our stuff into the house because we can't agree on who should take time off to pack everything up."

"Hire packers, my dear. Tell me, has Joel ever shared this kind of investigative detail with you before?"

"All the time."

"Then that's why you're mad. Makes perfect sense to me."

"And now I've got this competition thing going. I want to find out what happened to this girl, only this time instead of being motivated by the family, I've got this urge to win."

"Win?"

"Poor choice of words."

The food arrived, distracting Adrianne and sparing me the lecture about how the word "win" has no place in a relationship or a divorce. I tried not to watch Adrianne eat the catfish. I don't like catfish. We didn't talk much while we ate. When the waitress returned to refill our drinks, Adrianne glanced at me across the table and grinned. "Starving, dear?"

"I'm a healthy girl. Plus this is one of my favorite meals and I haven't eaten here since I've been boycotting." The Cracker Barrel restaurant chain had been in court twice—once with gay activist groups and once with black activist groups.

Adrianne sucked Diet Coke delicately through a straw. "I'm afraid I don't have a lot of information for you on Edgers."

Time for business, then. I ate the last of my tiny carrots, wondering how the restaurant cooked them to the perfect blend of sweetness and flavor. Maybe Joel could do it. I should ask him. After I won.

Adrianne pushed her plate to one side. "I spent some time with Mira Flanders—she's cleaned house for Cory's stepmother since Cory was five. The most interesting thing I got was that Cory kept his room neat, like a little marine, and was . . . how did she put this . . . *inflexible*. That he ate the same thing for breakfast the entire time she knew him."

"What did he eat?"

"Who knows?"

"How could you not ask?"

"I don't care what he ate for breakfast."

"Adrianne, what could be so good that someone would eat it every single morning for years?"

"Nothing, Lena. That's the point. Cory Edgers has always been a creature of habit, in the sense of someone who has to keep a rigid control of his routine. I could see him being quite difficult if something upset that routine."

"Did Mira Flanders say that?"

"No. She doesn't clean for anyone she doesn't like, which means she won't have anything overtly unkind to say. You have to read between the lines."

"What other things did you read?"

"Ummm . . . he dated a lot in high school. Thought he was quite the little man, until he met Amy McAlister, and then he fell madly in love, pursued her all through their senior year, and married her the summer after he graduated. She didn't graduate, by the way. Was kind of quiet and on the social fringes until she hit her junior year, developed a huge bustline, and got very wild."

"I didn't know he'd been married before."

"Oh yes. According to what I know, he was crazy about this little girl, and there wasn't anything he wouldn't do for her. I have it on good authority that she gave him holy hell after they got married. Most people in town blame her for the divorce, and think the world of Cory."

I shredded a piece of my napkin. "I've met him. I can see how he could give a good impression, if he wanted to. But he is not a good person, Adrianne."

"It's hard for me to judge."

I ate a bite of bread, even though I was full.

"Let me ask you something, Lena. Do you really think he killed that girl, Cheryl Dunkirk?"

"I don't know. I did at first. Now I think her disappearance is tangled up in some big ATF case, I just don't know what it is. But I have no doubt whatsoever that if he decided she was in his way, he'd have no qualms about getting her out of his way."

"How sure are you?"

"The truth? This guy scares the living shit out of me."

"My dear, you are nothing if not colorful." Adrianne tapped a finger on the table. "He's remarried, you know. I met his wife years ago. Have you talked to her? They used to live near the lake, but they moved. Cory always described her as something of a recluse, and said she didn't like to socialize."

"She's next on my list, if she'll talk to me. Which she probably won't."

Adrianne pushed her plate away. "You have some time this afternoon?"

"I can make some time."

"I don't think I've told you, but I have a new project, called Reach Out—funded by a federal grant, by the way."

"Congratulations."

"Thank you. We try to ease at-risk women back into the workplace. We mentor them, give them advice on schooling or job training that will get them an income big enough to actually support them. We're big on the little things, too. We help them get their hair done, their nails done, buy professional clothes, drive them to and from interviews. All those little things nobody thinks of that can make or break someone on the edge. Amy has been an alcoholic for the last fifteen years. She's been sober for six months—she's got the AA medal to prove it, and she just got her GED. I've got a home visit scheduled with her today. I'd bet she has an interesting insight on Cory Edgers."

The test lunch was over, and I'd passed judgment. There was never any kind of casual interaction with Adrianne Lindstrom, no matter how it might look from the outside. The southern good ol' boys had nothing on the steel magnolias.

Adrianne reached for her purse. "You want to go with me and see if she has anything to say about her ex?"

"They always talk about the ex."

I followed Adrianne along a complex switchback of country roads that had me confused after the first ten minutes. She drove her Mazda 686 just under thirty-five miles per hour, though I've heard they'll go faster. You would never know that Adrianne is a superhero.

I once saw her confront a six-foot-seven, ex-football player who had to weigh close to three hundred pounds. The image is one I'll never forget—the man with a tire iron in his fist, and Adrianne wearing one of her horrible sweaters, this one pink with brown teddy bears on the front. She was slightly stooped that day, arthritis worse than ever, and had refused to tell him where his wife was, though he knew and she knew that she could have told him if she'd wanted to. I had run toward them, with no idea what the hell I was going to do when I got there, but she'd held her palm up at me.

"This sort of nonsense is beneath you, Brent. I understand you're frustrated and panicked. I'm sure you think the only way to relieve the pressure is to see her and talk to her and make everything okay. But that's not love, my dear, that's an addiction or a temper tantrum, and neither are very pretty. Raging at her and being violent makes you feel better because it raises your endorphin level, but I'm not going to let you do that at Cherry's expense. I can offer you a Xanex if you'd like one. And would you please put that tire iron down? You're not really afraid of me, my dear, are you?"

And Brent, God bless him, put the tire iron down. Another one of Adrianne's judgment calls, and one I'd never have made, not having a death wish.

When I'd asked her about it later, she'd referred me to a book on male depression by Terence Real. "Society betrays girls around the age of eleven. But boys get worked over before they're even three years old, poor little lambs."

I figured Adrianne knew. She'd raised four boys alone.

Amy McAlister lived in a mobile home on a small grassy lot off a two-lane road that saw a lot of traffic. There were two cars in the gravel drive—a '92 Ford Escort, and a '99 Subaru. Adrianne pulled her little Mazda in behind the Escort and I parked my Miata in the yard.

The house was turquoise and rust where it used to be turquoise and white, and had been top of the line in the late seventies.

Stacked concrete blocks served as the front steps, and Adrianne had to take my arm and lean on me heavily to make it up and into the trailer.

Inside, a radio played Allison Krauss, and the stench of Marlboros was more like an assault than a smell. Everyone was in the kitchen, which was separated from the living room by a long bar. A woman on that divide between slender and emaciated sat on a stool with her head tilted back into the kitchen sink, and an overweight blonde with a blue smock over a white tailored shirt and loose jeans was massaging red dye into her hair.

The woman with her head in the sink held a burning cigarette between her fingers. "Is that you, Adrianne?"

"Yes, my dear, but don't get up."

The woman giggled. "I wasn't going to." Her voice had the husky edge of a long-term smoker.

"I've brought a friend. Lena, that's Amy with her head in the sink."

"Better than in the oven," Amy said. She waved the cigarette. "How are you?"

"And that's Milly there at the sink."

She looked at me over her shoulder. "I'm learning salon techniques and Amy is my guinea pig."

"Don't believe her," Amy said. "She's been doing my hair since high school."

Amy pronounced hair like *har*.

A young woman in her mid-twenties was setting out acrylic nails, red polish, little containers and sponges and a tiny professional drill. She had long black hair with a streak of white. She stood up and shook my hand.

"Good to meet you, I'm Elyse."

"But we call her Skunk," Amy said.

"Drown her, will you, Milly?" Elyse sat back down at the table. She took one of my hands and shook her head. "A biter?"

"Not usually."

"Want your nails done while you're here?"

"That's okay."

"Come on, we've got time. Milly still has to cut and dry and

God knows what else to Amy's hair. Sit right there." She pointed to a metal chair.

Adrianne leaned against the kitchen counter. "Go ahead, Lena. I hear it's better than therapy."

I knew I'd never find Joel getting his nails done while interviewing a background witness, and I wondered if that made me better or worse.

"We've all been wanting to meet you," Amy said.

"That's true." Elyse was looking at the size of my nail beds and matching each one to a white acrylic nail. "You sure have teeny hands. Sit down, hon, take the load off."

Milly looked at me over her shoulder. "We heard all about you from Adrianne and—"

"*Milly.* No names."

"Sorry. Anyway, we heard all about you."

"Are you working on a case?" Elyse asked. She cut the tip off a small bottle of glue, applied it to the edge of a white nail, and pressed it in place over my chewed-up nail.

"I'm here for your help," I said.

"Help with what?" Milly asked.

"Information. On Cory Edgers."

Amy lifted her head out of the sink. *"Cory Edgers?"*

Elyse applied glue to the base of another white nail. "You've surely come to the right place."

Amy McAlister's bustline had lost a certain amount of magnificence with severe weight loss. She sat at the table with a towel wrapped around her head, and though her face was drawn and angular, tightened by years of heavy smoking, she still had a certain prettiness that would stay with her forever. The cheekbones were classic, proportions nicely symmetrical. She had a bon vivant presence at odds with her air of being a woman with significant personal demons. There were books on the kitchen table—computer programming, French II, Algebra II, and trigonometry. A stack of spiral notebooks lay beneath. Fifteen years of addiction is a hell of a thing to fight, but Amy McAlister seemed like a woman who could pull it off. She had a cigarette in one hand, another burning in an ashtray, and an open bag of Skittles candies in front of her on the table. Sugar and nicotine to keep the cravings away.

"Cory Edgers loved me like you think you want a man to love you when you're a little girl." Amy glanced around the small kitchen, making sure she had everyone's attention.

It always happens this way. Interview someone, and they are reluctant to talk at first, but then the pleasure of being listened to, really listened to, begins to kick in and the next thing you know you can't shut them up. Amy McAlister clearly liked the limelight. This was going to be good.

"I had a crush on him since I was in junior high school, and he *literally* did not know I existed. I didn't have a lot of friends then, just one or two really close girlfriends. I wasn't shy, but I wasn't one of the cool kids, and I stayed out of the cliques. And then I grew boobs." Amy giggled. The sound of it made you smile. "One day I was a triple-A training bra, and the next a thirty-two D. My mama like to have a heart attack. Part of her was proud—the women on her side of the family had always had big *bosoms,* was how she put it. But we had to special order my bras, and suddenly boys started calling, and she went from glad I was making friends, to worried that the friends were all male.

"And I loved every minute of it, let me tell you. Lot's of girls don't like the attention, and I can understand the viewpoint, but it just wasn't me. I wore tight little T-shirts that stopped right over my belly button and I could walk down the halls and *turn* those heads, and I liked it, it made me feel powerful."

"You're an exhibitionist, Amy," Elyse said.

"Don't I know it." Amy took a long drag from her cigarette and blew smoke out of her mouth slowly, with a satisfied ecstasy that made me want to light up a Marlboro myself.

"I wasn't stupid, either. I knew it wasn't *love* they was wanting, but honey, my hormones were kicking in, and it wasn't *love* I wanted myself. Oh, Lord, boys that age—they don't know a lot, but there's something to say for enthusiasm."

Elyse shook her head, cheeks going pink, but Milly laughed out loud.

Amy squinted her eyes. "But the one boy I wouldn't have sex with was Cory Edgers. Tell you the truth, I didn't like him once he started noticing me. I thought he was boring. He was so regulated, so precise, everything had to be just so. And Mister Proper. Ask you for a date, tell you what time he was picking you up, and what time he was taking you home. He double-booked, too, and I didn't put up with that. He'd take one girl out from six to nine, the other from nine to twelve, and didn't care if both of them knew it. I must have turned him down a dozen times.

"But Cory, now, is the kind of man who can't stand being told no. The more I told him to go away, the more he wanted to date me. So I made up all kinds of *rules* for him. Like he had to wear a certain shirt, and get his hair cut a certain way, and eat what I told him for lunch, just to show me how much he really wanted to take me to a movie. And then when he'd do everything I told him to do, I'd call and cancel the date."

"You dog," Milly said.

Adrianne pushed away from the kitchen counter and settled into a chair. "Better listen to her, Milly, it wouldn't hurt to give Mark a little shake-up."

"I don't do that kind of manipulation," Milly said.

Elyse used a pair of scissors to cut most of the length off the glued-on nails. "And that's why you spend every Saturday night just sitting on the couch watching the TV."

Milly rolled her eyes.

This was a conversation that could last a year. I looked at Amy, who was lighting yet another cigarette. "So how did Cory finally get you to go out with him?"

"He took me horseback riding. He found out from my cousin that I loved horses, and that was the one thing I couldn't turn down. I mean, he did his homework. That's Cory all over." She set the Marlboro in the ashtray, grabbed the bag of Skittles and passed them over to me. I took as many as I could fit into my free hand and passed them back.

"You know, Cory really was good to me. We'd still be married if it hadn't been that I just didn't want to settle down, you know? Because when Cory really loves you, he will do anything for you.

But I drank and I run around on him a lot, and then I got pregnant. And when I miscarried the baby, Cory just give up on me. He wanted a family and losing that baby broke his heart. He blamed my drinking, you know, and smoking and being wild, and he was probably right. He's funny. He really did love me, but when he turned, that was it. He could barely stand to look at me after that. Didn't want a thing to do with me. And as far as I was concerned, it was a relief. I never did love him, not really. But he provided good, and he handled things for me, and it's nice sometimes to be looked after. It's just that when he does, he's got to have things his way. And let's face it, I'm an alcohol addict—the only thing I loved was Jim Beam."

"So you miss him ever?" Elyse said. "You wish you stopped drinking before the marriage broke up?"

"Can't quite put my finger on why, but I think the relationship between me and Cory would have been over a whole lot sooner if I'd been sober. But actually, the marriage ain't officially over. We never got a divorce. We meant to, we just never did get around to it."

CHAPTER SIXTEEN

Janis always tucks her hair in a John Deere ball cap when she goes to the meetings. She doesn't like the way the men look at her when she wears it down—long blond hair gives them thoughts she does not want them to have, not around her, anyway. Not that any of them would touch her. She is the liaison—she is the Rodeo Assassin's "woman," because Rodeo is too smart, too careful, and too mysterious to come to the meetings himself. But the word to the wise is that he is out there, watching.

It is dark out and very late. Nobody sees her leave.

It's a long drive. She makes it just as the sun comes up. She does not like to meet in the dark. Daylight is better, so they know she sees their faces.

There are four of them today. The spokesman, the one who stands a little in front, the one the others look to, has a gray crew cut and a smile like milk gone bad. He has a Smith & Wesson .38 tucked into the back of his pants. Janis smiles a little. She knows at least five true stories of people who carried a gun tucked into the back of their pants and shot themselves in the ass. Which is all these guys are good for. She hates them as much as she hated the Enemy.

They are all of them part and parcel of the whole thing. Every one of them had a role in Emma's death, from the cult members, to the Feds who would not help her when she asked, to the ones who wound up burning the whole thing down and ruining any chance of a happy ending in her life.

She is honest enough to know that she has no idea if she'd have handled Waco any better, once everything got out of hand. Too many bosses, too many opinions, too many rulebooks written by sideline experts. But she does know there didn't have to be a Waco. She does know she'd tried to tell them, all of them; she went for help and no one listened. She tried the local police, the Texas Rangers, the FBI, and the ATF. By the time she got to the ATF they were expecting her—just another nutcase from the cult fallout. We can't help you, I'm sorry, go home. She wonders sometimes what set the whole thing off, what turn of events turned the federal guns at long last on David Koresh and Mount Carmel? What took them so long?

Janis finds the survivalist groupies predictable, thus useful. All of them watching each other in their own bizarre universe of fanaticism, stupidity, surveillance, national security, and pissing contests. It is a pleasure to use the one to bait the other.

There's a new guy today. Janis doesn't like him. He talks too much, and he looks at her, which he thinks she doesn't notice. She wonders if he is a cop. He is too tall, too young, too pulled together and too buff to belong with the beer bellies and blowhards that made up the usual suspects. He seems a little stupid for any intelligent law enforcement agency to send undercover, but hell, nobody's perfect.

Lately Janis thinks of finding a little place near home, and just living quietly, riding a horse again. She has saved almost all of her money, and she knows that one of these days there will be a cop or a Fed she doesn't spot. She is prepared. And, being Janis, she is not afraid. The last Fed had been good, and gotten closer than anyone. The woman had looked like one of the usual types, a girl with big hair, tight jeans, and a hubcap belt buckle, hanging around the cowboys. She called herself Candy.

Janis had taken care of Candy on a Saturday night after the last show, and before the cowboys had their Sunday morning coffee.

She pulls a sealed envelope out of her jacket pocket and sets it down on the ground. The rule is they can't pick it up until she leaves. The only reason she made the rule was to have a rule. Dealing with Koresh taught her a few things.

Crew Cut looks at the envelope, then looks at her, and licks his lips. "Hey, girl, does he tell you the name?"

Janis does not like being called "girl."

"I bet you look in that envelope, don't you? Just so you know? I bet you can't help but look."

"Who told you to talk?" Janis asks. Even from several yards away she can see his complexion grow darker.

"It will happen in the next thirty-eight to forty-two hours," Janis tells them. "Make your first broadcast at midnight."

Janis turns abruptly and gets back into her truck, aware that she's added another chapter to the Rodeo Assassin Legend. Like all legends, this one has elements of fact and fiction. There isn't a "he" and Janis is herself the assassin.

She drives away, well aware that the buff guy has memorized the details of her truck. Except, of course, it isn't her truck. It belongs to one of the tourists spending the night near the fairgrounds, and Janis made sure he had enough Jack Daniel's the night before so that there is plenty of time to get the truck back before the tourist knows it's gone.

Janis takes off the ball cap and rolls the window down an inch. The cold air keeps her awake. She glances once into the rearview mirror, and sees the same dark brown Toyota that she saw just as she was leaving the meet. She has not seen it in the twenty minutes she has been driving since. There are no other cars and the road is long and flat, and yet for the last twenty minutes this car has stayed out of sight.

She decreases her speed to twenty miles an hour. The Toyota is there, edging closer. Janis chews her bottom lip, thinking that someone from the group is following. Which is not in the rules. It will be that new guy, the talker. And it is as if he wants her to see him, so she pulls the truck to the side of the road and waits. Whoever he is, he'll be sorry. She brings the cattle prod out from under the seat.

The Toyota approaches slowly, as if the driver is making up his mind. She could be wrong, Janis thinks, and whoever it is may pass her by.

The Toyota comes close enough for Janis to see the driver, a young woman, with curly brown hair. The Toyota pulls right in front of her truck, and the woman gets out of the car, slams the car door very hard, and faces her, hands on her hips, feet spread. Janis does not know this woman, who acts as if they have unfinished business of some kind. She gets out of the truck and leans against the grille of the pickup.

"So what's up?" Janis asks. She is almost amused, as well as annoyed.

"Who are you?" the girl says.

Janis does not reply.

"You might as well tell me. I saw you go into the woods. I saw him go into the woods. I know the two of you had some kind of assignation, and I want to know what about."

"Who are *you?*" Janis asks.

"Me? I'm Miranda. Cory's girlfriend. The woman he will marry as soon as the divorce goes through with the wife. And if he's been seeing you, I want to know it. And I want you to know exactly what you are up against here."

"Seeing him? As in . . . fucking him?"

Miranda's face goes dusky red. "So it's true."

"That I'm fucking him? No, it's not."

"You're lying. And why bother? Why else would he meet you like that at the crack of dawn?"

"If I told you, I'd have to kill you."

"Very funny. But don't give me that cop crap. This isn't his jurisdiction."

Janis drums a finger on the hood of the truck. So the son of a bitch really is a cop. She is turned sideways, looking at Miranda. A stupid cop, with a stupid jealous girlfriend.

"How long have you been seeing him?"

"This is the first time," Janis says.

"Did you sleep with him?"

"No."

"But you wanted to."

"No. But he definitely wanted to sleep with me."

Miranda is quick and she uses her nails. Janis feels the skin of her cheeks sting and bleed, and she sweeps her foot between Miranda's legs and drops the girl.

Janis is quick now, and strong, and she grabs Miranda by the skirt and drags her to the back of the truck. The girl is screaming, but it is rage and not fear, and she kicks like a calf being roped, connecting more often than not. Janis pulls the girl up by the collar of her shirt, and grabs both arms behind her back, making sure to cause a good amount of pain.

"Bitch."

"Tell me something I don't know," Janis says. She is out of breath. "Now be still, if you want to know who I am."

Miranda kicks again, and it connects, but then she stops.

"He's a cop, your boyfriend?"

"Yes, damn you." Miranda's chest is heaving and her face is red and swollen with tears.

"Federal?"

"Not yet, but he will be. He's working with the ATF. Why, what did he tell you? That he was already hired? He will be, don't worry. He's one of the best, believe me. And he's working on something that will put him at the top of the heap."

Janis nods, more to herself than to Miranda. Always trust that first instinct, she thinks. She'd known he was a cop on some subconscious level.

"I have some good news for you, Miranda."

"And what could that possibly be?"

Janis takes the cattle prod out of her belt. Miranda is listening now, and it is easy to hold her with one hand. "I'm not sleeping with your boyfriend, honey, and I reckon anything between us is strictly business. Unfortunately, Miranda, the business happens to be the big case he's been working on."

A singe and electric crack, and Miranda drops like a brick. The cattle prod has been enhanced, and it delivers one hundred thousand volts. Miranda will not be able to move for a while. Janis moves the girl's hair off her face. Her eyes are shut; she's out. Janis looks up and down the road, considering. There is plenty of wire in the kit, but by the side of the road is a bad idea no matter what time of the day. And the farther away the body is from the girl's car, the longer it will take for the cops to make an ID, and pick up a trail. But she will use the wire. So they'll know who it is. So the cop will know, if he lives that long. Janis chews her bottom lip. All she has to do is let the group know about the infiltration. They'll take care of him themselves.

Miranda isn't moving. Janis picks the girl up like a feed sack and loads her into the bed of the pickup. She brushes dirt off the hem of her Wranglers, and climbs back into the truck. Somewhere between here and there, she'll find a place.

Thirty minutes later, Janis takes a side road that leads to a patch of woods and a creek. Janis is tired. She drives off the little road through the field to the edge of the woods. The truck will leave tracks, the ground is damp; but she is too tired to carry Miranda across that field, and she'll be ditching the truck soon anyway.

Janis slings the double strap of a navy blue polyester satchel over her shoulder. Her kit. She closes the truck door gently, and walks around to the back.

No Miranda.

Janis frowns, circles the truck all the way around, and looks again. The back divider has been unlatched and let down. This kid has recovered from the stun in bizarrely quick time, and jumped out somewhere along the way. She is a mental, Janis thinks. Only a really crazy person could recover from a stun like that, and then have the guts to jump out of a moving truck. Janis looks back over her shoulder. She would like to go back after this girl. Likely she will find her, hurt or walking by the side of the road.

But it is getting late, and the owner of the truck will be waking up soon. The last thing Janis needs is for the truck to be reported stolen, especially since the man spent yesterday at the rodeo, and part of last night in a bar with her.

Miranda, she thinks. *I'll catch up with you later. You and the cop.*

CHAPTER SEVENTEEN

It is at worst a three-hour drive from Lexington to Clinton/Norris where Kate Edgers lived. It didn't seem kind to call her with a *hey, you don't know me but* sort of pitch that slammed her with the news that her so-called husband actually wasn't. Kate Edgers didn't know me; she wouldn't believe me. She might check my story out, and find I was right, but that wouldn't get me time and conversation.

It seemed reasonable at three this afternoon when I took the Raccoon Valley Road exit off I-75 to find her house and talk to her face-to-face. It was now past seven, pitch-dark and windy, and I was on some road called Kent's Ferry, which was patchy with ice, and clearly a death trap for possums, whose remains appeared regularly on the side of the road. I had no idea how to get back to the interstate, much less to the Edgers's house. On my right was a mobile home, with three cars in pieces to one side, and at least twelve dogs in and around the property. All of them were barking. I had just passed a sizable two-story house, newly built, with a circular driveway and a Ford Explorer out front. Before that was some kind of a chicken farm. Although I had lived in the South all my life, I had never been this far out of the real world. It was dark this far out from the city (*any* city) and patches of fog floated across the road. I felt sure I was going in circles, but nothing looked familiar, and there were no recognizable landmarks that meant I had been this way before.

I pulled off the side of the road and flipped the cell phone open. There was service. This was still Earth.

I dialed information and found that Bell South was alive and well. "Edgers, please. On Kent's Ferry Road."

Information gave me the number, then dialed it for me, and a woman answered on the second ring.

"My name is Lena Padget, and I'd like to talk to Kate Edgers, please."

"I'm Kate Edgers. I'm afraid I don't know you."

"Please don't hang up. I'm really lost out here." I didn't fake the panic in my voice. "I got off on Raccoon Valley Road at three o'clock this afternoon and I have been wandering around this mountain ever since."

"Where are you trying to go?"

"I'm a detective. I've been trying to find your house, to talk to you about the Cheryl Dunkirk case."

"I've already talked to all of you people."

"I'm private. Hired by the family to find Cheryl."

"I can't help you."

"If you don't want to talk to me about Cheryl Dunkirk, that's fine, but would you please God tell me how to get out of here? Right now, all I want to do is go home. There's a man down the road by a church, and he is standing out there singing about what the dead men say, and I don't want to go back in that direction if I don't have to because honestly, this guy freaks me out."

Kate Edgers laughed. "He's harmless. Your name is familiar. Lena Padget. Do I know you?"

"No."

"Then why is your name so . . . wait a minute, I read about you a couple of times in the papers. Aren't you the one that helps women and had the sister that died?"

"That's me."

"Did you come by yourself?"

"Yes."

"What kind of car are you driving?"

"A Miata."

"And you're not a reporter and you're not a cop?"

"A private detective, only concerned with Cheryl's family. And I'll go away if you'll just tell me how to get the hell off this mountain."

"My son and I were just sitting down to a pot roast dinner. If you'd like to join us, you're only about five minutes away."

Pot roast and people, bathrooms, telephones. "That would be wonderful."

"First let me explain my driveway," Kate Edgers says. "And be really careful on the way up."

I passed the driveway three times before I finally found the double mailboxes, one with reflective numbers down the post. The driveway was on the other side of the road, a short sweet break in the trees. "Driveway" was a kind word for a wide dirt track that had a smattering of gravel mixed in with mud and pot-holes big enough to give pause to an SUV. The Miata was small enough for me to go around most of them.

The track wound gently at a steep angle, but it was nothing I couldn't handle. The road leveled off and the trees gave way to a small clearing. There was a basketball goal on my right, and the glint of moonlight on water on my left. I put my foot on the brake and took a look. The pond was huge, I could see that even in the dark, and I thought I could make out the dark shape of a small dock. Beautiful in daylight, no doubt.

I put my foot on the accelerator. The tires spun, then achieved traction and I turned a corner and braked.

Kate Edgers hadn't exaggerated.

The road headed up at a ninety-degree angle, snaked sharply to the left and disappeared in the dark. Built on a clearing at the top, the house was a monster, brown brick and oddly shaped, some kind of homemade amateur architecture. There were security lights blazing on every end of the house, and lights in the windows, but darkness pushed from every side, and the woods were thick and close.

You think a lot about gravity when you drive up a road that is more like a ski lift, and you tell yourself that your car will not fall over backward and to think it might is foolish. The final curve had a sheer drop on the right and a deep rut on the far left, which is where I would have preferred to position my car.

Once the curve was negotiated, the track straightened out to level ground and the house. The front porch light was on. I got out of the car and looked back down the mountain, thinking that if down was worse than up I might never make it out.

A voice came out of the darkness. "The first time I came up that driveway, I cried. Of course, I knew I was going to have to live here."

A porch light went on, and I headed to it like an insect on a summer breeze. Kate Edgers stood on the porch—a tall woman, with dark blond hair pinned on top of her head, a genuine lop-sided smile, and a firm, calloused handshake. She smiled at me and shook my hand. I did not know how she felt about me, but I was very glad to see her.

"Come on in. The roast has been cooking all day in the Crock-Pot, so it ought to be good and ready."

A dog stood by her side, black, with a large head and wise eyes. He looked at me and wagged his tail. He looked wolfish and had the presence of a rottweiler.

Kate reached down and scratched the dog's head. "Don't worry about him. He looks scary but he's a baby doll, aren't you, Georgie Boy?"

I put a hand out and George sniffed it delicately, standing po-litely while I stroked his neck. He stood on the porch until both Kate and I were inside, and I felt like part of his herd.

It was a strange house. A stairwell on the right, with open back steps, led up to bedrooms and down to a basement. The foyer passed through French doors to a great room, where a wood-burning stove sat on a hearth at the right corner. The outer wall was all windows and French doors that led to a deck that circled the house. The view out over the mountain would likely be amaz-ing when it wasn't pitch-black dark. A boy of about four or five was on his knees in the middle of the floor, snapping pieces of wooden railroad track together.

"That's Leo," Kate said.

"Hi, Leo."

The boy didn't look up.

The smell of beef, potatoes, and onions permeated the house. It was warm inside, and good to be off the road.

"The bathroom's that way," Kate said, "if you want to wash up."

★ ★ ★

When I found my way back to the kitchen, Leo was sitting at the table, drinking a glass of milk, with George curled up at his feet. Kate waved me to a chair.

"Go on and sit. Everything's ready. You have no idea how thrilling it is to have company."

Kate put hot yeast rolls into a basket, offered me Coke, beer, or water, and sat down across from me at the table. The roast was fork tender. There were potatoes, onions, and carrots that were sweet and well done. Leo took two bites, then kicked his foot hard on his chair. So far he had not looked at me or said a word.

"Do you like being a detective?" Kate asked me.

"Some days yes, some days no."

Leo jumped down from the table, and Kate held his face between her hands. "Go upstairs and get ready for bed. You and George can read until I come upstairs."

Leo did not look at her, but ran up the stairs. George got up and headed after him.

"So Cheryl's family hired you?" Kate said.

"That's right."

"How are they?" she asked softly.

I shrugged. "You know how it is. It's hard."

"I wish I could help you out, but there's nothing I know about it. I've talked to the police from Lexington, the Commonwealth Attorney's office. Even the ATF. I'd help you if I could."

I nodded.

"Would you like some coffee?" Kate asked.

"I'd appreciate it. It'll keep me awake on the drive home."

"You're not as far out as you think. You can be back on seventy-five in fifteen or twenty minutes."

"That's a hell of a relief."

She got up and began rinsing a coffeepot. "Everybody seems to think my husband killed this girl. Is that what you think, too?"

"I'm not sure."

Kate looked at me over her shoulder. "Aren't you going to ask me what I think?"

"I didn't have the nerve."

She laughed. "Everybody else does." She sat down, resting both elbows on the table. "Cory isn't the easiest person. He's not good when he's frustrated. But I wouldn't be here if I thought he was a killer."

"I understand that."

"Do you think he's going to be arrested?"

"I honestly don't know. But I've met your husband."

"And?"

"And . . . and I can see how someone could have a favorable impression."

"You don't sound convinced."

"I only know him from the bad angles. And I have information that you don't."

"Which is?"

I looked at my feet. I really didn't want to do this.

"Which is?" Kate said again.

"Did you know your husband was married before?"

She nodded. "I saw her a couple of times when we lived in London. Amy McAlister. We never spoke."

"I spent some time with her and she told me that she and Cory never really got divorced."

Kate's face went slack, and she stood abruptly, went to the coffeepot and filled two mugs. She put cream and sugar on the table. "She's not exactly reliable, you know. She's an alcoholic. I always wondered if that happened before or after she married Cory."

"I checked it out, Kate. They never got divorced, which means you aren't legally married."

Kate laughed. "I'm sorry. I just don't . . . it's got to be some kind of mistake."

"Yeah, and the name of the mistake is bigamy."

"Why did you come all the way out here to tell me? So I'd get mad and spill my guts."

"Pretty much."

"Most people think Cory's a great guy."

"You're just not what I expected when I drove out here. You're younger than I thought you would be. And you don't look like one of those wives who—"

"Say it," Kate tells her. "One of those women who hang on to a man no matter what he does, because they are afraid to have a life of their own?"

"Something like that."

"What exactly is it you want from me? Because I've already talked to the police and the prosecutor's office. They won't tell me anything, by the way."

"Yeah, I hear you won't tell them the same."

Kate nods. "Why should I? Would you, in my place?"

"I'm not exactly sure what your place is, so I can't answer that. I guess I'd be careful, if I were you. No one's going to look out for you, including your husband, so you better take care of yourself. And Joel Mendez, have you talked to him?"

"Mendez. The detective?"

"Yeah. Just so you know, he and I are together in the romantic sense."

"As in biblical?"

"That, too, yes."

"Did he send you down here to talk to me?"

"He doesn't know I'm here, and he wouldn't like it if he did. Separation of church and state, you know."

"So who hired you then? Cheryl's sister?"

"Her stepsister and her father. They need to know what happened, and to make sure everything is done that can be done. It's a family thing. They're always going to have hope."

"They can't think this girl is still alive," Kate says.

"They can and they do."

"And you?"

I shook my head.

"Do you think my husband killed her?"

"I think it's possible. But not for the reasons everybody thinks. I don't believe it was over an affair. What do you think, Kate?"

Kate traced a ring of condensation on the table. "Why should I tell you that?"

"Maybe you shouldn't."

"I don't think I can help you on this. I don't really know how involved Cory is in this, but obviously I don't think he is a killer."

I nodded.

"And I just . . . I don't want anything to do with this. It's Cory's thing, not mine."

"Do you still love him, then?"

"I don't know. We've been married a long time and we have a son. And don't tell me I stay with him because I have low self-esteem."

"Oh, hell, Kate, those two words strung together are my least favorite ones in the English language. Look, I work with women who have bad husbands. It's my specialty, okay? And I am sick and tired of everything being dumped into the category of self-esteem. It's just the catchall, and it's meaningless. Women stay with crummy husbands because they think it's best for their children, because they're afraid to leave, because they don't want to be alone, because they want a meal ticket—there's a million reasons why. And none of them have a damn thing to do with self-esteem, and you don't look like a victim to me. I put you in the family re-sponsibility category. The minute you decide he's not good for the family, you'll cut him loose. Probably about the time we find out what really happened to Cheryl Dunkirk, if we ever really do."

"If I knew something that would help the family . . . I'd tell you that."

"Look, I'm not going to hound you about this, Kate. You have to make up your mind what you want to tell me, if anything at all. I just thought that since you hadn't come out in defense of the guy, you might be willing to tell me something, or anything that might at least lead to a body. It would be good for the family to be able to bury Cheryl, and not have to live with uncertainty all of their life."

"Yes. I really didn't think of it that way." Kate looked up at Lena. "Do the police have a case? Is Cory going to be arrested?"

"I have no earthly idea."

"What about the detective?"

"He won't tell me a damn thing."

"Then how can you expect me to talk to you? If I talk to you, and Cory finds out about it, don't you think he'll . . . I don't know. Do something?"

I leaned back in my chair. "Absolutely, I do. I'm glad you realize it yourself. If he did kill Cheryl Dunkirk, he can certainly come after you. Especially if he thinks you are any kind of threat. And even though you don't think he's a killer, you shouldn't take that kind of risk."

"So why would I tell you anything?"

I sighed "You might not. Revenge would be my motive, if I were in your shoes. But I'm kind of big on that sort of thing. And because of Cheryl's family. I would worry about them."

Kate took a sip of coffee. "I don't think I know all that much."

"Is there anywhere you could go if you needed to?"

"My parents."

"Can I give you some advice? Don't leave it to the last minute. If you decide you aren't comfortable here, or with him, take your son and go see your family for a while. Give yourself a chance to think, away from him, so you can find some perspective."

"I appreciate your concern, but—"

"I know. It's none of my business." I rummaged through my purse. "Here's my business card. That's my old number, here." I found a pen and put the new number down. "If I can help you out, give me a call."

"Sure."

"Thanks for dinner. And thanks for rescuing me. And remember what I said, will you? It's lonely out here."

CHAPTER EIGHTEEN

Kate's head rests sideways on the back of the couch, and her eyes are just barely open. She is drifting, and her mind no longer acknowledges the sounds and images that come muted from the TV. Leo is curled next to her, snoring softly. George is on the rug at Kate's feet, drowsing but alert, in the way of dogs who take the protection business seriously. Now and then he scratches and Kate wakes up enough to ask him why, as he has been cleansed of all biting companions. George gives her his full attention when she asks, then scratches again and settles back on the rug.

A cold front has swept in from Canada, and Kate and Leo have gathered kindling from beneath the canopy of wind-blasted trees, and stacked up logs from the woodpile. Kate has built a fire in the woodstove and closed off the French doors on either side of the great room, so that she and Leo and George are quite toasty. The three of them had settled in front of the television for an *X-Files* marathon—both boy and dog asleep before the conclusion of episode two.

On the other side of the French doors, the rest of the house was immersed in the chilled bluish dark that settles over winter nights. The scent of wood smoke, the glow of fire behind the glass door of the woodstove; these comforts were too pleasant to leave. Kate decided they would sleep downstairs tonight.

The neighbors at the bottom of the hill had brought Kate a bottle of red wine. It would be nice to have a glass, but she wouldn't. That morning she had woken up vomiting, the nausea striking at the precise moment her mind slid from unconscious to awake. There had been other indications, little things—a slight tingling in her breasts, feeling sleepy in the afternoon. The subtle and personal signs that told her she was pregnant.

By Kate's estimate she was six weeks along—it had been exactly that since the mishap. "Deficient condom" was how Cory explained it. Her gut told her he'd been trying to get her pregnant. *Why?* Kate wondered. To keep her vulnerable, to keep her in line? Kate wondered how she could earn a living and look after Leo, and deal with the physical strain of carrying another child. She wasn't sure she could do it. She wasn't sure she wanted to.

She had been in an odd state of mind since that strange visit from Lena Padget. She felt heavy and lethargic when she ought to be frantically worrying and finding out if she was, indeed, legally married to Cory Edgers.

In a small way she was excited. Did she really want to be married to Cory? If the marriage wasn't legal, she was free. She could walk right off the mountain, she could get her life back. She could go home to Kentucky. The lease on the house was in Cory's name. As soon as she got packed, she could go.

The urge was overwhelming—put some things in the Jeep, settle Leo and George in the back, and be home before breakfast tomorrow morning. Don't wait, the Padget woman had told her.

But it was so cold out, so cold. And she was sleepy. And she didn't want to leave Sophie alone on the mountain. She should do it right—pack up the house, hire movers, turn off utilities, and give her parents some warning that she was on the way. Not that the last was necessary. She could show up on their doorstep in the middle of the night and they'd be thrilled.

Kate was dreaming about breakfast in the big old kitchen at home when a low but sustained growl from George woke her. The sound of car tires on gravel permeated her consciousness. Someone was coming up the steep gravel drive—nobody drove up the mountain by accident.

George was up on his feet, making a beeline for the French doors, whining and looking at Kate. He grumbled low in his throat, and lowered his head. A ridge of fur rose like a stripe down his back and the slam of a car door sent him into a frenzy, his bark hoarse and fierce.

Kate was on her way to get the .38 she kept in the utility room off the kitchen. The gun was hidden behind the horse meds. The front door opened before she was halfway to the kitchen. George threw himself into the doors between the great room and the foyer, and they bulged outward with the force of his weight. Any second and he'd be going through the glass.

Cory Edgers paused in the doorway, keeping an eye on the dog. *My husband is home,* Kate thought. The black cloud for every silver lining. Kate noted how pale Cory was, as if he'd been ill. She put a hand on George's collar and pulled him back, but it was not until Leo woke up and shrieked "Daddy!" that George stopped barking and retreated.

Kate stood beside the couch, feeling so detached she might as well have been catching a glimpse of strangers through a window. There was the father lifting the little boy to his shoulders, a father who never talked to the little boy, or played with him, or picked him up for a hug unless there was someone to watch and notice. The little boy was smiling—a scene right out of Family 101. The weight was back on her chest, and she felt the spark of hope fading, felt herself retreating behind the façade of happy mommy, happy wife.

She had allowed herself to picture it, a life without Cory. Watch Kate leave the mountain. See her settle in that empty cottage on the family farm . . . there is Leo, and George and Sophie. Watch Kate raise her son in Kentucky. See the new baby in the crib. See how happy Kate is to be home, where she goes to her favorite grocery store and she knows where everything is on every aisle, where she goes to the movies at her favorite theater, where she runs into people she knows at Fayette Mall. See Kate sit in her mother's kitchen, anytime she wants. See it all slip away.

Kate sat on the couch, arms wrapped around her chest, grateful for the soft weight of George's muzzle, as he rested his head on her feet. It only took a look at her son's face, his glow in his father's presence, to make Kate realize how selfish it would be to break this family up if Cory was willing to make the marriage legal and give their life together another chance.

"So when did we get a pet?" Cory smiled, showing his teeth. He had always opposed getting a dog, mainly, Kate thought, because she wanted one. Kate braced her feet against the floor.

Leo scrambled away from his father, who only just managed to catch him before he fell and lower him gently to the floor.

Leo grabbed George around the neck, and kissed him on the head.

"Who is this critter, Leo? It's too ugly to be a dog. Has your mama gotten us some kind of a razorback pig?"

Cory leaned down to pet George, who growled deep in his throat. His smile took effort. "I guess he'll have to get to know me."

"Looks to me like he already does," Kate said.

"What's that supposed to mean?"

"Just joking." Kate realized that in less than a minute she had gone from contented comfort to beaten-down fatigue. How long had it been since she loved this man? Because going through the motions of loving him dominated her life, and she realized that she no longer even liked him. She had read the books and magazine articles; could this marriage be saved, how to keep the romance in your relationship, ways to please him in bed, increase your intimacy, the ten things men love to hear. All marriages had ups and downs, and seasons of desire and affection; but Cory, Kate decided, was not so much a soul mate as a seriously bad habit.

The habit opened his arms and grinned. "Hey, honey child, how's my girl?" Cory moved in on Kate with a smile that was not a smile, a look he reserved especially for her.

He hates me, Kate thought, *really hates me.* How could she not know this until now?

He was uncomfortably close, and his hand closed around her wrist. "In case you haven't noticed, I'm home early."

Kate used to wonder why Cory always kept a hand on her, just on the verge of uncomfortably tight. It made sense, now that she knew how he felt. Once the context changed, a lot of things made sense.

Cory opened his arms to give Kate one of the hugs that hurt, and her ribs ached before he even touched her, memories of all his past affections. His face was too close to hers. She could see that he had not been sleeping. The tiny lines around his eyes and nose were deeply creased and he looked as worn as she felt.

He crushed her close, pulling her up off her feet, holding her arms down and pressing close with his hips. Kate felt his erection through the thin sleeping shirt she wore. "You smell good," he murmured into her shoulder. "Katie, my Katie, have you missed me? Let's put Leo to bed and go upstairs."

Somehow George had worked his way between the two of them, and Kate took advantage and pushed away. She did not want to go upstairs, but she knew she would give in, she would fall down into that dark abyss of habit and expectation. She stretched her hand out just far enough to feel the fur on the top of the dog's head.

"Leo and I are sleeping downstairs tonight."

Cory was already on his way up. He stopped and looked at her over his shoulder. "What?"

"We were cold. We built a fire, and decided to sleep down-stairs."

"That's not practical, Kate. I want everybody upstairs in their room."

Kate smiled, like she was making a joke. She found that you could say terrible things if you smiled when you said them. "You go sleep in the bedroom. Me and Leo and George will sleep down here."

"Who the hell is George?"

"This is George. Leo's new dog."

"Dog doesn't look new to me."

Kate took a quick look at her son. Leo seemed oblivious to the conversation. He shook George's paw, tuning his parents out, slid-ing back into the niche of his private and solitary world.

"Kate, I am exhausted. It's been one hell of a week, and I've driven home all night just to see you." He beckoned her with his fingers. "Put the dog on the porch, or in the basement, and come on up to bed."

"You go to bed, then, Cory, nobody's stopping you. We're settled in down here and we're staying. You coming home when you find a convenient moment doesn't change my plans."

"Oh, hell, Kate. You're going to do that to me tonight? The overtime again?"

"That's not it."

"Don't punish me because I'm ambitious and I work hard. That's how I show my love to this family."

"Do you also show your love by taking me off the auto policy? And taking a life insurance policy on me that you don't even tell me about?"

"What the hell are you going on about? I did not take you off the auto policy, and we talked about the life insurance."

"No we didn't."

"Yes we did, Kate, twice. But, hey, I'll cancel the policy tomorrow if that's what you want." Cory opened the door to the woodstove. "Your fire's out. There's no point to this, Kate. Come to bed."

"We've got a good bed of coals, we'll be fine here."

Cory stared at the floor with his sad look, but Kate had seen it before.

"Okay, if that's the way it is, how about I get that fire started back up for you?"

"I can do it." *How polite I sound,* Kate thought.

"Are you just going to stay mad at me, Kate? Because of the working hours? I just walked in the door thirty seconds ago, and it doesn't seem like I've been here long enough to piss even you off. And if you want me to come home, you ought to make me welcome when I get here."

There was a time when that threat would have caught her. The easiest thing, the course of action that would keep the peace and restore the façade, would be for Kate to give in and go upstairs with him.

"Leo and I are having a campout by the fireplace. It's kind of a special thing. I promised."

Kate saw it in the set of Cory's shoulders, the tightening of his jaw, the argument that would come like wave after endless wave.

"Leo needs to learn to sleep in his bed. Look, Kate, if you're mad you're mad, I take your point. But grow up a little, okay? Don't act like a spoiled brat and sit down here and pout."

There were many things Kate could say, but she decided to say nothing. It was an intriguing idea, not trying to bring Cory to her point of view, not trying to compromise, or seek his approval. Why had this never crossed her mind before?

Cory looked at his son. "Leo, go on. Run on up and get in bed."

Leo curled up on the couch next to Kate and pulled the blanket over his head.

"It's three against one." Kate spoke softly and smiled, like it was all a pleasant joke.

And she wondered, really wondered, what it was that had been holding her. Was she that afraid of change? Was it something so superficial as refusing to give up the fairy tale that promises the prince and the princess live happily ever after? Was it just a sort of laziness or lack of energy that made her stay with what is at least familiar, or, even worse, was it that she chose this man, and would not admit she was wrong?

But no, it was none of those things. It was something very simple. Before tonight she felt that staying with Cory was the best thing for Leo. Now she wasn't so sure.

Cory looked down at the dog, who stared steadily back. Kate thought that George was like no other dog she had seen before.

Cory pointed a finger at George. "You better learn to like me, if you want to stay."

And it was over. Cory headed upstairs and Kate was All-Powerful, Goddess of the Night. Kate ran a hand over George's head. "You don't have to like him if you don't want to. And you don't look like a pig. You're very handsome."

Kate was up early the next morning. She had done farm chores too many years to enjoy sleeping in on the weekends. She kept to the downstairs part of the house, and Cory stayed upstairs. She wondered that he did not come down to get something to eat, but was relieved when he didn't. She had leftover stew for lunch, and a piece of potato bread with real butter. She was starving today, and after she got Leo down for his nap, she headed downstairs to finish up the last of the stew.

She was halfway down the steps when she heard Cory calling from the bedroom.

"Kate, *hurry.* Come quick. *I need you.*"

Kate stopped midstride and sighed, and ran back up the stairs. The blinds on the second floor were tightly shut, leaving the hallway in shadow. The bedroom door was open, and Kate ran through, only to be felled by the dressing table bench that was inexplicably right in the doorway. She fell headfirst, hitting her chin on the floor.

"Now you see what it's like."

Kate had bitten her tongue, and she swallowed a tinge of blood. Her chin was throbbing and tingly and it was going to be sore as hell. She got up on her feet and flicked the light switch. Cory was leaning up against the far wall of the room, arms folded, his smile patronizing and gentle.

"I didn't want to have to do that, Kate, but it seems like the only way to get my point across with you these days."

Kate took it all in; the neatly made bed, the strong smell of cigar, a wet towel on the antique dresser she had refinished herself. On its side in the entrance to the bedroom was the bench she left in front of her small dresser where she kept her makeup and perfume. It was a fragile piece, originally belonging to her great-grandmother; a mahogany frame supporting a cushion covered in musty-smelling, green, watered silk.

Cory has never liked the bench. He objected when Kate brought it into the bedroom, and continually hounded her about leaving it in front of her dresser, insisting she keep it wedged at the end of the bed. His justification was that he stubbed his toe against the mahogany bench legs when he walked past the dresser in the dark. Kate's suggestion that he turn on a light has never been considered satisfactory.

Kate saw it in her mind's eye: Cory carefully closing all of the blinds, turning off the upstairs lights. Placing the bench across the doorway and shouting for her to come quick. At this point her thought processes jammed. Kate was not even aware she had picked up the bench until she heaved it across the room, legs out.

Her aim was damn good, but Cory ducked and the bench hit the wall at an angle, gouging a two-inch scar, and splintering into five jagged pieces.

Kate turned and ran down the stairs, wiping the blood off her lip with the back of her hand. She could hear Cory behind her, and smell the cigar smoke that filmed his clothes.

"Kate."

She pretended not to hear, heading into her little feed and tack room to change into her oldest barn boots—the battered whiskey-brown ones, a half size too big so she could wear double socks in the winter and stay warm in the barn. The boots were cracked and streaked with dried mud, and the leather was so dry it looked thirsty. She stopped by the refrigerator to throw some carrots into Sophie's feed and took a carrot for herself.

Cory was waiting for her, blocking the front door, hands in his back pockets, rocking back and forth on his heels. Kate pushed past him and outside. Her heart was beating hard.

"Kate, we need to talk."

Not with a carrot in my mouth, she thought, heading down the drive to the barn.

"*Now*, Kate. This is a little more important than playtime with your horse."

Kate spit the carrot into the dirt and looked at Cory over her shoulder. "Nothing is more important than playtime with my horse."

Her hands were shaking; she walked very fast.

The usual peace eluded her until she was halfway through cleaning Sophie's stall. The mare had outdone herself, and the wheelbarrow was spilling over with wet shavings and manure. Kate took a rake and exposed the stained wet concrete, sprinkled powdery stall sweetener over the soiled areas, and raked clean shavings to the side of the stall. High time for a good airing out. It was breezy today, and sunny. A perfect day for it.

A shadow blocked the sun and Kate looked up. Cory stood on

the other side of the wheelbarrow, examining the ropes where she'd tied back the door.

"This won't hold, Kate. Didn't your daddy ever teach you to tie knots?"

She was across the stall in two quick strides and smacked his hand from the door. She clenched her fingers on the handle of pitchfork, choking on the words.

"This is my barn and you are not welcome. I will talk to you after I've had my time with Sophie, and not until."

Cory was silent for a long moment, and when he spoke his voice had gentled. "I'll help you, Kate. With two of us we can speed things up."

"No!" Kate grabbed the metal edge of the wheelbarrow just as Cory gripped the wooden handles. After a ludicrous moment of fierce tug-of-war, the soiled shavings slid over Kate's gloves, and the wheelbarrow tipped over on one side, dumping all the manure she had shoveled into a churned-up heap.

"What in the hell's gotten into you, Kate?" Cory kicked shavings off his feet. A mound of manure streaked the bottom of his khakis and stuck on the top of his shoe. He had worn casual loafers to the barn, and Kate looked at his feet with contempt.

"Idiot," she said, but quietly, so he could pretend not to hear.

"How did we get here, Kate? How did it come to this?"

Kate saw tears in her husband's eyes. Her hands began shaking again and she felt like the stall was shrinking, smothering her so she could barely breathe.

"No crying allowed in the barn, Cory. You might want to try something else."

Cory's face went blank, then hard like a brick, and Kate felt sick to her stomach. He'd almost had her; she'd been a hairsbreadth from being sucked back in. And it hit her like it never had before, that every move he made was nothing more than a calculated attempt to get what he wanted.

He walked away.

Has he always been like this? Kate wondered. It was as if she had been in a coma, and wakened to a world where everything had changed. Kate went back to work, she needed to be busy, and she righted the wheelbarrow, picked up the pitchfork and started cleaning up the mess. It was quiet again. The smell of horse and the physical labor regulated the beat of her heart, and kept her focused on the tasks at hand. The rest of her life faded. She way overfilled the wheelbarrow and was going to have to be careful not to tip it over again.

Kate's arm muscles were strong, and though the wheelbarrow was overloaded, she had it under control as she rolled it to the other side of the barn. She stopped at the edge of the manure pile and tipped the wheelbarrow down on its nose, letting the contents slide down the side of the mountain to the series of heaps from earlier loads. Later, she would spread it out a bit and plant grass to cover it over, to make a little oasis in the woods.

She righted the wheelbarrow and the feeling that one gets when one is not alone pulled her out of her world. Cory stood just a few feet away, watching her, and for some reason he had picked up the muddy sweater she'd hung on the side of the stall till her next trip to the dump.

Cory held the sweater up in one hand. "What is this, Kate?"

"It's a sweater, Cory, what do you think?" Kate was tired, suddenly; she wanted to curl up somewhere quiet and sleep.

Cory's eyes narrowed and his breathing got heavier the longer they faced each other. Kate thought about the pitchfork that was still in the stall. Then a rustle of dead dry leaves made her look up, and she saw George coming round the back drive to the barn. Leo was right behind him and heading their way. George ran to Kate, tail wagging, trotting sideways so he could let Kate pet him but still keep an eye on Cory, who stood motionless by the side of the barn. Leo sang to himself with that little chirpy noise he made instead of singing real words.

Cory turned his face away, and stared out over the mountain. "I mean where did it come from?"

"What's the big deal, Cory? George dragged it in."

"If that's true, how come you kept it? Why did you hang it on the side of the barn?"

"Because I wanted it out of his reach. I didn't want the dog dragging it up on the porch, or worse, in the house. Nor did I want to have to clean up shreds and pieces of it all over the yard."

"So you were just planning to keep it on the barn as decoration, is that what you want me to believe?"

"I don't want you to believe anything. I stuck it there till I could take it to the dump. Note the overflowing trash cans, in case you'd like to haul them off yourself."

Cory looked away again, then pushed off from where he had been leaning against the side wall, walking past her, passing close enough to shove her to one side when she did not move out of the way. "I'm going for a walk."

He headed down the steep driveway with the sweater still in hand. Kate watched him till he was out of sight, then climbed the ladder to the hayloft, so she could look out the little window and see where he went. But there were too many trees in the way, and she could no longer see him through the woods.

CHAPTER NINETEEN

That night, Kate was asleep on the couch in front of the wood-burning stove when Cory tiptoed by. She opened her eyes, and saw from the satellite television box that it was almost two A.M. She had not expected Cory would stay the night; had been puzzled when he did not leave.

Cory held his shoes in one hand and moved with great stealth. Kate pretended to be asleep, keeping her breathing normal. She had the impression he had stopped to look at her. It took everything she had to stay still. The feeling passed. A creak of wood told her he was taking the lower staircase to the basement. He would go out the back door, so she would not wake up. It was suddenly hard to imagine that she and Cory were man and wife. Legally, she supposed, they weren't.

Kate wondered where he was going. She wondered if she cared. Her stomach dropped and her eyes grew hot with tears. She held them in, in case he could hear. It was real now—her marriage, her fake marriage, was over. Two hours ago she would have said good. Now she was panicked, wondering if she'd made a terrible mistake, and she had to bite her knuckles and shove her face into a pillow to stop herself from running after him, from begging him to talk to her, to work things out.

Why sneak out in the middle of the night? To meet another woman? Why do that here, why tonight? Kate untangled herself from the comforter and scrambled for her shoes. It took time to lace up her boots. Her hands trembled, making her fingers clumsy, and she felt an overwhelming and urgent dread.

Wood coals glowed orange-red behind the glass door of the woodstove—goblin eyes, Leo called it.

Kate walked softly down the stairs to the basement. The sliding door was open a crack. She thought of the utility bill, then laughed. The account was in Cory's name.

The bulb in the security light behind the house had burned out, and it was dark, and hard to see. The woods in winter were drained of color. Kate was afraid—primitive fears, childhood obsessions—whatever it was, she did not want to go alone into the woods. She stood where she was, listening, aware of the thud of her heart, her own quick breaths, and the slide of gravel and boots on the driveway to the house. Cory. She moved slowly, trying to be silent, wincing whenever she dislodged a rock or cracked a twig. She kept to the edge of the tree line, and saw him, finally, a shadowed figure, heading down the drive.

Kate laid a hand on the rough bark of a tree, taking a moment to catch her breath. He was a stranger, this dark figure moving in the shadows. There was nothing familiar about him at all.

She moved forward, tripped, caught herself, then moved on. He had gone off the driveway and into the woods, making his way alongside the fence to Sophie's paddock. Heading to the pond. Kate moved faster.

The pond was halfway down the drive, and Kate had chased odd-looking trespassers away from it more than once. The owners swore you could fish there, though Kate had her doubts. But it was pretty. There was a small wooden dock; an upside-down canoe with a hole in the bottom rested in the weeds on the far side of the pond. She saw Cory walk out onto the dock.

He was facing her, though he couldn't see her. He had something in his hands. He stood for a long time, looking down into the water, a man in a world of his own. Then he glanced over one shoulder, and started wandering through the marshy weeds beside the water. Looking for something. Kate wondered what.

Cory moved slowly, carefully. Kate guessed that the mud was frozen and slippery. Once in a while he bent over and examined something on the ground. At last he straightened, holding on to a tremendous slab of rock. It was heavy enough that he carried it with both hands to the dock, setting it down on the slats of wood.

What the hell was he doing?

Kate watched, and then got it. He was tying something around the rock, something like a shirt, something with sleeves. The dirty little mud-stained sweater. The one she had hung on the barn. Cory lifted the rock that was bulky now, with the sweater tied securely around it, and heaved it out into the pond. Kate heard the splash, ever so faintly, from where she stood on the hill.

And she knew. The sweater belonged to Cheryl Dunkirk. The stains were blood, not mud. Even the dog had figured it out. Cory had killed that pretty girl, that intern. Why, she wasn't sure. There were so many possibilities, boiling down to one simple thing— Cheryl Dunkirk had gotten between Cory and what he wanted.

Kate did not even feel surprised. It was as if she had always known, from the day her mother called from Kentucky, as if she'd been falling and had finally hit the bottom of the well.

Cory stood on the dock, watching the ripples in the water; he seemed deep in thought, and Kate wondered why he stood so still and for so long.

Her back ached and she was cold, and she turned away and headed for the house.

Kate shed her muddy boots in the tack room and curled back up on the couch, staring at the woodstove without seeing it. She thought about Lena Padget and whether or not she should call. She could be jumping to conclusions. The sweater might not have had anything at all to do with Cheryl Dunkirk. She would call Lena tomorrow and ask what the girl had been wearing when she disappeared. Then she would know.

And as if to confirm her observation, the baby monitor crackled, and Kate heard voices from the barn.

A man and a woman. Hard to catch exactly what they said. A creak and a nicker from Sophie. Whoever it is, they were going into Sophie's stall.

"Are you sure he won't stomp us? That's happened to people when they got around horses."

The male laughter was familiar. "She not he. And this horse is so old you could push her over if she bothered you."

Just try it, Kate thought. *Sophie will knock you on your ass.*

Kate felt cold all over, and a slow anger flushed her cheeks. She could hear them, going into the loft. Her personal sanctuary.

"Do you think she knows?" the woman said. She sounded very young.

Cory's voice was hard and businesslike. "She's got no earthly idea."

If the monitor had been a two-way, Kate would have screamed in his ear.

"You sure?" the girl says. "She found the sweater. She's not dumb, is she?"

"She has two things on her mind, horses and kids. In that order."

"What did you do with it?"

"Don't worry about it, it's gone for good."

"It was cashmere," the girl said sadly.

"It was trouble, Mel, and you know it. Now com'mere."

"No."

"Okay then. You can go on back."

"No."

Cory laughed and Kate heard noises, and turned the monitor off. At least now there would be no more doubts, no going back and forth, and no more guilt about family unity. She would wait until Cory left, then pack up and go. She could get on with her life; she could go back home to Kentucky. It was that image that gave her a measure of peace. She curled up under the comforter, and began planning her new life.

But it was hard to concentrate, because she was wondering who the woman was, and if she was the first.

CHAPTER TWENTY

I walked through the maze of cubicles to Joel's desk at the Lexington Fayette County Police Department building on Main Street. It was raining and chilly, and traffic was picking up. I nodded to a few detectives I knew. As always, the noise level was muted, though everyone behind the desks looked alert. I was not sure why Joel's office always made me feel sleepy, but it did.

Joel was at his desk, coat jacket hung on a brass stand that I'd found in the same antiques store where we'd bought our table. I liked seeing it here. It made me feel like I'd put my mark on Joel's office.

He was studying a computer printout, and his shirtsleeves were rolled up one and a half turns each. He'd loosened his tie. A coffee mug sat on the edge of his desk. An open folder spilled pictures of Cheryl Dunkirk, her apartment, and her car.

"Hey, you."

Joel looked up and smiled faintly. From Joel this was equivalent to confetti and balloons. He rose to his feet and gave me a quick hug.

I have seen family pictures of Joel. At first glance, this slender man with tired eyes looks nothing like the sturdy toddler who stands between two proud parents, mother's skirt caught in the small fist. But look carefully and you will find the familiar expression, the focus, the look of wariness and speculation. It is as if the child knew what was in store—that some of it would be very bad and some of it would be very good. That he was bracing himself, and ready.

From the first moment I saw Joel Mendez in the carpeted maze of partitions where Lexington detectives work, I thought of him as the man with the tired face. I reached out and touched his temple, and he closed a hand over my wrist and shut his eyes. Gently I traced the lines of fatigue with a fingertip, as if my touch could erase the life experience that had put them there.

Joel shows a private face to the world, and until this case had never shut me out. I was the chosen one, and Joel always seemed to gather me close, as if he balanced his distance from the rest of the world by allowing no barriers between the two of us. I realized that this, more than anything else, had been what I missed.

"I have good news."

Now that I was here, in Joel's office, I wondered why it had taken me so long to make the decision to come. There had been no alternative. I was happier about it than I'd expected.

Joel smiled at me, with a calm acceptance that was somehow kind, and I felt like we were coming together again.

"I talked to Kate Edgers a while ago."

"She called you? Why?" He looked at me steadily, and I decided not to share any of the details of my trip to Tennessee to see Kate on the top of her mountain. And as quickly as that, we were miles away once again.

"She saw her husband with a pink cashmere sweater that may well have had bloodstains, and it sounds very much like the one Cheryl was wearing the night she disappeared."

Joel leaned back in his chair and closed his eyes. "Interesting. But it's hearsay and she can't testify against him." He reached for his coffee. "Lena, can I get you a cup of coffee?"

"Why don't you get yourself a whole pot? Are you asleep?"

"A spouse cannot testify against a spouse in court."

"You think?"

No response to the remark.

"Joel, listen. Kate saw him wrap the sweater around a rock, tie the sleeves in a knot, and throw it into a pond that sits about halfway down the driveway on their property."

Joel thought for a moment. "You believe her?"

"Absolutely."

"If it's true . . . what an idiot. Cops make some of the worst criminals. Okay, even without Kate's testimony, if it's Cheryl's sweater, on his property, that will nail it. The body will likely be close."

Joel leaned across the desk, put his hands on the side of my face and pulled me close. He kissed me hard, then turned to the phone.

"One other thing."

He stopped, hand hovering over the dial pad. "What?"

"You can have Kate's testimony. Cory Edgers never divorced his first wife, Amy McAlister. I double-checked, this is straight up. Kate and Cory Edgers aren't legally man and wife."

Joel frowned at me. "How long have you known that?"

I stared at him for a long moment. "That's the only thing you think of to say to me?"

"How long did you sit on that piece of information?"

I turned and walked away.

I was still in the lobby of the police building when my cell phone rang. The caller ID said *Miranda Brady.*

"Lena? It's Miranda."

I went through the double doors out onto the sidewalk. The wind was blowing, which made it hard to catch everything Miranda said.

"It looks like we've got him, Miranda."

"Him?"

"Your sister's killer."

"How? Who?"

"It's Edgers. There's no doubt."

"But Cheryl wasn't seeing him, she would have told me."

"Look, there are still a lot of details to put together. But it's him. With any luck he'll tell us where she's buried and you can put her to rest."

"Can you prove it?"

Odd question. "Yeah."

"How? Have you found some physical evidence?"

"The police have the sweater. The one Cheryl was wearing

when she died." They'd have it soon, anyway. "I'm sorry, Miranda, I can't go into it. Just trust me on this. He's nailed."

She was silent for a long moment.

"Feels weird, I know. You think you're going to be so happy, but you're not. It gets better, I promise. Do you want me to call your father?"

"No, I'll do it. He's been on the phone every night wondering if you'd come up with anything. This should give him some satisfaction."

"Tell him I'll put together a report, and call with details when it's pulled together."

"Great. Well done, I should say."

"Thanks." At least somebody appreciated me.

Chapter Twenty-one

Wilson tilted the wooden chair back against the wall and picked up his beer mug. His hand was sticky with barbecue sauce but it was pointless to clean it off because he was still eating. He figured he could handle one more beer before he'd have to switch to something nonalcoholic. Two at most. It was prom night and he was the host so he had to stay reasonably sober.

Nobody was falling-down drunk, but he was keeping an eye on the old guy sitting next to the woman with red hair. The two of them had put away a lot of beer. The guy got up to head for the men's room, and Wilson watched to see if he'd stagger. The man was amazingly sure-footed.

The entire group was spread out among ten tables, in groups of twos and threes, with one big group near the cash register. Twice, other customers had looked in the door, then turned around and walked out.

Billy's Barbecue was the perfect kind of place for this sort of gathering. Low-key, informal, wood booths along the back or a step down to the tables on the lower level. Wilson had just settled at an empty table near the men's room, which was not a coincidence. Wilson was a prom night veteran. He'd socialized his ass off, and was taking a break. Keeping tabs on the level of intoxication. Prom night DUIs were frowned upon.

It was going well. The locals loved prom nights; dinner and beer on the ATF, and a chance to discuss the case, trade opinions, war stories, theories. Ruggers had suggested it and authorized the expenditure and taken it out of the Nashville district budget. It happened often enough—a case solved when everyone got together in the same room to shoot the shit. Someone would come up with something he thought everybody else already knew. Sometimes it was the right push in the right direction, and enough cases were aided and abetted by prom night to make it a standard operating procedure.

Times like this made Wilson feel smug and superior to the FBI. You would never catch those guys having beers with the locals. You'd for sure never catch them picking up the tab.

Wilson picked up a barbecued rib, teeth scraping the bone to get the meat off. He was full but still eating. They didn't have barbecue like this in California.

He thought of Sel, and how much she would love this place. How she would have a healthy appetite for the barbecue and cobbler. Sel had grown up in Michigan, and currently worked as a chef in a bistro in Woodland Hills—a job she loved. She cooked, she surfed, she walked her dog. She talked about opening her own restaurant, but worried that it would take too much time away from the beach. In a town full of people who were never happy with how they looked and pursued the impossible dream of physical perfection, Sel was exotic in her personal contentment, and her seemingly oblivious lack of awareness of the California Code of Appearance.

Wilson dreamed of helping Sel run a barbecue place in Marina Del Rey. A southern barbecue place.

He looked across the room, watching Mendez. They'd met for the first time the day before in the muted but busy Lexington PD office. Mendez was different from the other locals. More reserved, watchful, giving the impression of a man who was tightly wound. Not a guy who took advantage of casual Fridays.

Mendez had been cordial, wary, but very open with the facts of the case. He had answered every question Wilson posed, addressed every issue head-on, no apologies, no fluff. The man was slender, and dressed very well. His tie was tight, even now, when everybody else was coming apart at the seams. His hair was a mix of black threaded with silver; he had brown eyes, and a faint white scar on one cheek. He did not have a hint of the resentment or inferiority complex Wilson occasionally found with locals.

It was funny, Mendez didn't talk much, get loud, or tell jokes, but somehow he put his detectives at ease. Maybe they were always at ease. They were southerners. Wilson noticed that Mendez listened a lot while making sure everybody had beer and barbecue. Besides Mendez and three other Lexington PD detectives, there were two local ATF agents there.

A few minutes before the gathering started up, Wilson had gotten a call from Nashville. An attorney representing Cory Edgers had been in touch—Edgers wanted to come in, to talk, to cut a deal. Wilson had been hoping the prom night discussions would give him a glimmer, something to burn Edgers with during the negotiation. No body made the whole thing difficult. But so far, nobody had come up with anything new. The barbecue had been great, the beer had been cold, and the case facts and theories had been the same old shit.

Edgers's attorney had requested both Wilson and Mendez be present and ready to "work things through." Which meant Edgers had something to give them. If it concerned Rodeo, Wilson could see where he and Mendez might have a difference of opinion. Mendez wanted premeditation and murder; he wanted recovery of the body. Wilson had his eye on the ball, and the ball was Rodeo.

The tab at Billy's came to four hundred eighty-nine dollars plus tip. Mendez had grimaced at the bill, but Wilson's jaw had dropped. You would never get away that cheaply in Los Angeles. They'd had their fill of beer and ribs, beans and deep-fried banana peppers, corn bread, Texas toast, blackberry cobbler and vanilla ice cream. Wilson fumbled through his wallet for the company credit card—the ATF American Express Platinum—and noticed that Mendez was standing by the wreckage of their meal, staring out the window. He seemed to be waiting.

"Did you want to order anything else to eat?" Wilson asked.

He'd signed the credit card slip, including a tip that brought tears of happiness to the restaurant staff.

Mendez gave him a small half smile.

Right, Wilson thought. *Why waste a whole smile when a half of one would do.*

Mendez looked antsy. If the beer had an effect on him, he hid it well. "Edgers and his attorney will be in before noon. Are you interested in thinking through some strategy, or would you rather do that tomorrow?"

"I'm still on West Coast time. I'm wide awake. Let's go get a clean table and sort things through."

Mendez looked over Wilson's shoulder at the kitchen.

"They won't be going home for another hour or two. They've locked the front doors but they said we could pick out a clean table and stay as long as we want."

Mendez followed Wilson up a level to the long pinewood booths. The beer was working in their favor; both of them more relaxed than usual.

"I answered all of your questions today," Mendez said.

Wilson leaned back against the cushion. He knew where this was heading.

"I feel like I'm somewhat out of the loop on your end of the case, and I wondered if you'd like to fill me in. I think as it stands that you and I are going to go into that negotiation tomorrow with two different agendas."

"I had that same thought. Give me a quick rundown on what you do know. I can make sure everything you have is accurate and fill in the blanks."

A waiter appeared, left a pitcher of beer and two clean glasses and told them it was on the house.

"I know Edgers was involved with Cheryl Dunkirk—professionally and personally. I know Edgers is not legally married to the woman he says is his wife. I know he killed Cheryl Dunkirk and tied her bloody sweater to a rock and threw it into a pond on his property. The last two aren't confirmed."

Wilson felt his stomach go tight. "Who's been holding out on who?"

"The last two came in today, still being checked. I also know Cheryl's disappearance is somehow crossing one of your ongoing investigations, and that whatever it is, it's big."

Wilson poured beer into both glasses, shoving one toward Mendez. "Is that why Edgers is coming in? He knows about the sweater?"

"Your guess is as good as mine."

"Has there been a leak?"

"Let's just say the evidence came from a leak."

Wilson sat back in his booth, shredded one of the paper towels Billy's provided for cleanup. "Okay, Mendez. This is what I've got. There have been five federal agents assassinated in the last five years—three were FBI, two were our guys. All of them were present at Waco during the firestorm."

Mendez reached for his glass. Took a long swallow. "Go on."

"The killer keeps the same MO. Stuns them with some kind of high-powered Taser, binds their hands and feet with baling wire, strangles them with baling wire."

"Torture?"

"Doesn't look like it. On the other hand, the method of execution is pretty up close and personal."

"So you're not thinking this is a hire job."

"We don't think so. Right on the heels of every death is an Internet radio broadcast with the name of the victim, location of the body, details of the kill. Information that could only come from someone who either did the job, or was in communication with the one who did. We tracked the data streams, and have come up with a different survivalist group each time. What these groups have in common is they're loosely organized, ineffective, small-timers. It's never the same group twice."

"So the killer is using them to draw fire."

"Not bad for a local guy." Wilson looked up quickly and saw that Mendez hadn't taken offense. Stupid joke. Too much beer. "Your office do much with geographical forensics?"

"We've got some people training at the University of Tennessee in Knoxville. Nothing formal, nothing up and running yet. The sniper investigation your people did in the D.C. area put the spot-light on it, so we may get some funding on down the road."

Wilson balled up a paper towel from the roll at the end of the table. "We work with a marine intel group out at Pendleton, and they spent a lot of time on this. Kept coming up with the same re-sults—the killer had no discernible geographical base. We inter-preted that to mean that the killer was not a single person, but some kind of networking conspiracy with these groups. And then more data came in and we started to get another picture—a geo-graphical route. We pounded the computers for anything that runs that particular track and came up with the U.S. Pro-Am Markus Bourbon Rodeo."

"Stun gun. Baling wire. Large animals—bulls."

"The Rodeo Assassin. We still haven't got anything solid on the Waco connection. But we had an agent working undercover at the Markus Bourbon Pro-Am, and she was certain she'd identified Rodeo's girlfriend, a rodeo clown named Janis Winters, who func-tions as a sort of liaison between the survivalist groups and Rodeo himself. That was the last we heard from our agent before we found her body."

"Same way as the others?"

"Down to the last detail. Except for no Internet radio stream." Wilson rubbed his eyes. "In the meantime, we get an intern here in Kentucky who disappears, and one of the last things she did be-fore she went missing was have a conversation with her ex-boyfriend, who used to be an ATF intern himself. She tells him that a sheriff by the name of Cory Edgers, who'd been mentoring her since she'd gotten the intern job, and who had actually gotten her into a bit of trouble with her boss, had told her that he was working undercover on a big case that involved the murder of federal agents. She told the ex, Robbie, that she thought Edgers was bragging to impress her, but that a lot of what he said sounded pretty real. She also said he knew who the next victim was going to be, and that he would bring "the big guys" in when he'd made his case. He was going to make a big splash, and get himself hired on with the ATF. He told her the name of the victim.

"She's conflicted, not sure what to do, wondering if it's all a come-on and a lot of crap. She's on the job a couple of weeks later when she hears about a federal agent down in Alabama, dead, same name as Edgers told her. She freaks, goes to see Robbie the ex, who tells her to go straight to the S.A. in charge and tell him everything. But she's adamant that this Edgers is into something that's over his head, he's a good cop, she's not going to get labeled a snitch before she even gets out of college. And for all she knows the operation is legit and the S.A. knows all about it."

Mendez looked down at his fingernails. "Did she tell the ex what she was going to do?"

"No. But he said it would be like her to give Edgers a chance to go to the S.A. himself."

Mendez looked across the table at Wilson.

"What?" Wilson asked.

"I interviewed Robert Little myself. He didn't bring any of this up."

Wilson took a breath. "I know that. He thought he was doing the right thing."

"Little is a law enforcement grad student. He's familiar with the concept of obstruction of justice. This bit of information was crucial to the investigation. I could have gone to the grand jury and had Edgers indicted on that alone."

"I know. That's why we kept it from you." Wilson studied Mendez, saw no change in complexion, no sign of anger, no telltale pulse beating in the temple or the side of the neck. Unemotional, matter-of-fact. Formidable. "If you'd gone to the grand jury we'd have shut you down."

"You'd have tried."

"I give you that. But I'm bringing you in now. That's the whole reason I'm here, to manage the Kentucky end of this, and work directly with you. It takes a little time to get the groundwork laid and the task force moving. Everything's in place. One of our agents lost her life tracking this guy, and she was close. It wouldn't make sense to shrug that off and say 'oh, well.'"

"Point taken."

Wilson took a deep breath. "As soon as we got the word from Monica Clive, our agent, we matched up times and locations of deaths, with times and locations of Rodeo performances, and cross-referenced with rodeo personnel. There are always some guys that don't go on the payroll, and get paid under the table.

"The girlfriend, Janis Winters, is a hit on every one. After Agent Clive was killed, we freaked, we figured Winters would disappear and Rodeo would go underground. We kept a very loose, very discreet surveillance. Winters stayed put. We went over the videos Monica took. Edgers shows up in the very last one."

"Edgers does? What is he doing? Is he in contact with Janis Winters?"

"Nothing we can see. But that's not definitive."

Mendez scratched his chin. "So is he really trying to work the case, or is he in with the killer?"

"That's the question."

"Why kill Cheryl Dunkirk?" Mendez asked.

"Either he's working with the killer, and she knew too much about it. Or he's working the case, and he screwed up and let an agent get killed without warning us, and he didn't want to lose his career and opportunity to be a Fed. Or he was having an affair with her and it was a crime of passion."

"Or he didn't do it."

"That's possible, too."

Mendez's cell phone rang. "Excuse me," he said, answering. "Yes. Yeah. Good."

Wilson was tired and his mind drifted to Sel. Meeting her had been one of those weird, self-made miracles. Wilson had sweated through months of physical therapy till he could walk, albeit with a limp, and he was getting back in shape, but his swing and shag dancing days were over. It depressed him, looking at the surfboard that was as familiar to him as his own face. It was too good a board to be out of the water, and too sweet to sell to someone who would not treat it right. So Wilson started spending days off walking the beaches, looking to give the board to the first good-looking female surfer he could find.

Wilson found her at Zuma Beach. He knew she was the one as soon as he saw her go out. He'd climbed the steep pathway that led to the rock overhang, his leg throbbing and stiff. He'd stood on the edge of the rocks, breathing heavily, sweat runnels sliding down the side of his flushed face, and watched her through the binoculars hanging on a string around his neck.

It was chilly enough that there were very few diehards on the beach. The girl wore a thigh-length skin suit. Her hair hung in dark wet spirals, and she rode that board with a grace and balance that somehow made her free. She had good form, and an East Coast style, and simply seeing the way she stood, the way she held her arms, brought it all back to Wilson, the joy of being out.

"Okay," Mendez said. "I'll talk to you later."

"Hey, don't hang up yet, Joel. If that's your girlfriend, maybe she'd like to come down for some food."

"That was the sheriff's department in Anderson County. They'll get the paperwork together for us to drag the pond on Edgers's property."

"Oh. Well, you can still call your girlfriend."

Mendez hesitated. "I'm sure she already ate."

When Edgers arrived at the Lexington Police Department with his attorney at precisely ten o'clock the next morning, Wilson and Mendez were freshly shaved, showered, and had consumed their first two cups of coffee. The four men met in a small conference room; gray carpet, cream-colored walls, a muted and silent chamber. This was no overheated worn-out room with green walls, ugly tile, and a two-way mirror, a confining claustrophobic square where cops and perps and attorneys yanked their ties loose and screamed at each other. In this room cops and perps and attorneys only wished they could yank their ties loose and scream at each other.

Cory Edgers had arrived in uniform, and he gave Wilson a long slow stare. Wilson returned a lazy look, hiding behind the California dude image, noticing that the man was the kind of spit-and-polish law enforcement his boss back in L.A. drooled over. Wilson glanced over to Mendez. If the man had an opinion, it did not show on his face.

Mendez had already briefed him on Edgers's attorney.

Lexington-based, though he'd been raised in Bowling Green, Vernon Carminsk ran a one-man firm specializing in the representation of white-collar criminals. Many of his clients were innocent; just as many weren't. Carminsk was short, stocky, with dark blond hair and a pretty good suit. He shook hands with Mendez.

"Joel."

"Vernon. This is Agent Wilson McCoy of the Los Angeles office of Alcohol, Tobacco and Firearms. Here as requested."

"Appreciate your time," Carminsk said. He glanced at Edgers and pointed to a chair. Carminsk emitted the faintest hint of cologne; a light but masculine scent. He opened a briefcase, took out two files, handed one to Mendez, the other to Wilson.

"Just a moment of background, if you'll bear with me."

In Wilson's opinion, Edgers had made a wise choice in attorneys. Carminsk had a cordial but direct professionalism that would carry over to his clients. He gave the impression of a man who was straight up, uninterested in legal tricks and posturing, and intent on getting things sorted expediently. He'd be a breath of fresh air in L.A. And a jury would follow his every lead.

"You both know my client, Deputy Sheriff Cory Edgers. You know that he has been in law enforcement for ten years, that he has a good record, and the solid reputation of a hardworking family man. You also know that for the past year he has been on temporary assignment with the Lexington ATF office." Carminsk looked at Wilson. "Mr. Edgers was flattered by the confidence the ATF showed by hiring him to work for them on a temporary basis." Carminsk leaned back in his chair.

"Mr. Edgers is atypical of my clients. Most of them, understandably, want *one,* not to go to jail; and *two,* not to lose their jobs. I can honestly tell you that Mr. Edgers never focused on either when we first talked. . . ."

Slippery word, focus, Wilson thought.

"Mr. Edgers's main concern was in getting a very complicated situation resolved in the best way possible. Mr. Edgers is law enforcement through and through. Whatever else you may think of him, I don't think you can disagree with that."

Wilson tipped his chair back. He was not an early riser on the

West Coast, and it was agony getting up on the East. But he'd been out of bed before the alarm went off that morning, and had been edgy and on the mark and now he was struggling to stay awake. He checked his watch. Might as well time things and try to come up with the average period a southerner talked before getting to the point.

Carminsk held up a finger. "My client has an amazing story to tell you. He has information that is critical. He very much wants to talk to you both—he and I are in agreement on that. On the other hand, I represent the man, and I want to make sure he is looked after."

Wilson looked to Mendez, expecting him to make the usual *Tell me what you know and we'll see* reassurance. Mendez said nothing. No one said anything.

Carminsk cleared his throat. "I don't want Mr. Edgers to talk to you unless we get some guarantees about the repercussions of what he's going say."

"What do you want?" Mendez asked.

"Involuntary manslaughter for the death of Cheryl Dunkirk; ten years total, six served, four probated. Minimum security prison. Immunity for any further charges that might come out of this discussion and subsequent investigations. And by that I include state and federal charges."

"Too broad," Mendez said. "Is he willing to locate the body?"

"No. Mr. Edgers does not know where Ms. Dunkirk is. Nevertheless, he feels a certain amount of responsibility in her disappearance. You'll understand when you hear his story."

Mendez looked over at Wilson, and said, "Excuse us." Wilson followed him out of the room and a ways down the hall.

Wilson leaned back against the wall. "How do you read it?"

Mendez was thinking, staring at nothing in particular. "He killed her. He wouldn't take the manslaughter charge if he hadn't. He won't tell us where the body is, which means that whatever story he and Carminsk have come up with is crap, and won't be borne out by forensics. That says to me it was a premeditated killing. And that he wants to cover his ass in case Cheryl is ever found."

"He could get the death penalty; an intern is still a Fed. And even if it didn't merit that, a federal sentence would mean no parole." Wilson folded his arms. "Why does he think we'd agree to anything this stupid?"

"I think he has something for you."

"Something that's worth a sweetheart deal?" Wilson said.

Mendez put his hands in his pockets. "Without a body, I don't have much. We'll get some matches out of Cheryl's car when the DNA results come back from the state lab, but those can be accounted for; Cheryl and Edgers spent time together. I don't have a case; I might never have one."

Wilson wondered how it was he'd gotten comfortable working with Mendez so quickly. As if they'd been partners for months. "What did you think of the 'family man' remark?"

"A little much for a bigamist."

"Have we been out here long enough?" Wilson asked.

Carminsk was talking softly to Edgers when Wilson and Mendez sat back down. "What's it going to be?" Carminsk asked.

Mendez looked at Wilson, who shrugged. "When you start harping on Mr. Edgers's reputation as a family man, your credibility starts to fade. Bigamy's illegal even in California."

Carminsk just barely skipped a beat, but Wilson had seen it. The old client-does-not-tell-his-attorney-everything glitch.

"It's a technicality, something Mr. Edgers wasn't even aware of until recently. He thought it best to get this matter of Cheryl Dunkirk resolved before he took steps to make the situation right."

Damn good, Wilson thought. *Right off the cuff, vague enough to cover almost everything.*

Mendez scooted his chair back. "Let's not waste any more time. Give us the story. There won't be an agreement until we know what you've got."

Carminsk looked at Wilson. "What if Mr. Edgers could give you the Rodeo killer?"

"What do you mean 'give'?" Mendez asked.

"Name, location, and pictures. The shots will help your case, they won't make it. They show the killer putting things into a pickup truck. They show the stun gun and the baling wire. We can also give you the name of the next victim on the list."

"Who?" Wilson asked.

"Do we have an agreement?" Cory said.

It was the first thing he'd said. Carminsk winced and gave him a look.

Mendez looked at Carminsk. "I'm going to walk out for ten minutes and get the paperwork going to have your client arrested for conspiracy to commit murder."

"You can't make that stick," Edgers said.

"I'm willing to give it a try."

"Not another word," Carminsk said, pointing at Edgers. He stared at his client, waiting for what, Wilson was not sure. Edgers was clearly not big on taking advice, much less orders. "Tell them your story."

Edgers tilted his head, as if organizing his thoughts, took a deep breath, and began.

The suspicions, Edgers admitted, were true. He had indulged in a brief affair with Cheryl Dunkirk; he knew it was wrong. He ended the affair about the time he got a lead from an old high school buddy about a survivalist group. The buddy swore the group was involved in the murder of an FBI agent. The friend had hung out with the group, been involved in a few "projects," and was worried. He didn't want to go to the police; he didn't want to be a party to murder. He went to his old buddy Cory Edgers.

Edgers promised the friend he would keep the information to himself until he was sure there was something to the story. Cheryl knew Cory was working on something undercover, and she wanted to be involved. She wanted to make a splash, so that she would look good, so that she would be guaranteed a job.

"She was competitive, even with me," Cory said. "She wanted to be the intern everybody remembered."

Also—she was young and inexperienced, she thought she was in love, and she was pregnant.

They fought it out the night she disappeared. She'd picked him up and they'd gone for a drive. She'd started in on him about being involved in his investigation of the survivalist group. Again, he told her no, to stay out of things. If the story was true, then the situation was dangerous. If it wasn't true, Cory needed to protect his friend.

She'd threatened him. Said she would go to his wife, that she would tell everyone about their affair. She would have the child and if he did not do as she said, she would make the child's life, Cory's child's life, a living hell.

He'd gone ballistic. He admitted it. She was going to take it all away; his career, his family. If she had his baby, they'd be tied together forever. He'd live in constant worry about whether or not she was abusing the child.

They'd fought. She'd gotten furious, left the car, and taken off. He'd looked for her, couldn't find her. Eventually he drove the Mustang back home and put it in the parking lot of her apartment house. She'd never been seen again. He felt responsible for leaving her behind.

Edgers took a breath, hands making fists. "That's it. That's what happened."

"What a crock of shit," Wilson said.

Carminsk held up a hand. "I don't think that sort of comment is constructive, Agent Wilson."

Edgers spoke as if solely addressing Mendez. "The rodeo killer is named Janis Winters. She works as a clown with the rodeo circuit. She has everyone convinced she's just a liaison, but she's it. She's the killer. Give them the pictures."

Carminsk reached into his briefcase, and put a brown envelope in the center of the table. Wilson opened the flap, and took the photographs out, flipping through them slowly, then handing them to Mendez.

Janis Winters was blond, younger than he'd expected, not hard-looking at all. Pretty. A professional quality long-range telephoto lens had caught her slinging a knapsack into the back of a green pickup truck, unzipping the sack. Inside, a small roll of wire, a tool that looked like it might be a wire cutter. Another set of shots of Janis Winters taking a stun gun out of the bag and tucking it inside her coat.

"Who's the next target?" Mendez asked.

"Do we have a deal?" Edgers said.

"Who is it?"

"I don't know the name," Edgers said. "Somebody out of Nashville."

CHAPTER TWENTY-TWO

The ATF office in Nashville was actually in Franklin, which is an offshoot of the city; suburban, expensive, and new. Wilson sat in the little cubicle that the assistant S.A. had offered him, and looked at his watch. Alex Rugger was supposed to have met him three hours ago to orchestrate the capture of Janis Winters.

Wilson drummed his fingers on the table. Footsteps no longer made him look up; he'd been faked out a dozen times already. He was tired and his leg was aching, and he'd had a little too much beer at the barbecue the day before. The time zone change was catching up with him, as well as the driving he was doing from Nashville to Lexington, Kentucky. Other than mountains, Wilson couldn't see much difference between the two.

"You're Wilson?"

Two men stood outside the cubicle. They gave him the glazed smile that Wilson figured was the hallmark of a southerner, and since Wilson had figured out that southerners smile at everybody, he knew it didn't really mean a thing. Kind of like Californians, he decided, wondering if you could find honesty in the Northeast.

The black man, thick in the middle and balding, put out his hand. "I'm Bennie Krupp."

"Nice to meet you," Wilson muttered. He knew he should stand, but he didn't trust the leg just now, and he didn't want these men to see. First impressions were critical, and he wanted them to look at him as a fully functioning member of the team.

"I'm Ronald Bishoff." Bishoff was white, red-haired, and skinny. He had a long neck, and probably a pencil dick. Wilson rubbed his eyes. He'd better take some Advil before he killed the next person who wandered by.

"We thought we'd give you a briefing," Krupp said. "Move things along."

"I thought Alex was going to do that." Wilson realized he sound whiny, like a girl who'd been stood up for a date. He was feeling like an annoyance all of a sudden, instead of a part of the investigation.

"Yeah, Rugger was supposed to be here this morning, and he hasn't called in. The assistant S.A.'s trying to track him down. Until then, she says we might as well start filling you in. Sort of a briefing-lite."

Krupp and Bishoff exchanged looks and a laugh, and Wilson doesn't even bother to look pleasant over a joke he'd heard a million times before. Something had struck a note with him. The assistant S.A. tracking Rugger down. Something wrong with this scenario. These guys were nervous, too.

"Hey, don't bullshit me, okay? What the hell is going on here?"

Krupp looked angry and Bishoff blushed. "Look, Wilson, it's a big investigation. We're taking care of the Tennessee end, and the assassin. You're handling that intern business up in Kentucky and keeping an eye out for overlap. No need to get ahead of yourself on this."

"That's not what I'm talking about, and you know it."

Wilson stood up, shoving the chair under the little desk. He walked away from the two men, keeping the limp to a minimum, which was usually painful, but he didn't feel a thing.

"Self-important California asshole," one of the men said—it sounded like Bishoff. Wilson wouldn't disagree.

It was a long walk to the office he wanted, but Denise Asher was good enough to welcome him personally when he arrived at her open door. She was the assistant S.A., in charge of all Nashville agents. Wilson liked her. She was down-to-earth and matter-of-fact, and at the moment she looked tense. Wilson waved from the hallway. She didn't snub him, as he feared, but motioned him in.

She held the phone to her ear, said okay, and wrote things down.

"Yeah," she said. "I'll get back to you." She hung up and leaned back in her chair.

"Problems," Wilson said. Not a question. "Where is Rugger? Has he got something hot?"

The woman shook her head. "No, that's not the problem. The problem is we don't know where he is."

Wilson felt it in his gut, like someone had kicked him in the stomach. "When? I mean, when was he last seen?"

"Last night. Coming out of a Target, not seen exactly, but talking on a cell phone to his wife. He'd stopped in to get some notebook paper and a protractor for one of his kids. He told his wife he was on the way, and that he was hungry, and that's the last thing she heard."

"And she's just now telling you this?"

Denise Asher raised an eyebrow. "No. We got people on this last night."

The phone rang again, and Wilson knew it was bad news before Asher picked it up. She said her name, then just listened.

"Oh God," she said finally. "No, just get an ambulance out there. Don't make her do anything. I'm coming out myself. Hey, don't worry about that. Compassion, until I get there. I know. I know."

Asher hung up the phone and looked at him.

"Dead?" Wilson asked.

"Wife found him just a little while ago. She suddenly started thinking that maybe he went to Wal-Mart, not Target. She went out herself, and found the car. Locked, but she had a key. The front seat was soaked in blood, nobody in the car. She opened the trunk." Asher hid her face in her hands. "Come on, Wilson, you can ride out there with me."

Wilson tried to get the names and ages of Rugger's kids straight in his mind on the ride out. Rugger had invited him to dinner, and he'd met all of them just days ago, but he had the feeling that he was missing one of the daughters. He finally asked Asher, who filled him in. There were four of them. A boy in high school, fifteen. Kyle. Two daughters in middle school; Amy, fourteen, and

Sandy, thirteen. The youngest, eight years old. Kevin—the one who needed the notebook paper and the protractor.

"He still have that old sheepdog?" he asked.

"Boris? No. Boris died of bone cancer three years ago. They have a German shepherd now, though Alex swore he would never get another dog. Boris the Second."

"Boris the Second," Wilson echoed.

"There's a cat, too. Natasha."

Rugger's wife was so calm and matter-of-fact that Wilson felt afraid for her. She sat without a fidget in the back of an ambulance, a blanket wrapped around her shoulders. There was blood on her shirt, a white oxford shirt, oversized, probably a cast-off from Alex. Sel was always stealing Wilson's shirts, and she liked the white ones best. The shirt was smeared red, and the woman's jeans were stained dark along the thighs, and blood had dried on her hands.

"Hey, Wendy," Asher said. Friendly and calm.

"Denise, hi."

Asher took the woman's hands without flinching, then turned them palms up. She looked at one of the ER techs. "Think we might get her cleaned up a little?"

"She won't let us," the man said. He was Hispanic, and had a low voice. "I didn't want to upset her more than we had to."

Wilson nodded, it made sense to him, and Asher turned back to Rugger's wife.

"Do the kids know anything yet?"

Wendy shook her head. "No. I thought I'd better talk to you first, before I went home. I'm not going to want to leave them after I break the news."

"That was smart."

Wilson heard cars and voices, the arrival of the forensic team. Doors slammed, but he did not turn around. He was riveted by this woman, Wendy, Alex Rugger's wife.

"I told you the wrong place," Wendy said, and laughed. "Alex always teased me about screwing things up. You know, I'd ask him to meet me at Cracker Barrel, and then go to Bob Evans. He always said that's just part and parcel of marrying a college professor. He could always figure it out, you know, if he went somewhere and I wasn't there. He knows how my mind works, and he'd find me. Of course, when we all got cell phones, it wasn't so much of a problem."

Asher nodded. "So anyway, I was embarrassed to call you, Denise. Stupid, you know? I was just so worried, because Alex always calls me, he never makes me upset. So I just came right on out. I had to. And I was so relieved, because I didn't see the car at first. But I drove all the way around, and I found it here, on the side. Alex would never have parked here. Whoever did it, they moved the car."

"That's good, Wendy. The longer they were in the car, the more things they fooled with, the more evidence they'll leave behind."

"That's what I figured."

"Listen, Wendy, have you called your sister?"

"Oh, yeah. She's on her way to the house. Actually, I called her before I called the office. Who was it I talked to?"

"Carol."

"Yeah, Carol." Wendy took a deep breath. "If you don't need me here, Denise, I'd better go see to the kids, before it hits the news. They're pretty worried about their dad. And with my sister over there, they'll know something's up."

"Let me go with you," Asher said. "And Wendy, don't you want to clean up a little? It's a little rough, seeing the kids with—"

"Oh, Jesus, yes. What is the matter with me?" Wendy laughs. "I guess we all know what is the matter with me. I know I'm acting strange, but to tell you the truth, I just don't feel a damn thing. You're going to think I'm crazy or I don't love him but—"

"No, no," Asher said. "The less you feel, Wendy, the more you loved him. Your mind is just protecting you right now. It'll come soon enough. Come on, let's get you cleaned up, and get some of that blood washed off, then I've got a big coat we can throw over you till you can get that shirt off, too."

"Denise, I know you don't have time—"

"Of course I do. I'll be right back."

Wendy looked up at the ER tech. "I guess you get your way. You have one of those wet wipe things?"

"Right here, sweetie. Right here."

Asher crooked a finger at Wilson, who followed. A perimeter of barriers had already been set up, but the scene was relatively quiet. Three men detached from a huddle and made a beeline for Asher. She stopped to listen. Wilson kept walking.

"No, leave him be," he heard Asher say to someone behind his back.

Alex Rugger's car was sitting parallel to the back of the store. The trunk was open, the small bulb glowing. Rugger's eyes were wide open, and he was still in a shirt and tie, only the shirt was drenched with blood. The wire had been wrapped so tightly and fiercely around his throat that his head sat oddly upon his shoulders. His hands, bound in front with wire, were crusty with blood, something Wilson had not seen in other crime scene photos. He wondered what was different here. He looked closely, and saw that the left wrist was cut clean to the bone. Autopsy results, histamine levels, all indications in the past were clear that the other victims were unconscious when they were killed. Alex Rugger was conscious, and struggling. Wilson realized he had touched the man's wrists, and gotten blood on the fingertips of his right hand. He said a small prayer in the back of his mind, just for Alex Rugger. Then he said one for each of Rugger's children.

CHAPTER TWENTY-THREE

Janis chews grape bubble gum to stay awake. She can't hold another cup of coffee, and in truth she doesn't need one—she hasn't slept since she got the note.

> I know what you've done. I know you have done it six times. I know you are Rodeo and not a girlfriend. It's in your best interest to meet me tomorrow night at the Tennessee Welcome Center and rest stop at the Kentucky-Tennessee border. I will be at the top of the pathway behind the buildings. Come alone. Be there at two am.
>
> There is a way out if you want it.

Janis had thought she'd gotten a glimpse of Miranda in the stands, but hadn't been sure. Later she'd spotted the cop; that night she'd found the note. As far as Janis is concerned, the cop and Curly Girl are in way over their heads. But she still hasn't figured out their agenda.

If her luck holds, the two of them will come together. Janis exits from I-75 into the welcome center. It won't be dark for another three hours. She pulls into a parking place next to a Ford Suburban that houses two annoyed looking women and six children around the age of nine. Some kind of school field trip, Janis thinks.

The parking lot is half full, and hers is just one of several pickup trucks. Driving a pickup around Tennessee and Kentucky is equivalent to piloting a stealth bomber. No matter how big you are, nobody notices you're there.

People stream in and out of the welcome center, using the bathroom and picking up brochures. A long trail of vending machines are lined up behind the main building, partway up the path where Edgers wants to meet. This cheers Janis up. She never remembers to bring anything to eat when she is working and always winds up hungry. She twists her hair up on top of her head and covers it with the ball cap—this one is her oldest and most favorite, a pink cap from Banana Republic. Long blond hair attracts a surprising amount of attention and if Janis lets her hair down over her shoulders every man in the place will remember her. She wears two sweaters under the old barn coat to bulk up. Loose jeans and old barn boots, hair hidden in the hat, sweaters adding thirty shapeless pounds, and now she is invisible. Janis locks up the truck and heads into the welcome center to use the ladies' room.

The center is rank with cigarette smoke. Janis smoked for an entire week the month she turned sixteen when Mama told her she was old enough to make up her own mind. It wasn't like her mother to step aside without an opinion and Janis had waited a full three weeks before going out to buy her own package of Virginia Slims. And then the guy at the 7-Eleven wouldn't sell her the cigarettes, and her mother had gone in and gotten them for her, figuring that if she wanted to allow her daughter to smoke, state and federal law had nothing to do with it.

Mama hadn't said a cross word, and had even remembered to get her a book of matches, which pretty much took the fun out of it. And since Janis spent most of her spare time in a barn where she'd die before she lit up (unless her mama caught her and killed her first) the whole thing got pretty pointless. She didn't want to be like the Dozer boys, who had to run out to smoke every fifteen minutes like they'd die if they didn't. Plus it made her mouth feel weird and coated her tongue and ruined her taste buds. Plus it was a detriment to French kissing, which was something Janis particularly enjoyed.

She stops at the vending machines and buys a cup of hot chicken soup, though she is sweating under the coat and sweaters. It is sunny out and the temperature has climbed into the forties. But it will be cold tonight.

Janis stocks up with a can of grape soda, peanut butter crackers, and M&Ms. She stares down into the parking lot. Pretty full, and the windows of her pickup are illegally tinted black. She can steal a nap after she prepares.

She sips the soup, puts the vending machine hoard in the front seat of the truck, then walks up the asphalt pathway that leads steeply to a wooded area. The grass near the vending machines is a designated dog-walking area, and a woman with a basset hound on a leash is encouraging her dog to "get on with it or forget the whole thing." A boy and girl, brother and sister, throw a ball to a Border collie who seems more interested in herding the two of them together than catching the ball.

Janis grins, thinks about her brothers.

Keep your mind on your work, she tells herself, as she leaves the top of the path and heads into the woods. Her daddy used to say that to her, and now she says it to herself. She wonders if her dad is taking his blood pressure medicine with the same silly jokes; she wonders how her mother's roses are wintering over. She wonders if Chris and his wife will break up or stay together, and if Dale will keep that new job.

She hasn't called home in such a long time. Sometimes, on Sunday afternoons, she wonders if they're all still getting together for a big meal after church. She pictures how Mama used to look at them around the dinner table during Sunday lunch and give that special smile to her dad, who would grin back, like their garden variety family was some kind of miracle. And daddy would chime in with the usual *Well, hey, how perfect is this?* God, how that used to embarrass her when she'd bring a date home.

Janis is used to being homesick. Like most girls raised in Texas, Janis does not understand why anybody would want to live anywhere else.

But since Waco, Janis has felt incapable of staying in one place anymore, and the pro rodeo life has suited her very well, satisfying both her restlessness and pursuit of the Quest. She'd known the minute she'd read the note that the Quest was over. She had not expected the sense of relief, the surge of freedom and release. She'd walked away from everything without a second look, gotten rid of the stolen truck as soon as she'd picked up all the caches of money she'd stashed in bank safe deposit boxes between Tennessee and Texas. She drove the old truck into Lake Pontchartrain and paid cash for a pickup of her own. She had a little piece of land out in west Texas, bought and paid for three years ago when she'd had a bit of a scare, and she planned to go there, spend some time training a few horses. No single female alone on a piece of land could slide by without attention, but it would be on a local level, and she could pack up and leave anytime. Or stay forever. Or maybe . . . maybe even go home.

She hadn't seen anyone from home in over three years. No doubt people from her old life came and went without recognizing her, but on one particular Sunday afternoon two years ago, she'd been walking past a hot dog stand in an old pair of jeans with her hair tied back and no clown makeup on and Mr. Biggers had recognized her right off. No surprise, he'd known her all her life. But it was good to see this neighbor whom she'd known since she was knee-high to a grasshopper, as he liked to say.

"Good Lord," he had said. "I can't believe it's you, honey. You have no idea how much we all miss you. How come you never get home?"

Luckily, Mr. Biggers never stopped talking long enough to look for an answer and Janis had just stood and looked at him, seeing how the years had added wrinkles, taken away hair, left him with a tremor. He'd never been a good-looking man, and yet the aging just made her feel that much more affection for him.

He shook his head and grinned. "I'll never forget you and Dandy winning that rodeo scholarship to Texas A & M."

Janis felt her smile fading, but he kept on talking.

"Everybody in town thought you were so cute."

"I take after my mama."

A master stroke. Biggers had grinned. "Yes, little girl, you do. And nothing's changed, honey. Every man in town is still half in love with your mama, including myself, as you well know." Mr. Biggers shook his head, and stared into space, and his smile faded, too. "How many years has it been, now, since—"

"Eight," she'd said, thinking eight years, two months, and a day.

"God, seeing you sure does bring back the memories. The older I get, the more I realize that memories may be the only thing you get to keep, till you get so old those go, too."

In the way of southerners, it had taken him forty minutes to tell her good-bye, and she hadn't been in any hurry to rush off. But the whole time she'd stood there listening to him she'd wondered what Mr. Biggers would say if she told him she *wanted* to get old enough for her memories to go away; if she told him that sweet Emma stood at the end of Janis's bed nearly every night. Sweet little Emma, with eyes burnt out like black sockets, and scars all over her face, holding little Crumpet in a burnt blanket, because no one would take Janis seriously, and then when they did, they had shown no mercy, no mercy at all. What would he say if she told him she lived for the day she did not wake up remembering how hard she'd tried and how badly she'd failed?

Janis sleeps too long; it is well past dark when she wakes. And even though she feels the quiet and the lateness of the hour, she keeps her eyes squeezed shut, holding tight to that last stream of consciousness where the dream still drifted. She'd been riding Dandy, just the two of them out in a dusty field in Texas, it had been so real. She could feel the horse surging forward in an easy lope— loping on Dandy was like being in a rocking chair. She could smell his own particular horse smell; throw his saddle blanket in a pile of other dirty horse blankets and she could pick his out by the scent.

There are tears on her cheeks, and Janis sticks her tongue out, tasting the salt like a little girl. She is going back to Texas, and she'll be riding again by summer. The Quest is over. She is almost done.

★ ★ ★

The welcome center traffic has thinned to almost nothing; there are two cars in the lot—one on it's way out. Earlier, Janis moved her truck to the Kentucky side of the interstate and walked a mile or two, crossing all lanes of fast-moving traffic like a child playing hopscotch. It is eleven twenty-five and Janis has been sitting cross-legged at the edge of the tree line since ten. She is warm enough, wrapped in sweaters and the barn coat. Outdoors at night, Janis is in her element. When most elementary-school kids were doing their homework in front of the television set, Janis was in the barn. When she was older, juggling dating and going to school, nighttime was the best time to get the chores done for a girl who did not like to get up any earlier than she had to. Janis always preferred the sunset to the sunrise. Most of the boys she dated were farm kids of one kind or another, and they'd come over to "help her with her barn chores." They really came in hopes of getting her alone up in the hayloft.

Not that she'd let them help, not after she and Mama brought Jim Dandy home. The gelding belonged to no one but Janis, that was clear from day one. Dandy was a nervous horse, and things had to be done a certain way to make him comfortable. He had three water buckets, because he drank a lot and got worried when the supply went low. He had a fan for hot days, his own mineral block, and a stall ball that he ignored. Janis kept him six inches deep in cedar shavings, no matter how much it exasperated her mother, with an extra three inches layered in front of the back window, where Dandy would stand all day watching for Janis.

Mama had spotted the gelding at a racetrack in Sarasota, being worked as a companion horse, walking the skittish thoroughbreds from the barn to the track. Mama had said something curt under her breath when she saw him. Mama was Irish and she knew a good horse when she saw one.

There are more horses per capita in Ireland than anywhere else in the world, her mama would say. Then her father would say, *There are more Texans in Texas than anywhere else in the world,* and Mama would look annoyed. The Irish, her father often observed, have no sense of humor on the subject of the Irish.

Mama had seen the horse pass while they sat in the stands, and she'd announced that the gelding was out of Jenny's Fancy and maybe Doc James. How Mama could tell such a thing from so far away, and how she could remember the quarter horse lines when her heart was really with thoroughbreds, was just one of the many amazing things about Myra Winters.

You had to be able to believe six impossible things before breakfast to survive a single day in the Winters's household. When Janis and her siblings compared Myra Winters to other mothers they sometimes laughed and sometimes swore, but there was nothing they could do about it. Their mom wouldn't do the work on their science projects, lead Brownie troops or Cub Scout packs, or make snacks for kids in the afternoon. She'd actually laughed the day Dale told her that Ron Jerrold's mother made Rice Krispies treats when they went to his house after school.

Learn how to make them yourself, she'd told him.

She expected the whole family to pitch in on indoor as well as outdoor chores, and she never asked anybody's permission or opinion on anything—ever. Janis remembers a sleepover for Peggy Gifford's fourteenth birthday, and how they all sat around and bitched about their mothers. Judy Something-or-other said she thought Mrs. Winters was completely cool, and much more interesting than anyone else's mother. Then Peggy said she over-heard her mom and Mrs. Hatcher talking, and her mom had said that Mrs. Winters could get away with anything because she was Irish. And Mrs. Hatcher said it was more likely because she had big boobs. Everybody laughed, including Janis, but after that Janis didn't like Mrs. Hatcher, who had no boobs at all, and she quit baby-sitting for the Hatchers' four "darlin' boys."

At the track that day, nobody asked why Mama, who came to look at thoroughbreds, was obsessing about a quarter horse. Janis was thirteen years old at the time, and getting to be a pretty good trick rider. She was just getting into barrel racing but wasn't much good at it yet. She was good, however, at being a thirteen-year-old pain in the ass, with a smart mouth and a burgeoning interest in slender boys with brown eyes. Mama had clearly decided to redirect Janis's thoughts and energies.

Still, it came as a complete shock when her mother looked at her father and said *I'm buying* from all the way up in the stands.

"What you going to do with another horse, Myra?"

"We need a good barrel horse. And anything out of Jenny's Fancy is a good bet, if you ask me."

Janis remembers how the whole family had turned and looked at her. Everybody knew about the plan. Janis had decided she wanted to go to vet school at Texas A & M when she was eight years old, and had never wavered. Farm finances were always scary, and college was a hopeful but not guaranteed possibility. There was good money in barrel racing events; that's how Janis planned to work her way through school.

"What do we need some old barrel horse for?" Bob Winters had looked at Janis over one shoulder and given her a wink.

In spite of having a family bet of two dollars on Dog in the Manger to win, place, or show, the Winters family abandoned the racetrack and trooped to the barn. Dandy was tied outside in the blistering sun. He was fretful and underweight and in serious need of having his hooves trimmed and his teeth floated. Mama stood in the barn doorway with that look on her face that made the rest of the family nervous.

Janis remembers that one of the stable guys asked them their business, and her mother dismissed him with a command to fetch the owner. It was clear that there was something about the horse's flank Mama did not like, and Janis remembers her mother whispering to her father about a *pitchfork,* and *it happens all the time when there are idiots in the mix.* And though her mother had made the comment under her breath, Janis saw a couple of the hands look up. Mama could be very embarrassing, and she was not one to back down.

The owner did finally come out, and Janis had nightmares about him for the next year. He was a skinny man with a bald greasy head, and jeans that were loose and sagging on his butt. He had a napkin around his neck, and something sticky at the edge of his mouth, and he'd dismissed their mother with one terse remark that none of the kids heard. Her mama got that funny little smile that meant somebody was in trouble, and she asked Daddy to take the kids out, and said she would meet them by the car in an hour.

"I'm not going to leave you here, Myra."

Janis remembers her father's exact tone of voice. And she was glad; she did not want to leave her mother alone in this barn.

But Mama just smiled at him and waited, until he gave her a quick kiss on the cheek, begged her not to hurt anybody or bring on any lawsuits, and herded all the kids away. They'd had snow cones, and stood by the car sticking their tongues out to see whose tongue had turned the most blue. Janis had been keyed up and anxious, and got tired of looking at tongues and eating snow cones, and could not seem to be still. So Chris had hoisted her up on his shoulders, and said he could beat Dale to the forsythia bushes even while carrying their sister's fat butt. Janis remembers being so mad at Chris and swatting his behind to get back at him, but it only made him laugh and run faster. Dale beat them by a mile. Nobody could run like Dale.

"You'll get the horse," Dale told her as they finally stopped to catch their breath. And Chris told her he was psychic and had a feeling that the horse would be coming home with them that day.

Chris and Janis had degenerated into part real, part play fighting with sticks for swords, when Dale grabbed Janis and told her to look.

She would never forget her mother that day—how she had smiled with utter serenity, leading Jim Dandy across the parking lot with nothing but a rope around his neck, because the owner wanted to charge her twenty dollars for a frayed nylon halter, and Mama had said it was in sorry shape and not worth a buck.

Janis remembers catching her breath, and the feeling she had in her stomach. Dandy was sixteen hands, with massive hindquarters and dainty feet, and he was already bringing his head down and going quieter after an hour or less with Myra Winters. How beautiful they were, almost magical, her mother and that horse— Mama wearing that little navy sheath dress and low heels, her hair in a French twist, with sunglasses perched on top of her head. Janis knew then why Daddy called her mother *sprite*.

"Young lady, come over and get your horse. He's bonding with me, and I'm not the one."

"Well, go on then, Janis," Dale said. And Chris gave her a nudge.

They'd had horses of their own for a while now. It was Janis's turn.

Janis had been careful, walking over with unhurried confidence, coming in from the side. She was going to take her time with this. She was going to do it right.

She spoke to the horse and put a hand on his neck, telling him how beautiful he was in her horse voice, which was a calm voice, a bit matter-of-fact, a bit soothing. Dandy had skittered sideways, and Janis knew he was wary and afraid. She took the lead rope from her mother, who said, matter-of-factly, *Good, Janis,* and Janis had used her fingertips to massage little circles into the horse's neck, just like her mother did with her favorite thoroughbred.

"Looks a little big for a barrel horse," one of the brothers said. Janis thinks it was Chris.

And her mother had winked. "Riding this boy at a canter will be like sitting in a rocking chair."

"Lope," they'd all shouted, because although Mama rode hunt seat and dressage, the rest of the family rode western because it was *for God's sake,* Texas *after all.*

"One thing now, Janis," her mother had said, and Janis listened but did not look away from the horse. "Be very careful around this horse when you have a pitchfork. And never let anyone ride him but you."

And her father had said something under his breath, and her mother had laughed in that low throaty way that made people stare.

"Yes, I know, Bob. And generally I agree that either the horse or the rider should be experienced, but I think this is a good match. I've got a feeling about this horse."

Janis has sifted through this memory so many times it no longer hurts. But she misses Dandy still, after all these years. How agile he had been—impressing the judges who looked askance at his large muscled rump and thought *good luck.* He was as good as the smaller wiry competitors, and he drew the eye; he was flashy. Janis and Dandy earned purse after purse, until Janis had a secure college fund, not just for herself, but for all the Winters kids.

There are no cars in the parking lot of the welcome center when Edgers's Saturn creeps in, running without lights. It is past midnight. Janis wonders again what it is that Edgers has in mind.

Whatever it is, she is ready. Janis has two guns and four quick loads in the deep pockets of her coat. The killing kit and all of her papers, her computer, are at the bottom of Lake Pontchartrain in the stolen truck. Luckily, in Tennessee, guns are as easy to come by as fireworks and fried food, and she'd stopped at a flea market in Pigeon Forge to buy what she needed.

The flea market had the usual selection.

She'd avoided the Lorcin L-22s, which were half-assed pocket plinkers, and inaccurate to boot. Most of them self-destructed anyway, after going through a couple hundred rounds. Janis wasn't big on Lorcin guns, or anything manufactured by Standard Arms, which had picked up where Lorcin left off when they'd gone out of business in '98, but there were so many of them floating around, cheap and available, that they made a good choice for a low-profile murder weapon. She'd settled on a Lorcin L-9 milli-meter, after checking to see that the magazine wasn't glitchy, as they sometimes were. She had talked the seller down to forty-seven bucks because in the world of gun buying he would be more likely to remember her if she hadn't tried to negotiate.

She'd come across the Davis P-380 by chance. It wasn't a bad bet for reliability and price, and was a good, rudimentary shooter, common enough if she had to use it. It would be a decent backup gun, always a wise idea when you used a Lorcin. The Davis had cost her seventy-eight bucks. Even with the ammo, she'd spent less than two hundred dollars. It had been a good day—bargain hunt-ing at the flea market, catching a long look at a couple who were actually getting married at a drive-through wedding chapel in Pigeon Forge, just down the road from Sevierville. The area was overflowing with wedding chapels, welcome centers, antique markets, and signs for Dollywood. A strange place, even when you considered how far south it was. They didn't have anything quite like it in Texas that Janis can remember.

The guns are loaded, the Lorcin in the right pocket of the barn coat, the Davis in the left. Janis chews her lip, waiting. The Saturn pulls into a spot along the far left side of the lot. The engine con-tinues to chug for a full ten minutes before it cuts off abruptly and a man gets out of the car. He is wearing black, *secret agent man,* and he goes to the trunk, and takes out a rifle case. Janis, fingering the half-assed Lorcin in her right pocket, is annoyed. She wishes she'd bought a Mack ten.

The man looks around; he is alert, not nervous. Clearly this is Cory Edgers—the height and the air of smug competence give him away. Janis finds the game of murder tag less complex than she expected, finding so many people to be across-the-board lazy, and often enough, not overly bright. She'd expected to be caught early on in the game, but had eventually reached the conclusion that she might get the chance to retire someday.

Janis gets to her feet just as the cop starts up the pathway. She stretches. She has been frozen in position for an hour and a half.

When the target is about two hundred feet away she decides that she'll talk to him first.

He is heading just for the spot behind the trees where she'd found the Almond Joy wrapper. His, she figured. No doubt he'd done a reconnoiter before writing the note.

The cop, like an ex-Eagle Scout, carries the gun properly, broken in the middle, and through the crook of his left arm. Janis takes the Lorcin out of her pocket, right arm draped down her side, waiting for the cop to get closer. She raises the gun, aims, fires.

The bullet hits the cop in the left elbow and passes through the bone. He groans and drops the rifle.

Janis frowns. She was aiming for the shoulder. On the other hand, the cop was moving, albeit slowly, and it is very dark. The force of the bullet causes him to turn and face her, giving Janis a quick window of opportunity where he is vulnerable. She closes one eye and fires again. The second slug slams into the cop's abdominal cavity and he drops like a rock.

Janis bites her bottom lip. It is a fine line to walk, trying to keep him alive and conscious for a short amount of time, but making sure he can't use the rifle. Better he winds up dead and quiet, than talkative and able to shoot. Janis errs on the side of caution.

She checks once over her shoulder. If Curly Girl is in the car, she's sitting tight. Janis is pretty sure he is alone, and she walks over to look at him.

She takes the rifle before she even looks at the cop, checks the load, snaps the weapon together, and aims it at the cop, who is crumpled sideways and still. Janis nudges him with the muzzle of the rifle, but he does not move. She takes the butt of the rifle and thumps him hard in the spot where blood gushes from the stomach wound. He groans but does not move. He is unconscious, likely in shock, and can't be counted on to wake up soon, if ever.

Janis shrugs. She fires two more times, obliterating the cop's face. She is close enough to be hit by spatter. She steps back into the trees and watches his car—a crappy Saturn. If Curly Girl is there, she's still not coming out. Janis gives it fifteen minutes, then pockets her gun, sets the rifle down, and drags Edgers back into the woods. He is heavy, and the position puts an awkward strain on her back. She can't do anything much about the blood trail, but with the body out of sight she might get a few extra hours give or take, before the body is found.

Janis checks the cop's pockets, taking the wallet and the cell phone. She straightens up, takes a minute to look around, see if she's left anything behind that she shouldn't. The cop's right eye is still intact, but rests an inch away from the socket. She has put an eye back into a socket once before, helping Bones Jones see to a couple of team ropers who'd gotten into a bar fight with three Argentine tourists. Jones, ostensibly the resident rodeo vet, required to be on site by Pro Rodeo animal welfare rules and regs, has a sideline business of treating patients who don't care to have their gunshot wounds reported by the local ER, or who simply have no health insurance. There are a growing number of clients in the second category, and Janis was the vet's second pair of hands. She was good with the animals, even the human ones. Sometimes she was the first pair of hands when Jones lost the ongoing wrestling match with Jack Daniel's.

Car keys, Janis thinks, and goes back through the cop's jacket, finding them in a pocket she missed.

She walks down the pathway to the Saturn. She is tired and unhappy. She needs to track Curly Girl down—the last person who knows Janis is Rodeo. She doesn't have much time—not with Rugger dead, and what is left of the cop lying at the edge of the woods. She needs to disappear.

Janis keeps a hand on the Lorcin, preparing to fire right through the fabric if Curly Girl really is in the car. She is exposed as she approaches, but she is short on time, and she doesn't think the girl is there.

The front seat of the Saturn is empty save for a neatly folded map and a pair of cop sunglasses. A quick check of the backseat reveals handcuffs, a straitjacket, and ankle cuffs. Edgers had been making plans. Bringing her in? Playing supercop?

Janis shrugs. She'll never know. But Edgers has brought a lot of hardware, and she feels flattered.

It takes less than an hour to get back to the truck. Traffic is threadbare, and the highway is easy to cross. Janis is relieved to settle into the front seat, turn on the engine and the heater, lock the doors. She stows the rifle in the back section of the extended cab, covering it with a blanket. She unfolds the half-eaten bag of M&Ms, sucking the candy coating off one by one while she takes out the cop's cell phone and spends over twenty frustrating minutes of trial and error before she can access his messages.

"Babe? It's me. I'm halfway there, hon, and I just realized I left the directions at home. I'm sorry . . ." A girlish laugh. "I think I can find my way to the house, but I'm not sure I remember which exit. Is it Emory Valley Road or Raccoon Valley? Give me a call, studly, and let me know. Good hunting, by the way. I'll be waiting for you at the Dairy Queen by the exit. I'll be the cute one drinking Cherry Coke."

Janis smiles. The message had been left two hours ago. Maybe she'll get lucky, and Curly Girl will live long enough for a short conversation. Janis sheds the barn coat and one of the sweaters, then peels the ball cap off her head, shaking her hair out and pulling it into a low ponytail. She's hungry. She considers stopping at Waffle House on the way.

CHAPTER TWENTY-FOUR

I have not been able to sleep since that afternoon in Mendez's office. I talked to Brady, typed up a summary of everything I'd done on the case, and spent another afternoon at the movies. The only source of information I had concerning developments in the case came from the newspapers, and there was nothing there. Edgers hadn't been arrested yet, and I wondered why.

My nightmares were back—deadly quiet now, full of silent open-mouthed screams and the vibration of running feet. People's lips moved but no words came out.

All my dreams involve strangers who need me to help them escape. We are behind enemy lines in a nameless war, and I have to get everyone on the train that will get us over the border to safety, whatever border that is. My charges come in twos and threes, bringing their children, their dogs, their grandmothers. Some of them are in wheelchairs, some are pregnant. The faces change; the only constant is they are all helpless; they use crutches, they can't hear, they are too afraid to move. They won't leave without the family cat or the rabbit they've raised since birth.

Roughly half of these dreams end badly and the bad ones tend to repeat. My psyche launches the sequence again and again until I know who waits outside the door. I know that one of the children will fall off the train if I don't get to the window now, and shut it tight. The body will still be there behind the couch, but if I am careful to get everyone through the room quickly, then the mother won't see and refuse to leave, and we can all get away this time, without being caught.

Mendez is deeply asleep beside me in our bed. He worked late tonight, stayed at the office through dinner, and avoided my eyes once home. We don't talk unless we have to. Twice I've come across him sitting on the edge of the bed, looking at nothing in particular. He eases away from me to his side of the bed even in sleep, and I curl away from him to mine.

I don't know what finally woke me the next morning, only that I sat up suddenly, wide awake. The house was quiet and I felt that disconnected confusion you get when you seriously oversleep. I usually wake when Joel gets up in the morning, and it was strange to be so suddenly alone, save Maynard, who was curled on my pillow over the top of my head.

The clothes Joel left draped over the footboard were gone. Even Joel finds it difficult to be neat without the majority of our furniture. The shirt and pants are missing, he has left the tie. I walked down to the kitchen. The coffeepot was clean and empty. There was no water in the sink. I padded back upstairs and looked into the bathtub drain. No dark curly black hairs. Joel had left in a hurry, no shower, no coffee, in the shirt and pants he wore the day before. Whatever it was that was critical enough to get him out of bed so quickly, he did not see fit to share with me.

Events were moving along all around me, and I was out of the loop.

I picked up the phone to call Miranda. I still had the key to Cheryl's apartment and I was ready to give it back and be done with it. I pulled on the shirt and jeans I wore yesterday and paused just long enough to brush my teeth and put on enough makeup to keep from scaring the unwary stranger. I would drop by Miranda's apartment, and if she wasn't there I would leave it in the mailbox or shove it under the door. Then I'd be done with the whole business, which sounded pretty good to me.

Miranda lived in the Lamplighter apartments on East Reynolds Road, right next to the Landsdowne post office. She rents what is called a garden apartment, which means basement in less friendly terms. The parking lot was small, there are only four buildings, and I didn't see Miranda's car. She was in the first building on the left, and I knocked on her door with little hope that it would be answered.

It wasn't.

The mailboxes were the locking kind, and there was no room under the door for a key. I have a girlfriend, Kay, who lived in one of these apartments after her first divorce. It was easy enough to get in. I shoved the front door hard with my right shoulder and the door swung through the frame. I had the grace to be slightly ashamed, but it didn't stop me from going inside.

The apartment had the aura of a fake smile plastered over a less than friendly face. The carpet was tan and new and the walls were cream-colored and relatively unsmudged. Miranda had hung a depressing array of posters—recent movies, most of them bad, and a few obscure heavy metal bands with softly pornographic names. The place was clean enough, which surprised me, though I'm not sure why. The faint but unmistakable aroma of McDonald's scented the air.

"Hello?"

No one answered, but the phone rang. In three rings the machine picked up, parroted Miranda's canned message, and I heard Miranda's father on the line.

I picked up the extension on the wall in Miranda's tiny kitchen.

"Paul? This is Lena Padget."

A pause. "I guess you and Miranda are wrapping up the details. Can I speak to her, or would you ask her to call me in the next hour or two?"

"She's not here."

"What's going on? Is something wrong?"

"No, I just came by to drop off the key to Cheryl's apartment. The door was unlocked, so I thought I'd just leave it on the kitchen counter."

"I wanted to talk to you anyway. Do you know what the details are on Edgers's plea bargain? How easy is he getting off?"

"What are you talking about?"

"Ah. I'm sorry. I've been indiscreet. Miranda told me you asked her to keep things quiet until everything settled out."

"Keep what things quiet?"

Brady was silent for a long moment, and when he spoke his

voice had a flattened quality. "Miranda called me yesterday and told me not to come down this weekend. She said that Edgers had confessed to killing Cheryl, and made a deal with the police, and that it was all over. I take it that's not the case."

"Paul, excuse the question, but I don't think Miranda was telling you the truth."

"No, she was, I just got off the phone with Captain Mendez. But he wouldn't give me any details, just confirmed that there had been a deal, and that Edgers would be giving himself up in forty-eight hours. Lena? Are you there?"

"I'm here. Who told Miranda about the plea bargain?"

"She said you did."

I thought about that. None of the thoughts were useful. "Let me get back to you on this, okay, Paul?"

"Catch me on my cell phone, will you? I'm on the way out. Do you have a pen?"

I looked around the kitchen cabinets. No pen, but a notepad. I ripped the first sheet off, then gave it a second look.

Miranda had written down explicit directions to Kate Edgers's house on the mountain.

I let Brady give me his cell number but I did not bother to find a pen and write it down. Why would Joel tell Miranda and not me? And why would Miranda tell her father that *I* gave her the news? Maybe she'd gotten her information from someone other than Joel.

But it wasn't a good thing, Miranda on her way to see Edgers's wife. I had Kate's number in my case notebook, but she didn't answer.

And then, my feeble brain, long clouded by sympathy and concern for the family of victims of violence, particularly the sisters in the family, at last put the pieces together. Miranda, always jealous of Cheryl, would be instantly drawn by any man in Cheryl's life—particularly a man Cheryl looked up to, and admired, and maybe even had a crush on. It made sense now that Miranda had lied, and defended Cory Edgers, and misled me from beginning to end. Miranda was in love with him—so much so, that she had stood by and almost let him get away with killing her sister.

Past time for me to get some distance from my clients. There are no good guys, there are no bad guys, there are only guys.

CHAPTER TWENTY-FIVE

The little trailer was dim inside, even with both lamps on, and Wilson opened the crimson curtains over both windows to let in the blaze of sunlight. The temperature had risen to fifty-two degrees, which seemed to thrill the locals. Wilson was cold.

Rodeo had left bits and pieces of furniture and kitchen utensils, a few dishes, and a dead fig tree, but the clothes—everything else—all were gone. She went by the name of Janis Winters, but no such woman existed in the Social Security registers, no such woman had a birth record, or paid taxes, possessed a passport, or had any credit card or bank accounts. She did own a truck, which was sitting beside the trailer, hopefully containing enough forensic traces to identify this woman who had not officially existed before she vanished.

Why now? Wilson wondered. It can't be a coincidence that Rodeo disappears within twenty-four hours of Cory Edgers handing her over. He had called Mendez in Lexington, and told him to pick Edgers up instead of letting him surrender in the presence of his attorney and in the eye of the news media tomorrow at noon.

It was odd to come face-to-face with the mundane details—that the Rodeo assassin was the same woman who seemed to survive on yogurt, bananas, and Spaghetti-Os. The walls were marked where pictures and newspaper articles had been hung, then ripped away. Wilson had gotten statements from two people who had heard talk about Janis Winters's obsession with Waco and David Koresh, and about a sister named Emma who had perished in the flames. Nashville was trying to match the sister with the list of Waco victims.

So far Wilson had gotten nowhere with the cowboy Janis had supposedly been intimate with. The kid had managed to both tick him off and stir his admiration by giving the simple statement that Janis was a sweetheart, and gentlemen did not talk about their women, then he'd completely shut down. Wilson had pushed further and elicited a phone call from an attorney paid for by the kid's father, who was evidently wealthy, sophisticated, and in a very bad mood. The "clowns" Janis had worked with swore up and down they barely knew her, but their eyes said *she's one of us, buddy, and you can go to hell.* Wilson had never known a serial killer to draw this much affection. It reinforced his faith in the stupidity of your average guy on the street. Every time Wilson closed his eyes he saw Alex Rugger's wife sitting in the back of that paramedic unit, shirt drying chocolate brown with blood.

He had called Sel twice last night, and she hadn't been home. She hadn't returned his calls, either. No doubt she was working long hours at the restaurant, or maybe the waves were good. He just wanted to hear her voice.

Sel was the breath of fresh air in his life, an unpredictable mix of innocence, wisdom, and practicality. He could never anticipate her viewpoint. Wilson had given her the surfboard that first time they met, along with a handy explanation calculated to generate her sympathy and overcome her reluctance to take a gift from a stranger. It was no problem getting her to meet him later at a small café in Marina Del Rey. He'd known she was from out of town the minute she'd agreed; a local girl would have been more cautious.

Marina Del Rey was home for Wilson. He'd grown up just down the road in Playa Del Rey, and misspent countless hours of his youth blading off Venice Beach—another activity relegated to his past. It was dark by the time Sel arrived, a half-hour late. The air had gone crisp, like fall in New England, and Wilson was sipping a beer, listening to the surf from Venice Beach, and calculating the odds of getting laid.

What he didn't factor in was the effect Sel would have on him. He'd fallen in love within ten minutes of sitting across from her at the small round table. Although she noticed the candles flickering in the center of the table, and the starched white linen tablecloth that snapped in the breeze swirling in off the beach, Wilson noticed nothing but Sel.

His one-night-stand plan had not accounted for the confidence he felt when she tilted her head while he talked, giving him all of her attention; the effect of the intelligence in her brown eyes; or the way she pushed the dark, shoulder length hair from her face. He was captivated by the way she talked about surfing. The way she let him know, with a simple squeeze of her hand, that she understood how it would feel to give it up.

Wilson stood at the edge of Janis Winters's little kitchenette and saw that one small picture of Koresh had escaped notice, and was hanging on the side of the refrigerator and out of view. Winters had drawn devil horns in over the top of the man's head. Hard for Wilson to imagine this streak of light mischief from the same woman who excelled at cold-blooded execution. As always, a killer's humanity jarred him. It was perfectly logical that a murderer shopped at Kroger's like everyone else, ate Twinkies and Whopper burgers, but the details always stuck in Wilson's mind.

Where is she? Wilson wondered. *Who is she?*

He'd put an APB out on a Dodge Dakota that had only just been reported stolen from a bar no more than a half mile down the road. One of the locals had gotten drunk at a sports bar called Boots, gone home with a girl he'd met shooting pool, and woke up the next morning with a hangover, and a new girlfriend to hide from his wife. The girl had driven him back to Boots, but the truck hadn't been in the lot. They'd spent the next twenty-four hours trying to remember where they might have parked it before they finally notified the police. The Dakota had been sighted once, in Louisiana, but the sighting was made by an off-duty cop on his way to the ER with his youngest son, who was bleeding profusely after catching a football with his nose. The pickup hadn't come up on the radar since.

Since the Dakota had disappeared the same time Janis did, Wilson figured she'd taken it with her. Her stun gun, her baling wire, all the tricks of the trade, were gone. Just her pickup truck—well-known and covered with Pro-Am Rodeo parking stickers—and the trailer were left behind. He figured Janis Winters had a good chance at disappearing if she ditched the truck and got out of the game. The possibility made his stomach hollow.

Odds were she wouldn't, but this one was hard to predict. Her motive eluded him. Clearly, she had no sympathy and a great deal of contempt and hatred for the Branch Davidians. But it was the law enforcement guys she was killing. Whether or not she would quit would be a whole lot easier to predict if he knew why in the hell she did what she did in the first place.

When the next team of investigators arrived, Wilson stepped out of the trailer. His cell phone rang. Mendez, according to the caller ID.

"You pick Edgers up?" Wilson asked. He appreciated Mendez. He was not the kind of southerner you had to be polite to before you got down to business. Wilson wasn't feeling particularly polite.

"Somebody else got to him first. His body was discovered at roughly one this morning up in the woods behind the Tennessee Welcome Center between the Kentucky-Tennessee border. Long-haul trucker sleeping over, taking his dog out for a late night walk. Corpse was still warm. Shot four times: once in the arm, once in the stomach, twice in the face. Looks like a nine millimeter from the wounds. Time of death between eleven and one A.M."

"Face shots close range?"

"Very. Killer finishing him off."

"You sure it's him?"

"No wallet, no cell, but it's his car, and yeah, I'm sure it's him. One of his eyes was the right color."

"You sensitive bastard, Mendez."

"Nothing on him in the way of weapons. He didn't return fire but he may have been hit before he could. There were no weapons in his car, either, so I'm thinking the killer has them. Guy's a cop, and a hot dog, he'd have something. There were wrist cuffs, ankle cuffs, and a straitjacket in the backseat of Edgers's car."

"What the hell is that about?"

"He was obviously meeting somebody."

"Yeah, but was it Match.com or Murder Inc.? No Taser and no baling wire? Because Miss Rodeo is long gone."

"One thing you should know, Wilson. Word's out about the Edgers's deal."

"The magical mystery grapevine of law enforcement."

"I didn't tell."

"I didn't think you had, and it sure wasn't me. Hell, for all we know it was Edgers." Wilson stepped sideways suddenly, to dodge a man leading a horse. The man gave him an amused smile, but Wilson had no interest in getting within kicking range of animals that weighed over a ton. "Mendez? You still there?"

"Yeah. Your office had any calls from the media about Edgers confessing?"

"Not that I know of. Yours?"

"Not a whisper. Maybe it *was* Edgers who spilled it."

"Who'd he tell?"

"Cheryl Dunkirk's sister. Miranda Brady."

"That doesn't make any sense."

"It might make a lot of sense. Cory Edgers was murdered last night at the welcome center that happens to be at the halfway point between Lexington and Kate Edgers's place. Maybe Miranda caught up with him."

"You think this sister is capable of something like that?"

"She struck me as self-centered. Edgy and a little off."

"Maybe a couple loose connections?"

"Definite possibility. The more I think about it the more I like it. It would explain the shooting—arm, stomach, anything to bring him down. Then two bullets right in the face."

"She sounds pretty pissed off." Wilson rocked backward on his heels. "You think she might be heading for Edgers's wife?"

"Unpredictable."

"It doesn't seem likely, but I think I'll head that way. I'll give Kate Edgers a call, tell her to leave or lock up, and I'll have the local boys look in."

CHAPTER TWENTY-SIX

K ate was in the hayloft when she heard a female voice call her name. Her heart jumped. The deputy had insisted she stay locked in the house. Something to do with Cory. Kate figured if Cory wanted to kill her he'd have done it already, but she'd stayed locked up most of the day. She'd come out only to see the horse. She'd called her mother a couple of hours ago, said the hell with packing, would they please come get her and Leo and bring the horse trailer for Sophie. And she'd warned her mother to expect George.

Kate looked out the tiny window just under the roof. Just a girl, alone, maybe twenty-one or twenty-two. She did not recognize her. The girl called out again, unaware that Kate was studying her through the window at the top of the loft. The girl's hair was brown, long and coarse, naturally curly or permed. Her calves looked thick beneath the denim skirt that hung just over her knees. The length was wrong for her height and the waistband cut her off in the middle, giving her a tight, uncomfortable look. She would be pretty enough in the right clothes.

Kate didn't know her. She did not look dangerous. And, on second look, she seemed familiar. Probably one of Don and Cathy Madison's grown daughters.

Kate put the utility knife in her pocket and headed down the ladder. She latched the stall door on her way out of the barn and looked over her shoulder.

"Can I help you?" Kate brushed hay off her shirt and out of her hair.

"Is Cory here?"

"Cory?" Kate folded her arms, feeling uneasy. "No, he's not."

"I knocked on the front door."

Kate grimaced. Leo was no doubt awake again. "Cory isn't in the house. He isn't here, I told you."

"He was supposed to meet me." The girl's voice had gone so petulant Kate expected her to stomp her foot. "You're Kate, aren't you? I recognize you from the pictures."

The girl smiled, making her round face rounder.

"Do I know you?"

"I think you do. My name is Miranda Brady."

The girl reached into her coat pocket and pulled out a hand-gun. A .38 Smith & Wesson; just like one Cory had. And Kate remembered where she'd heard the distinct, little girl voice before.

"You were in the barn with my husband the other night, weren't you? I heard you on the baby monitor."

The girl pointed the gun at Kate's stomach.

Kate put her hands in her pockets, fingers closing around the utility knife. "What are you doing here?"

Miranda moved closer. She had a dark complexion; her skin had large pores. Kate could see eruptions of whiteheads scattered across the dusky forehead. The girl held the gun in one hand, and furiously chewed the nail of her little finger on the other.

"You look like a nice person," Miranda said.

"I am a nice person." Kate took the utility knife out of her pocket. There was something about this girl—a weird aura of self-absorbed entitlement, a subtle taint, like meat just before it turns.

Miranda chewed her bottom lip. "I wonder if this is going to be hard."

"If *what* is going to be hard?"

"Killing you."

Kate stared at her. "Just because you're having an affair with my husband? He's left, gone, not coming back. All yours, Miranda."

"But that's your fault, isn't it?" The girl lifted her chin. "No life of your own, always complaining about his hours, never caring how hard he works, refusing sex. You invented and obsessed over problems with his son just to get attention. I know all about you."

"Whatever it is you think you know, take it with you and go. Cory isn't here, and he's not coming back."

Miranda stopped chewing the nail, and moved even closer. "You don't believe I'll do it?"

Kate grabbed the muzzle of the gun and twisted. She was six inches taller than Miranda, and she had large hands, strong with outdoor work. She could feel it when Miranda flexed her finger and fired. The bullet thudded into the dirt three inches from the end of Kate's Ariat barn boots, and close enough to Miranda's peg-laced hiking boot to abrade the leather.

"What in the hell do you think you're doing?" Kate felt light-headed she was so angry. She snatched at the gun again and Miranda leaned into her, bringing the gun barrel up against Kate's stomach. Miranda closed one eye, drawing a bead.

"Let the knife drop," Miranda said.

Kate complied.

"Good." Miranda tilted her head to one side. "You have no idea who I am, do you?"

"My soon to be ex-husband's slut."

The girl did not seem to hear. "I'm Miranda. *Miranda Brady.*"

Kate knew that name. "You're the sister? That's why you look familiar. Your picture was in the paper. You're Cheryl Dunkirk's sister."

"I know what you're going to do, Kate. I know you can't be trusted. I'm not going to let you ruin everything now that we've come this far. Now that Cory and I have found each other, now that we're together, I'm not letting anything mess it up."

"You must be crazy. Don't you get that my husband killed your sister?"

"My mother died, you know, when I was a baby girl." Miranda's voice was nonchalant. "I don't even remember her. It was me and my dad, and we did fine, till he decided to get married again. Up and out of the blue, pulls me out of school, moves me from Pittsburgh to Kentucky. Do you know what it was like for me growing up? Motherless, and then my father gets remarried, and to my stepmother who already has the world's most perfect daughter. Cheryl likes living in Danville, Cheryl wouldn't be happy in Pittsburgh, why should Cheryl have to change schools in the middle of the year? Miranda can just go to any old school, who cares? Cheryl is two years older, so it makes sense that she should have a later curfew, that she needs a car, and that the music should be turned down because she's *studying*. It's not even my house with Cheryl's mom taking the place over, even though my dad paid for the whole thing. This is *Cheryl's* town, and everybody loves her, she's everybody's friend, and she's so kind, trying to include the little sister. Not a real sister, a *step*sister."

"So you're jealous?" Kate took a step backward. "Did you help him? Were you there when he killed your sister?"

"My *sister* introduced us; me to Cory. I could see there was a thing between them, that she was attracted to him. She told me about it. That's one reason she had me meet him—to see what I thought.

"And when I saw him the first time . . . it just happened. We fell in love the exact minute we saw each other."

"They had a clip of you crying. On CNN. I saw you on the news."

"I know, I have it on tape." Miranda chewed some more on the nail. "It wasn't like you think, it wasn't like anybody thinks. Cheryl was out to *get* Cory. She's the one who *started* the whole thing. We were all together that night. Cheryl took me along, for protection, to make sure Cory didn't get out of hand. She said she needed to see him one last time. She was going to warn him, to tell him to go to the S.A. in charge and tell him everything.

"I mean, who in the hell is she, Saint Cheryl? Why does she get to dictate the terms, to ruin a man's career, when he's spent weeks trying to work a case? He let her in on the details; he was going to make her part it. And what kind of trust did she show him? She said she'd give him twenty-four hours before she went to Hardigree herself. She was going to ruin his career, she was going to humiliate him. What did she think would happen? Did she think Cory would be a good little boy and say *yes ma'am?*

"It's not like Cory planned it, he just panicked. They were yelling at each other, and he pushed her down in the seat. He couldn't let her report him. I was right there in the back and I could see how hurt he was, how scared. Cheryl was taking away his dreams, everything he ever wanted, everything he'd worked toward for so long."

"You didn't help her?"

Miranda looked at Kate, but she was seeing something else. "She wasn't my blood sister, she was my stepsister. But we grew up together; we were close. I couldn't watch it. She was getting hurt, she couldn't breathe. And I kept thinking, what if someone was hurting me like that?

"Then Cheryl went nuts. I think if she had just kept her head, he would have stopped. But she was strong, she fought like crazy, she kicked the windshield out. It was scary. She was so desperate, like some kind of animal.

"I got out of the car and I ran around to her door. I think I was going to drag her out, get her away. But then . . . then I thought, no, she's too far gone. It's too late to save her. But I couldn't let her suffer."

Kate tried to take another step backward, but Miranda brought the gun up, and she froze.

"Cheryl's got this baseball bat, it's always in the backseat, she plays pickup softball with some guys she knows at Woodland Park. I don't remember picking it up, but I had it." Miranda looked at Kate. "I hit her one time, and that was all. At first, you know, it seemed like she was so strong, that nothing could kill her, and then . . . just that one time. She turned out to be just as fragile as a baby bird. My sister. Do you have a sister?"

Kate shook her head. She did not have a sister. All things considered, she wasn't sure a sister was a good thing.

"It's funny, you know, but I miss her. And sometimes I feel . . . I keep seeing Cory wrapping her head in that little pink sweater." Miranda put one hand to her throat. "Do you know that when something like this happens to you, nothing really changes? That's the part that surprised me the most. You still have to buy eggs and fix toast and count calories. And you look in the mirror and you look the same. Nobody sees anything different when you go back to work. I think about that a lot. But it can't be for nothing, right? It's got to be a destiny thing. It's Cory and me; it's fate."

Miranda moved close enough that Kate could smell the mint on her breath, and by the time Kate registered the muzzle of the .38 between the buttons of her shirt, Miranda had already squeezed the trigger, and the initial spatter of blood fell like a fine aerosol spray on Miranda's skirt.

Miranda, mesmerized by the puppetlike way Kate jerked backward, was aware of the heat of the muzzle of the .38, and the sensation of Kate's body absorbing the velocity of the close-range bullet. In her mind she replayed the satisfying thunk of the impact, when the bullet struck Kate with such swift and devastating force. It was Miranda who cried out, caught between the intensity of taking a life, the sweet satisfaction of control, and the loss, once again, of the woman she could have been. Miranda's biggest fear was that no one would understand why she did what she did. She could only be happy with Cory at her side; only Cory could heal her hurts, only Cory could calm her panics.

It shocked Miranda, the gush and volume of Kate's blood. She rocked back on her heels, studying the hole torn in Kate's stomach.

Kate's awareness of time had breached the narrow focus of day-to-day existence, and events that rippled through her consciousness were like memories, whether they had happened yet or not. She saw the mountaintop receding. She saw Leo at the moment of his birth; just a glimpse, because the vision was overlaid by a late summer afternoon in Kentucky, and the sight of Leo—a grown-up, slender Leo—leading a colt who was skittish and mysteriously traumatized, and pathologically unable to control his fear. And somehow the colt grows quiet, sensing safety in the hands of Kate's son, who kept the lead rope slack and walked ahead; still confident, and still without words.

Kate was confused, wondering if she saw the life that was, the life that will be, or the life that could have been. She was drifting, and did not hear Leo scream.

Miranda did hear the scream and it brought her to her feet.

Leo had run from the house wearing only one shoe, and his left foot had turned blue from the cold. The sensation connected him, a bridge from the here and now to his internal world that was a whirlpool kaleidoscope of sound and sensation. Leo paused at the top of the hill and Miranda aimed the gun, waiting for the boy to come closer, her finger just starting to squeeze. Something made her turn her head—a noise, a flash of movement observed out of the corner of one eye. She saw George just as he launched himself from the rise of the driveway. Miranda aimed and fired and the bullet took George on his right side, singeing the fur and traveling through one rib. Because the shot caught the dog at an angle, it penetrated no further and exited three inches from the point of impact.

George felt no pain; a creature of instinct, obeying the genetics of wolf, he was aware of nothing but the feral intent to kill.

Miranda whirled and ran, confirming George's decision that she was prey, and he brought her down, sinking his jaws in the back of her neck and left shoulder. Miranda's screams were piercing and guttural, which excited George further. She dropped the gun, and her hands scrabbled over the dirt, only to find not the gun but two small, booted feet. A burst of electric shock knocked Miranda and George backward into unconscious oblivion.

CHAPTER TWENTY-SEVEN

J anis checks the dog first—the shock was worse for him than the bullet wound, but he is breathing and semiconscious, eyes open to little slits. She checks Miranda. The girl's eyes have rolled back in her head. Janis leaves her and goes to the woman, to Kate. She can hear the little boy making his way down the hill, but he does not say a word and neither does she.

Wreckage and too much blood is what Janis thinks when she gets to Kate. But Kate is still breathing, and Janis sees the blood ooze in a lazy spurt, which means an abdominal artery that is nicked or severed. Janis slides two fingers, then three, into the opening of the wound. She closes her eyes, picturing the layout of internal organs, but she cannot find that rogue end of the artery— she needs a larger opening.

The utility knife is on the ground by Kate's right hand, and Janis takes it. She senses the presence of the little boy. He stands a few feet away, one shoe on, the other foot bare. He wears a sweatshirt and a pair of pajama bottoms and a hat with ear flaps bent down.

"Go check on the dog," Janis says. Intent on enlarging the wound, Janis does not look back up, but she is aware that he moves, finally, and heads for the dog.

The incision brings more blood but not much, and Janis has enough leeway to get her whole hand inside the body cavity. Kate does not move, but she breathes. Janis is methodical and unhurried. It is her lack of fear and steady plodding that has always impressed the vet. Shut everything out except exactly what you are doing, he always told her; always surprised when she did.

Janis has it, finally, the artery taut and rubbery between her fingers. If she lets it slip out of her grasp it will curl up and away and she won't get a second chance.

There are no clamps, so she ties it off, easy, slow, both hands inside Kate's abdominal cavity. Janis does not rate Kate's chances of survival, which depends on how long she can sustain the massive blood loss, how much internal damage there is, how soon she gets to an ER, and whether or not Kate will survive the onslaught of bacteria Janis has left behind in the abdominal cavity.

Janis's hands and wrists are slick with Kate's blood. She wipes them on her sweatshirt. This whole thing is turning messy. She checks her cell phone. No service. She will take care of Miranda, quickly, then call 911 when she gets to her truck.

Miranda hasn't moved. Janis grabs the neck of the girl's sweater and drags her down the path. She glances back once at the little boy.

"Your dog will be fine," she tells him. She's not so sure about the mom. *Too bad,* Janis thinks. She likes a woman who keeps a neat barn.

Even going downhill, dragging Miranda is hard work, and Janis is in a sweat by the time they make it to the side of the pond. The sun has dropped and it is dusk, and full dark will come instantly, as it does in the mountains.

Janis drops Miranda in a thick patch of saw grass. Miranda whimpers and cries. Janis grabs her by the hair and dunks her head in the water. Miranda sputters and her eyes open.

"Stay," Janis says. She goes down on one knee and holds her nine millimeter to Miranda's throat. "I know you shot that woman. I know your boyfriend's a cop, and you know who I am. Just for curiosity's sake, what are the two of you up to?"

Miranda tosses her head in spite of the gun. "I won't tell you a damn thing." Her speech is slurred and she shivers. She is coming out of the shock of current slowly.

"I expect you haven't seen him today."

"What do you mean? What did you do to him?" Miranda's eyes fill with tears. "Where is he?"

"First you tell me what I want to know. Then I tell you what you want to know."

Miranda swallows against the pressure of the gun at her throat. Closes her eyes as if she can make Janis go away by not looking at her. "We were going to blame it on you."

"Blame what on me?"

"His wife. We were going to kill his wife, and bring you down here and make it look like you did it."

Janis smiles. "That explains the straitjacket and the cuffs?"

Miranda's eyes go wide. "So you did meet him. Did you hurt him? Where is he?"

"Do you want to see him?"

"Of course I do." Miranda tries a smile. Ever hopeful.

"Done." Janis shoots Miranda through the heart.

Janis pauses, takes a breath, then steps back and puts the gun in her jacket pocket. She is bending over to roll the girl into the water when she hears a car coming up the drive. She checks quickly to make sure Miranda is dead—the vacant eyes confirm the kill. Janis slips into the woods.

CHAPTER TWENTY-EIGHT

It never failed to amaze Wilson, the way people on the East Coast could move from state to state with a speed and ease unheard of out west, where one had to either cover a significantly higher number of miles, or wrestle with continuously clogged traffic, or both. The southeastern states were relatively small to a California boy, the interstates wide open and free of traffic. Rodeo had been able to move in and around the Southeast like a ghost.

Wilson had changed into black-and-green Cammies, a black sweatshirt, and lace-up hiking boots. He wore a blue Kentucky Wildcats ball cap he got in the hotel gift shop—he bought one for Sel, too. He'd wrapped an ace bandage thickly around his leg.

He opened the bottle of Advil resting on the front seat, unscrewed the cap of bottled water, and swallowed four extra-strength gel caplets. Bad for the stomach, good for the pain.

Wilson turned the rental into what he hoped was Kate Edgers's driveway. The sheriff's department was supposedly on its way out, but he didn't see any sign of them.

A Glock, holstered, lay on the seat near Wilson's leg.

The driveway began to wind and get steeper, and Wilson looked ahead, mouth open. A good thing he had four-wheel drive. He could see that the gravel drive led up the mountain to a hideous, brown-brick house. Someone had nailed a basketball goal to a tree on the other side of the drive. A battered Miata was parked on the grass at the edge of the drive. Wilson parked his rental behind the Miata. He slipped his arms through the holster straps, double-checked that the Glock was fully loaded, and slammed the door of the Ranger.

He cupped his hand. "Hello?"

A woman, crouched near the side of the pond, stood up when she heard him call. Wilson headed in her direction. He recognized her—she was the woman who'd been at that kid, Rob's house, asking about Cheryl Dunkirk. Her name was Padget, Lena Padget. He walked toward her, noting every detail of the scene, the edge of the woods, the grassy slope and pond, a small wood dock, an overturned canoe.

"It's Wilson McCoy, isn't it?"

The woman had the kind of southern-inflected contralto that could launch a man's fantasies into high gear. Her hair was dark and curly, and hung two inches above her shoulders. Her eyes were very blue, her face very white. And she had blood all over her shirt.

"Hey, are you okay?"

"I'm fine, but she's not."

She, Wilson thought. *Rodeo?*

Then he saw the small round hands that snaked from behind a tree stump. Wilson crouched down awkwardly, trying to bend the bad leg, but it wouldn't cooperate, and he had to sit instead of balance on his heels. He studied the girl with detached care, and in the back of his mind, he said a small prayer, just for her.

A sudden intake of breath made him look up. The detective had no color in her face, and he got awkwardly to his feet, thinking she was going to faint on him.

"Best sit down," he said.

Lena looked at him, then back down at the body, and sank to her knees. Her heart was beating so hard and fast he could see the motion through her sweater.

The woman had been shot one time, through the heart.

"Do you know who she is?" Wilson's voice was gentle.

"Miranda Brady," Lena said. "My client." She turned her back to him, as if she could not bear to watch him examining the body. "I don't understand this. I thought she came out here to—"

"Go after Edgers's wife, right?"

"For a dumb California blonde, you sure do know a lot."

"You were right, though. She was after Kate Edgers. But while she was going after Kate, and you were going after her, she was being hunted by—"

"By?"

"Another party,"Wilson says.

Lena nodded. "And this other party. You were hunting him?"

"That's right. Except it's a her."

The corner of a piece of paper peeked out over the top of Miranda's skirt pocket. Wilson snapped latex gloves on, and pulled the paper out.

"What the hell."

Padget looked at him. "What is it?"

"Marriage license. Cory Edgers and Miranda Brady? That puts a whole new spin on things, doesn't it."

"I should have figured it out earlier. Another illegal marriage for Edgers."

"So you now about that, too?" Wilson got slowly to his feet, almost falling back again when he lost his balance. The leg was worse than ever.

Wilson looked down at Lena. "I just don't get why the hell she hired you."

"She and Edgers made the most of it, believe me."

Wilson checked Miranda Brady's feet. Hiking boots. Size eight, from the looks of them, distinctive soles. He checked her hands for defense wounds. Found a bite where the blood had barely dried. He pushed her hair off her shoulders, and rolled her to one side. "Jesus." Something had clamped its jaws around the girl's neck, tearing the flesh, sinking teeth so deeply into the shoulder that Wilson could see the glint of bone. All of the wounds were thickly encrusted with blood. "The Edgerses have a guard dog?"

"They've got a family pet."

The ground was soft and muddy, and Wilson looked for prints—the kind made by Justin cowboy boots, ladies size six and a half. No luck. He got his cell phone out of his pocket. Found no service. "Dammit."

"Who is this person?" Lena asked him. "Who are you after?"

When Wilson didn't answer, Lena waved a hand up the hill, where she could just barely see a glimpse of the top of a barn over the tree line. "There's a woman up there, with a small child, and they're pretty isolated out here. Is this guy—this woman—going to go after Kate Edgers? Can you at least tell me that?"

"She's not interested in Kate, I promise you. And the deputy sheriff drove out here early this afternoon—made sure she was okay. She promised to stay locked up in the house."

Wilson, bent double over the soft muddy ground, found what he was looking for—the heel print of a cowboy boot.

"Which way did you come in?" Wilson asked.

"Down forty-five. Past that church and the weird man who stands in the road and sings."

"I came from the other end. Did you see any pickup trucks parked along the road, anything parked pretty close by?"

Lena frowned. "There's a tan pickup, I think it's a Ford, but it has Tennessee tags and a flat tire. There's also a green Chevy, extended cab, but it had Louisiana plates."

"That's her," Wilson said, thinking that sometime in the near future he was going to have to call the Louisiana state cop who'd spotted Rodeo's pickup on his way to the ER.

Wilson took Lena by the shoulders. "Look, Miranda's body is still warm. The blood hasn't even dried. Rodeo can't be more than fifteen minutes ahead of us, if that much. We need to get her now, or she'll slip away. I'm going up in the woods, after her. I want you to go to the Dodge and wait there. Hide, so she won't see you if she comes walking out of the woods. *Don't do anything* if you see her. She's killed seven federal agents we know of, and she killed Miranda Brady. Likely she's the one who killed Cory Edgers. Take my cell—call if you get service. That number there, the first one on the phone list."

"You got all that?" Wilson asked.

"Yeah. I got it."

"Lena, hear me on this. On no account are you to—"

"I said I got it." Lena turned away, then stopped. "Cory Edgers is dead?" She looked back over her shoulder to see Wilson disappearing through the trees.

It was full dark by the time she made it down the driveway.

CHAPTER TWENTY-NINE

The last of the daylight disappeared less than fifteen minutes after Janis killed Miranda. The dark hit suddenly, as if someone had thrown a blanket over a dim and flickering light. Janis does not stumble; she has eyes like a cat. She moves with care and caution, walking alone in the woods, circling behind the big ugly house and following the ridge down to the road where she left the truck. Janis is cold, but she does not regret tucking her coat around the woman and the little boy and his dog.

She is not afraid, but she is tired. Weary to the bone. Tired in her soul. She thinks of long summer nights, playing kick the can with her brothers. Where are they? Why doesn't she see them anymore? Something has happened, she can't remember what. Just that it is bad.

She is worried about something. What is it?

She cannot find him, her Dandy, that's what it is. How could she have forgotten that? She'd walked into his stall, holding the apple cut into sixths just as he likes, and he was not there. Someone had put another horse in Dandy's stall. Did they think she wouldn't notice? Did they think she was stupid? The other horse, the imposter horse, had butted his head against her arm, and she stopped herself just before she smacked him. He was a horse; he didn't know he was in the wrong stall. She gave him half the apple.

Why can't she remember? Why can't she remember where Emma is and what happened to her? She has the disoriented and disconnected sensation of one who has been plucked from one life and set down in another. There is no continuity. She knows she has lost things, people, places, Dandy, but she does not know when and how. She knows that she can't go home, even though it is what she's been imagining since she left the rodeo. And already that life has receded and she feels like a stranger to the person she was as the rodeo clown.

Janis does not know how to get away from these feelings, and she does not know how to resolve them. She can't quite work things out, and she is beginning to question what is and isn't real. The people she loves have been replaced with imposters. Have they done that with Dandy, too?

Preoccupied as she is, she notices the small red eyes ahead of her on the ridge. The possum scuttles off into the brush. Janis needed just that glimpse to focus. The only reason a shy possum might make the choice to come toward her up the ridge would be if there was something worse waiting at the bottom.

Hidden in the darkness, shielded by the trees, Janis pauses no more that forty feet from the road. She sees the dark shape of her truck. She watches and waits, and sometimes she thinks there is movement or the murmur of a voice, but she cannot be sure. But she knows—somehow, she knows—that someone is down there waiting for her to go for the truck.

Janis points her gun in the air, fires, then emits a wailing, drawn out scream. And then she runs, uphill, drawing whoever it is who waits for her, away from the truck. With any luck she can circle back and drive off while the follower is still bumping into saplings. She will need to be fast. There may be others coming.

Over the sound of her own ragged breathing, Janis can hear she is being followed by one of them, if not two. She veers farther right, then crouches and waits. The noise of the follower draws her, and she gets a first glimpse of her enemy, who is small and lithe, stopping now to listen.

"Wilson?" The enemy is a woman, and she is smart. She is heading back down the hill to the truck. Janis forgets she is tired and goes after the enemy like the predator she is.

A heavy blow knocks Janis to her knees. The enemy must have

heard Janis coming up from behind, because she was hiding, waiting, holding the heavy stick. Her shoulder blades will be black and blue, Janis thinks, and she is pissed. Janis pitches forward, face to the dirt, waiting for the enemy to come closer, something an enemy can never resist.

Janis grabs the enemy's ankle, and slams her head into the enemy's knees. The enemy makes a noise as the air goes out of her lungs. She has gone down quickly and hard. It catches her wrist when Janis raises her arm; it is strong, but not strong enough. She pins both of its arms, but the enemy is quick and it bites. The teeth are merciless, and Janis loses her balance, and both of them slide over the edge of the ridge.

Janis is falling, it is steep, and she cannot stop the momentum. The enemy is falling, too, it is getting away. Janis grabs a skinny tree, and hugs it like a lover. Her heart is slamming, and here comes that old headache, her constant companion; she's ripped out a fingernail, and bruised if not broken a rib.

Janis is so tired. That anger that she calls her tantrums is gone, and she doesn't care if the enemy gets away. She tries to look at her forearm where the enemy bit, but it is too dark to see. She touches it carefully; the bite hurts more than the rib. She wants to head for the truck, but there is something she has left behind. She can't remember what it is. She left it at the barn, right, the barn. Is it Dandy? Is that where Dandy is? Janis sobs deep in her chest. What if she never finds him? What if she never sees him again?

Nobody but Mama knows how scared Janis used to get. Sometimes, after a bad fall, her legs used to shake so badly she could hardly get up in the saddle. She used to make over ninety thousand dollars a year barrel racing as a teenage girl, and she was elected Sweetheart of the Rodeo when she was twenty years old. No Sweetheart of the Rodeo was ever afraid of a horse. Dandy would never hurt her, Dandy never did. They were both scared, but when it was the two of them together, they were safe as rocks.

Wilson moved quickly, plotting a trajectory in his mind. He climbed down off the ridge, losing any semblance of a trail, and followed a steep slope back in the direction he'd come. He moved as fast as he could and still stayed on his feet, but it was taking him too long, and he was making too much noise. He stayed with it, grimacing. The presence of pain was already making itself known over the buffer of the Advil. The leg had been getting too much of a workout.

Damn, he was awkward as hell. Before Waco he would have moved down this slope without breaking a sweat. Before Waco he could crouch on a surfboard and run his hand on the wall of water moving his wave, right in the sweet spot of the curl.

The worst thing was facing it, knowing Chesterfield was right, that his leg was a problem in a crunch. He moved as swiftly as he could but even the girl could outdo him. She might be a sociopath, but she was also a girl.

Wilson kept the pain in a separate compartment. He was aware enough to dread the long hours it would take to get it back in control, the spaced-out exhaustion and relief of pain medication. But worse was giving up. Knowing he no longer belonged in the thick of an investigation like this; that ethically, he would have to retire to the sidelines, the minor gun buys, the endless paperwork. He'd be pretty useful doing computer analysis and research for the active agents.

So much of what he loved in life had been taken away when the bullet tore through his thigh, penetrated the bone, and shattered. It always used to amaze him the way doctors could pull someone through when they were horribly, tragically hurt. You saw the documentary on television, found out the patient lived, and never thought about it again. Wilson knows that the story is not over after the first dramatic hours in the ER. Welcome to a lifetime of trouble. Old bullet wounds never die.

A split second's difference in Waco . . . he could be dead. A lot of them were dead—agents, women and children in the compound, and so many of them innocents, sucked into the cult by their own tragedies, with no way out once inside. Who was really to blame for it? All of them human, stumbling through the drama of their own lives and ripe for mistakes, all of the pathways converging. Somewhere in that night of oily black smoke and no heroes, was the story of Janis Winters.

But his story was in there, too. The story of Wilson—who can no longer dance or surf or do his job. The story of Alex Ruggers, who died with a wire around his neck, struggling so hard his wrists were sliced to the bone as he died slowly, and suffered. And no doubt that somewhere in an inside pocket of the clothes the Medical Examiner cut away from Rugger's body were pictures of his kids, his wife, his dog.

Janis hears someone moving up on the ridge, quieter than the other one. Another enemy, a big one this time. Janis has adrenaline now and it renews her. Where before she could barely hang on to the tree and keep from sliding down that steep mountain slope, now she moves in spurts, strong and ready, making her way back up to the ridge.

Up at last, and back on her feet, Janis stops to listen. There is so much noise, coming from down the slope. Which one is it? It is hard to keep track of two. She needs to be high, she needs to be above them, and she sees what may be a shortcut that will take her past a switchback on the trail. She can wait there for both of them.

In the darkness, Janis can't see that the offshoot of trail only peters out, and she has to backtrack and find her way back to the ridge. The big one has gotten ahead of her, and is blocking her way on the path. Janis is not afraid. She is never afraid anymore.

She can't see the face of this enemy, but she can tell that it is a he, and the enemy comes toward her. *Come and get me,* she thinks. *I'll be waiting.* But she does not take the gun out of her waistband.

The enemy does not see her as she stands behind a tree. It is too dark. She knows who he is by the limp—a Fed, another Waco veteran, another name on her list. His face is shadows, and he seems to bring the darkness with him, and he sees her, finally. They are ten feet apart on the trail.

The enemy has a gun, and he points it at her. Janis knows what to do. It is just like when she played out in the fields with Chris and Dale—once they get the drop on you, partner, you have to play fair, don't you, or the boys won't let you back in the game. Girls on sufferance only.

Janis puts her hands up, and the bullets catch her, one-two-three. She is thrown off her feet with a force that is familiar—because it happens so fast, because she is helpless; and because this is a place she has been before. She has missed her chance to get it under control, it's bad horsemanship and her own damn fault, she should have been ready for it, not smiling at that cowboy who is up-and-coming on the team roping circuit.

Ah, God, it is happening now, the nightmare, her foot caught in the stirrup, she is being dragged. No, no, no she can't make it stop, she is going so fast, her back is hurt, her muscles won't obey. She feels her body flip, and the left foot is still tangled, something has to give, and she hears the bone in her leg snap. She is facedown now, and her forehead seems to explode in showers of fireworks . . . oh, she remembers this well.

How strange the mind is, how odd the ways it finds to protect. She has been here all along, it isn't over, a memory of the past, it is still happening—the thing she has always dreaded, being dragged. All of those other things, just hallucination, the blood and the wires and the haze of pain before the anger takes her under like a monstrous wave crashing over her head. Thank God it is all just a bad dream, she's hurt her head, and Dandy, her Dandy, is stopping, people are screaming, one of them is her. Mama's voice, talking to Dandy, keeping him still; only Mama could stop this horse, she must have run so fast, she was way back in the stands, Mama is magic, Mama will save the day, Mama is screaming *cut the leather cut the leather* . . .

"Catch Dandy," Janis whispers.

And the man who leans over her, who checks the pulse at her neck, does not understand what she means, but he does understand she is dead, and he says a small prayer in the back of his mind, just for her.

CHAPTER THIRTY

Wilson was aware that Lena was standing just up the pathway looking down. He felt his muscles jerk, it was uncontrollable. He wondered how long she had been standing and watching.

"You okay?" he said.

"Nothing that can't be cured by a hot bath and a Band-Aid. So that's her? Your killer?"

"That's her."

"Is she dead, then?"

"She's dead," Wilson said. He took the cell phone out of his pants pocket, and flipped it open, but there was no service at the top of the mountain. He expected as much. "We'll head for the house, make sure everything is okay there, get a team out to round up the bodies."

"Shouldn't one of us stay here?"

"Yeah, but I don't want to and I bet you don't either."

"I'm cold," Lena said.

Her voice sounded funny, Wilson thought. "Are you sure you're okay?"

"Maybe a little shook up."

"You and me both. Come here."

She moved down the path toward him and he took her hand. His leg hurt with an intensity that guaranteed he would not sleep for nights to come.

"Look," she said.

There were lights, down on the road, and the wail of sirens that meant help on the way. Wilson hugged her, for no particular reason, and she slowed her pace to his.

"Here," she said, draping his arm around her shoulders for support. "It's not all that far."

They came out of the woods at the halfway mark on the driveway, where the land flattened, and the pond waters looked black in the dark. The barn was lit, and there was a small checkerboard of emergency units—cops, paramedics, the sheriff's department.

Halfway up the drive they can see the lights in the barn.

Wilson felt a prickle on the back of his neck.

"Stop back here," he told her.

"No."

He wanted so badly to get the weight off his leg. It was a tedious thing, throb throb throb, he couldn't think of anything else.

"Maybe you should stay here and let me go," Lena said. But they both continued up the hill and were sweating by the time they made it to the barn. Wilson was leaning harder and harder on Lena's shoulder and she staggered under his weight. Wilson heard the murmur of voices, mostly men. *Mayhem,* Wilson thought, his mind adrift.

Wilson saw Kate Edgers first. She was on the ground in a pool of blood so thick and large he could not believe she was alive. But she must have been, because someone had hooked her up to an IV drip and she was being loaded onto a stretcher. He blinked, trying to take it all in. A little dark-haired boy, face stark white, was held by a middle-aged woman who was sitting on the hood of a pickup truck that has inexplicably come up that mountain drive with a horse trailer. A man, probably her husband, brought a cup of something hot to the woman and the boy, though the man looked like he could use something himself. He leaned inside the window to stroke the head of a large black dog. All of them watched the stretcher as Kate was loaded into the van. The man kissed the woman, gave her his jacket, and took the boy from her arms. She got into the back of the van—one of the medics gave her a hand. The lights flashed, and the unit pulled tamely away in a crunch of gravel.

He saw Mendez, just as the detective turned and spotted the two of them, and his leg gave out as Lena surged toward Mendez. Wilson landed with no dignity and great annoyance on his rear.

Mendez headed for him, but Wilson waved him off.

"I'll stay down here, if you don't mind."

Mendez grinned, looked over his shoulder, and saw two paramedics running toward them. "You hurt bad?"

"Nothing a cold beer won't help."

Joel put his arms around Lena and held her and Wilson watched them with open and vulgar curiosity. He missed Sel.

"Wilson?" A car door slammed and Wilson looked between the two medics. The S.A. from Nashville. She was wearing low heels and a skirt and a long coat, and was already giving orders.

"I want overtime for this," Wilson said, when she came close.

"Dammit to hell, it's been a long night." she said. But she sounded confident and Wilson heard car doors, heard her start giving orders, and he closed his eyes, relieved, and finally off duty.

He knew that the minute he got back to California and put his arms around Sel, his world would quit spinning out of control, and he would be able to center, and be steady. But he had much to do before he could go home.

CHAPTER THIRTY-ONE

Two days after Wilson McCoy brought down the Rodeo assassin, Joel asked me to accompany him back to the mountain were Cory Edgers used to live. Miranda and Edgers were still in the custody of the morgue, and Kate Edgers was still listed as critical in ICU.

The Andersonville sheriff's department, in a joint operation with the Knoxville office of Alcohol, Tobacco and Firearms, was providing the equipment and manpower, if not the budget, to drain the pond where Kate Edgers saw Cory Edgers sink Cheryl Dunkirk's bloodstained sweater. As ponds go, this one was man-made and small, no more than twenty feet across.

I sat on the dock, leaning up against Joel, who had wisely left his suits behind and dressed in jeans and a sweatshirt. The jeans were very clean and neat, and the sweatshirt was almost new, but there was mud crusting the edges of Joel's hiking boots, and with that I had to be content.

"When are you going to throw this shirt away?" Joel asked me, plucking at the sleeve of my most comfortable denim.

"Throw it away? Feel how soft this is, Joel. Do you know how long it takes to break a shirt in this good?"

"Ten years?"

"Good guess."

He kissed the side of my neck, which surprised me, because he is rarely demonstrative in public. I was feeling quite daring as it was to lean up against him while we sat on the dock in the midst of an official police operation.

I turned sideways so I could see his face. "Thanks for inviting me."

"You're easy to please, Lena. Most women want expensive bistros, wine, a dozen roses. Tickets to the opera from time to time."

"You know what I mean."

He didn't say anything.

"I'm sorry, Joel. About the way things have been between us over this whole thing."

"Do you wish you hadn't taken the job?"

I thought about it. "No, not really. How long are you going to hold a grudge?"

"About as long as it took you to break in that shirt."

The noise of the pump had run most of the crew away. There was nothing to do but wait, and pretty much everyone except me and Joel was taking a long lunch at someplace called Golden Girls.

"I was kidding, Lena. About holding a grudge. It's not that I don't think you have the right to do your job. I just felt betrayed."

"Betrayed?"

"I'd been trying to find Cheryl Dunkirk and getting nowhere for two months. I was failing not just locally, but on a national level, including sound bites on CNN where retired cops critiqued the whole investigation." He shrugged, then smiled. "Some of what they said made good sense—for some reason that was even worse. Then you get hired by the family, and blithely inform me that you're on the case, and it's clear you expect to breeze in with your good old girl network and save the day."

"Joel, how can you say that?"

"I'm not saying that's necessarily the way it was. I'm saying that's the way it felt."

I looked over at the pond. The water level was down by a third. The water looked murkier, and seemed to be draining at about the rate of evaporation.

"Lena? Don't you have a comment or something?"

"Yes, but you actually expressed a feeling, and I'm afraid to say anything negative, because if I do you may never express another one."

He rubbed my shoulders. "Tell me. You'll spontaneously combust if you don't."

"You make me feel like I have to apologize because I had the confidence to go into the investigation. But Joel, you have to realize that one, I don't work in the public eye, and two, I knew the groundwork. Although, I have to tell you that even if I did work in the public eye and even if you hadn't laid the groundwork, I wouldn't have been afraid to take it on."

"I'm not supposed to be surprised, am I?"

"But to be fair, I did find myself feeling competitive. When you talk to me about investigations, including this one, you always dismiss my opinion like it was nothing. It gets under my skin. I wanted to beat you on this one. I wanted to win."

"Win?"

"Yes, I know, poor choice of words."

I closed my eyes and turned my face to the sun while Joel absorbed my last remark. I knew that in less than a year he'd respond. I looked out at the pond, and watched the water ripple toward the pump.

"Joel?" I looked at him over my shoulder. His eyes were closed. "Joel, are you asleep?"

"Almost."

"So what do we do now?"

"Nothing."

"But how do we resolve this?"

"We don't. We communicated."

"Is that all there is to it?"

"I think so."

"Oh. Do you feel better?"

"I don't know. Maybe. You?"

I closed my eyes, thinking. "Yeah, I do."

"Lena, do you see the way the water is rippling there, right dead center."

I looked to where Joel was pointing. "There's something there. What do you think it is?"

Joel squeezed my shoulder. "Hard to tell at this point. The crew should be back soon."

"Is it Cheryl?" I asked.

"I think it might be."

The crew straggled back within the hour, and we waited for the water to drain. A sodden rag rug, tightly bound with duct tape, lay in the mud in the center of the pond floor. I stayed on the dock while Joel took off his shoes, rolled up his jeans, and squelched through the mud. He had a utility knife, and slit one band of duct tape. He was bent almost double, and he straightened suddenly, and nodded. He glanced at a deputy sheriff.

"That her?" the man asked.

"I think so."

"I'll get a van out, sir."

"Thanks," Joel said.

Dusk was falling by the time Cheryl was brought up from the pond and loaded into a mortuary van. The duct tape had been slit, the rug unrolled, and the body identified. Cheryl could not be lifted from the rug due to skin slippage. It surprised me that the body had stayed down on the bottom of the pond, but Joel said that a corpse wrapped and taped in a rug would be so heavy with water that it would sink and stay put.

And so we found Cheryl Dunkirk at last, Joel and I, as well as a measure of peace to calm the upheaval in our relationship. As it turned out, Joel and I were a little more human than we'd realized, and neither of us held the moral high ground.

It strikes me, sometimes, that Cheryl and Miranda shared a temporary burial spot there at the pond on the mountain. Sometimes I wonder if a certain restlessness of spirit remains, or if the older spirit forgave the younger, and somehow helped her along.

CHAPTER THIRTY-TWO

The ATF office in Nashville was starting to feel too familiar, Wilson thought. It was past time for him to go home. Sel had sensed a change in him, though he did not think he acted any differently. Now she was entirely upbeat, full of good news and reassuring tidbits, and comforting reassurances that she missed him and would welcome him back whenever he got home. No guilt, no pressure, no worries. A part of him was gratified by the kid gloves and supersensitivity, but the rest of him felt sidelined.

He had gone through all the motions of wrapping the case, filling out the paperwork, answering question after question from the investigative team. Nothing was like he thought it would be, not the least of which was the way he felt, which was so detached that he had the sensation he was watching a movie of himself rather than being himself.

He checked his watch. In fifteen minutes there would be a forensic post mortem of Janis Winters's life and motivations. Wilson would be there, as well as the assistant S.A., the local forensic psychologist, and the forensic autopsy tech. The post mortem was officially a committee, and would generate an official report, based on their findings and conclusions. The report would be disseminated to appropriate parties throughout the agency and considering the nature of the case, read again and again through the years. The rumor mill had it that someone from Winters's family would be making an appearance but Wilson hoped the rumor was crap. Most families of serial killers liked to be left alone.

Just the remote possibility that someone from the family would be there made Wilson dread going into that conference room. But he was interested in meeting the forensic psychologist, as they had had many conversations on the phone. The man with the voice, Wilson called him. In Wilson's imagination he was short and cuddly like a teddy bear, with a thick mop of curly brown hair.

He heard footsteps outside the little cubicle the Nashville office had hospitably made available for his use, and the S.A. of the entire Tennessee and Kentucky office wandered through the door.

Wilson finally felt something. He felt nervous. But the S.A., tall and slender and confident, was also as friendly as hell.

"Wilson McCoy, good, I was hoping to catch you before the meeting. Thought I'd let you know that the evaluation of the shoot came through okay. I'm sure you had no doubt that it would turn out, but it always feels better when it's confirmed. They'll get to you in writing on this pretty quick here." The man winked. "I've got enough pull to get the word early, so I thought I'd pass it along to you."

Wilson stood up and shook the man's hand. "Thank you, sir. Much appreciated. Will you be sitting in on the meeting?"

"Nope, I wish I could, but I have a flight to catch, so I'll have to wait for the report. And I've been briefed already."

Of course, Wilson thought. Nothing would go on in that committee today that this man didn't already know.

"Just wanted to make sure everything was cleared up on your account before I hit the road."

"I appreciate that."

"Good job, McCoy," the man said, slapping Wilson's shoulder. He nodded, then headed at a good clip down the hall.

Wilson looked at his watch. Plenty of time, except he was pretty slow on his feet right now, so he might as well go. The ATF conclusion that the shooting of Janis Winters was justified was a relief for a lot of reasons.

Wilson was early to the conference room, but not the first to arrive.

"You're Wilson?" the man said, standing up to shake hands. "I'm Mark Christian. We've talked?"

The forensic psychologist was a surprise. He looked more GQ than cuddly, though the voice was still the same. He was in the room alone, and looked like he'd been there for a while.

"Good to put a face with the voice," Wilson said. He wondered where Christian bought his suits.

"I wanted to take you aside before the meeting—"

But whatever Dr. Christian was going to say was cut off by the arrival of the Medical Examiner. Not a mere forensic tech, but a distinguished ME from Minnesota; she looked to be between fifty and sixty-five, had white hair that was cut short and combed carefully back, and a pointed chin. She wore a plum-colored suit and pantyhose and low-heeled black shoes. Wilson thought frumpy until she smiled at him. There was a brightness in her eyes, and kindness in her face, and Wilson, like everyone else who met Marian Windsor, forgot he thought she was frumpy within the first five minutes of knowing her. She had received twelve marriage proposals in the last decade alone, and if she were to keep count, which she did not, her lifetime total so far would be sixty-three. She lived alone with her two cats, Frank and Beans, but was rarely home; she was either working or letting someone take her out to dinner. Marian Windsor had an active social and sexual life.

Wilson looked over at Christian. "Somebody told me that someone from the family was coming to the meeting. I take it that's just a rumor."

Christian looked panicked. "No, that's only a rumor. Anything like that would be a really bad idea."

Wilson liked it that this man said "really bad idea" instead of stringing together a more technical and jargonized opinion, which would amount to the same thing in words more difficult to spell.

"Her mother was very willing to help, though. I talked to her at length." Christian said.

Wilson imagined that Janis Winters's mother found Christian's voice a selling point—the man had the richest, most comforting voice Wilson has ever heard. It would be impossible for a voice like that not to go into counseling.

The door opened and the assistant S.A., who Wilson now

called Denise, walked in smiling, nodding at each and every one of them. She took her place at the head of the table, and picked up the phone. All of them had notepads and a glass of water.

"Sandy? Oh, Robin. Hon, for God's sake get us some coffee in here, would you? No, no, that's great. Thanks." She looked up at the group. "Coffee's on the way. Let's go."

Wilson wondered why she was so cheerful. He took three Advil gel capsules, downing three-fourths of his glass of water.

Christian opened his briefcase and handed each of them a file that was full of pictures. "This one's off the charts, folks. I've never had another one like it."

Marian Windsor was nodding. "In case anyone wonders why I'm here, it's thanks to a federal grant specifically created for the purpose of compiling physical information on level-four killers through physical and psychological forensics. It requires permission of the family, which we do have."

"As I said, the mother was very cooperative," Christian says.

"Why is that?" Wilson asks.

Denise looked up. "Good question. What did you make of her, Mark?"

Christian put his fingertips together. "I liked her. Intelligent woman, Irish, though she's been a U.S. citizen for the last thirty years. I can't be an expert on her from the short amount of time we spent together, but my gut says she is well adjusted, and a good mother. Nothing she did would make you change your mind."

Wilson opened the file and took the pictures out one by one, laying them in a line on the table. He was careful to keep them straight, edges just touching. As if controlling how they were placed would draw the sting of seeing the three-dimensional life of Janis Winters.

"Very pretty girl," he said. He didn't mean to say anything at all. But his comment had them all opening their files. And the life of Janis Winters began to unfold.

Her baby picture was ludicrously adorable. She was held by an older boy, Wilson assumed a brother, and she had huge blue eyes, and white-blond curls, and the kind of chubby baby face that made maternal women go weak in the knees. Wilson had never desired a child of his own, but Janis Winters's baby pictures gave his heart a tug.

This mother was formidable, Wilson thought. Wise of her to provide the pictures. He understood what she was up to. She would put her daughter in the best light possible, which was not easy with a daughter who nearly decapitated federal agents with a stun gun and wire.

Another picture showed Janis at age six wearing denim overalls and a cowboy hat, holding a toy six-shooter she aimed at the photographer. The overalls were worn at the knee, and delicate as she looked, it was clear that she was strongly influenced by the two boys, brothers, who stood behind her. Even at six, she was no fragile flower afraid to get out and mix it up.

Wilson went to the next shot. "Who is the woman holding her on the horse?"

Christian raised an eyebrow. "That's the mother."

Wilson looked across the table at Christian to make sure it wasn't a joke. He had been expecting a worn-out sort of farm wife, with brave woeful eyes—not this petite, dark-haired creature with the upswept chignon, the outrageous smile, and the radiant pleasure she took in holding her daughter in front of her on the horse. She wore riding pants and high black leather boots, and a white tailored shirt that was open at the throat. You could see the glint of a necklace. The barn in the background cost more than the average house.

Christian held up a picture of Janis Winters as Sweetheart of the Rodeo. The picture was vintage Texas. Janis wore a glittering cowboy hat over long curly hair, and held a bouquet of tiny pink sweetheart roses. She was astride a massive paint horse, and her smile was toothpaste commercial quality. There was nothing in that young and and exquisite face that hinted of dysfunction or hard times, nature or nurture.

Denise picked up her copy of this shot and slipped reading glasses on her nose. "This is her? This is Rodeo? She looks like an angel, not a serial killer."

"She was," Marian Windsor said.

The anger came so hard and quick Wilson felt nauseous. The

door to the conference room opened abruptly and a man carried in a tray with coffee cups, cream, and sugar. A woman followed with a huge stainless steel pot. The fragrance of strong coffee permeated the room.

"You make it yourself?" Denise asked, and the man grinned and admitted he did. He was young and carefully dressed, and had a cowlick that likely caused him agonies of embarrassment every day. Wilson thought that if he had a cowlick like that he would burn it off before he'd be seen in public.

Christian waved the picture of Janis Winters on a horse. "This is where the trouble began."

It is as if he said once upon a time. The attention of everyone in the room was riveted.

"Agent Wilson McCoy picked this case up four weeks ago. At that point Janis Winters had killed five agents. Two with the ATF, three with the FBI, all of them present at Waco. The first thing our profile indicated, and let's face it, we're talking common sense, was a vendetta. Wilson, why don't you take it from here?"

Wilson stopped for a minute to gather his thoughts. He had already worked out everything he needed to say, and everything he needed to keep to himself, and he took a sip of water and began.

"When I was assigned to this investigation, we had two problems. The big one, the vendetta against federal agents present at Waco. The other, a missing intern in the ATF office in Lexington, Kentucky, and a strong indication that a member of local law enforcement, working on task with that office, was involved."

Everyone in the room knew the broad outline of the case, and Wilson gave them details. The survivor groups, the dovetail of killings in cities with the appearance of the Markus Bourbon Pro-Am Rodeo, a link established through the killer's use of baling wire. He took them swiftly and succinctly down the path of the investigation; the confession of Cory Edgers and information of his involvement with Rodeo; making an actual ID of the killer, frustration in the inability to link her to Waco. The discovery of a sister, Emma, involved with the Branch Davidians, and present when the compound erupted in smoke and flames. There was no positive ID of an Emma Winters in the death rolls, but interviews with survivors of Waco confirm the presence of a woman named Emma, who had a child, a son—both fitting the profile of Winters's sister and nephew.

At the time of the last three assassinations, Janis Winters lived in a trailer and was employed by the Markus Bourbon Pro-Am as a rodeo clown. She was considered fearless on the job, and flaky out of it. She had few people she was close to, and the ones she did know had all been told the tragic tale of what had happened to Janis's beloved sister Emma. According to the few witnesses who knew Janis well enough to spend time with her in the trailer, she kept stacks of notebooks along with pictures and newspaper articles concerning David Koresh and the Branch Davidians. She was said to be compulsive about getting her sister's story down on paper. Her writings were said to be almost solely concerned with her guilt and frustration at not being able to rescue her sister Emma, and her obsession with finding a horse named Dandy.

"I didn't know about the writings," Marian Windsor said. "But it's a common manifestation."

"Manifestation of what?" Wilson asked.

Christian leaned forward. "Let me get back to that," he told Wilson. "At this point the ATF has a slam dunk in court. We've matched Janis Winters's DNA to several samples taken from three kill sites. We have witness statements that Winters was often seen with baling wire, and although we have not been able to recover the Taser, a rodeo veterinarian has confirmed in a deposition under oath that he helped Janis Winters take an ordinary Taser and increase the voltage. At the time he was under the impression that she needed the Taser for self-protection. The man, who goes by the nickname Bones Jones, is a long-term alcoholic; however, his deposition is rated highly credible. The physical evidence is there, the motive is there, we've got a sworn statement from a law enforcement witness that Janis Winters is the assassin Rodeo; however this witness is dead and his statements are compromised. To date we have six witnesses from various fringe survivalist groups who will swear that Janis Winters approached their group under the guise of Rodeo's girlfriend, and delivered the information on the next target. Future prosecutions are planned in regard to the survivalist groups." Christian frowned and rubbed the back of his neck. "There's only one thing wrong with the whole scenario."

"Which is what?" Wilson said.

"Janis Winters didn't have a sister."

Janis Winters had won the Sweetheart of the Rodeo pageant, Christian told them. He paced across the small room, then stopped, back to the wall, folded his arms, and told them the story in that soothing, mesmerizing voice.

The accident happened on the final day of Janis's reign. And her name wasn't Janis Winters. Her name was Laura Bass. And though she had enjoyed being a rodeo queen for a year, Laura was more than happy to hand over her rhinestone studded cowboy hat to the next girl in line. She had earned scholarship money for college, still planned to be a vet, and had enough purse money from barrel racing with Dandy to see her way through and then some. It had been a great year, a fun year; she had traveled and met a lot of good-looking young men, but she was bored with it and ready to give one hundred percent to school. She hadn't had much time to ride Dandy, and she was tired of explaining to certain people she invariably met that being a rodeo queen might be a joke as far as they were concerned, but that it did involve the ability to control two thousand pounds of horse and perform all-around skills such as calf roping, trick riding, and barrel racing. It also required a certain charm and beauty and brains that was said to be found almost exclusively in a woman from Texas. The benefits included a generous college fund, numerous business contacts, a new Mustang convertible, and a hellacious wardrobe. And how many other girls of nineteen could say they'd ridden a horse in Amsterdam, Singapore, and Montreal?

Laura was all smiles now that it was over. She waved to her mom, who sat in the stands eating a hot dog and drinking a beer, and it was hard to tell, but she was sure that her mother winked. As usual, Mama was ignoring the attentions of some man who was trying to steal a moment of her time. Mama was not unkind, but she did have a tendency to be crushing when she was bored.

According to tradition, the pageant ended with a parade—all the contestants on horseback, led by the incoming and outgoing sweethearts, who rode their horses side by side. Every year the parade got bigger, including more and more cowboys, on horseback of course, a handful of male and female trick riders, always popular with the crowd, clowns, little kids on recalcitrant ponies, and Olieka men on their little bikes. Pageantry, Texas-style, and a hell of a lot of fun, and pretty much anybody who wanted to make a reasonable donation could advertise their products with a float.

There was never a consensus on what started the wreck and spooked the horses, even after the videotapes had been studied frame to frame. Theory and speculation were thick and unrelenting, and stories ranged from a cherry bomb thrown at the legs of the horse ridden by the new winner by the unsportsmanlike boyfriend of one of the runners-up, to a clown waving a pitchfork, with each story alternating between favor and scorn. The only thing agreed on was that it started a chain reaction that is not uncommon in horses, who react to the panic of other horses with as much enthusiasm as they'd have for a fear they'd found on their own. Horses are, after all, herd animals, and their survival depends on a mutual tribal agreement that all members can cry wolf, and that when one of the herd takes off hell-for-leather, the rest of them are going to run as well.

The new rodeo sweetheart lost her rhinestone cowboy hat but not her seat. It was a close thing, with the horse an inch or two from falling over backward and crushing the slim young woman, but the rodeo queen proved the committee's choice true by not jerking her horse's head up, keeping loose hold of the reins, and hanging on like a tick.

The palomino pony directly behind Laura and Dandy executed a rather neat little sideways crow hop, and his rider, already cranky at being a mere third runner-up, had his head turned to one side in no time, and kept him in a tight circle so no matter where he wanted to run, he couldn't get much of anywhere. And when he got the hops out of his system and made it clear, hell yes, he was listening to whatever it was she said, she took him through fifteen minutes of maddening figure eights to remind him that spooking on *this* girl was always going to be more trouble than it was worth.

One could speculate forever about which young woman was the best rider in the bunch, but there was no question that Laura Bass was certainly in the running. Dandy had pulled this maneuver on her before—that maddening and contentious wheel and bolt, where he whirled in a sudden one-eighty turn and took off for all he was worth. And at sixteen hands and eighteen hundred pounds of muscle and speed, Dandy was worth quite a lot.

To a champion barrel racer like Laura, keeping her seat during such a piece of equine misbehavior was nothing compared to the hair-raising turns they executed during competitions, where Laura had a little crowd-pleasing trick of grabbing a handful of dirt—keeping her seat in a split-second whirl was more a matter of instinct than anything else. Her thighs would grip and her pelvis and hips would rock forward with the motion of the horse, and she'd ride the bolt out far beyond the point where Dandy wanted to keep going, till he was covered in sweat and sorry, so very sorry, he had started the whole thing in the first place.

But Laura had been on the road for a year, traveling and performing rodeo queen duties, and Dandy had spent a frustrating amount of time bored in a paddock, or frustrated in his stall. He tolerated Laura's mother, flattened his ears at anyone else, and generally stayed in a funky bad humor. He did not understand that Laura had rodeo queen duties, and by the end of the year, neither one of them were at the top of their form.

Another complication came in the presence of Hal Mercado, riding his quarter horse gelding, Storm. Hal was an up-and-comer on the team roping circuit, and he made a point of showing up wherever Laura might happen to be. Laura was just starting to notice the way he always seemed to be around, and they were just at the stage of exchanging that certain kind of smile. While another cowboy would have already been taking her flowers and asking her out, Hal was patient, and liked to play the line like the fisherman he was. Hal was used to women coming to him.

Clearly this sort of lazy behavior was not going to catch the attention of Miss Laura Bass, and Hal had decided to turn his courtship up a notch. To do so he came up with the novel notion of riding sideways behind the line of watchers, grinning at Laura and making it clear he had her in his sights.

Still, Laura might have pulled things out of the fire if her left rein hadn't broken.

One minute she was trotting along looking at that good-looking cowboy Hal Mercado, and the next she was off balance, with no reins, and her right foot already out of the stirrup. In a split second Laura knew she could go one of two ways. Kick that left leg free of the stirrup and take a fall, or keep her seat and get that horse back in line. For a girl like Laura it was hardly a tough call, and she leaned back and grabbed a handful of Dandy's mane, and was just getting settled down deep in her seat, when the horse slipped, and Laura went sideways over the left side, hitting the asphalt hard. With her left foot caught in the stirrup, Laura landed with her back arched, cracking a not so critical vertebra directly under her bra. If she hadn't arched her back, the odds were high that she'd have spent the rest of her life as a paraplegic.

Still, being dragged by a runaway horse was even worse, and the odds of being killed were pretty steep.

Miraculously, Laura survived, with a crisply broken leg, one cracked vertebra, two shattered ribs, and multiple head trauma. And her injuries would have been worse if one, Hal Mercado had not forced his agile little bay to cross right in Dandy's pathway, ensuing in a collision that broke Mercado's ankle and permanently lamed his favorite horse, and two, if Laura's mother had not made it down from the stands in near record time, grabbed Dandy's bridle, and stilled the frantic horse. All in all it was a pretty close call, witnessed, in living color, by the ATF forensic committee, courtesy of a videotape loaned by Laura's mother and made possible by a talented cameraman who had at the time been a virtual new hire at Channel 5.

Wilson listened to Marian Windsor in something like a daze. If the other members of the committee noticed that he turned his pictures of Laura Bass facedown on the table, they made no comment. Marian Windsor drew a large cartoon head on a piece of notepaper. The nose and the half smile made it clear that this illustration was a side-angle view. She didn't bother with ears. Wilson found her drawing something of a relief from the usual power-point presentation. Maybe because she was so unself-conscious about her medium.

"There," she said, holding the paper up. She had labeled the brain functions according to location. Personality and thought were located behind the forehead, and she had circled them and put an exclamation point beneath.

"I've had Laura's medical records, the ones from the accident, and eight months after, when she disappeared. Your average ER doctor has just started realizing in the last few years that the worst thing about head trauma, depending of course on the initial injury, is the secondary injury.

"Laura suffered blunt trauma here, on the back of her head—see here, where the vision functions are. Because she took the initial impact on her back, before her head hit, she'd have had something of a concussion, and gotten her bell rung, but likely the complications would have been minor. The worst of her injuries occurred not on impact, but when she was dragged across the asphalt road. You saw the way she got flipped when the horse veered in the other direction. That's when she really got hurt. Her leg snapped, a pretty clean break, by the way, and according to the X rays, it healed up great. But she hit her head hard, right here on the forehead, and then she actually bounced because the horse was still moving, and hit it in the same location, again and again.

"There was a great deal of swelling to the prefrontal cortex, here. This area of the brain governs the higher order executive functions—social awareness, moral conscience. Personality. One of the things we're finding is that subjects with severe antisocial personality disorders have a certain amount of damage to this area of the brain. Laura suffered an intercerebral hematoma that shut off the blood supply to this part of her brain.

"Her care was pretty competent. The hematoma was surgically drained, she was watched, tested, and the cell death was kept to a minimum, considering the severity of the trauma, but a lot of brain cells were compromised. Another complication in an injury like this is the way the trauma sets certain biochemical events in motion. You get the formation of free radicals that target the fatty acids of the cell membrane, the result being cell death. Nobody really understood that at the time Laura suffered this injury. They figured that the cell damage she suffered from the hematoma was it. It wasn't, of course.

"When the mural circuit is damaged, the prefrontal cortex can no longer interpret feedback from the limbic system—which means that the signals from her brain that govern the free expression of emotion aren't interpreted and filtered by her social awareness and moral conscience, and the end result can be intensely violent, aggressive behavior. There is no guilt, and no thought for the future, no consideration of consequences.

"Laura's mother said that after the accident Laura became absolutely fearless. She used to be afraid of heights—that was no longer the case. Rattlesnakes—Laura wouldn't hesitate to pick one up. No fear whatsoever on horseback. And Wilson, you said that one thing all the people who knew her as Janis Winters and worked with her at the rodeo commented on was how she had no nerves and no fear when she was out in the ring, drawing the attention of a bull or whatever kind of raging animal is involved in a rodeo show."

Wilson saw Christian hide a grin. He could see the humor; Marian Windsor had areas of complete mastery, but rodeos weren't one of them.

Marion pushed hair out of her eyes. "My suspicion, when I heard the details of the case, and looked at the statements from Laura's mother concerning the personality changes that started after the accident, was that there was significant and increasing damage to the amygdala. And when I took a look at Laura's brain during the autopsy, I found *that*—see, right here?" She held up the drawing, but she had made so many circles and exclamation points that Wilson could make no sense of which brain cell did what. On the other hand, he was willing to take the woman's word for it.

"This pair of almond-shaped structures," and here Marian added ovals to the drawing, "see, situated here between the cerebral cortex and the limbic or emotional center of the brain. Significant damage there—which explains why Laura lost all fear. This area of the brain controls survival and fear." She looked up and smiled at all of them. "Make sense?"

Everyone nodded while Wilson wondered what all of this really meant. Because he was afraid that it meant that he had executed the Sweetheart of the Rodeo.

Christian was watching Wilson, and Wilson scribbled on his pad like he was making notes. He had the ridiculous suspicion that Christian could read his mind, which made him feel acutely uncomfortable. *Paranoia,* he thought, wondering where the paranoia brain cells might be.

"Here's what happened when Laura went home." Christian flipped through his notes, squinted at his own handwriting, then looked back up. "At first, Laura is brave and good-natured, but privately tells her mother that she is afraid to ever get back on a horse. Her mother says don't worry, we'll work it through like we always did before. Then Laura gets better. Physically, she's young and tough and has an incredible constitution and ability to bounce back.

"Her mother notices that she stops hanging out with her friends. She talks to Laura, and some of the kids she knows pretty well, and thinks that Laura is having memory problems, which make her feel alienated and off balance. And she's having attacks of jealousy, about everything, her friends paying more attention to one girl than another, her boyfriend talking to anybody else. Finally, either Laura drops out of the group, or they drop her. She starts having temper tantrums, and there's never any clue as to when and why they hit.

"And her mother is devastated when she realizes how deep Laura's memory loss goes. She keeps thinking that the memories will start coming back, but what really happens is that it gets worse, and Laura compensates by making things up to fill in the gaps.

"The last month Laura was home she got it into her head that someone had taken her horse, Dandy, and substituted another horse, and that was what had caused the accident. Her mother went out to the barn with Laura time and time again, showing her how the horse really was Dandy, but Laura would say, OK, sure, but never really believed her.

"And one day Laura's mother got up in the morning, and realized Laura was gone. Nobody, the family, and our own investigators, have been able to find out where she was the following five years. The family hired private detectives and ran ads, and looked everywhere a girl who loved horses might wind up, but nothing ever came up.

"Six weeks after Waco, Janis Winters surfaces, and gets hired from one rodeo circuit to the next as a clown. Her instincts are good, she is absolutely fearless, and she continues to be the only reason some cowboy makes it out of the ring in one piece. So her little oddities get overlooked. She lives in a trailer, and mainly keeps to herself.

"And she's changed so much—physically and personality-wise—that nobody really recognizes her as the Laura Bass who used to be a pretty good barrel rider on the local circuit near Higman, Texas.

"The interesting thing is she has acquired a sister, Emma, and a secret sorrow that she confides to anyone who gets close to her, that Emma was involved with David Koresh and the Branch Davidians and died at Waco. And her trailer is full of every last word that's ever been written on the subject, including the rantings and ravings of splinter survivalist groups she runs across on the Internet.

"Why the fascination with Waco? The dates are pretty interesting. She disappears, then resurfaces three years before the whole Waco incident starts up. And she tells people that her sister went away and got tangled up in a cult, and that the authorities refused to help her, and that she's going to get her sister out herself. And she is obsessed with cults, and spends her time researching them.

"While there was no Emma, some of the cult survivors we talked to do remember a Laura, who was pretty much picked up off the streets. Laura was pregnant when she was taken in, had her baby there at Mount Carmel, and stayed about eighteen months after the baby was born. She started fighting with Koresh, because she wanted to leave, but he wouldn't let her take her child. No one we talked to has information about exactly what happened, just that one morning everyone woke up and she was gone.

"We do, however, have reports of a Laura Bass talking to the Texas state police and the Waco sheriff about a baby she said was kidnapped by the cult. She told them she'd been to the FBI, the ATF, and the Texas Rangers. We're still looking for something in our records, but we don't have any reports filed. Because she could not come up with a birth certificate, or anyone who'd actually seen her with a baby, she was written off as a nutcase. But the autopsy confirms that Janis Winters did give birth to a child."

Christian gave a nod to Marian Windsor. "We went back through the records of unidentified Waco victims—as you know, many of them were children. We ran a comparison with Laura's DNA and got a hit. We've confirmed that a male victim, age approximately five years, died of asphyxiation at Waco."

Wilson wanted very much to leave. He knew the others were studying him. Because his prefrontal cortex was in pretty good shape, and there was no interference with the feedback from his limbic system, he stayed put. He tried to think of Rugger, which he managed for a while, but it was not an image he was fond of, and he finally focused on Sel, and the way she looked that first day he saw her working the surf at Zuma Beach.

Wilson kept Sel in mind. She was the target. He just needed to get home.

CHAPTER THIRTY-THREE

Joel had no idea that I was sitting in the Cracker Barrel in Corbin, Kentucky waiting for Wilson McCoy, who had agreed to buy me a late breakfast. As usual, I was late, but Wilson was later, so I sat in the nonsmoking section at a table for four in front of the window. A vigorous stream of sunlight lit the room. I sipped my coffee and watched the parking lot. The waitress brought me a basket of biscuits, in case I got hungry waiting for Wilson, and I opened one up and ate the soft bread from the middle, plain, without jam or butter. It was very peaceful, arriving first and having a few moments to myself. I wondered if I had been missing out by arriving late everywhere I go. Maybe the reason some people were habitually early had more to do with peace and quiet than punctuality.

A spiffy new F-150 truck painted hot-rod red pulled into a prime parking space right in front of the restaurant—you couldn't get closer unless you had a handicapped sticker. I did a double take when I saw Wilson climb out of the truck—he looked so local, in blue jeans and a blue Kentucky Wildcats ball cap. And driving a pickup truck on purpose? But it had to be Wilson, because of the limp.

The waitress led him straight to my table, her cheeks newly flushed, and I could not hear what Wilson said to her, but she tossed a look at him over her shoulder, and I saw him grin. There was no hiding Wilson's West Coast flair—evident in the fit of the jeans, Ralph Lauren; the black sweater, a blend of silk and wool.

He sat across from me, leaned across the table, and kissed my cheek.

"Hello, Lena."

"Is that really you in the ball cap?"

He took the hat off for a moment to show me the dyed blond hair and dark roots, twirled it on one finger, and put it back on his head. "See my truck?"

"I did. With utter amazement. You better get back to Los Angeles, dude, or before you know it you'll 'be spending your retirement money on a tractor and forty acres. As it stands, you could almost pass for a native."

"Sticks and stones, Lena."

The waitress arrived with coffee for Wilson, and a warm-up for me. I ordered my usual breakfast, sourdough toast, hash brown casserole, and today, bacon, and fresh squeezed orange juice.

"How about you?" the waitress asked Wilson.

He closed his menu and looked at her. "You pick it out for me. You know what's good here, don't you?"

She chewed the end of her pen. "You hungry?"

He nodded.

"Stand by," she said, and headed off.

Wilson took a gulp of coffee, black of course. I was glad he'd had the wisdom not to ask for espresso. "I was disappointed you wouldn't meet me back at the mountain. I wanted to see where you guys found Cheryl Dunkirk."

"I will never set foot on that mountain again. And stop complaining. I drove an hour and a half to meet you here."

"Only because I'm buying and it's Cracker Barrel."

"To tell the truth, I figured you'd be in L.A. by now."

"You're my last stop; then I'm free. I'm taking the red-eye out of Nashville tonight."

"Seems to me I'm a little out of your way."

"Well, hey, I wanted to thank you for all that help on the mountain. It didn't seem right not to talk to you again after you helped me out of the woods and dumped me on my ass in front of the barn."

I laughed and put my glass down.

"Did orange juice go up your nose?"

"No, Wilson, it didn't." I wiped my mouth with a napkin, striving for dignity.

Wilson looked over my shoulder, eyes growing wide.

"What?" I asked, looking over my shoulder. Our waitress was headed to the table with a tray heavy with food.

"Tell me that isn't for us."

"You told her you were hungry."

It was worth the drive down to watch Wilson's face as our waitress—Patty, according to the name tag—set country sausage patties, bacon strips, grits, pancakes, three eggs over easy, and another basket of biscuits in front of Wilson. She set a small bottle of maple syrup on the table, and a little dish with foil-wrapped pats of butter.

"Be sure and put some butter on those grits while they're hot," she told him, patted his shoulder, and left.

"Is that all you're eating?" Wilson asked me.

"At the time I ordered I thought I was going all out. Until I saw what you were getting."

"Do you people always eat like this?"

"You people?"

Wilson put his napkin in his lap. "I'm from California. We're afraid of food."

"You're just afraid you'll like it."

"Truer than you think." He poured syrup on the pancakes, speared the butter pat, hesitated, then put it on the top pancake. But he didn't eat.

I chewed bacon and sipped coffee and got tired of waiting. "Come on, Wilson, old son. I know why we're here. Let's get it out in the open."

He put his fork down. "So you *did* see."

He meant did I see him aim his gun at Rodeo, see her hold up her hands, and see him shoot her anyway, three bullets one right after the other.

"No, Wilson, I didn't see a thing."

His looked at me with a sad sort of summing up. "You better think about that."

"I have thought about it, Wilson, you think I'm brain dead? You think being from Kentucky makes me the village idiot?"

Wilson tilted his head sideways. "I haven't been in this part of the country all that long, but I have noticed that where the West Coast has a Starbucks on every corner, you guys have a Baptist church. I always thought people were joking when they called this the Bible Belt. I can't help but think this thing might weigh on you, and that maybe one of these days you'll want to get it off your chest." He glanced out the window. "I don't feel like waking up at night having to worry about that. If you think it's a possibility, let's just go to the S.A. here in Lexington, and let him know the whole thing."

I thought of Jeff Hayes. "The truth is, Wilson, I've been in a similar situation myself, and I understand pretty well how you feel."

"What's your story?"

"I don't have a story, Wilson. And neither do you."

He didn't look at me, just kept staring out the window. "That sure is a pretty truck."

"Eat your breakfast. You've only got twelve hours to make your flight."

He grinned at me. "Hey, Lena, if you're ever in California—"

"I promise not to look you up."

CHAPTER THIRTY-FOUR

Wilson felt almost otherworldly as he entered the elevator at the end of the parking garage. The smell of oil and exhaust stayed with him until he stepped into the lobby of the building on Sepulveda, and took yet another elevator to the ATF floor. He was feeling displaced by his time on the East Coast, and the things that happened while he was there. He walked through the heavy outer door that shielded the inner workings of Alcohol, Tobacco and Firearms, Southern California-style, passed the cameras, raised a hand to the receptionist. He threaded his way through the hallway and the cubicles, feeling nostalgic. Details caught his attention. How thin the carpet was beneath his feet. A scuff mark that had been on the wall ever since he could remember. Stupid stuff, all of it vivid.

Vaughn Chesterfield stood in the doorway of his office, waiting for him like always, and Wilson wondered if the man ever really intended Wilson to think he was late. Maybe Chesterfield just liked to stand there when he knew someone was on their way. For all Wilson knew, it could be some kind of Connecticut welcoming ritual. He was beginning to get an appreciation for the cultural differences from one part of the country to the next.

Today Chesterfield had a friendly smile and the kind of welcome where your superior officer shakes your hand with his right, while squeezing your forearm with his left. It is the kind of greeting given to a soldier who has done a difficult job, and done it well. Wilson looked Chesterfield in the eye, but the spark of resentment in his heart died before it was fully formed. Chesterfield was not grinning, he was not slapping Wilson on the back. He was not even smiling that big. Whatever anybody said about the ATF, Wilson was aware that the organization had managed to put some intelligence into the mix of management. Today, which was the last time he would see Vaughn Chesterfield, Wilson almost liked the guy.

The sentiment appeared to be mutual.

Vaughn waved Wilson to a seat, moved around the desk, and settled into his own chair. As always, Vaughn wore a tie and a pressed white shirt. For some reason, Wilson decided he liked that.

Vaughn studied Wilson for a long moment, then leaned back in his chair. That Vaughn would allow himself to relax with Wilson in the room meant a barrier had gone down.

"Tough job out there, Wilson. You did it well."

Vaughn glanced at Wilson's bad leg like a man who cannot resist the compulsion, but he made no comment. Wilson was grateful. He knew that people were showing friendly concern when they boomed out *Hey, Wilson, how's the leg?,* but since it was clear exactly how the leg was, *bad,* Wilson would just as soon not include his daily dose of pain in the general social chitchat.

"You want some time off?" Vaughn asked.

Wilson had nothing to say to this question, though the offer didn't surprise him. The Nashville office, during their bout of debriefing slash counseling, let him know that in this kind of situation, a short leave of absence was recommended and offered with no strings. It was one of the few times the ATF would give you time off with a pat on the back.

"To tell you the truth, Wilson, I thought Rugger was going to put you on the fringe of this thing. Sort of ease you back into the field, see how things worked out. None of us saw how this thing would blow up on you like it did."

Hearing Alex's name jarred Wilson. Chesterfield noticed.

"Son, I'm going to give you some advice. You sit in that chair and you wince when I say Alex Rugger's name. I don't blame you for feeling that way. I saw the photos. You saw the reality. Blood in a picture is a shadow on paper. Blood on your hands from a man you like, a man you respect and consider your friend . . . that's another thing."

Wilson took a deep breath, but it did not relieve the ever-present heaviness in his chest, the weight that settled like darkness when he pointed his nine millimeter at Rodeo and shot her three times in the chest. Why couldn't Chesterfield have broken the ice with him before all this happened? He'd been a good enough agent then. He'd given a hundred and ten percent, tried to follow the rules, tried to please.

Too late, he wanted to say.

Wilson had no illusions about how the ATF felt about rogue agents. He used to feel the same way himself. He probably had more in common with Rodeo now, than he did with the man across the desk.

"Don't second-guess yourself about this, Wilson. You made a decision out in the field, and in the moment. It's been looked at every which way by the investigative team, and you're in the clear. Don't judge yourself harshly." Chesterfield rubbed the bridge of his nose.

"It's too easy to think back on these things, to come up with different outcomes, with other things you wish you'd done. And if you do, and you will, I want you to put yourself in the shoes of Janis Winters's next victim. I want you to think about how that wire would feel around your neck. I want you to think about this guy's funeral. I want you to picture a closed coffin, because nobody wants this guy's wife and kids to see how his head no longer fits on his neck. And I want you to think that you did what you had to do. And someday I want you to let it go."

Wilson did not know what to say to all this, so he punted and said nothing at all.

"You're entitled to some time off here, Wilson. I think you should take it."

Wilson pulled an envelope out of his pocket. Sel had beautiful stationery. Heavy linen paper, matching envelopes. Wilson had typed the letter on his personal computer, and used the white paper and cheap envelope he bought at Walgreens on his way home from LAX.

Chesterfield reached across the desk to take the envelope, and he frowned while he read the letter inside. He read it slowly, and he read it twice, then sighed and sat forward in his chair.

"Why?"

Wilson looked rueful and brave. "The leg, sir. I know you and Alex Rugger had some reservations about the limitations I might have. I know I've waited seven years to get back in the frame. But the truth is, and it's time I faced it, I'm no good out in the field."

"There are other possibilities here, Wilson. Other kinds of assignments. All of them crucial to the job."

"Not for me, sir."

"I can't change your mind?"

"You can't, but I appreciate that you tried."

Chesterfield stood up and shook Wilson's hand, and made the kind of noises that management makes.

"What are you going to do with yourself, Wilson?"

And Wilson gave him a genuine smile. "I think I'm going to open a restaurant."

Chesterfield raised his eyebrows. "Hell, Wilson, I didn't know you could cook."

"I can't sir." Wilson nodded, and headed out the door.

Chesterfield sat for a moment, thinking this over, then he put his head out the doorway to call Wilson back. He wanted to talk to the man more, see if maybe a leave of absence would be acceptable, but it was already too late. For a man with such a sizable limp, Wilson moved quickly, and Chesterfield got a quick glimpse of the bad leg and the well-cut hair, before Wilson turned at the end of the hallway and was gone.

Chesterfield closed his office door, which usually stayed open, and sat in his chair, turning it around to stare out the window at the traffic on Sepulveda. He couldn't help but notice the brand new pickup truck, teal blue, extended cab, oversized tires. He watched it squeak through a yellow traffic light, and whistled, thinking he wouldn't mind having a pickup himself, maybe after he retired.

CHAPTER THIRTY-FIVE

Tonight Joel and I are hosting the official housewarming party for our new cottage. Joel is down in the kitchen cooking, and whatever it is smells wonderful all the way upstairs, where I am still soaking in a hot bubble bath. I have a little neck pillow now and a foot cushion so I can stretch out lengthwise and not float away. In a few minutes I will get out and get dressed. I have been soaking too long as it is and my hair, which is pinned on top of my head, will be too curly.

We sent invitations out to our housewarming party three weeks ago. McFee sent immediate regrets, but I called him, and I'm hoping he'll come.

Kate's mother called me yesterday. Kate is out of the hospital and recuperating quickly. Her father went to both Edgers's and Miranda's funeral, but she says he won't talk about it. Yesterday they found Leo in the stall of a rather bad-tempered stallion, but the horse was matter-of-fact and Leo was sitting cross-legged under the feed bin building some sort of structure with straw. It was George who alerted them. Kate's mother had been sure Leo was taking his nap, and confided that her grandson has an uncanny ability with locks and requires more supervision than she is used to, and she couldn't be happier. When Kate is well enough, she and Leo were going to move out to one of the old farmhouses on the acreage.

Joel tells me that the Bass family managed to get Laura buried in private with no publicity at an undisclosed location in Texas, and that they had consented to Wilson's request to attend. Joel was amazed to learn that Wilson quit his job at ATF, got married, and opened a southern-style barbecue restaurant in Marina Del Rey.

The Dunkirk investigation changed my relationship with Joel. What we have together is different now, something more complex. We are closer, though we are aware that there are things that each of us hold close and secret, and do not share. I still look forward to taking Joel for granted, but I don't worry now, that if I make a wrong step the relationship will break. I'll communicate and Joel will express a feeling every year or two and we'll manage. As a matter of fact, Joel is getting almost too good at communication, which has resulted in us hiring a cleaning service that comes once a week.

When I first started taking the kind of cases I do, I admit I saw things in black and white, with good guys and bad guys and no shades of gray. I did not think about clients like Miranda Brady. I know I will be more careful to keep a distance between myself and the people I try to help. It is still a struggle, trying to keep up with the finances and barter system, and I have cultivated the art of living in the moment, and not worrying about bills down the road, trusting that things will work out one way or another, which, Joel tells me, is the worst kind of financial planning he's ever heard of. I tune him out when he brings up retirement.

I don't think you can immerse yourself in the drama of other people's lives and come through clean and unmarked. But I think there is a need for someone like me, someone who is not a cop, someone who has been to the dark places and come through okay, someone who used to be a victim herself.

This is not the life I pictured. I had thought that my days would be more organized, more routine-oriented, certainly smoother. Do the job, pay the bills, curl up at night with the man you love. I figured that by now I would at least have gotten the linoleum off the bathroom floor and painted the hallways and the kitchen and the bedroom.

Life never follows the rules. But Joel and I did the packing together, and have moved all our furniture in. And the living room walls have two new coats of red, just in time for the party. It looks terrific.